Touch of S

Karissa Laurel

Touch of Smoke
Red Adept Publishing, LLC
104 Bugenfield Court
Garner, NC 27529
http://RedAdeptPublishing.com/
Copyright © 2019 by Karissa Laurel. All rights reserved.
First Print Edition: February 2019
Cover Art by Streetlight Graphics

And before Solomon were marshalled his hosts,
of jinn and men and birds,
and they were all kept in order and ranks. (Quran 27:17)

Chapter One

Mama, I'm Coming Home

THE DAY I LEFT EVANSVILLE, I twisted my rearview mirror until it reflected the ceiling of my daddy's '61 Apache and not the road behind me. Refusing to look back, I set my sights on the yellow lines winding down the middle of Highway 19 and followed them out of the Smoky Mountains as if I were Dorothy trailing the yellow brick road to Emerald City. But once I got there, I had no intention of clicking my heels and whispering spells to carry me back home.

I'd sworn I would never return to Evansville and its misty gray mountains. Those insidious valleys and hollows attracted secrets, holding them in confidence until they festered and infected everyone and everything, breaking hearts and ruining lives. And I'd sure as hell never go back to Owen Amir. If deceit were a contagious disease, then he had been ground zero.

But there I sat, three years later, idling on the shoulder of that same highway, in that same Chevy pickup.

I'd told myself I'd only return when hell froze over, and I was going to have to eat those words. Outside my windshield, the mountains blazed in a frenzy of autumn colors. Fire rained down in the shapes of fall leaves: scarlet maples, smoldering-amber oaks, flaming-yellow poplars. A persistent gray mist, like smoke, enveloped the distant ridgeline, and if the temperature dropped another few degrees, the whole place might, indeed, freeze over.

Welcome to Hell, also known as Evansville, population 3,413—give or take a few.

2

I rested my forehead against my hands clenched around the steering wheel and gritted my teeth, keeping back my tears with sheer stubbornness and determination, which was also how I'd managed to make it this far without turning back. My truck had seemed to roll to a stop on its own, some unseen barricade preventing its entry into town—an invisible boundary built of heartache, fear, and painful memories. *If I turn around and leave, no one will ever know I was here...*

But the universe conspired against me.

A tap on my window jolted me from my musings. I squealed, and my foot slipped from the clutch. The truck chugged, lurched, and fell silent. "Dammit." I stomped the emergency brake before I trundled backward down the mountain.

Scraping hair out of my eyes, I rolled down my window and forced a smile to my lips. A sheriff's deputy grinned at me in return. His broad-brimmed hat shadowed a familiar face lined and wrinkled with age. Silver hairs glinted in his thick Wyatt Earp mustache. "Rikki Albemarle," he said. "I'd recognize those crazy red curls anywhere. Never thought I'd see you around these parts again."

"That makes two of us, Mike." I clenched the steering wheel tighter, resisting the urge to smooth my wild coils. It wouldn't help. My hair had a life of its own, and the moisture in the air made me look as if I'd been French-kissing a car battery.

"Your mom didn't say a word about you coming home."

"It's a surprise."

Mike Heinlein's fuzzy eyebrows arched. "Oh? Well, try not to give her a heart attack. We still need her—she's on the schedule tomorrow."

I blinked at him stupidly. "You mean she still patrols, even after...?"

His face paled. "She's not as fond of serving civil processes as she used to be, but she'll make the rounds on occasion. Kiss hands, shake babies." He winked to assure me he was joking, as if I couldn't tell. "Election season is coming up, and she wants to make sure people haven't forgotten about her."

"Is anyone running against her?"

Mike's smile dimmed, and disapproval showed in his expression. He obviously thought I shouldn't have to ask such questions about my own mother. A daughter ought to know. "Why don't you ask her yourself?"

"I'll do that," I said. "I'm heading to her house right now."

"You remember how to get there, or do you need an escort?"

Heat flooded my cheeks. *Please, God, no.* "I think I can find the way."

"Be sure to stop in and see Rose. Let her fix you a sandwich... a cup of coffee at least."

Mike's wife, Rose, ran the diner on Main Street and had a chicken salad that made grown men shed tears of joy. She'd also baked birthday cakes for me every year of my life until I'd moved away. "Of course I will."

Deputy Heinlein tapped his brim in a brief salute and strolled to his patrol car. I started my engine, shifted into first gear, and released the parking brake. The truck shimmied and sputtered as I pulled onto the highway and rolled past a carved wooden sign welcoming me to Evansville. *Here goes nothing.*

A wide banner hung over Main Street, announcing Evansville's upcoming Fall Leaf Festival. For two days, hundreds of tourists would tramp through town, visiting arts-and-crafts booths, music pavilions, street performers, and food vendors. As I drove by, a construction crew was setting up a stage in the center of Wallers Memorial Park, a couple of acres of groomed grass in the center of town, surrounded by a short jogging path.

At the third stoplight, I turned left and followed a two-lane street up a steep incline known locally as Water Tower Hill. A mile or two later, I turned left at the Pentecostal Holiness church and hung a right at the rear corner of Evansville High School's football field. The yellow goalposts jutting up from the field's opposite ends reminded me of my mom's favorite old joke: "What do the Evansville Panthers and the Pentecostal Holiness preacher have in common? They can both make two hundred people jump from their seats and yell, 'Jesus Christ!'"

I stomped the gas pedal and rolled onward, heading out of town at the opposite end from which I'd entered. After cruising a winding road leading farther into the mountains, my truck bumped over a rutted dirt driveway that dead-ended in a clearing—a three-acre plot tucked up against a backdrop of tall pines marking the Great Smoky Mountains National Park boundary. White smoke bloomed from the chimney of a modest clapboard cabin nestled among those pines. Lights burned in the cabin's windows, chasing away gloomy shadows lurking beneath the eaves. A swing hung from the rafters at one end of the front porch, and a pair of perpetually empty rocking chairs hunched together at the other end.

My truck's brakes squeaked as it rolled to a stop. My mom would fuss if she heard it. She'd accuse me of neglecting my dad's beloved old truck, Dolly. If she'd had a choice, my mother never would have let me take his Apache in the first place, but I had run away with it, betting the sheriff of Twain County wouldn't press grand theft auto charges against her only child, no matter how irrational she thought I was at the time.

Inside the house, I found my mother exactly where I expect-ed—halfway through a bottle of rosé and sacked out in her recliner with some old sitcom blaring on her big screen. Remembering Deputy Heinlein's warning about giving my old lady a heart attack, I tiptoed outside, leaving her undisturbed. Besides the fear of scaring my mom to death, I wasn't fully prepared to talk to her yet. We'd parted on regrettable terms, and I didn't know the words that could mend our rift. So much depended on her and what she had to say, and that was something I couldn't predict in the countless imaginary dialogues I'd held with her over the past three years.

After unloading my luggage onto the front steps, I brushed away cobwebs and settled on the old porch swing. Its chains creaked and popped as they accepted my weight. With a push, I set the swing rocking in a gentle rhythm and slumped in my seat.

My phone rang, its shrillness disrupting the peace. With numb fingers, I slipped it out of my pocket and grimaced at the image on the caller ID screen. Dr. Joseph Khan's profile picture grinned at me: dazzling smile, dark eyes, and dusky-bronze skin. He was handsome, charming, and brilliant, but something about him set off a subtle alarm. My instincts might have been issuing a legitimate warning, but my ability to evaluate romantic risks was as damaged as a smoke alarm with a faulty wire.

When I thought of Joseph, the words he'd spoken to me the last time we were face-to-face played on repeat: *I think it's best if you take some time to focus on* you, *Erika*. Always he called me Erika, never Rikki. *If we put our relationship on hold, there'll be fewer distractions, and you can channel all your energy toward recovery.*

His understanding of our "relationship" differed drastically from mine. He wanted more—a commitment and intimacy—but he might as well have been asking a dried-up old dairy cow to produce milk. I couldn't give him what I didn't have. And even if I did, I wasn't sure he was the one with whom I wanted to take those risks. He was persistent, though, and didn't like taking no for an answer. At some point, I was going to have to make my feelings—or lack thereof—clear, but I had few friends left, and I hated to chase away a potential ally.

Not in the mood for drama tonight, Joseph.

With a quick thumb swipe, I sent his call to voicemail and zipped up my coat, tugging my hood over my unruly hair and shoving my freezing hands deep into the fleece-lined pockets. The mist that followed me up from the foothills had gained weight and substance, thickening into a gray, soupy mess, and I thanked my lucky stars I'd arrived before sundown. Driving at night strained my eyes *and* my nerves—mountain roads had a way of making unanticipated drops and turns after dark.

The swirling fog and the porch swing's hypnotic rhythm drew me back through my memories, back through time. I'd come to Evansville for several reasons: to find that elusive *closure* everyone always talked about, to finally exorcise the ghosts and demons that had followed me out of town three years before, and to find answers to questions I'd avoided as long as possible. Questions that refused to be ignored any longer. Questions spawned the day Owen Amir cruised into town on his Ducati Diavel and interrupted my ordinary, predictable life.

Chapter Two
Tall, Dark, Handsome Stranger

THREE YEARS BEFORE...

Rose Heinlein refilled my glass from a pitcher of sweet tea and shoved aside my book stack. She set my plate on the counter—potato salad and a grilled pimento cheese sandwich, both 100 percent homemade. *Yum.*

"Can't you stop studying long enough to eat?" she asked.

"Not if I want to pass." I set down my pen and met her blue-eyed gaze. Rose looked a lot like Little Debbie, if Little Debbie were thirty years older. "Final exams start in two weeks."

"Why haven't you been studying all along? Seems kind of late to be cramming in a whole semester's worth of material."

"I *have* been studying all along." I nibbled a corner of my sandwich, and cheese oozed from the crusty bread and dripped on my plate. I scraped up an orange drop and popped my finger in my mouth. "Or maybe I could quit college and come work for you. You could teach me how to cook like you do. Don't lie. I know you put crack in all your food."

"Oh Lord, no." Rose flapped her hand at me. "Don't say that."

I paused in the middle of scraping up another pimento cheese blob. "Don't say what? That you cook with crack?"

She laughed again. "No. Don't joke about quitting school. Don't wind up in a diner like me and pregnant before you're old enough to buy a beer. You're too smart for that. Twenty years will go by"—she snapped her fingers—"just like that. Before you know it, you'll be looking back on your life, wondering what in the heck you've been doing all this time. If you look back on twenty years of nursing, that might be something to be proud of. Twenty years of making sandwiches and meatloaf... not so much."

"Don't say that, Rose. You're the heart of Evansville. The diner's important to this town. That's not something you can dismiss. You raised a great family too." I'd grown up with her son, Luke, who'd joined the army not long after he graduated high school. Last I'd heard, he was somewhere in the Middle East—Iraq, or Afghanistan perhaps.

Her cheeks colored, and she looked away. "Well, now..." My compliments had obviously flustered her. Not that half the men in town didn't compliment her every day and propose marriage despite the fact that Deputy Heinlein was her husband. "My pecan pie never saved a life."

"I wouldn't be so sure. I bet it's brought many a desperate man back from the brink." I laughed when her blush deepened into bright crimson. "This town loves you. *I* love you. That's all that matters in the long run, right?"

She scrubbed the heel of her palm across her watering eyes and turned away mumbling something about "the mouths of babes."

The bell over the diner's door rang, announcing the arrival of a new customer. Rose looked up from her spot behind the counter and opened her mouth to call out her usual greeting, but her words died in her throat. Color drained from her face, and she wobbled on her feet. I dropped my sandwich and reached for her. "Rose... *Rose?* Are you okay?"

She ignored me. Her gaze had locked onto something, or someone, behind me. She clutched at her chest and gasped. I turned around, searching for the source of her shock, and found two young men standing in the middle of the diner with all eyes on them, as though Ron Weasley and Harry Potter had apparated out of thin air. One of them, brown-haired and blue-eyed, grinned. His shaggy hair and thick beard stumped me for a moment, but his disguise clearly hadn't fooled his mother.

"Luke Rey Heinlein." Rose's tone was the one every mother used on misbehaving children. "What in God's glory are you doing here?"

Luke Heinlein? Think of the devil, and he doth appear... or something like that.

"I wanted to surprise you," he said. Luke smiled so big it was a wonder his face didn't split wide open.

Everyone watched the exchange between mother and son like a crowd at a tennis match, heads swinging back and forth, observing each action and reaction.

"Well, you did," she said, breathless. "You got me good. Does your daddy know about this?"

Luke held out his hands at his sides and shrugged. "No, ma'am. I stopped here first."

A beat of silence and then, "Don't stand there like a bump on a log. Come give your momma a hug."

The whole diner sighed as the two embraced, but my attention drifted to the unfamiliar young man who had stood silently at Luke's side throughout the exchange. He apparently noticed me staring, and his dark eyes locked onto mine. His lips spread into a cagey, flirtatious grin, and he winked. I snorted and turned my attention back to my lunch. With an exam in the morning and at least three chapters to review between now and then, I had no time for flirting with a cocksure stranger. Not even a ridiculously handsome one.

The air currents around me shifted. Hairs rose on the back of my neck, and an electric hum filled the air. So did the scent of something smoky—not cigarettes but the faint odor of burning oil and incense. I paused, pen hovering over my notebook, and focused my peripheral vision. A masculine hand—long fingers, blunt nails, an antique signet ring on the middle finger—drummed a quiet rhythm on the countertop beside me.

"Sorry to bother you," my neighbor said, his voice deep and a little gruff. "But could you pass me a menu?"

I looked up, realizing Luke Heinlein's mysterious companion had taken the empty barstool beside me. He pointed at a pile of laminated pages stacked on the counter and arched an eyebrow. Shaking off my daze, I handed him a menu and focused on my textbook. Having grown up surrounded by a slew of mostly look-alike mountain men, I'd never mistake Luke's friend for a local, and his aura was immediately distinctive. Unique. Magnetic.

Amber undertones warmed his dusky skin, and black hair fell in a thick swath over his forehead. The corner of his mouth curled up in that flirtatious grin again when he caught me peeking at him. "Got any recommendations?" He motioned to the menu.

I paused, processing his request. *Quit being stupid, Rikki. He's not the first guy to ever strike up a conversation with you. Just because he's a little prettier than average doesn't mean you get dumb and nervous.* "I-I like the pimento cheese." I mentally smacked myself. *I like pimento cheese? Really?*

The stranger's gaze dropped to my plate. "Must be good," he said. "You didn't leave a crumb."

My warm cheeks flared hotter, and I peered down at my biology notes so he wouldn't see my blush. "Yeah, well... It's kind of iconic around here. Rose won a blue ribbon for it at the state fair." *Could I sound any more like a hillbilly? Better shut up now, or next I'll be telling him about Jim Tucker's prize-winning heifer and Betty Gidley's famous blackberry cobbler.*

"Well, that's all the endorsement I needed." He flashed a genuine smile.

"Her tea's good. A little too sweet for me, but everyone else seems to like it that way."

"Maybe I'll try it. Don't get much cold sweet tea where I come from."

"And where's that?" The words rolled off my tongue before I could stop them. "I don't mean to be nosy. I just—"

"You mean you can tell I'm not a local?" He blinked at me, all big-eyed and melodramatic.

I suppressed a laugh. "It's the accent. Dead giveaway."

"Don't tell anyone, but..." He glanced around the room as if checking for surveillance. Lowering his voice, he whispered, "I'm a Yankee. Never thought it was a big deal before, but we did pass a Civil War monument on the way into town."

"Are you a soldier too?" I threw aside my former reservations about being nosy. "I'm guessing based on the fact you came in with Luke. Figured y'all might be army buddies."

He nodded, and a lock of dark hair fell over his eye. He raked it back. "Yeah. I'm in Luke's unit."

"You don't sound so happy about it."

He flinched, a surprised look washing across his face. "No, no... Luke's a great guy."

"You were overseas with him. Iraq or someplace like that."

He shrugged. "Yeah, someplace like that."

"But you're home now?"

He glanced around the diner, taking in the people and the old, worn fixtures. "Not quite home but close enough." His gaze settled on me, and electric flashes of excitement crackled in my nerves. Good Lord, he was a handsome man. "I'm Owen, by the way." He stuck his hand out. "Owen Amir."

I took his hand, but we didn't shake. He simply held my fingers, and I let him. "Erika Albemarle. People call me Rikki."

The corner of his mouth quirked. "Rikki?"

"What?" I pulled my hand loose from his.

"I guess..." He shrugged. "I guess I wasn't expecting it. Rikki's a little uncommon for a woman, isn't it?"

"I'm named after my dad."

"Was he hoping for a boy?"

I balled a fist. "Were you hoping for a fat lip?"

Laughter burst from Owen's throat. He leaned back and rubbed his eyes as he chuckled. I gritted my teeth and stared at my empty plate.

"I'm sorry, Rikki." He leaned closer, and his smoky scent whisked by me again. He lowered his voice. "I'm not normally so rude."

"What do I care? You're just some stranger passing through."

"No, I'm not. And this wasn't how I wanted to start things off, offending the locals on my first day in town." He fidgeted with the old ring on his left middle finger. "You should let me make it up to you—let me prove I'm a nice guy."

His grin was so damned charming, it worked like a magic spell. "What do you mean?"

"Let me take you to dinner tonight."

I scoffed. "Are you for real?"

"I'll be on my best behavior." He laid his hand over his heart as if making an oath.

I studied him again, his bright smile, the dark stubble dusting his square jaw, the way the overhead lights glinted off his hair in blue-black streaks. *Don't say yes. This one's a guaranteed heartbreaker.*

Owen leaned closer, his dark eyes locking onto mine. "Okay." I hadn't realized I was going to agree until the words left my mouth. "Dinner. Tonight. My choice."

His voice dropped lower, practically purring. "Just tell me when and where."

I scribbled an address on my napkin and slid it to him. "Be there at seven."

"Should I iron my suit, or are jeans okay?"

"Oh, definitely jeans." In a rush, I gathered my books and tucked a loose red curl behind my ear. I needed to leave, to get away from Owen before he talked me into selling my soul. Something about the glint in his eyes suggested that was a real possibility. "And if you have a pair of boots you don't mind messing up, I'd advise you to wear them."

A flicker of interest crossed his face. Before he could question me further, I fled, escaping the diner into a warm spring afternoon. The heat of his stare through the windows burned my neck and shoulders as I walked away.

Dear God, what kind of trouble did I just agree to get into?

Chapter Three
All Work and No Play

I SHOVED MY PITCHFORK into a mound of soiled hay and grunted as I heaved the pile into the wheelbarrow at my side. My back protested but not as much as it had when I'd started this job months before. Mucking stalls in Jack Huddle's stables was hard work, but it paid good money, and I sank every dime into my college savings fund.

Grunting, I forked up another mound as the barn door cracked open, letting in a cool gust of fresh air. Owen's dark head poked in. He glanced around the room, and when his gaze lit on me, he smiled, stepped inside, and pulled the door closed behind him. Until the moment he arrived, I wasn't sure he was going to show up. I'd been preparing myself for disappointment, trying to convince myself not to care either way. But at the sight of his earnest grin, relief spilled through me like a warm shot of whiskey, proving I'd cared more than I wanted to admit.

Beneath a black leather jacket that looked as soft as butter, Owen wore a thermal T-shirt unbuttoned at the neck, revealing an elegant collarbone and a hint of amber skin. My fingers twitched, responding to a subconscious urge to touch him, there, in the hollow of his throat. He was a stranger, and while I didn't yet know if he was a shallow jerk or a kind and brilliant soul, the baser part of me responded to him on an instinctual level that had nothing to do with logic or reason. We'd shared no more than a handful of words, but he was already shaking my foundations, and they weren't the steadiest to begin with.

15

He cracked a wry grin. "I didn't know what to expect when I pulled up in the driveway. Unless this is some kind of equestrian-themed restaurant, I'm not sure what's going on here."

I motioned to the hay. "Isn't it obvious?"

"You're getting revenge on me for my rudeness at the diner and making me work for my supper?"

I laughed. "Maybe a little. But no, I brought supper." I pointed overhead at the hayloft, where I'd stashed a tote stuffed with sandwiches. "A picnic, I guess you could say. I didn't have time for anything else."

He grinned, revealing a dimple—only one, in his right cheek. "*Or...* you were looking for an excuse to get me up in that loft with you."

"I have a feeling you wouldn't need an excuse."

He chuckled. "You're probably right."

"But be assured, it *is* just supper. If you don't get my meaning, I'll be happy to introduce you to the business end of my pitchfork." I pointed the sharp tines at him for emphasis.

He raised both hands in a defensive gesture. "I got the message. Don't worry."

"I'm almost done here. This is the last stall. Why don't you go up and unpack my tote bag? It's just some turkey subs and a couple bags of chips, but the cookies are homemade."

"Did you make them?"

"Yeah, but don't get excited. My baking has never won me any blue ribbons."

He plucked a hay strand from the tail of my braid and twirled it between his long fingers. "Why don't you let me help? Two hands are better than one... or something like that."

"If you're sure." I handed him the pitchfork, and he heaved soiled hay into my wheelbarrow as if it were a pile of feathers.

"So, this is your place?"

"Nope. Just a part-time job."

He raked up the last little pile of straw and chucked it in my wheelbarrow. "Where do I dump this stuff?"

I crooked my finger, and he followed, pushing the smelly mess down the barn's wide aisle. A pair of horses poked their heads over the high stall doors and sniffed inquisitively as we passed.

"You're a student, though, right?" he asked. "I saw the books on the counter at the diner."

"I'm transferring from the tech school and starting the nursing program at UNC in the fall."

"UNC? That's in Chapel Hill, right?"

"Yup." I opened the barn door and gritted my teeth against a blast of cool night air. "I'll be moving at the end of summer."

Under the glow of an exterior floodlight, Owen wheeled the dirty hay around the barn's backside and dumped it at the edge of a huge pile that Mr. Huddle would either compost or burn, depending on the need. We scurried back into the barn and scrubbed our hands clean in the big work sink.

He grinned when he caught my gaze. "If you want to be a nurse, then why are you mucking horse stalls?"

After drying my hands on an old rag, I climbed the ladder into the loft, and Owen joined me. "This is only *one* job." I sat, folding my legs beneath me, and grabbed my sandwich. "I have more. I'm an EMT with the county service, and sometimes I babysit for my mom's deputies—the ones who have kids, obviously."

Owen paused, sandwich halfway to his mouth. "Your mom's *what*?"

"Deputies." The curse of being the sheriff's daughter meant people often kept me at a distance, possibly afraid I'd tattle if they broke the speed limit or drank a beer before their twenty-first birthday. I wondered whether Owen would react similarly once he knew the truth.

If only he knew that being the sheriff's daughter was the least of my flaws.

I spread my sandwich wrapper in my lap to keep hay, horsehair, or manure from contaminating my supper. "My mom's sheriff of Twain County."

His mouth fell open. "She is?"

"Yup. Second time she's won the election. I think she plans to make a career of it."

Owen set down his sandwich, leaned back against a hay bale, and groaned. "Of all the girls I could have asked to dinner, I had to pick the sheriff's daughter."

"It's a small town, and there aren't that many girls you could've asked." I poked at my sub roll, shoving a loose turkey slice into place. "Put one red marble in a bag with five or six blue ones, chances are good you'll wind up selecting the red one."

He reached over and fingered a bright-auburn curl that had slipped from my braid. "And you're the red marble?"

"It's, uh, probability." I swallowed. "If you give me your criteria, I could give you the actual odds."

"Let me guess. You're studying statistics this semester."

"Got an A on my exam too."

"What do you mean by 'criteria'?"

"Age, physical preferences, that sort of thing. You tell me what kind of girls you'd be willing to take to dinner, and based on our town's population, I'll tell you your chances of ending up with me." If my statistics talk didn't bore Owen out of his mind and bring our date to a screeching halt, then I'd add a point in his favor under the "kind and brilliant soul" category in addition to the point I'd already given him for helping me shovel hay.

He shook his head. His smile faded, and his expression turned intense. "I don't need to know my chances."

"No?" I picked at the crust on my sub roll. "Why not?"

"That takes all the fun out of it."

His confidence was intimidating. I cleared my throat and changed the subject. "What about you?"

"What *about* me?"

"What's your story? Your name is Owen Amir, you come from somewhere up north, and you're in Luke Heinlein's unit in the army—"

"*Was* in the army."

Glancing up, I met his stare. The sparkle of humor in his eyes had dimmed. "Was?"

"Our commitment ended. We served our six years, and now we're out... mostly. We're pretty much regular civilians again."

"Oh, I doubt that." My poor sandwich had succumbed to my nervous jitters and sat in a crumbly pile in my lap. I balled up the remains and stuffed them into my tote.

"What's that mean?" He popped the last bit of his sub in his mouth and waited for my answer.

"*I* am the regular civilian here." I pointed at myself. "I go to school, go to work, and hang out with my friends in my very limited free time. I've never been to another country, and I've certainly never seen active combat. In fact, you and I probably have almost nothing in common."

Owen rooted through the tote, found the ziplock bag of cookies, took one for himself, and handed one to me. "Do all civilians work the same jobs?" he asked. "Do they practice the same religions, have the same interests, attend the same schools? Everyone's different, but most of us have more in common than we think—soldiers or not."

I broke off a cookie chunk and nibbled it. "I get what you're saying. But I still think I'm right when it comes to you and me."

He dipped his head and peered at me through thick black lashes. My heart stuttered, skipping a beat or two. "Then why are you and I here right now, together?"

We were there because I thought he was charming, confident, and gorgeous as sin. Because during the five minutes we talked at Rose's Diner, he had triggered something within me, an instinctual attraction—I blamed it on hormonal urges or animal magnetism. Lust at first sight. Maybe my head and heart weren't quite convinced, but my body was insisting it wanted more of him. I shrugged and blushed. *Too much damned blushing.*

"No, really," he said. "Tell me."

"Because you seemed... interesting."

"Interesting?"

And unbelievably appealing and sexy. "Yeah. *Interesting.*"

His shoulders shook in silent laughter. "I guess it could be worse."

I broke off another cookie chunk and inspected it. "We've got one thing in common at least."

"What's that?" He cleared away the last of our trash and stuffed it in my bag as he waited for my answer.

"We both like chocolate chip cookies."

"And Rose Heinlein's pimento cheese." He chuckled. "There have been successful partnerships founded on much less than that."

I leaned back against a hay bale and stared up at the barn roof. "Told you her food was great."

"Tea *was* too sweet, though."

"It's not for the fainthearted."

A thick silence settled between us, acting like a dam against the flood of questions welling inside me. While I could have stayed up all night, interrogating Owen about his past—his war experiences, his personal life—hunting for deeper commonalities than a shared appreciation for cookies and pimento cheese, something told me it was too soon to pry like that. That same voice warned that if I asked those kinds of questions, he had the right to ask them of me in return, and

I wasn't willing to bare my soul to many people, least of all a stranger. "Owen?" I asked.

He shifted closer and leaned against my hay bale. "Hmm?"

"Of all the places in the world you could have gone, why'd you come to Evansville?"

His shoulder pressed against mine, and I felt him shrug. "Wanted to get away from the world for a while, make a fresh start with my life now that it's not promised to the army. Luke talked about Evansville so much, I thought it might be the kind of place I needed."

"You're looking to get away, and I'm looking to get out." I chuckled sadly. "Talk about bad timing."

He huffed. "It's the story of my life."

After Owen helped me shut down the barn for the night, I followed him to the side yard, where I'd parked my dad's rugged old Chevy. A sinister black motorcycle crouched in the shadows on Dolly's far side. I would have missed the bike altogether if he hadn't thrown his long leg over the seat. The sexy, sleek machine fit his personality. *Oh yeah, it* totally *fits.*

"Why am I not surprised?" I asked.

He patted the small seat behind him. "C'mon. Let me take you for a ride."

"Kind of chilly, isn't it?" My pulse tapped an erratic rhythm—a mixture of eagerness and fear.

Owen zipped his leather jacket to his chin, slipped on a pair of gloves, and fiddled with something near the handlebars. A moment later, the motorcycle roared to life, and a tingle of delight shimmied up my spine. "Hold tight to me," he said. "I'll keep you warm."

I studied the clear night sky as I debated. Stars winked and twinkled, a million diamonds in a sea of black. The nearly full moon shone like a spotlight. "I have a biology exam first thing in the morning and an all-night shift with the EMS. I should probably go home."

His smile widened. "You probably should. But where's the fun in that?"

"Do you have a spare helmet?"

"No. But you can wear mine."

"You take chances with head injuries?"

He rapped his knuckles against his temple. "Made of rock. Just ask my mother."

I eyed Dolly and her big boxy cab. She looked as if she could withstand a nuclear blast. *Am I going to shun the safety of all that Detroit steel for a quick thrill on the back of Owen's bike? Hell yeah I am.*

"Okay." I stepped closer. "I've never ridden one of these things before. Tell me what I need to do."

He tugged his helmet off his handlebars, slid it over my head, and adjusted the chin strap. "Keep your feet on the pegs no matter what. Never put them down, even if we stop. Hold tight to me and keep your weight forward. When we hit a curve or a turn, the bike will lean. Don't fight it, but don't shift your weight either. It'll throw us off balance."

I stiffened and pulled away. "Wow, that's complicated. You're sure this is safe?"

He pulled me close and tugged up the zipper of my Carhartt jacket until it stopped at my throat. "Trust me, okay?"

"Famous last words of a fool."

He barked a joyous laugh that was genuine and full of life. "Throw your leg over and hold on, Rikki. I'll give you a ride you've never had before. And if you stick around, I promise it won't be your last."

While muttering curses about his cockiness, I levered my leg up and over the seat. When I sat, the bike sank beneath me, but I managed to swallow my squeal as I slid my arms around Owen in a loose embrace. He grunted, wrapped his fingers around my wrists, and pulled my arms snugger around his trim waist. "*Hold tight,* I said."

My heart spun like a pinwheel, but I complied with his demand. He shifted his weight, drawing the bike up straight. He cranked the throttle and revved the engine. We rolled along Jack Huddle's driveway at a slow pace, but my blood rushed in my ears as though we'd jumped tandem from an airplane.

"Ready?" he shouted as we approached the highway. He gave me no chance to respond before the bike dipped to the right, he gunned the throttle, and we shot off into the night.

As we rode, Owen occasionally stroked my knee or drew a warm finger over my knuckles as if reassuring himself I was still behind him. I never asked where we were going, assuming he had no destination in mind, but we wound up on a familiar length of road—a stretch of Highway 74 winding alongside the Nantahala River. Moisture thickened the air. The scent of fresh water—moss, minerals, and fish—intensified. This time of year, this area was mostly empty, but in another month, tourists would invade, filling the river with paddlers eager for white water adventures.

I tapped Owen's thigh. He slowed his bike, and I pitched my voice above the roar of river and motorcycle engine. "Take a right up here at the next road."

He nodded and eased off the throttle, slowing as we neared the turn. He leaned, and the bike coasted around the corner, rolling onto a narrow road that crossed a bridge suspended over the water. I tapped his leg again and pointed at the concrete barrier between the road and riverbank. "Pull over there."

He stopped the bike parallel to the road and dropped the kickstand with his heel. When the motorcycle settled, he flicked the ignition switch, leaving only the river's throaty growl to echo in my ears. I tugged off my helmet and handed it to him. He slid off his seat and followed as I strode toward the bridge, a concrete-and-iron structure spanning a shallow but wide bend in the river. Twenty feet below, the water tumbled over jagged rocks, forming eddies and white-capped waves. Moonlight sparkled, dancing and jumping in the currents.

I stopped midway across the bridge and leaned against the railing, peering at the dark waters. Iron beams formed two pairs of arches on both sides of the bridge, adding support and improving the aesthetics of an otherwise utilitarian hunk of concrete. "The old bridge burned a while back. Big fires destroyed the Smokies a few years ago. It came up through here, wiped out a bunch of the rafting cabins and outfitters. Took a while to rebuild, but you can't keep mountain folks down for long. They're stubborn and industrious."

"You brought us here to show me a bridge?"

I flicked on the flashlight app on my phone and held it under my chin, casting my face in dramatic lighting. "I brought you here to tell you a ghost story."

Owen chucked and leaned against the railing. Instead of looking at the river, he pinned his attention on me. "You like scary stories?"

"Not necessarily." I stepped back, raising a finger to ward him off when he reached for me. "Uh-uh, this bridge is bad luck for couples."

"Are you saying we're a couple already? You move fast, Miss Albemarle."

I shoved his shoulder and ignored his teasing smirk. "I'm saying if you're going to live in Twain County, you should know some of the local lore."

He cocked his head and folded his arms on the bridge railing. "Do tell."

"Have you ever heard the tragedy of the Nantahala Lovers? It's our own local Romeo and Juliet story." I frowned and bit my lip. "Or maybe I should say it's our own local Hatfield and McCoy story, since this is the mountains, and the families are hillbillies instead of Italian nobility."

Owen chuckled. "Isn't hillbilly an offensive term?"

"Only if you're not from around here."

"So, *two households, both alike in dignity, in fair Twain County, where we lay our scene...*"

I gaped at him. *He's hot* and *nerdy?* My heart pitter-pattered.

"What?" He shrugged. "I read."

"Shakespeare?"

"The desert gets really boring when you've been stationed there long enough. Reading is a good way to pass the time."

I digested that curious bit of information and kept going. "Well, instead of the Montagues and the Capulets, it was the Harrises and the Dietzes. And instead of the Renaissance, it was the forties."

"So their families were sworn enemies, but the two teenagers fell for each other, anyway? Star-crossed lovers and all that?"

With a nod, I pushed away from the rail and strolled closer to the bridge's opposite end. "This is the part you might find interesting, though. Their parents hated them being together, as you'd expect, but it was World War II, and they figured it wouldn't be long before Bennie Dietz got drafted. And he did. They *didn't* expect Dorothy Harris to sign up too."

"What do you mean?"

I flinched. Owen stood mere inches behind me, but I hadn't heard him move or make a sound, not a crunch of grit under his boot heel or thud of a heavy footstep.

"Women didn't fight in those days," he said.

I poked his chest. "More of them fought than the history books would lead you to believe." Backing away again, I crossed to the opposite railing and stared upstream. Low-hanging branches shadowed the rushing water, blocking the moonlight. An uneasy feeling crept over me, as though spirits watched us from those dark places. "But you're right. Dorothy wasn't a soldier. She served as a nurse. She was stationed at Pearl Harbor on the day Japan attacked."

"She was killed?" His voice was soft, reverent.

I nodded. "Bennie lost a leg during a battle in France not long after. He came home and heard the news about Dorothy." I patted the bridge railing, which rose to just above my navel. I could climb it, but it would take some effort. "Dorothy's family had buried her in a private family plot. They refused to let Bennie come onto their land to visit her grave."

"Even though he was a wounded veteran?"

"The animosity between those families was deeper than any notion of patriotism or sacrifice. Besides, people had different feelings about wounded warriors in those days. Life was never going to be easy for Bennie. One night he couldn't take the pain anymore—from his injuries and from his broken heart." I latched onto one of the arching cross support beams and hauled myself up, balancing on the narrow railing.

Owen grabbed at me. "Rikki, what are you—"

I stepped away, released the arch support, and continued my story. "Bennie came out here to this bridge—managed to climb up on the railing somehow."

Owen grunted when I wobbled. "You're making me nervous."

"What is it? A twenty-foot fall? It might not mean instant death, but I guarantee there would be broken bones, and Bennie wasn't in the best shape to begin with, physically speaking. Was probably drunk too. If the fall didn't kill him right away, then the water finished the job."

Maybe I was trying to show off a little. Taking risks like this wasn't like me, but it added drama to my story. Owen, however, was clearly distraught. "Rikki... *please.*"

"What are you afraid of? You're the one racing around mountain roads at night with no helmet."

"One of us should be the responsible one. I nominate you."

Sighing, I relented and crouched, preparing to jump down, but Owen moved fast, throwing his arms around me. He dragged me away from the railing and set me on my feet at the center of the bridge. His breath puffed a staccato beat in my ear, and his smoky scent was intense. "Are you *nuts?*"

"I'm sorry. I was just trying to spice things up a bit."

He cleared his throat and scrubbed a hand over his face. "Next time, leave the spice for cooking, okay?"

Chagrinned, I dropped my chin to my chest. "Okay."

"So..." He pushed a loose curl behind my ear. "I thought you said this was a ghost story. Are you saying Bennie haunts this bridge?"

I squirmed out of Owen's embrace. Reluctantly, he let me go. "No. It's Dorothy's ghost. Folks have said they saw a woman in white standing on the railing, searching the water for her lost love. Whenever anyone tries to approach her, she disappears. And young lovers caught on the bridge together have been chased off by terrifying, ghostly howls."

"Well... that was tragic and hardly the right tone for a first-date story."

I snorted. "Like you could do better."

"Actually"—he buffed his nails against his chest and studied his cuticles—"I can."

"*You* have a ghost story?"

"Something like that." He held his hand out. I took it and let him lead me back to his bike. He sat sideways on the saddle and pulled me between his outstretched legs. "This one takes place in the mountains, too, but not in the US. This happened in the Jibal al-Khalil, the Judean Mountains, near Hebron, in Palestine."

My curiosity sharpened. Drawing from stereotypes—his deep-bronze skin, his dark hair, his last name—I'd suspected Owen's ancestral roots were Middle Eastern, likely Arabic. His telling a story set in Palestine suggested my assumptions might've been right.

"The violence between Israel and Palestine took a toll on that area, and there are more than a few abandoned villages hiding there in the mountains—places a little boy might like to explore whenever he could sneak away from his elders. The fact that the elders had forbidden the little boy from going into those houses only enhanced the appeal."

I chuckled. "Was the little boy's name Owen, by chance?"

"Shhh." Grinning, he pressed a finger to his lips. "Listen. One day, the little boy's older brother dared him to go into one of those empty old houses late at night, after their elders had gone to sleep. And he didn't want to admit it to anyone, but he was really scared because he'd heard those houses were haunted. The jinn like to live in these kinds of places, and they like to play tricks on foolish children. So, this boy, he knew his brother was waiting, and his brother would tease him—maybe even beat him up if he didn't go inside. He said a little prayer to Allah, asking for protection.

"He made his way through this house—he's only got an oil lamp lighting his way. And he managed to make a circle through the house without any problems. He was looking for a souvenir, something to take to his brother to prove he'd completed the challenge. On his way back to the front door, he spotted a shelf. On the shelf was a dusty old jar."

I bit my bottom lip, anticipating the end of this story and wondering where it was going to lead. I'd half expected Owen to tell me another tale about lovers, maybe one with a happier ending, but his story was way more intriguing than mine. The way he told it—his voice and tone and the tension in his muscles—made me feel as though this was something that had truly happened rather than a mere folktale.

"Little boys are innately curious," he said.

"Are they?"

"You don't have a brother?"

"Only child."

"Spoiled rotten, then, aren't you?" he teased.

I brushed my knuckles against his chin and brought us back to the story. "The little boy opened the jar, didn't he?"

He clicked his tongue. "Of course he did."

"What was inside?"

"What do you think?"

"A... how did you say it? A jinni? Like Aladdin and his lamp."

"This isn't a Disney movie." He sniffed. "The jinn are rarely so benevolent as a blue Robin Williams."

"So, was it a jinni?"

"It was." Owen threw his leg over the seat and sat backward on his motorcycle. He patted the pillion seat, gesturing for me to join him. Careful not to kick him or upset the bike's precarious balance, I climbed up, sat, and hooked my feet around the pegs. We faced each other, and the moonlight shone brightly, illuminating his brow and the bridge of his nose while drawing dark shadows over his eyes. "Having been kept captive in the jar for so long, the jinni was *furious* with humans. It vowed to kill whoever released him. The little boy begged for his life, but the jinni was merciless. So, the little boy tricked the jinni into returning to the jar."

"How did he do that?"

He sniffed. "I really wish I knew."

I laughed again, surprised by his sudden petulant tone. "Maybe the little boy wished him back into the jar?"

"The jinn don't grant wishes, but they do make deals. I suspect the little boy offered the jinni something he couldn't refuse. But whatever it was, the details have been forgotten over time.

"So, trapped again, the jinni pledged to reward the little boy with something very valuable if he released him. The boy agreed, and the jinni told the little boy where he could find a ring. A very powerful ring—powerful enough to protect him against the jinn, maybe even powerful enough to control the jinn."

"Did he find the ring?"

Owen traced a finger across my knuckles. "The legend says he did. The boy found the ring in his great-grandmother's jewelry box."

I feigned outrage, gasping dramatically. "Did he *steal* it from his grandmother?"

Owen shook his head. "She caught him in the act, but when he explained the story, about what had happened with the jinni in the mountains, his grandmother gave him the ring and told him to never take it off unless he was to pass it to one of his own sons or daughters one day."

"Did it protect him from the jinn as promised?"

"By all accounts, yes, it did."

Owen wore a curious ring on his left middle finger. Its age and wear suggested significance—a family heirloom, maybe. Perhaps this legend traveled from parent to child when the ring was passed down. If I was right, then his tale seemed a personal thing to have shared with someone he barely knew.

"Thank you for the story. It did seem to have a happier ending than mine. Nobody died in it."

His voice was strangely cold when he replied. "No. Not yet, anyway." He blinked and forced a tight smile. "That story wasn't about me, by the way. I was born in New York. So were my parents."

"You're as American as apple pie, huh?"

He stretched, popping his neck, then stood and repositioned himself facing forward. "You'd be surprised." He settled on his seat again, drew the bike up straight, and flicked the ignition switch. The Ducati growled. "My *sitto* makes an excellent apple pie."

Chapter Four
Fire on the Mountain

I LOST COUNT OF THE days, swept up in a whirlwind of exam preparation—joining my best friend, Mina Rhee, for study cram sessions that involved borderline-lethal doses of caffeine and sugar—and long, hard hours in the back of the Twain County EMS's ambulance. I had clocked out, turned off my radio, and was climbing into my truck at the end of my third shift in a row when Roberto, a lead paramedic, dashed out of the station, yelling for me. "Rikki, hold up!"

His anxious voice made my Spidey senses tingle. Whatever he was about to say next wouldn't be good news. "What's going on?"

"Wildfire on Raven's Knob. Fire departments from around the county are already on the scene."

My pulse switched from an anticipatory lope to a desperate sprint. "Injuries?"

He shook his head. "Not yet, but we're going to head out to back up the firefighters and be there just in case there are civilian casualties."

I followed Roberto to the ambulance. My fellow EMT, Bonnie Jo, was climbing into the passenger seat, leaving the jump seat in the back for me. "It's pretty sparsely populated out that way."

Roberto opened the rig's back door for me, and I climbed in. "And for that," he said, "we should be grateful."

Raven's Knob was a stubby peak with a bald, rocky hump at its crest. A rudimentary park and campground clung to the north-facing side. A narrow rural road snaked around the mountain, and two dozen or more families had built homes and farms along that route. A nearby meandering creek might've discouraged the fire from spreading farther west and north, but on the east side, there were acres of vulnerable pastureland and national forest.

Our sirens screamed through the countryside as we raced toward the fire. Normally I tuned them out, but tonight the shrieking stripped my nerves like an exposed wire. I gripped the edges of my seat, ground my teeth, and repeated a steady litany of prayers under my breath. My gut clenched as I thought of the fire that had swept through the Smokies several years before and the devastation left behind. Twain County had escaped the worst of the damage, but I wondered whether we would be so lucky this time. *Please, God, don't let this be another fire like that one.*

The cloying scent of burning wood intensified as we neared Raven's Knob. Roberto shut off the siren and slowed to a creep. The other emergency vehicles' lights strobed through our rear windows, lighting the interior in bright red and blue streaks. He lowered his window, and I recognized the voice shouting at us. *Of course, she'd be here.*

I unhooked my seat belt and squeezed my shoulders through the narrow port between Roberto's and Bonnie Jo's seats. "Mom?"

She touched the brim of her Smokey-the-Bear-style hat, something she usually reserved for formal occasions. Most days she just wore a ball cap embroidered with a sheriff's office patch. Tonight she'd apparently wanted to appear more official. "Rikki."

"How bad is it?"

"Could be a lot worse. Buddy Thompson's running this show, so everything's in capable hands. My crew's mostly here to direct traffic, relay communications, help with evac."

Buddy Thompson was the head of the local National Forest Service office, and his crew would have primary jurisdiction. Fine by me; the forest rangers were trained for handling these kinds of emergencies. Mom and her deputies were better equipped for dealing with stubborn homeowners, media, and the local lookie-loos.

She pointed at my paramedic in the driver's seat. "I was just telling Roberto to go another mile or so and stay out of the way as best you can but be prepared for whatever. Don't expect too many civilian problems—my guys got most of them to clear out ahead of the blaze. You and the other paramedic crews will mostly be here to treat any overzealous types from the county fire and volunteer departments. There's got to be at least a hundred of them out there stomping all over that mountain, playing at weekend warrior." A sneer wrinkled her nose. "One of them is bound to bite off more than he can chew."

She stepped back from our rig and motioned for us to continue down the road. "Stay safe out there, gang."

"Be careful, Mom."

She nodded, and I watched her fade into the gloom as we pulled away. I held my place, squeezed in between Roberto and Bonnie Jo, staring out the front window. Smoke swirled across our windshield in grayish wafts, thinner than fog but still reflecting our headlights. Ambulances from other stations around the county lined either side of Raven's Knob Road. We pulled onto the shoulder behind a rig from the Six Springs Rescue Squad. I also spotted ambulances from the Silverton Township and two other county stations.

Roberto parked, and my eyes watered the moment I encountered the smoky air, but I blinked away my tears and followed Roberto's flashlight beam toward a group of paramedics and EMTs gathered near a county ambulance from a station near the western border. A young man sat on the rear step, slumped over, his hands on his knees as he inhaled deep breaths from an oxygen mask. Ashes dusted his dark hair, and sweat ran in gray rivulets down his brow.

"Too much excitement?" I asked the young woman standing next to me. I'd seen her before in some of our in-service training classes but didn't remember her name.

"He should be fine." She shrugged. "They'll patch him up and send him home. He's the first, but he won't be the last."

As the night wore on, more firefighters came in, suffering everything from smoke inhalation to burns on their extremities. Most were treated and sent home. A few were taken to Twain County General for further assessment and observation. Roberto, Bonnie Jo, and I mostly stood around, perfecting the art of hurry up and wait.

I had established a perch on our ambulance's rear step and sipped from a thermos of coffee while Bonnie Jo's latest patient claimed a spot beside me. A volunteer firefighter from Six Springs, he complained of feeling dizzy and weak. Bonnie Jo wrapped a blood-pressure cuff around his bicep, inflated it, and pressed a stethoscope to the inside of his elbow. She listened to his pulse with her eyes closed. I was tempted to close my eyes, too, and give in to the urge to doze off, but a mob of excited voices startled me out of my stupor.

After stumbling to my feet, I raced around the corner of the ambulance and approached a group carrying an unconscious man. Roberto beat me to him and issued orders in a commanding voice, telling the group to carry their friend to our rig. One man from the posse hung back, watching as the others followed Roberto. He looked like most of the others, dusted in a patina of gray and black that disguised his face and hid the true shade of his light hair. His T-shirt hung from bony shoulders, and its logo revealed he was a member of Silverton's volunteer fire department. He caught me staring and narrowed his eyes. "You a paramedic?"

"EMT."

"Close enough." He crooked his finger. "I need you to come with me."

I crossed my arms over my chest, holding my ground. If he needed my help, I would gladly give it, but I wouldn't follow him into danger without knowing the risks. "Where to?"

"Buckley homestead. You know it?"

"Not personally, but I know it's a big beef farm up the road."

"Can't we walk and talk at the same time?" He marched off, heading toward the front of the ambulance procession.

I debated holding my place until he finished explaining but didn't want to risk wasting time that was better spent helping someone in need. I jogged to catch up with him.

"Buckley Senior won't leave. Says he's got to defend his cattle. Fine, don't nobody have a problem with that. 'Cept now there's an offshoot from the main fire creepin' down the mountain toward his house. We got firefighters at the scene, but Buckley and some of his family are trapped behind the fire line. We need medical response to get as close as possible and be prepared for the worst."

"You're going to need a whole lot more than just me."

"Already got a team put together." He pointed at a group of EMTs rushing down the path ahead of us, flashlight beams bouncing. "Hurry and catch up."

I rolled onto my toes and sprinted behind them, but as I raced past the last ambulance, reaching a string of civilian vehicles, someone shouted my name. "Rikki?"

"Luke?" I recognized him leaning against his truck, illuminated in the light of the lantern perched on his hood. Soot and ash coated him head to toe, same as everyone else. "What are you doing out here?"

"Owen and I were hanging out at the house when Dad got the call. Decided we'd follow him out here and see if we could help."

"Owen?" I searched the darkness around Luke's truck. "Where is he?"

Luke pointed up the road. "Went with a group of firefighters up to the Buckley farm about an hour ago. Haven't seen him since."

"That's where I'm headed now." Two ambulances blasted past us, presumably carrying more EMS staff and supplies to the farm. I pointed at the volunteer from the Silverton fire squad. "Fire Marshall Bill there said there's a group at the farm trapped behind the fire line."

Luke flinched. "Oh God..."

"You wanna come with?"

"Do you really have to ask?" He grabbed his lantern and climbed behind the wheel. "Get in, Albemarle."

I jumped into the truck bed and said a prayer for Owen. When we reached the house, Luke zoomed past the other crews and ambulances, driving around to the backyard. As soon as the truck stopped, I jumped out. Luke caught up to me, and we loped toward the woods on the hill behind the Buckley farmhouse. He'd brought his high-powered Maglite, and its beam bounced off the billowing plumes of smoke.

My eyes watered, and I coughed. "Maybe this isn't such a good idea. I'm sure I could find a spare respirator somewhere."

"I already asked for one. There aren't any extras except for what you might have on your rig. You want to grab one of those?"

"No." I shook my head. "Save those for our patients—somebody who needs it more than I do."

He dug a square of red fabric from his pocket and passed it to me. "Here, put this on. It might help."

I tied the bandana around my face, covering my nose and mouth while Luke twisted the scarf around his neck so it covered his head, leaving only a slit for his eyes. I'd seen soldiers wearing those same scarves in every news report about the American military in the Middle East.

"Won't be much help if we're overcome by smoke." I coughed again.

"What help are we if we wait back at the house with everyone else?"

"The alive kind."

He stopped abruptly, and I stumbled into him. "He can't stop talking about you, you know."

"Who?"

"Owen."

"This isn't really the time to talk about it." And it wasn't, although that didn't stop me from feeling a moment of satisfaction from Luke's admission. It was only fair that Owen couldn't stop talking about me—I certainly hadn't been able to stop thinking about him.

Luke shrugged, and his flashlight beam swept through the smoky trees. "I'm just saying there will never be a second date if you let him die in this fire."

I hacked a derisive sound. "If I *let*—"

"Stay here if you want." Luke stepped deeper into the woods, and gauzy smoke curled around him like a beckoning spirit. "But I was trained to never leave a man behind, especially when that man is Owen. He's like a brother to me, and I owe him my life."

"Luke."

He kept going.

I stomped my foot. "Luke!"

He paused. "What?"

Grumbling, I hurried to catch up. "Wait for me."

We weaved through trees and bracken, following our noses and the occasional distant shout or flashlight strobe. The crackle of hungry flames rose to a steady roar. My nose and throat were clogged, and my eyes spilled a constant stream of tears. The intense heat baked moisture from my skin. Ghostly shadows of fire crews danced before us like hellish demons. The angry buzz of chainsaws seemed to vibrate in my teeth.

"We're never going to find him like this." I tugged Luke's sleeve.

Ignoring me, he cupped his hands around his mouth and shouted. "Owen! Owen Amir!"

"Owen olly oxen free," I muttered under my breath.

Luke swung his flashlight back and forth in an arc and bellowed like an angry elephant. "Owen Amir!"

"Might as well be yelling for a needle to come out of the haystack."

"Needles don't have ears." He leaned back and called again, raising his voice to the heavens.

My eyes were bleary from dust and exhaustion. Twenty or more hours on duty without a real break or any rest was taking its toll. I hated to give up too easily, but with my throat closing up and my eyes swelling shut, I didn't know how much help I could really offer. I grabbed Luke's arm. "Look, dude. I don't know what you're hoping—"

A huge shadow stumbled into Luke's flashlight beam. I yelped and skittered back.

"Luke." The shadow spoke with a raspy, dry voice. "What the hell are you doing here?"

My heart stuttered, skipping a beat as my vision cleared long enough for me to recognize the speaker. *What are the odds? Not sure my statistics class prepared me for this kind of calculation.* "Owen? What's a nice guy like you doing in a place like this?"

Owen grunted. "It doesn't surprise me to find *you* here, Luke, but dragging Rikki into a situation like this—"

"He didn't drag me. I'm EMS. This is my *job*."

The flashlight beam cast his face in harsh contrast when he gave an apologetic wince. His shadow groaned, and only then did I realize he hadn't come alone. He was supporting the weight of another man who swayed on his feet. I rushed to his side and shoved my shoulder under the man's armpit, although Owen likely didn't need my help.

"Can you two get Mr. Buckley some help?" Owen asked. "I've got to go back for the others."

Mr. Buckley slumped against me, and my knees buckled, but I caught myself before I fell.

"I'll bring the others out to you, okay, Rikki?" Owen paused and brushed his knuckles along my jaw. "Be careful, though. Stay safe."

"You can't go back in there."

"Yes, I can. I'll be fine." He pointed at my patient. "Just get him some help."

"There are ambulances in the drive at Buckley's house. Bring out anyone you find, and I'll make sure they get treatment."

Owen paused and nodded before retreating again into the smoke and shadows.

"Luke, I know you want to go with him, but I can't carry Mr. Buckley by myself. Help me get him to the driveway, then you can go back for Owen."

Luke opened his mouth as if to argue. But he stopped, bit his lip, and hauled Mr. Buckley over his shoulder with a grunt. We hustled the old man down the hill into the flat yard behind his house. Another team had spotted us and rushed to take Mr. Buckley from Luke. They carried him to the nearest ambulance and went to work checking his vitals.

Luke left without a word, rushing up the hill and disappearing into the tree line. I paused long enough to guzzle a bottle of water and scrub a wet towel over my face and eyes. An audience of medical personnel had surrounded me, asking questions about how we'd come to find Mr. Buckley. I explained what happened, and we set up a rotation, with two people at a time going to meet Owen and Luke or whoever else came out and ferry them back to the ambulances we'd set up as an impromptu field hospital in the Buckleys' front yard.

We received and treated two more members of the Buckley family before it was my turn to climb up the mountain again, this time with Roberto at my side. Dawn approached as we waited, minutes ticking by as slowly as cold molasses, both of us too keyed up and anxious to make small talk. Finally, after what felt like hours, Owen lurched out of the gloom, Luke at his side, carrying another man between them.

"This is the last one," Owen said. "You lead the way, Rikki. We'll bring him down."

"Okay, but then you'll let me take a look at you."

Roberto's flashlight cut through the murky light. Sunlight struggled to find its way through the smoke. I had lost track of the time but figured I had been at it for close to twenty-four hours. If I didn't stop soon, they'd be finding a spot for me in the back of one of those ambulances.

My feet felt like concrete blocks. A root caught my boot and tripped me. Owen latched onto my arm, catching me before I face-planted. "It's not me you should be worrying about. Don't take this the wrong way, but you look wrung out."

"I'll be all right." I waved him off and slogged down the hillside, following Roberto. Luke and Owen handed off their patient, but before I could order Owen to let me check him out, a band of firefighters descended the mountain, announcing the fire had been contained. The crowd cheered, and relief crashed over me like a tidal wave, swift and overwhelming. It knocked me off my feet, literally.

Before I hit the ground, Owen caught me and swept me into his arms, holding me steady while I recovered my footing. "Luke, give us a ride out of here, will you?"

"What about you?" I mumbled. "You need to let Roberto check you out."

"Really, I'm fine. Relax and let someone worry about you for a change."

Too tired to argue, I relented. Owen helped me shuffle to Luke's truck. If I had been in better shape, I would have objected to being lugged around like a sack of potatoes, but he was gentle when he lifted me into the passenger seat.

"Take the keys," Luke said. "Get her home. I'll hitch a ride with somebody else."

I pried open an eyelid. "You sure you're okay, Luke?"

He winked and flashed a wicked grin. Ash, soot, and the weak dawn light painted both young men in sickly, sallow hues, but they hadn't suffered any obvious damage. "I might be hocking up black loogies and picking ashy boogers out of my nose for the next few days, but I reckon I'll live."

I groaned. "You are *so* gross."

He was still chuckling when Owen climbed into the driver's seat and slammed his door shut. "Can you stay awake long enough to give me directions to your house?" He cranked the engine, whipped the truck around, and sped out to the main road.

"I'll stay awake, and you tell me what compelled you to take a risk like that. Are you hoping to join the local fire department or something?"

"No, I don't want to be a fireman, but helping out in critical situations is just what I'm trained to do. A soldier runs toward the fire, not away from it."

"You're not a soldier anymore. It's not your responsibility."

"I guess you can take the boy out of the army, but you can't take the army out of the boy. You can't tell me that even if you quit the EMS, you wouldn't still help people if they needed it."

I rolled a shoulder. "Giving someone the Heimlich maneuver is not the same as rushing into a raging forest fire."

"And yet, there you were, doing that very thing." He squeezed my hand. "You were a hero tonight, Rikki."

"Speak for yourself, Superman. Besides, how could I get a second date with you if I let you die in that fire?"

He barked a surprised laugh. "So, that was your motivation, huh?"

"Seemed like a good idea at the time."

"I've been trying to get you to go out with me again for the past two weeks, but your schedule has been overloaded."

"My biology exam is the day after tomorrow... wait. What's today?"

He snorted. "Technically, it's Tuesday."

"Ugh. Then my exam is *tomorrow*. But when I finish it, I'm done with school for the rest of the summer."

He reached over, wrapped an arm around my shoulder, and pulled me closer. I snuggled against him, soaking up his reassuring warmth. "Then maybe you'll have some time for me?" he asked.

"Maybe, if you're lucky."

"I'm feeling pretty lucky right now."

I smiled and rested my head on his shoulder. "You're not the only one."

Chapter Five
No Expectations

I DROPPED MY FINISHED biology exam booklet on the stack on the proctor's desk and resisted the urge to skip out of the classroom, whistling a victory song. *Nailed it.* Or at least I thought I had. The weight of school pressure lifted from my shoulders, and I felt fifty pounds lighter, though I knew the feeling wouldn't last. Fall semester at UNC would be a hundred times worse when my course load focused on the heavy-duty sciences and practical medical procedures.

I leaned against the classroom door, and it opened into a hallway cutting through Twain County Community College's small science building. Mina Rhee, my best friend since grade school, slouched against the wall across from me, her gaze unfocused and empty as she twirled a strand of long black hair around her finger. Her low-slung jeans and cropped T-shirt revealed a glimpse of rib tattoos. In Evansville, such a thing had once been scandalous, but Mina had confessed to getting a thrill from shocking our town's old biddies.

I, on the other hand, wore a comfortable old pair of Levi's and my shabby Doc Martens. No glamour but no scandal either. When I was little, I'd wanted to be just like Mina, but once I realized my future was destined for a closet full of hospital scrubs and nonslip shoes, I lost interest in trendy fashion, to Mina's perpetual disappointment.

She glanced up as I approached, and the vague, unfocused look on her face disappeared. "Rikki." She bit her lip. "How'd you do?"

I'd rocked the test, but Mina's worried expression kept me from saying so. "I think I did okay. How about you?"

She fell into step beside me, leaving behind a faint trail of Miss Dior Cherie's jasmine blend as we strolled to the exit. "If I passed, it was all because of you. I'll owe you my firstborn child or something."

"What do you mean?"

"All that time you spent helping me study. I don't know what I'd do without you. You're more than my BFF. You're, like, the benevolent goddess of exam preparation."

I frowned. "That's a lame superpower. I'd rather be able to fly or turn invisible."

"Still..."

I squeezed her arm. "I'm sure you did great. You've done well all semester, haven't you?"

"Yeah, I guess." She and I pushed through the exit doors and stepped into a bright spring afternoon—the perfect weather to accompany my good mood. Exams had ended, and the only thing standing between me and UNC was a few months of summertime freedom—at least when I wasn't working. My bank account would need a lot of padding before I left for Chapel Hill, and the EMS station manager had promised to give me all the hours she could spare.

"You want to get lunch?" I asked as we crossed the small courtyard, heading for the parking lot.

Mina glanced at her phone. "It's kinda early."

"Yeah, but I didn't get breakfast this morning, and I have at least an hour to kill until my shift starts."

She inhaled as if preparing to answer, but her mouth fell open, and her eyes bugged. I followed her stare, which had landed on a tall, dark figure in a black leather jacket, sitting astride a nightmare of a motorcycle parked beside Dolly. Warm tingles of delight washed over me from the roots of my hair to the tips of my toenails.

"Who the hell is that?" she whispered. "Wait, is that... *him*?"

I hadn't seen Owen since he'd taken me home from the fire and helped me stumble into bed. He'd taken off my boots, drawn the covers over me, and kissed my cheek as I sank into a coma-like sleep. When I'd woken up half a day later, I'd discovered a text message from him—Shakespeare, of all things.

Enjoy the honey-heavy dew of slumber.

I would have reached out to him sooner, but I'd promised to help Mina study, and we'd spent the evening gorging on pizza and biology trivia. Owen's presence there in the school parking lot was an unexpected but welcome surprise. *Very welcome.*

Owen shifted on his bike, and his signature grin spread across his lips. Black sunglasses shielded his eyes, but I remembered the way the stars had seemed to reflect in their dark depths.

"Oh," Mina said, breathless. "Oh my..."

"You can say that again."

"Hey, Rikki." Owen flicked a quick two-fingered wave as we approached.

I tried not to smile like an utter idiot, although that was how I felt. A couple of hours in his company and I was like an infatuated tween at her first boy-band concert. "What are you doing here?"

"You owe me a second date. Thought I'd take you to lunch before you went to work."

"When you told me about him, you left out some crucial details," Mina whispered.

"Like what?"

"Like exactly how *fine* he is." She punched my shoulder and raised her voice, backing toward her car. "Call me later."

"I'd have asked you to dinner instead," Owen said, still sitting astride his bike. "But I won't be around tonight. Or most of next week either. I've got some business out of town."

"Bored of Evansville already?"

He slipped off his sunglasses and peered at me through thick lashes. Amber flecks, like fool's gold, glinted in his dark eyes. "Oh no." His voice was low and full of suggestion. "Things are starting to get *very* exciting around here."

"You came all the way here to ask me to lunch?" Twain County Community College was near the county's most southwestern edge, almost at the limits of the bordering town of Millsboro. My school wasn't on the way to anything, so Owen had likely come here on purpose, solely to see me. How could I be so lucky?

"How else was I going to get ahold of you?"

I could've listed a dozen ways I would've liked him to get ahold of me, none involving telephones or scrawled notes left on windshields. "Meet me at Rose's Diner?"

Owen's gaze dropped to his lap, and his thumb toyed with the old ring on his middle finger, spinning it around his knuckle. "You don't want to ride with me?"

"I would..." Oh, how I'd loved having Owen between my legs the night he'd driven us out to the Nantahala Bridge, his back pressed against me as we soared over winding mountain roads, like spirits unrestrained by gravity, but sensibility won out. "But it would take too long to bring me all the way back here. The diner is closer to my house, and I have to get home and change before I go to work."

"Too bad." He clicked his tongue. "There *will* be a next time, though. I like having you wrapped around me, Rikki." He slid his sunglasses in place. "Meet you there, okay? I'll get us a booth." He straightened his bike, flicked the ignition switch, and gunned the motor. After revving the engine several times, he shot away as swiftly as a bird, one of those big predator types, a raven or a black eagle.

I released my pent-up breath in a wheeze and crumpled against my truck door. "You spent your whole life itching to leave this town," I told myself. "Now's not the time to start looking for a reason to stay."

The drive to the diner gave me time to settle my nerves and harden my defenses against Owen's ridiculous allure.

The last time we were together, I'd wanted to plumb his proverbial depths, but beneath the bright light of a clear spring afternoon, romance gave way to reason. *Is it possible to enjoy his company without getting attached? Can I even take that risk?* Nothing would keep me from attending school in the fall, and there was no point in moving to Chapel Hill with a broken heart.

I parked Dolly in a spot beside Owen's motorcycle, near the diner's front door, and killed the engine. The reflection in my rearview mirror revealed my curls were tangled around my head and shoulders like a ruddy lion's mane. Finger combing only made things worse, so I hissed a silent curse, dabbed on a coat of lip gloss, and climbed out of the truck.

When I stepped through the café's front door, an almost empty diner greeted me, and the tension in my shoulders eased. Owen made me nervous enough on his own. At least I wouldn't have to eat lunch with him under the scrutiny of the whole town.

As I eased into a seat across from Owen, Rose brought over a pair of menus and set them on the table.

"Rikki?" She cocked her head to the side and furrowed her brow. "When Owen said someone would be joining him, I didn't think it would be you."

"Um, surprise?" I waggled my fingers at her.

She gave him a serious look, her eyes narrowed. "You make friends quick, don't you?"

"What can I say? I'm a friendly guy."

Rose patted my shoulder. I'd known her long enough to recognize a fake smile when I saw one, though. "Well, don't get too friendly with this one. Rikki's leaving for school soon." Her phony smile drooped. "I'd hate to see you waste your time."

"*Rose*," I said, trying for a gentle rebuke.

Her gaze slid over to me. She read the plea on my face, and her shoulders sagged. "I'm sorry, honey. That was rude. Rikki's been like a daughter to me since, well, for a while now."

Owen gave her his flirtatious grin, dimple and all. "Don't apologize. I'd be protective of her, too, Ms. Heinlein."

"Don't talk about me like I'm not here," I grumbled, staring holes into my menu.

"I'll get y'all some tea. Be back in a sec."

Owen snickered. "Should we tell her it's too sweet?"

"Never. Just take it and say thank you. It's not so bad if you let the ice melt a little first."

"I thought my teeth would rot after one sip."

I chuckled. "One glass won't kill you. I promise."

Rose returned with our tea glasses and took our orders. Then she disappeared into the kitchen again, leaving Owen and me alone in the empty dining room. I fidgeted with my napkin and studied the diner's décor as if I hadn't seen it a thousand times before—the antique Coke signs, red-checkered tablecloths, and scratched linoleum floor.

The diner had been my home away from home for years, especially the years after my dad died. My interest in nursing most likely stemmed from the countless hours I'd spent in the hospital with him. While the doctors swept in and out, discussing things in quick, emotionless terms, the nurses held his hands and talked to him. They laughed and listened to his stories. They eased his pain, cleaned his messes, and dried his tears.

They'd also been the ones who hugged me, supplied books and puzzles for the long, quiet hours, and snuck me cookies from the snack bar. By the time my father passed away, I'd seen more of the nurses than I had of my own mother.

Owen's foot kicked against mine. "You got serious there for a minute. What's on your mind?"

I plastered on a smile. No way would I start a relationship—or whatever this was—by bringing up the morbid subject of my father's death, and certainly not over lunch. "Someone walked over my grave, I guess."

His brow puckered. "You sure you're okay?"

"Sure, I'm sure."

Peering at me as if he suspected there was more going on in my head than I'd admitted, he leaned over and laid his open palm on the table. I interpreted the gesture to mean he wanted my hand, so I gave it to him. He folded his darker fingers over my pale ones, and the contrast was stark. And lovely. *So much for being on guard.*

"I almost regret having to go away this weekend," he said.

"You don't know me well enough to miss me yet."

"True, but it doesn't change the way I feel."

Owen's frankness was refreshing and, if I was honest, a little daunting. I wasn't sure I was capable of returning the favor. I could lay much blame for my sorry love life at my own feet, and while most men in my hometown had good hearts, nearly all of them had been poured from the same mold, one that hadn't equipped them for dealing with me—someone with trust issues, a debilitating fear of losing the people she was closest to, and plans that were too big for this small town to satisfy.

"Owen, I like you. A lot." He hadn't balked at eating a picnic supper in a horse barn and had helped me shovel hay. He'd shared ghost stories with me. He'd risked his own safety and worked tirelessly to save strangers from a forest fire. He'd asked questions about my life and seemed more interested in finding out about my dreams and goals rather than the best way to get into my pants. And he'd quoted Shakespeare, for God's sake. "Even though I barely know you."

His dark brows knitted together, and his grip tightened. "But...?"

"But I'm leaving in a couple months. I don't plan on coming back. It seems like a bad idea to invest much time into... well... whatever this is."

He leaned closer. "I hear you, and I understand. So, how about this? What if we see how things go? No expectations, no long-term plans, just go wherever the road takes us."

I'd gone where the road took us that night I'd ridden on his motorcycle, and much of my heart remained there with Owen. His suggestion made sense on the surface, but I sensed heartbreak lurking underneath. "I don't know..."

"Look, I'm not going to push you into anything you don't want, Rikki. Maybe we don't know each other very well yet, but I respect you *and* your ambitions. I'd never want to get in the way of that."

"Okay...?"

"Whatever happens next is up to you. If you want to see where things lead, meet me under the water tower next Sunday night. Eight o'clock. If you're not there, I'll get the message, and I'll leave you alone, okay?"

I bit my lip. "Just like that? I no-show and you drop the whole thing?"

"I can take a hint."

"That's really understanding of you."

"I know." His dimple winked at me. "I'm pretty great that way."

I laughed, and it broke the serious mood that had enveloped us. Rose returned with our plates, and we dug into our food while we talked about my exams and the latest on the Raven's Knob fire. News reports were saying that officials suspected arson, but no suspects had been named. When Rose took our empty plates away, Owen insisted on paying our bill, and he walked me to my truck.

He patted Dolly's faded blue hood and gave her an appreciative look. "This is a serious truck."

I squinted at him. "I hope you're not implying I can't handle it."

"I wouldn't dare."

"Good, because I've been driving Dolly since I was sixteen. My mom said anyone would have to be an idiot to hit me in this truck. She'd shake it off and keep rolling."

"Dolly?"

"I know." I rolled my eyes. "My dad was slightly obsessed with Dolly Parton."

Owen grinned and waggled an eyebrow. "Who could blame him?"

"Well, you can't live in the Smokies and not love Dolly. I'm pretty sure it's against the law or something."

We stood in awkward silence for a moment, both of us probably pondering how to part. Owen quietly swore, pulled me against him, and pressed his lips to my temple. "I'd kiss you for real"—his voice was low, rumbling, and full of heat—"but I'll save it for next Sunday." He stepped back and walked away.

With wobbly knees, I climbed into Dolly and started the engine. Eyeing my reflection in the rearview mirror, I gave myself a hard look. "Girl, you got a lot of thinking to do between now and next Sunday. You better make the right choice."

Chapter Six
Unhappy Girl

PRESENTLY...

The overhead porch light blinked on, and the front door banged open beside me, jolting me from my reminiscing. My mom stepped onto the porch, and her gaze shot immediately to Dolly. She paused, shook her head, and faced me. She hadn't changed much—still looked like Rizzo from *Grease* but with a sleek pixie haircut. I halted the porch swing and heaved myself to my feet. "Hey, Momma. Long time no see."

Smudged mascara ringed her eyes. Wrinkles infested her red blouse, and when she exhaled, her breath smelled of wine. "Glad to see the truck's still in one piece."

"A nuclear holocaust couldn't kill Dolly."

She studied me from one narrowed eye. "You eat yet?"

"Nah. Been driving all afternoon."

"Well, c'mon." She shuffled to the door. "Got some chili in the fridge. I'll reheat it for you."

I followed her inside, into the kitchen. Supper was a safe, neutral topic—a good way to break the ice. Besides, I'd skipped lunch on the road, and now my stomach was growling. "Did *you* make the chili?"

"Hmm," she said, an affirmative mutter. "One of the boys brought me some ground venison. It's pretty good. Not too gamey."

I climbed onto a stool at the kitchen counter and watched her stoop in the refrigerator. She hauled out a big Dutch oven, set it on the counter, and heaped chili into a pair of bowls. "Might've gotten it a little too spicy, though."

"That's okay. I like spicy."

"Hmm." She shuffled to the microwave with a bowl in each hand.

A few minutes later, she joined me at the counter. Steam billowed from my bowl, and I blew on it as my stomach growled.

Mom handed me a spoon. "All I got is milk, beer, and wine. Or water. You'll have to go to the store if you want anything else."

I swirled my spoon around my bowl, and the piquant aroma of chili, cumin, and garlic tickled my nose. "I'll do some shopping tomorrow."

She paused, spoon halfway to her mouth. "You gonna stay here that long?"

"You think I drove all the way up here just to turn around and drive away in the morning?"

"Don't know what you're planning to do, Rikki. Haven't seen you in a long time."

A fist clenched my heart and squeezed. She'd opened a door, and I could hear my therapist's voice urging me to walk through. I rested my head in my hand, my elbow bent on the table despite the rules she had tried so hard to ingrain in me. "I know, Mom. It was easier that way."

I thought she'd ask me why I'd come back, what made me break my promise to never set foot in Evansville again, but she merely grunted and spooned up another bite of chili. Good old Mom, clinging to denial and obliviousness as usual. She'd always been more of a roommate than a mother, anyway. It seemed nothing much had changed.

We finished supper in stilted silence, and I took our bowls to the sink and rinsed them. "You got room for me, ol' lady?"

"Your bedroom's pretty much the way you left it."

A time capsule of my late teen years, then. Great. "I'm going to take a bath and head to bed. The drive wore me out." So had the apprehension over seeing my mother again and wondering how she would take my sudden reappearance on her doorstep. I hadn't expected hugs, but I'd hoped for more than cold indifference. I would have even welcomed her anger because that would have meant she felt something.

Instead, all she gave me was static—a disconnected phone line.

Facing my mom again was a big reason for coming back but not the only one and certainly not the most compelling. I'd run to get away from ghosts, painful memories, and a monster intent on consuming me. The ghosts weren't necessarily real, but the monster surely was. For three years, he'd lived in my nightmares, feeding on my dreams until my life was crumbling.

If I was ever going to get my life back, I was going to have to exorcise that demon, and the only way to do that was to come back to Evansville and challenge him face-to-face. *Helluva lot easier said than done, though.*

WARM BREATH BREEZED across my cheek, followed by the brush of warmer lips and hotter hands trailing up my abdomen, between the valley of my breasts, stroking the length of my neck, my jaw, my ear. Wriggling with delight and desire, I uttered a moan and threaded my fingers in dark, silken hair.

He reversed and traced a path in the opposite direction, drifting down... lower... *lower.* Firelight flickered over him, drawing living shadows on his skin, painting pale light over the planes of his shoulders and back.

Bucking against him, unable to hold still despite the firm grip he had clamped around my knee, I groaned and called his name.

"*Owen.*"

Glancing up, he met my stare, and heat burned in his gaze. Blue flames danced in his dark eyes. In one heartbeat, he was a gorgeous being of life and light, but in the next...

He was no longer flesh and bone but a creature of shadow, fury, and wrath.

Teeth, claws, and violence.

The monster roared, and I woke up panting, sweaty, and aching from passion poisoned by fear.

I turned over, stuffed my pillow over my head, and tried to rid my mind of the disturbing images in my dream, but it was no use. The visions were persistent, domineering, forceful. Experience had taught me it would be a long time until I drifted to sleep again.

At least this time, I woke up before I started screaming.

WHEN I FINALLY PEELED my eyes open, the rich aroma of fresh coffee and hot bacon greeted me. Weak early-morning sunlight filtered through the blinds in my bedroom, signifying I'd made it through another night. Sitting up, I rubbed my face and grumbled when my back protested the torture of having slept all night on a mattress that was well over twenty years old. Somewhere in my bags, I'd packed a bottle of ibuprofen, but I left it behind as I shuffled to the kitchen. Coffee tended to go a long way toward solving most of my problems, anyway.

"Morning." Bleary-eyed and puffy-faced, I shambled into the kitchen.

Mom arched a single eyebrow at me and turned back to her frying pan, where bacon sizzled and popped, and sang me country love songs that made my toes curl. "Bacon's almost done," she said.

My mouth watered, although I almost never allowed myself such indulgences. Coffee might have made me its slave, but I ate a careful diet designed to keep my cholesterol and blood sugar low. Working in the health care industry had made me cautious, which was a nice way of saying "paranoid."

Mom eyed me as if reading my thoughts. "Eat a lot, okay? You could use some meat on your bones."

"Yeah, well, if you've seen as many heart-attack victims as I have, you tend to find the value in fiber. But I'm not going to refuse a good plate of fried pig every once in a while."

Mom pounded her chest. "Eat it almost every morning, and my ticker's still going strong."

I grabbed a clean mug from the drain rack, filled it to the brim, and sank onto a stool at the kitchen island before taking a long, glorious sip. The pleasure of it went straight to my head and made my scalp tingle.

She scooped bacon from the pan and set it to drain on a paper towel–lined plate. "You want an egg?"

"Sure. If you don't mind." I swallowed my protest when she cracked the egg into the bacon grease. If I was going to commit dietary sin, I might as well go all the way.

After breakfast, I urged Mom to leave the dirty dishes to me. "I'll do the shopping and make us supper tonight too." I'd make my move then, prepare her favorite—chicken-fried steak and mashed potatoes—to soften her up a little before I hit her with a heavy round of emotional artillery.

"Hmm," she said in agreement as she trundled down the front porch steps in boots, jeans, and sheriff's jacket—the only part of her outfit paying heed to her position as the county's head lawman. As rain started to fall, she tugged on a ball cap embroidered with a replica of the sheriff's office badge. Fat, cold droplets pattered on the porch's tin roof. *Plip, pop, pop.* She climbed into her old—though not nearly as old as Dolly—Crown Vic and drove away with a brief wave out the window.

I stopped by the kitchen for a coffee refill then trudged into the bathroom and frowned at the mirror. Humidity had wreaked havoc on my curls, and they sprang wildly about my head. Years before, I'd started suspecting my hair was kinky, and not in a curly way but in a BDSM way; it rebelled against me simply because it enjoyed being beaten into submission.

"How about we try more for Julia Roberts in *Pretty Woman*," I said to my reflection. "Less Ronald McDonald."

My reflection stuck her tongue out at me. Then she laughed. *Hussy.*

Instead of fighting it, I weaved my hair into a quick braid and swiped on mascara, but there was little to be done about the dark circles under my eyes. Satisfied with my grooming, or lack thereof, I shuffled to my bedroom, where I tugged on my faded old Levi's—jeans that had withstood every fashion fad since high school—laced up my black butt-kicker boots, and shrugged on my wool peacoat. The outfit reinforced the tough-girl attitude I'd need to propel me through the day.

My trusty old truck chugged to life on the second crank, and I patted her dashboard. She purred beneath my palm, and her tires spun gravel as we roared down my mom's driveway. "Just like the good old days, huh, Dolly?" I punched the radio's power button and tuned in to the local country station. "When in Rome..."

I pulled into a parking space on the street in front of Rose's Diner as a large man in coveralls and a trucker hat walked out. He paused beneath the red awning over Rose's front door, probably contemplating the rain. Stiffening his shoulders, he lumbered up the sidewalk, his jaw clenched in grim determination.

I met my own gaze in the rearview mirror and wrinkled my nose. *You can do this.* Gritting my teeth, I slid from my truck into the pounding rain, ran for the diner's front door, and collided with an exiting customer. "Oof," I grunted, stumbling back.

The man I'd crashed into grabbed me and held me steady while I regained my footing. "Sorry," he muttered. "Oh, man, I'm really sorr— Wait. Rikki? Is that you?"

I raked sodden hair from my face and looked up into a pair of familiar eyes, blue like a Carolina sky on a clear summer day. "Hey, Luke." Dread swirled in my stomach. The last time I'd looked into those eyes, they'd been filled with fear and desperation. "Thought I might bump into you here, but I didn't think it would be so literal."

Luke Heinlein gaped at me, speechless.

I waved at his face. "Luke?"

He blinked and shook himself. "What are you doing here?"

"Coming to see your mom."

He stiffened and let go of my arm. "You sure she wants to see *you?*"

I shoved my hands into my coat pockets and hunched my shoulders. A cold shiver of guilt rippled through me. "I've come to apologize, if that means anything."

"She almost died, and you virtually ignored her. Now you show up on her doorstep like nothing's happened."

Mom had told me about Rose's heart attack, and I'd sent her a get-well card and flowers. But I hadn't visited. Not even Rose's near-death experience had brought me back. *God, I'm a selfish jerk.* But I didn't say that to Luke—he'd probably figured out that much on his own. "You know why I left," I said. "You know why I stayed away."

"I know a lot more than you think, and *I* didn't run. I'm still right here."

"You didn't lose your best friend... on top of everything else."

"You think I didn't care about Mina? Didn't miss her as much as you? I was in love with that girl since she was in high school."

An angry growl rose in my throat. "I loved her since the first day of kindergarten, when she punched Thad Miller in the face for pulling my hair and calling me a clown." I'd never had a sister, but

Mina had been family to me, as close as blood. Closer. She'd been my heart, ripped from me still beating and bleeding. It wasn't the first time I'd suffered such an injury either. That I was still capable of walking and talking was a small miracle—or maybe I was merely a zombie who'd gotten good at convincing people I was human.

Luke's eyes went wide and round. His grim expression lightened, and he snorted. "She was a force of nature. I won't argue with that." He shifted his weight and pursed his lips. "So, apologizing to my mom was your only reason for showing up in Evansville after all these years?"

"No." I shook my head. "I'll give you three guesses, but I bet it'll take you only one."

"Hmm," he said in a way that reminded me of my mom. "Good luck with that."

"Where is he?"

Luke hacked a cold, hard laugh. "Like I'd tell you. You want to see Owen again? You'll have to do it without my help. I have loyalties, and none are for you."

Heat flared in my cheeks, and I clenched my jaw. I wasn't sure why I had expected anything different. Mom took me in because, well, family. Apart from Owen, the rest of Evansville owed me nothing. But for Luke to still be loyal to Owen after everything that had happened... I couldn't reconcile it.

My gaze dropped, and I nodded. There was nothing I could say. Owen was a wall, and Luke and I stood on opposites sides.

"It wasn't his fault," Luke said.

"If that's true, then why has he never explained himself?"

Luke scowled, giving me a look of disgust. "That's not the right question, Rikki. The right question is why should he have to? You were always looking for excuses to run away from him, and you were so quick to doubt him."

"I was there." Heat—a memory of roaring, hungry flames—washed over my skin. "I saw what happened."

"Don't forget that I was there too. I saw everything, but you only saw what you *wanted* to see." He threw his hands out at his sides. "People like to believe truth is black and white, but it's not. It's relative, colored by your perception. You wanted to believe Owen was a monster, and so that's what you made him out to be. Your perception bent things to fit that narrative, and you've held onto it like a security blanket ever since. If you can't let go of it, you'll never know what actually happened that night." He shook his head dismissively as if he'd already decided I was a lost cause. "Owen was not the monster you think he was."

"Then what was he?"

"If you want to know, you should ask him yourself."

"Would he even talk to me?"

"I don't know. I'll tell him you're in town if you want. Can't say what he'll do with that information, but I'll tell him."

My stomach squirmed. "You don't have to."

"I know. But I will. We could use a little excitement around here."

"Excitement?"

"I'm being diplomatic."

"Is that something you learned in the army?"

"No." Luke shook his head and walked away. "I learned it from Owen."

Chapter Seven
Heartache Tonight

THREE YEARS BEFORE...

Ms. Weatherly relaxed against the stretcher pillow as Toni and I loaded her into the back of our ambulance, but she didn't release my hand. I climbed into the rig beside her, and Toni, our team's paramedic, clambered in behind me. Roberto, who'd taken driving duties for the night, glanced at us over his shoulder. "Ready, ladies?"

Toni gave a thumbs-up, and the ambulance lurched forward.

My patient sucked in another shallow breath, and her eyelids fluttered closed. Her heart rate had been low, but we'd managed to stabilize it. As we raced the short distance from Brightleaf Nursing Home to Twain County General, my thoughts shifted away from Ms. Weatherly, drifting toward Owen and our pending meeting under the water tower. *If* I decided to show up.

He'd said we wouldn't place expectations on each other, but meeting him at the water tower *was* an expectation, maybe the first of many, despite our best intentions. Giving in to him might be like sliding down a slippery slope that started out fast and fun before crashing in a mud puddle of heartache at the bottom. Unbidden, my memory recalled Owen's lazy grin, his sparkling eyes, his lips brushing my cheek. My eyelids fluttered closed, and I imagined those same lips, warm and urgent, pressing against mine. A flame lit in the pit of my stomach, and my fingers clenched, grabbing for something wisdom insisted I shouldn't want.

As I contemplated my complicated romantic situation, Ms. Weatherly's grip on my hand eased. I let go and leaned back to get a better look at my partner as she worked. Toni was a burly woman with dark-brown skin. Silver strands threaded the short hair at her temples. A long-term EMS veteran, she made our rig less of an ambulance and more of a mobile emergency room.

The familiar tang of disinfectants and cleaners greeted us when we rolled through County General's sliding doors with Ms. Weatherly's stretcher. An ER nurse slipped in to take my place, reassuring the patient with a calm, firm voice. Offering a brief prayer for the charming old lady, I retreated from the exam room and headed outside to grab a private moment before our crew loaded up and returned to the station.

Under the portico where we'd parked the ambulance, I pulled out my cell and called my best friend.

"Rikki?" Mina asked as she picked up the phone. "Why are you calling me from work? You *never* call me from work. What's happened? It must be something desperate or horrible. Oh God, I can't stand it. Give me the bad news, quick, like you're tearing off a waxing strip."

"Quit being so dramatic."

"But that's what you love most about me."

"No, I love that you massage my feet after a hard day at work and keep Cap'n Crunch stocked in your pantry just because it's my favorite. I put up with the drama because it's part of the package."

She harrumphed. "But really, why are you calling?"

"It is sort of an emergency."

"Let me guess. You have that meet and greet with Owen tonight and you're getting cold feet."

"In"—I checked my watch—"four hours, I've got to make a decision about whether or not I'm going to show up."

"Do you honestly have to think about this? Did you *see* how fine he was?"

"This is the worst time to be getting involved with someone. I'm leaving for Chapel Hill at the end of summer."

"Who said anything about 'getting involved'? Rikki, I love you, but you take life way too seriously sometimes. What have you got to lose?"

"Besides my heart?"

"They grow back. I should know. I've lost mine a half dozen times."

I gnawed a ragged cuticle on my thumb. Constant hand washing had ruined my chances of ever having a decent manicure. "There's something different about this guy."

"Hmm." Her tone was as grim as mine. "Never heard you say that before."

"I know."

"So, it could be serious."

"That's what I'm afraid of."

"Hmm," she said again.

"Mina, tell me what to do."

"You already know what I think you should do. Put on that outfit I bought you for your birthday and go get the guy."

"I am *not* hiking up Water Tower Hill in a miniskirt."

"So, you're going?" Her voice had gone high and breathy.

I'd probably made up my mind the moment Owen offered me the option, but at least I could convince myself I'd given it serious contemplation. "Lord help me, I think I am."

Mina squealed until she ran out of breath, then she cleared her throat. "What time does your shift end?"

"Six."

"That doesn't leave us much time to get ready."

"Us?"

She made an exasperated sound. "Like I'm going to trust you to dress yourself. You'll wear dirty jeans and some raggedy old shirt if I don't intervene."

I didn't contradict her because she was right. "But I don't want to look like I'm trying too hard either."

"Trust me, okay?"

"Just don't make me regret letting you in on this."

THE END OF MY SHIFT came and went, and my replacement failed to show up. No one could get in touch with her, which left me stuck with a second shift. I kicked an ambulance tire and cursed, venting my frustration.

Toni blinked and raised an eyebrow. "Oh my."

"I had plans tonight, and if Bonnie Jo doesn't show up, I don't know what'll—" A familiar, shrill alarm cut me off. "Dammit."

Toni shook her head and clicked her tongue. "Not your lucky night, is it, girl?"

She unclipped her radio's shoulder mic and responded to the dispatcher while I sucked up my disappointment and shoved it aside, focusing instead on the latest emergency. Roberto, who had already claimed his spot behind our rig's steering wheel, winked as I climbed aboard and settled into the jump seat behind him.

"I thought your shift was over," he said.

"Blame Bonnie Jo," I said as Toni squeezed her girth into the passenger seat. "What do we have, Boss?"

She threw a sour grimace over her shoulder. "Car wreck on 441. SUV decided to wrestle a tree."

"What happened?"

She grunted. "The tree won."

I LEANED AGAINST THE hallway wall outside County General's ER and slumped to the floor, my hands pressed against my eyes, fighting back tears. That night's call hadn't been my first visit to a vehicle crash, and it certainly hadn't been my first encounter with death. Regardless of how many times I'd witnessed tragedy, each loss of life hurt but especially when the victim was someone I knew. This time, it was a local man who'd been a good friend of my father. I'd gone to school with his daughter, and now her dad was gone, just like mine was.

Releasing myself from guilt and blame, even when death was imminent and inevitable, was proving to be my greatest shortcoming as a medical professional. I snorted and wiped my face on my shirtsleeve. *And you think you can handle nursing in an oncology ward?*

Part of me had pursued the EMT job because I was driven to help people. I couldn't save my dad, but I could save others. And maybe the idea of racing to an emergency like a superhero thrilled my ego—I was my mother's daughter, after all. I'd also hoped repeated exposure to trauma might work like a vaccination, helping me develop an immunity against the pain of working with terminal patients.

But if that were so, then my vaccine wasn't working.

That night, I felt as if my chest had been cracked open and packed with jagged ice shards. If a method for avoiding pain existed—other than drowning in a bottle of pills or alcohol—I hadn't yet discovered it. Instead, I white-knuckled it until the wound healed over, all the while wondering, *If I do this job long enough, will my heart eventually be composed of nothing but scar tissue?*

Maybe then, things like this wouldn't hurt so much.

My cell phone buzzed against my hip. I tugged it from my pocket and answered. "Mina?" Sniffling, I rubbed my nose on my shirtsleeve again.

My best friend's irritation came through as a heavy huff. "I've been waiting at your house almost an hour. You're going to miss your date with Owen. Or did you change your mind about him?"

"No..." I hadn't changed my mind, but I couldn't transition to going on a date with a virtual stranger when I'd spent the last hour coated in blood. My psyche wasn't made of rubber, and my emotions wouldn't bounce back that fast. Death and romance went together like oil and water. Tonight was not the night for motorcycles and making out, and I said as much to Mina.

"Oh, Rikki, I'm *so* sorry." She released a long, heavy sigh. "Look, why don't I go grab a pint of Chunky Monkey? You can put on your pajamas, and we'll eat ice cream and be sad together, if you want." She'd always known the best balms for treating my heartaches. "I'll call Luke and see if he'll track down Owen and give him the news so he doesn't think you stood him up."

"I could just text him."

Mina shook her head. "Let me take care of it. Luke owes me a favor, anyway."

"He does?" I twirled a loose curl, and it locked around my knuckle like the finger-trap party favors I used to get at birthday parties as a child. Gritting my teeth, I jerked my finger free. "How did that happen?"

"He came home on leave to take me to prom and promptly got drunk, puked all over my dress, and passed out before we got to the dance."

"Ha!" I barked a sharp laugh. "I remember that night. Luke definitely owes you, but I'm surprised you've never called in a favor from him before."

"I have. Lots of times. He might spend the rest of his life trying to make up for that night."

I grunted, rolled to my feet, and stood. "Okay, yeah, ice cream sounds great."

"How much longer before you get home?"

"I gotta get back to the station, clean the truck, make sure it's re-stocked. It won't take long."

"I'll go grab the ice cream. Call me when you're on your way."

NEARLY AN HOUR LATER, my best friend and I lay on my bed-room floor, devouring a carton of Ben and Jerry's. My mom had gone to a friend's house to play bridge, leaving Mina and me alone to com-miserate and gorge on Chunky Monkey. I licked ice cream from my spoon and stared at the glow-in-the-dark stars stuck to my ceiling. "Nights like this make me think I must be crazy. I should think about being a pharmacy tech like you. Pill bottles never break your heart."

Mina snorted. "You wouldn't say that if you saw an Oxy junkie begging for a refill."

"Maybe..." I whirled my spoon like a magic wand. "Maybe I should move to Vermont and become a Ben and Jerry's taste tester."

"Now you're talking."

"I'd be the size of an elephant in a week."

"But you'd be so, so happy."

I was leaning over to shove my spoon back into the carton when a knock at my bedroom window made me jump like an electrocuted frog. I shrieked, clasping a hand over my chest as my heart rammed against my sternum.

Mina pointed across the room with a shaky finger. "Somebody's at the window."

Whispering, I said, "Tell me something I *don't* know, Captain Obvious. Go see who it is."

"This isn't my room. *You* go see who it is."

With my pulse still pounding in my ears, I crept to my bed and knelt on the mattress. Slowly, I slid back the curtain, pulled the blinds apart, and peeked at the darkness that had fallen over my backyard. A flashlight clicked on, illuminating a face peering back at me. I dropped to the bed with a wheeze of surprise.

"Who is it?" Mina asked.

"Luke Heinlein... the freak." I rolled off the bed, and Mina followed me from my room and down the hall.

"Maybe he wanted to cheer you up," she said.

"By scaring the crap out of me?"

I turned on the porch light and opened the front door as Luke jogged up the steps. A shadow shifted behind him, stepping into the light.

Owen.

My heart lurched into my throat. I swallowed, trying to force it down, and stepped back from the door.

With his hands shoved in his jean pockets and his shoulders shrugged up close to his ears, he glanced up and met my gaze. A glimpse of taut flesh and the curve of a hip bone peeked between his shirt hem and his jean's low-slung waistband, and I felt a bit guilty noticing how tempting he was. Owen looked uncomfortable and reluctant to be there. Instead of meeting under a water tower for a late-night make-out session, he'd been dragged to my house to navigate a minefield of heavy emotions. Poor guy.

"What are you two doing here?" Mina folded her arms over her chest and shoved out her hip.

"Coming to check on you." Luke chucked a thumb over his shoulder, pointing at Owen. "He said we should leave you alone, but I told him you might want some company."

Owen rolled his eyes and scowled at the porch ceiling. "If they wanted company, they would have told us." He met my eyes again and shrugged. "I tried to tell him, Rikki."

"No," I said, finding my voice. "It's okay. Y'all come on in." Stepping aside, I waved them in. "Mom has some beers in the fridge. Help yourself."

Luke, smiling and oblivious, accepted my offer and strode through the doorway, heading for the kitchen, and Mina followed him. Owen tentatively stepped into the foyer but stopped near the door as if expecting me to change my mind and kick him out. "You're sure it's okay? Luke told me what happened. I understand if you don't want company."

"No. Really." I waved aside his explanation. "Now that you're here, I'm glad you came."

The corner of his mouth turned up, but the smile didn't reach his eyes. "I'm sorry about everything. Epic bad timing, huh?"

"Story of your life, right?"

The little smile fled. "Is this a sign of things to come—that the timing will never be right for us?"

"You were the one who said, 'No expectations.'"

"I did say that, didn't I?" His gaze dropped, taking in my old high school volleyball T-shirt and ragged jean shorts. He studied the wild red mane coiling around my head and reached out, fingering a curl.

Luke returned, toting a solitary beer, and I pointed at his bottle. "Hey, get one for your buddy."

"He doesn't drink," Luke said. "He's a... what do you call it? A teetotaler?"

I cocked my head at Owen. "Really?"

He shrugged, obviously unnerved by the sudden scrutiny. "It's not a big deal—"

"It isn't," I agreed. "I have sweet tea. I could make coffee."

"Coffee would be great."

"C'mon." I motioned for him to follow. "You can help me."

In the kitchen, I set Owen to measuring coffee grinds while I took down mugs and poured water in the carafe. "Hope store-brand stuff is okay. We don't get too pretentious about things around here."

"Coffee is mostly all the same to me. Learned not to take too many things for granted. Especially the simple things."

I slid out a stool at the kitchen island and sat as the coffee's aroma perfumed the air. Owen leaned on the counter beside me, close enough to share his warm, smoky scent. I ignored the voice inside my head urging me to touch him, stroke his knuckles, or brush the loose lock of hair off his forehead. Instead, I knotted my fingers together, braced my forearms on the countertop, and studied the pale freckles dotting my wrists. "The army teach you that?"

"Life taught me that. And yeah, the army sort of reinforced it."

"Working for the EMS will teach you not to take things for granted too."

He leaned closer. His arm pressed against my shoulder, and his closeness was an unanticipated pleasure. "Death's never easy, is it? Old, young. Sudden or long-suffering."

"Nope. Never."

His voice softened. "You want to talk about it?"

I looked up and met his stare. The amber flecks in his dark eyes flickered like dozens of tiny flames. A few days before, I'd assumed he and I had nothing in common. Now I wasn't so sure. "Have you seen a lot of death? In the army?"

He glanced away. "We signed up for it. Thought we knew what it meant, what to expect."

I unlocked my fingers and laid my hand over his. "The man who died tonight wasn't my first. The first was my dad." I stopped and swallowed. "Cancer. Five years ago. I was fifteen. Feels like it was yesterday."

Owen flipped his palm up and laced our fingers together. His hands were warm and a little rough. "Oh... I'm so sorry." He flinched, and his face tightened as if he'd tasted something bitter. "That's what everyone says, though, isn't it?"

"Sorry is better than nothing. Better than ignoring or forgetting or acting like it never happened. Acting like it's no big deal. You'd be surprised how many people dismiss grief as if it's a cold. A bad case of allergies or something."

"I'm actually not surprised. The things people have said to me after I came home from the desert..."

"Yeah. People can be assholes."

Owen chuckled, but it was a sad, joyless sound. We sat in an air of gloomy silence until the coffeepot spat and hissed, announcing the end of its brewing cycle. I hopped out of my seat and crossed the kitchen. "I'm sorry for being such a downer." I poured coffee in both mugs. "I knew I wasn't going to be good company. It's why I didn't meet you at the water tower tonight."

He accepted a mug from me and dumped in a heaping scoop of sugar from the bowl on the counter. "But you would have?"

I ducked into the refrigerator, searching for milk. "Would have what?"

"Come to the water tower."

After snagging the milk jug, I backed away from the fridge and faced him. "Yes. I was planning on it." The drawn, tight look on his features relaxed. He let out a long breath. *Had he been worried I wouldn't?* I passed the milk to him and shut the refrigerator door. "I'm glad Luke talked you into coming here, though."

His eyebrows rose, and his lips parted. "Really?"

"You're a good distraction."

He traded his surprised look for something more cunning. "I can be a *really* good distraction, Rikki. Maybe you'll let me prove it to you sometime soon."

I hid my blush behind my coffee mug. "I'm free again on Thursday. Have to work every night until then, though."

"Thursday night is days away, and you and I don't have time to waste. The end of summer will be here before you know it, and I intend to make the most of it."

I ignored the way his words had lit a warm fire low in my belly. "You barely know me."

"Maybe, but I like what I've seen so far. Enough to know I want to spend more time with you. Get to know you better." He winked. "See what *else* there is to like."

Coffee sloshed over my fingers as I fumbled my mug. I muttered a string of curses under my breath as Owen sprang to my rescue, grabbing a dish towel. He took the mug from me and blotted my hands. Then he wrapped his fingers around mine and peered into my eyes. "Do I make you nervous?"

"No." I shook my head, but it was a lie. Owen made me nervous and excited and scared and eager, all at the same time. "But I'm not used to people being so blunt."

He tugged my hands, and I stumbled closer, falling against him. He released my fingers and wrapped his hands around my hips. I swallowed, trying to shove down the dry lump lodged in my throat. His smoky scent filled my head, and his heat enveloped me like a ghostly embrace. He was tall and lean, but he seemed to take up twice as much space as he should have.

Against my will, my lashes lowered. "You know what my daddy said about boys like you?"

He tensed.

"He said sometimes the wrong boy is the one who knows how to say all the right things."

He grunted a sound of dissent low in his throat. "I'm more than just words. If it's action you want—"

"Rikki!" Luke bellowed from the living room, breaking the tension. I pulled away, gasping for air that didn't smell like Owen. "Where the hell is the TV remote?"

Owen's mouth puckered into a frown, and he lowered his voice so only I would hear his next comment. "Are you afraid of getting close to me?"

Crossing to the kitchen doorway, I glanced at Mina and Luke. She smacked him on the back of his head, and he winced. "Way to ruin the mood, idiot," she grumbled.

I pointed at the side table beside my mom's recliner. "Check that drawer, Luke." I looked back at Owen. "I'm not afraid, just fond of my personal space."

He raised his hands as if surrendering. "You can have all the space you need."

I held his gaze, searching for an indication of his intent. *Was he teasing, or had he meant what he said?* I returned to the kitchen island, intentionally placing the counter between us, and settled onto a stool. His dark eyes followed my every move. "Tell me more about yourself, Mr. Amir. You've decided to come to Evansville to get away from the world for a while. Now what?"

Owen folded his hands around his own mug and stared into his coffee's dark depths. "Well, Ms. Albemarle, I'm going to start a business."

Surprised, I gaped at him. "What kind of business?"

He glanced up and released one of his easy grins. "Why don't you let me show you?"

Chapter Eight
Shattered

DESPITE MY EARLIER heartache and belief that my spirit couldn't rebound quickly enough to enjoy the company of anyone other than Mina and a pint of Chunky Monkey, I found myself behind Dolly's wheel with Owen in the passenger seat. He'd angled his long, lean frame into the corner of the cab so he could watch me while I drove. Taking up more than his share of the space, he sprawled over the bench seat, one knee bent near my hip, the other leg stretched out, nearly reaching my foot as I worked the pedals on our drive into town.

Owen extended an arm across the seat back and snagged one of my curls. He toyed with a loose ringlet, twining red strands around his long fingers. Even that slight touch turned my insides into warm, melted butter.

"Take a right at the next street," he said without taking his eyes off me as we rolled down Main Street.

He'd refused to tell me where we were going, and I'd refused to let him drive unless he revealed our destination first, so he compromised, agreeing to feed me directions in small doses. I flipped the turn signal and tugged on the wheel, and Dolly's tires skidded as she rounded the sharp turn, going entirely too fast.

Owen chuckled. "If you're Thelma, does that make me Louise?"

"Nah. You're clearly Brad Pitt in this scenario."

He raked his fingers through his dark hair. "Don't tell me you prefer blonds." He pointed at a spot farther down the road. "Take the second left and pull into the parking lot on your immediate right."

74

I gave him a hard look from the corner of my eye and followed his directions, slowing as we bumped over the rutted entrance to the parking lot of an abandoned furniture warehouse. After shifting into neutral, I stomped Dolly's stubborn parking brake, slumped against my seat, and studied the derelict building illuminated in the headlights. "You're opening a furniture warehouse and distribution center?" I clicked my tongue. "Seems unlikely, but what do I know? Maybe you have a thing for credenzas and love seats."

Owen tugged another of my curls and released it before heaving open the passenger door. The overhead light flicked on, revealing a quick flash of his dimple before he turned away. "No, just a thing for redheads."

Leaving the engine running and headlights on, I followed him outside, and the slamming truck doors disrupted the quiet evening. With his hands shoved in his rear jean pockets, he stood in place, studying the old brick warehouse the same way he might've scrutinized a masterpiece hanging in the Louvre. To me, the building looked like nothing more than a tired old hobo waiting for a gravy train that would never come.

"Is this where you're going to lock me up while you torture me to death?" I snickered. But the longer Owen stood there, staring in silence, the more my paranoia insisted that coming to an abandoned warehouse in the dark with a virtual stranger was maybe less of an adventure and more of a dangerous impulse.

Owen raised his hands, positioning his fingers like a photographer framing his shot. "Picture it, Rikki. New windows, fresh paint on the trim, some pressure washing for the brick. Resurface the parking lot, put out some potted plants, and it'll look like new."

"*What* will look like new? You still haven't explained what you're planning to do."

When he spun to face me, Dolly's headlights cast him in stark contrast, dark shadows and a blinding white smile. "I'm planning to do whiskey. Moonshine, to be exact."

"M-Moonshine?" I wheezed. "I thought you said you don't drink."

He jabbed a finger against his chest. "*I* don't drink, but I don't mind making a few bucks off the people who do."

"Moonshine's something the mountain folks do up in the hollers far away from public scrutiny. You don't make it in the middle of town in an old warehouse."

Grit and loose gravel crunched beneath Owen's boots as he eased closer to me. His denim-clad knee brushed against my bare one, and his smile turned sly and cunning. The sparks in his eyes blazed. "I'm not talking about illegal stills and evading the tax man like in the old days." He tossed up his hand, gesturing at the warehouse. "This is going to be a microdistillery and bar. I'll make small-batch corn liquor and distribute it locally... *if* my luck goes the right way."

Owen curled his fingers around my shoulder, pulling me against his side, and turned me toward the warehouse's front entrance. He leaned down, bringing our faces even as we studied the old building. "We'll serve signature cocktails, and there'll be a café, too, like those microbreweries popping up everywhere, but more unique."

I snorted. "What do you know about making moonshine, Mr. Yankee Teetotaler?"

Tilting his head, he captured my gaze with his dark, bottomless eyes. His grin revealed that irresistible dimple again. With his lips hovering inches away from mine, his breath was warm and sweet as if he'd been sucking honey-flavored candies. "I don't know one damned thing about making moonshine," he said, "but I have a partner who does."

I leaned back and arched a skeptical eyebrow. "What partner?"

"That's why I was out of town for the last week. I was talking to a guy, a vet from my unit who lives in Tennessee. He'll be my master distiller—his family's been in the business for decades."

"Well, if he's going to be the master distiller, what are *you* going to do?"

Owen's confidence and charm nearly convinced me. If he put his mind to it, he could probably sell ice to an Alaskan. If I wasn't careful, he'd soon have me buying everything he was offering with his suggestive grins. Smirking, he tapped his temple and put on a thick mountain-boy accent. "*I'm* going to be the brains of this here operation."

Taking my hand, he drew me across the parking lot while describing his renovation plans in detail. His enthusiasm showed in each gesture and wave. His passion was heady, and the more I listened, the more he intoxicated me, his words themselves becoming moonshine.

"Have you thought up a name for it?" I tugged him toward the front door.

"Thought I'd call it Moon Runners. I've already hired someone to design a logo."

I realized he couldn't have made this much progress in the short time he'd been in Evansville. "You've been thinking about this for a while, haven't you?"

He jerked his chin in an affirmative gesture. "Been working on this for a few months. Started looking for locations before our discharge orders came through."

"Will you show me around?"

He cocked his head and narrowed his eyes. "In the dark? Won't be much to see. It's still a wreck in there. Junk everywhere. It's not very safe."

"We'll stay in the doorway if that makes you feel better."

Owen huffed and shook his head but fished in his pocket until he found a small key ring. He selected an old brass one that he jiggled into the bolt lock over the warehouse's rusty door handle. "Would have told you to put on jeans and boots if I'd known you wanted to go inside."

Glancing at my shredded jean shorts and low-cut Chuck Taylors, I thanked Jesus I'd recently boosted my tetanus shot. "Not asking for a grand tour. Show me what you can from the threshold."

Owen shook his head again, but he shoved his shoulder against the heavy door. It squealed as it gave way, swinging open on rusted hinges. I pushed past him, stepping farther into the room, but stopped at the edge of the small illuminated square thrown by Dolly's headlights. "Just give me the general idea."

His boot steps echoed in the open space as he moved behind me. Taking my shoulders, he shifted me until I faced the warehouse's rear, where the light failed to reach. "The back wall there"—he pointed, leaning over my shoulder—"will be where we'll line up the distilling tanks." He wrapped an arm around my waist and spun us around like partners in a slow dance. A warm thrill raced through me as his lips brushed my ear. "And over there will be the café."

My pulse throbbed in my ears, my chest, my lips. It wouldn't be enough, these limited touches, these coy games, this not-so-subtle flirtation. With Owen, my options were sink or swim, and no matter how much reason and logic urged me to do otherwise, I was sinking, utterly drowning in him. I stumbled back and fought for a breath to clear my head, but my heel connected with an obstacle hidden in the shadows. I lost my footing and squeaked a feeble protest as gravity waged war against my balance.

The moment I was certain I would hit the floor and smash my tailbone, Owen grabbed my arm and yanked. Still off balance but with the added element of momentum, I plowed into him, tackling him to the floor.

Or that was what *should* have happened.

Instead, the world jumped up and swirled around me in a blur of blue sparks and shadows, air roaring in my ears like a tornado. I blinked, and the impression of someone—or some*thing*—huge, dark, and beastly burned behind my eyelids. When the dizzy moment passed, I found myself back on my feet, upright, and firmly wrapped in Owen's arms. His heat blazed against me, filling my head with his smoky scent until I felt drunk and woozy.

"What...?" I shook my head and cleared my throat, but the intoxicating sensation remained. "What just happened?"

"You stumbled. I caught you."

"No." I squirmed, and he dropped his arms, releasing me. A thousand minuscule candles seemed to flicker in his eyes, giving them an otherworldly aura. I inched back, my steps wobbly. "We were falling. We should have hit the floor."

His lips twitched. "I'm quick on my feet, Rikki. Give me some credit."

Squinting, I studied him, his wide stance and the set of his jaw, full of self-confidence. He rolled his broad shoulders and grinned, obviously enjoying my scrutiny. Again, his presence seemed larger than the mere height and width of his physical body. Like a cowl and cape, dense shadows draped over him, and they seemed tangible enough to touch. When I reached out to stroke them, Owen drew back.

The shadows fled.

I shivered.

With no better explanation than to assume an overdose of adrenaline and desire had colored my perception, I dismissed my concerns and shrugged, heading for the door. "You're not quick on your feet. You're The Flash on steroids."

His laughter followed me into the parking lot, but it was callous and more than a little cold.

The drive to my house was quiet, the atmosphere between us thick. If humans had animal instincts, then the wild creature inside me was insisting the man sitting in the passenger seat was more predator than appearance suggested. Something about Owen had changed. He was a tiger, I was his mouse, and I should run before he swallowed me whole. When I caught him staring at me, the dark look on his face implied he might do that very thing, given the chance.

I cleared my throat and reached for conversation, for something civilized, human, and less carnal. "Why'd you join the army?"

He flinched and blinked. The sinister feeling eased. "Nine-eleven."

Surprised, I gaped at him. "But... I was just a little kid then. You couldn't have been much older."

"I wasn't, but it was a big deal to me, even then."

"I think it's safe to say it was a big deal to everyone."

"Yeah, but for me, it was more than that. It was personal."

A cold echo of grief, a remembrance of emotional pain, reverberated through me. Maybe I should've stopped there and changed the subject. Instead, I tightened my grip on the steering wheel and plowed ahead. "Did you... did you lose someone that day?"

In the glow of the dashboard lights, I watched him scrub his face. His eyes remained closed after his hands fell away. "An aunt. She worked in one of the towers."

My throat tightened. "You were close to her?"

"No, not so much. But I saw what losing her did to my family. She was my dad's little sister, and it devastated him. The next day, my uncle went to the local army recruiter office and signed up. Said he wanted to show the world that not all Arabs hate the US. We were patriots just as much as any other family."

"How long has your family been in the US?"

"Since both sets of my grandparents fled Palestine in the fifties."

"And you followed in your uncle's footsteps and joined the army?" I kept my eyes glued to the road, fearing if I looked at him, he'd refuse to talk.

"I idolized him. Thought he was a hero."

"He was, wasn't he?"

From the corner of my eye, I watched Owen shrug. "I guess. I wish he would have told me the truth, though."

I waited for him to expound, but he said nothing more.

"The truth about what?" I asked.

Owen shifted, drawing himself up straighter. He stared out the passenger window, gazing into the dark forests lining the winding mountain road. "The truth about how difficult it was going to be for people like us. Didn't matter that my parents and I were born here and only practiced Islam when my grandparents were around on holy days. We worked ten times harder to prove ourselves. Every move we made was questioned and doubted because of our ancestry and religion."

A cold fist clenched around my heart. "I can't even imagine—"

"No, you can't, and I'm not asking you to. I'm out now. It's over, and I'm trying to move on."

"So... you regret it?"

He slipped his ring over his knuckle and spun it around several times. He often fidgeted with it in thoughtful or tense moments. He was quiet for so long, I thought he wouldn't answer, but as I steered Dolly onto the gravel drive leading to my house, he sighed. "I don't regret it, no. I'm proud of my service, and I still love my country. But sometimes I mourn the dumb, innocent kid I was before. He died over there in an Iraqi desert. I buried him, and he'll never come back home."

After I parked Dolly in her usual spot, Owen walked me to my front porch. He kept one hand shoved in his back pocket and the other balled in a fist at his side. His gaze remained glued on the path.

His earlier arrogance had vanished, and my heart ached for him. I knew firsthand about the loss of innocence and the bitter taste of emotional pain, although mine was a different flavor from his. We'd have to find more things that we had in common, or we were going to wind up being the two most tragic young people in Twain County. *They'll have to start calling us Hamlet and Ophelia.*

When we reached my front porch, Owen plastered on a smile, though it lacked its usual sincerity and charm. He took both my hands in his and stroked a calloused thumb across my knuckles. "Sorry I ruined the mood. I was supposed to be cheering you up."

"I was the one who decided to ask personal questions. There's a risk of stirring up ghosts when you go that route."

Brushing a brief kiss across the back of my hand, he eyed me with a warm look that tingled in my toes.

"Thanks for trusting me with your story," I said, a little breathless. "I guess it's rare that people are willing to do that, especially with someone they've recently met."

"I can't seem to help myself around you. You have a way of getting between my cracks."

"Are you afraid of me?" I grinned, throwing his earlier question back at him.

He let loose a sharp laugh. "A lot of things scare me, Rikki. You most of all."

Dumbfounded, I blinked at him. "What could I ever do to you?"

"I think... you could shatter me completely." Pulling away, he stepped back and retreated several paces, heading for his motorcycle. Only then did I notice Luke's old Ford truck and Mina's red Mustang were gone. Their absence was a relief. After a full day of riding emotional roller coasters, I wanted nothing more than to retreat to my bed and pretend Owen's sudden aloofness hadn't left a chilly place in my heart or that something strange hadn't happened in that old warehouse.

"I'll call you." Owen turned his back and crossed the remaining distance to his bike.

His motorcycle snarled and roared to life. Before he rolled off into the night, he flicked a brief two-fingered salute in my direction. I waved back and wondered what he meant when he said I could shatter him.

Not likely. Cuz I'm sure he's going to shatter me first.

Chapter Nine
All Apologies

Long after Luke had walked off, I stood on the sidewalk outside Rose's Diner, staring through the window, watching Rose scurry around the dining room, busing tables as the morning crowd thinned. She was more at home among the checkered tablecloths and Americana than at any other place in Evansville, including her own house. Her dark hair had gained a few more silver strands, but otherwise she hadn't changed.

Wonder if she'd say the same about me?

I screwed up my courage, pushed open the door, and hovered at the threshold until I spotted an empty booth. After sliding to the end of the bench seat, I hunkered close to the wall and ducked behind a menu. James Bond would get to keep his day job, though, because I sucked at espionage.

"Heard you were back in town." Rose appeared at my table, tapping her pencil against her notepad as a scowl carved deep lines around her mouth. My heart cramped, and I resisted the urge to drag her into my arms and hug her until she squawked. Her severe frown was enough to discourage me from trying.

"How did you know?" I asked.

"Mike told me he rolled up on you sitting at the town limits, trying to work up your nerve." Her stern expression sat uneasy on her face. Rose was made for smiles and laughter, not cynicism and bitterness. She huffed and pointed at the menu. "You want something?"

"Um, how about a coffee and a chance to explain myself?"

"Coffee's fresh, but we're all out of pity."

A blush pooled in my cheeks. If my surrogate kid had moved away without saying goodbye, stopped talking to me for three years, and hadn't reached out to me when I'd had a medical crisis, I'd be hurt and furious too. "Not asking for forgiveness. Just a chance to clear the air."

She gestured to the dining room, where the tables were mostly empty but in need of clearing. "Does it look like I got time for chitchat, Rikki? Come back into town unannounced after three years of playing dead and you think everyone's going to drop what they're doing and give you a welcome-home party?"

The shame I felt when she first spoke cooled as her words poked my sore spots and stirred my defensive reflexes. "Give me five minutes. I can come back later, when you're not so busy."

Her nostrils flared as she exhaled. After glancing around the room, she paused, waved at a young girl in a Rose's Diner T-shirt, and raised her voice. "Molly."

The girl, who was serving pancakes to a table of hungry men, glanced over her shoulder and gave us a questioning look.

"I'm taking a quick break," Rose said. "You keep it under control, okay?"

Molly nodded and turned back to her customers as Rose squeezed into the bench across from me. She glanced at her watch. "Three minutes. You got one minute for each year you were gone. Better talk fast."

I opened my mouth and froze. A million times, I'd imagined picking up the phone and calling, explaining myself, throwing myself at Rose's mercy. In all those years, I'd never managed to find the right words. Even though I sat before her, finally face-to-face, nothing had changed. "I don't know what to say."

She grunted, rolled her eyes, and shifted to scoot out of the booth. "I should have known—"

Grabbing her hand, I tugged her back. "Wait. I'm sorry. About everything. About leaving and never calling, never coming back to visit, never saying goodbye."

Rose leaned close and lowered her voice, nearly growling. "I had a heart attack, Rikki, and all I got from you was a card and some roses. You were like a daughter to me, and you abandoned me when I needed you most—"

"I *know* what I did," I whispered, trying not to draw the attention of the patrons around us. "And I know what I *didn't* do. I've made a list of each one of my failings, and it plays on repeat in my head each night before I go to sleep and each morning when I wake up." The list of my wrongdoings was the soundtrack to my nightmares.

Rose's face crumpled into a harsh parody of pity. "Am I supposed to feel sorry for you? Luke was in the Middle East for months on end, but he still managed to make the occasional Skype call. You were only four hours away in Chapel Hill."

"You're not supposed to feel sorry for me." I slumped against my seat. "No, I want to explain myself. That's all."

She pressed her lips into a thin line, folded her arms over her chest, and gave a meaningful look at her watch.

I let my head fall into my hands. "I'm on paid suspension from my job. It was a mercy. They had every right to fire me."

"The straight-A student and Twain County's most valuable employee?"

"I know..." Picking at a peeling spot on the Formica tabletop, I drew my shoulders in and sank further into my seat, hoping I could disappear if I made myself small enough. "I'm losing it—no. Strike that. I've *lost* it."

"Lost what?" She leaned closer. Despite her animosity, she was obviously intrigued.

"Everything. A good job. Most of my relationships. Maybe even my mind."

"What's going on? All that perfectionism finally backfired?" Her words were cutting, but her soft tone conveyed empathy.

"No. Well, not entirely." I didn't know how to tell her, without sounding like a drama queen of the highest order, that I couldn't sleep. When I did, night terrors ripped me awake, screaming and scrambling to escape scenes of death and distorted, twisted shadows oozing violence and whispering malicious threats. No hospital would abide an oncology nurse who resembled Death's handmaiden and shuffled the halls like a mindless wraith. No employer would tolerate an employee who turned to self-medication when prescriptions failed to cure her ills.

"You know that old saying?" I asked. "Curses are like chickens. They always come home to roost."

Despite my failure to put everything into words, Rose seemed to sense my distress. *And* my sincerity—she'd always been good at sympathizing, even when she was still angry and hurt. She covered my hand, stopping me from picking away more peeling tabletop. "What curses are roosting with you? Your dad's death?"

I bobbed my head but couldn't quite meet her eyes.

"Your mom being so distant?"

"Her too," I croaked.

"Mina?" She said her name so quietly I almost missed it.

"Yes." I swallowed, resisting the burn of tears in my throat. You'd think after three years, I could hear her name without wanting to bawl my eyes out, but being in Evansville brought the past closer, made the absence of loved ones more vivid. "Her most of all."

Slowly, haltingly, I ground out the words, telling Rose how my coworkers, my therapist, *and* my employer had all handed me my ass and ordered me to get my shit straight.

"So..." Rose twisted her lips into a contemplative pucker. "Are you going to try to fix things with Owen too?"

"I don't know what I'm going to do with Owen." *How can I mend things with a monster?* "But I need closure if I'm ever going to let it go. The way things were left..." I shook my head. "It did a lot of damage. More than I realized at the time."

"What did he *do*?" Rose squeezed my hand. Her brows pinched together. "You still haven't told me what happened to make you sever all ties, run away, and never look back. He clearly loved you. Why would you leave him like that?"

The words to explain it clung to my tongue with claws and spikes and nails. Despite my heart's willingness to confess, my body refused to obey. Rose waited several more seconds, giving me one last opportunity, but when I said nothing more, she tapped her watch. "Time's up. I gotta get back to work."

"I'm going to talk to him." I reached for her wrist, stopping her. "Please, let me talk to him first, and then I'll come back and tell you everything."

Her eyes narrowed. "You've never once lied to me. You've avoided and evaded, but you've always spoken the truth. In the three years I've known Owen, he's been nothing but wonderful to this town and to my family, but you were my favorite girl first. So, if something happened, I'll believe you, but I think Owen deserves your consideration."

I shrugged and released her wrist. "I don't know if I can give him that. He has a lot to answer for."

She snorted and slid from the booth. "Then you two still have a lot in common."

"Will he be at Moon Runners?" I asked, following her.

She stepped toward the closest table of dirty dishes and started stacking them together. "He doesn't spend much time there anymore. Luke runs most of the daily stuff now."

"So where will he be, if he's not there?"

She glanced at me over her shoulder and huffed, her nostrils flaring wide. "The one thing you've never been, Rikki, is dumb. You know where to look for him, *if* you're serious about it."

She disappeared through the kitchen doorway, leaving me standing in the diner with Molly and a table full of men who had devoured more pancakes than should have been possible in the short amount of time I'd been there. Reluctantly, wishing things had gone better with Rose, I left the diner and returned to my truck.

Sitting in Dolly's cab, I let my vision go unfocused and hazy as I contemplated my next move. Rose was right. I wasn't dumb, and if Owen wasn't at the distillery, there was one other place I was likely to find him. My blood chilled, and a cold finger stroked the length of my spine. Could I go back there? To his innermost sanctum?

Like most of the Appalachian Mountains, the Smokies attracted isolationists and recluses for a reason. Countless nooks, crannies, and valleys offered places to hide, retreat, and disengage from the world. Sometimes people disappeared in those niches and never reappeared, and there I was, considering delving into the deepest heart of those shadowed hideaways.

He won't welcome me. I might go in and never come out again, but at least it would mean an end to the nightmares.

My phone rang, waking me from my disturbing thoughts. The sky had clouded over as though the weather was reacting to my mood. Absentmindedly, I swiped the accept button and pressed the phone to my ear. "Hello?"

"Erika? I've been trying to get in touch with you. Haven't you gotten my messages?"

I cringed. *That'll teach me to not check caller ID first.* "Hello, Joseph." I exhaled. "Reception is spotty up here. I told you that."

"So there are no landlines?"

I closed my eyes and pictured Dr. Khan. With his eternally bronzed skin and brilliant white smile, his mere presence had made most patients and hospital staff weak in the knees. For months, he'd pursued me, but the flame between us never ignited. Maybe there was nothing left of my heart to fuel that fire. Or maybe it had to do with the flutter of uncertainty I felt in his presence. Sometimes I thought he was a little *too* interested in me.

"What do you want me to say?" I asked. "I've been focusing on myself and channeling my energy into recovery. Wasn't that how you put it?"

Joseph snorted loud enough for the sound to carry over the phone, but his tone was light and playful. "Sarcasm and Erika Albemarle go together like peanut butter and jelly."

"Miss me?" I couldn't help teasing him. He'd been patient with me. I should've cut him loose already, but his persistence was charming... when it wasn't annoying.

"I do." He spoke frankly, without a hint of humor. "I thought giving you some space was the right thing to do, but now...?"

I worried a ragged cuticle on my thumb with my teeth. "Now what?"

"Now I'm not so sure."

"Dr. Khan admits to not being sure about something? Hold on a second while I make a note of it on my calendar."

"Erika, stop. I'm serious."

"I'm aware. But I don't know what you expect me to do about it."

"I don't expect you to do anything other than stay in touch like I asked. I wasn't sure that ancient hunk of rust could get you there in one piece."

"Well, I haven't checked in with any of my *other* colleagues since I got here."

Thunder rumbled. I pulled my thumb from my teeth and glanced at the sky. The clouds had gone from gray to deeply bruised. Banners advertising Evansville's Fall Leaf Festival snapped in the rising wind, and the trees lining Main Street danced and swayed. Mother Nature inhaled a deep breath and exhaled a rain gust that pounded like bullets on Dolly's steel roof and hood. *"Ancient hunk of rust" my ass.*

"What's all that noise, Erika?"

"I'm going to have to call you back. This storm came from nowhere, and I can barely hear you." Part truth, part convenient excuse to get off the phone. Joseph stirred uneasy feelings in me, reminding me of the turmoil I thought I was leaving behind when I left Chapel Hill.

"I'm worried about you." Another thunder boom muffled his words.

"It's only a storm. I'll be fine."

"That's not what I'm talking about."

I shifted, pressed in Dolly's clutch, and turned the ignition key. The old truck coughed once and chugged to life. "You told me that before. Nothing's changed."

"Lots has changed," he said. "You're actually trying to do something about it."

"How can you be so sure?" The storm brought in a cold front, and the temperatures plummeted like a penny dropping from the top of the Empire State Building. I fiddled with Dolly's dashboard, flipping knobs and levers until warm air blasted across my feet. "Maybe I'm just running away again. I have a habit of doing that, you know."

"You said home was the source of your problems. If you're running away, you're doing it all wrong."

I chuckled, closed my eyes, and pressed my forehead against the steering wheel.

"Do you miss me, Erika?"

If we'd been apart for weeks, rather than days, I still wouldn't have missed him—not like he wanted. A small handful of people haunted me in their absence, but none of them were Joseph Khan. "I haven't been gone long enough to miss you."

"Ouch."

"I warned you. Getting tangled up with me is a bad idea." Not giving him an opportunity to respond, I ended the call, tossed my phone onto the dashboard, and shifted into reverse. A brief glance in the rearview showed me the street was empty. I backed out, shifted into first, and stomped the gas.

Dolly's wheels slipped once, twice, before catching. We chugged uphill toward the florist shop at the other end of Main Street. The list of ghosts I needed to face while visiting Evansville was long. Some of them might require bloody sacrifices before they were appeased, but I hoped at least two of them would be content with flowers.

Chapter Ten
Just Like Heaven

THREE YEARS BEFORE...

Barefooted, standing in the EMS station's driveway in my black sports bra, jogging shorts, and yellow rubber gloves, I hosed down an ambulance and attacked its tire rims with a stiff brush and a canister of abrasive cleaner. As I scoured the ambulance's fourth and final wheel, a rumble of thunder growled in the distance, but no clouds spoiled the perfect blue sky. Rocking back on my heels, I searched for the source of the sound and recognized the familiar, flat-black Ducati Diavel turning onto the service road leading to the station.

Delight pooled warm in my stomach.

Over the past two weeks, we'd called and texted and met for two brief coffee dates at Rose's Diner, but despite our efforts, we'd been like those two proverbial ships always passing in the night. He'd started renovations at the distillery, and I'd been buried under an avalanche of EMS work. We'd been too busy to make formal plans, so his appearance was a sweet surprise, and my heart danced like an eager puppy left alone too long. Instead of wagging my tail at the sight of him coasting to a stop in the station's driveway, I stood, blanked my face, and tried not to mind the gray soap scum dripping from my gloves.

Owen pulled off his helmet and combed back his dark hair. He caught his bottom lip between his teeth as his gaze dragged over me, lingering on my curvier places. "If you'd asked me yesterday, I would have said it was impossible for a pair of yellow rubber gloves to ever be sexy, but now I can see I would've been very, *very* wrong."

I raised my water hose and aimed at him. "Don't get too hot and bothered, or I'll have to cool you down." If he kept looking at me with those dark, hooded eyes, I'd have to hose myself off as well.

Grinning, he threw up his hands in surrender. "Not a bad idea, but I can think of better ways to do it."

"Do what?"

"Cool down." He shrugged off his leather jacket, draped it across his motorcycle seat, and approached like a stalking cat. His snug T-shirt hugged broad shoulders and a defined chest. My mouth went dry as I imagined the planes of bronzed muscle underneath. Faded jeans rode low on his hips, revealing a flash of dusky skin my fingers itched to touch. *Is he as warm as he looks? Warmer?*

Clearing my throat, I dragged my mind away from thoughts of running my hands across Owen's bare skin and pasted on a smile. "What are you talking about?"

"Mr. Michener's pond."

Pond? Is he talking about swimming? Skinny-dipping? My heart rose in my throat and throbbed like a hot, glowing coal. "I-I don't think I've ever heard of it."

"It's off the road, tucked up in one of the hollers outside of town."

"Hollers?" I arched an eyebrow. "Adopting the local lingo?"

"Just trying to fit in."

Owen stopped inches away. His dimple flashed, and I was done for. If he put his hands on me and said he was dragging me to hell, I would have asked, *How fast can we get there?*

"You're not working tonight," he said. "That's what you told me last time we talked, right?"

"I did say that." And heavily implied I'd be available to hang out. Apparently he'd taken the hint.

"Then you're free to spend the rest of the day with me?"

"I, uh..." I cleared my throat. "I've got to rinse the soap off these wheels before it dries."

As if he'd heard my thoughts and decided to bestow mercy on me, Roberto strolled from the garage. "I'll finish it for you, Rikki." His gaze swung between me and Owen before he gave me a knowing wink. "You're not even on the clock anymore. Get outta here before a call catches you."

"Sure you don't mind?"

Stepping closer, he took the hose's spray nozzle from me. "You did the hard part. All I gotta do is rinse her off and put her away, right?"

I tugged off my yellow gloves and dangled them before Roberto's face. "You want to borrow these? I understand they make the guys go crazy."

A flush lit his cheeks. "No, thanks." He patted his rounded belly. "I have enough trouble beating them off as it is."

I glanced at Owen. "Let me grab my shoes and my truck keys, and we'll head out."

His smile fell, and he seemed disappointed. "I don't know, Rikki." He brushed his knuckles down my arm from shoulder to elbow. Goose bumps rose in the wake of his touch. "I think I'd like to have you tucked up against me just the way you are."

The coal in my throat turned hotter but not hot enough to burn away common sense. "Ride your bike with this much skin exposed?" I motioned to my bare feet, bare stomach, pretty much bare everything. "I don't think I'd look good in road rash. The only other clothes I have are my uniform, and I'd rather not put that hot thing on, if I can help it."

Owen's lips puckered into a frown, and he sniffed. "I guess you have a point." He stepped away and strode to his bike. "Be quick, okay? It's getting hot, and we've got a long ride."

I hurried inside the station, tugged on a spare EMS T-shirt, and grabbed my bag, my keys, and a couple of old towels from the shower room. After shoving my feet into my Chucks, I rushed to my truck and climbed behind the wheel. Owen fired up his motorcycle as Dolly's engine turned over. He rolled to the main road, and I followed at a careful distance, admiring the way his lean body hugged his bike.

I pictured him wrapped around me the same way and briefly regretted insisting I drive my truck, road rash or not.

Owen hadn't lied when he said we had a long ride. He led me away from town on a winding road that climbed steep mountains and tumbled into valleys. Shifting his weight with subtle adjustments, he handled his bike like an extension of himself, and I could've watched him for hours. *Hell, I could watch him clip his toenails for hours.*

At a spot not far from the county line, he raised his hand and waved. His right blinker flashed, and he turned onto a weed-infested gravel drive surrounded by a thick forest. He slowed, taking care to maneuver his bike over the worn path, and I followed him, bumping and creaking as Dolly crept over ruts and potholes.

A quarter mile in, the overhanging trees opened, revealing a clearing and a small pond with a short wooden dock. Behind the pond, the landscape rose in a steep hill topped by a charming cabin. It was a daydream—or a set from the most romantic movie scene imaginable. As I rolled to a stop and turned off the truck's engine, a thousand questions tumbled onto my tongue.

Owen's motorcycle fell silent. He tugged off his helmet, smoothed back his hair, and tucked his keys into his pocket. Grinning, he strode to my window and leaned in, smelling of warm leather and sweat and the ever-present undercurrent of smoke, for which I still hadn't found an explanation. Tobacco carried a distinctive aroma, a subtle dried-fruit sweetness, but Owen smelled like cold winter nights and camping trips.

"What is this place doing here?" I asked. "How did you find it? Is this *yours?*"

Instead of answering, he opened my door and jerked his chin toward the pond. "C'mon. I'll tell you all about it."

Grabbing the towels I'd borrowed from the station, I hurried to keep up with his long-legged strides. He paused at the dock's edge and unlaced and kicked off his boots. I stopped beside him and toed off my sneakers. Barefooted, Owen and I strolled to the end of the dock, and he raised his arms in a gesture encompassing all our surroundings. "The guy who sold this place to me was named Michener. Tom Michener—that's why he called this Michener's pond—but I'm thinking of calling it *El Jannah.*"

I scanned our surroundings—lush greenery and wildflowers blooming in an array of vibrant colors: creamy trilliums, golden violets, blue phlox, fire pinks, and rust-red columbines. Birds whistled and crickets chirped. The pond, rimmed in white stones, sparkled crystalline clear. Even the air smelled sweet, like fresh water and cut grass. "What does it mean?"

"It's the Islamic term for paradise. Heaven."

"Very appropriate." The Smokies had always been beautiful, but this place was ethereal, magical... *enchanted.* Awed, I shook my head. "It's unbelievable."

His smile turned shy, and he shoved his hands in his pockets. "You think so?"

Nodding, I tossed our towels onto the dock and sat at the edge. Easing my feet in the water, I gasped and gaped at him. "The water's even warm."

He dropped into a crouch beside me. "It's fed by an underground hot spring."

"Of course it is."

"Why do you say that?"

"This place is too good to be true... sort of like you."

He flinched and leaned back on his heels. "If you think that, then you don't know me very well."

"I don't know you at all, really." I stared into the distance. "Not as much as I'd like to."

Owen grunted and dropped to his rear. He rolled up his jean cuffs and dipped his feet in beside me. "Then let's change that. A question for a question. You can refuse to answer, but if you *do* answer, it must be completely honest. Sound fair?"

I bobbed my head. "Fair enough."

"You're already one up on me, so I get to go first."

I glanced at him from the corner of my eye and caught the smirk he flashed at me. "Okay, shoot."

"You asked me why I wanted to be a soldier, so now I want to know why you want to be a nurse."

The warm coal that had been burning in my throat from the moment he showed up at the EMS station turned cold and dropped to my stomach. "My dad."

His smile disappeared, and his expression darkened. "I suspected it was something like that. You said he died when you were younger?"

"Cancer." I swirled my foot through the water, stirring ripples that spread until they broke against the pond's distant edge. "I want to go into oncology so I can help people like him. The nurses who took care of him were amazing."

"There's more than one kind of hero in the world, I guess."

I leaned over and shoved my shoulder against his. "Some wear armor and carry guns. Some don't."

"I'm no hero, Rikki." He ducked his head and took my hand in his. Like sunlight peeking through rain clouds, the physical connection eased the gloomy mood that fell over us at the mention of my father. "Just a guy who thought he had something to prove."

"Tell me more about it. About your service. Only the parts you *want* to share, of course."

"It was six years. That's a long story."

"Where did you serve?"

He tugged my hand, pulling me closer. At the same time, he eased back until he was lying on the dock, face up, with me sprawled on top of him. Low and steady, his heart thumped beneath my ear as I curled myself to fit him, reveling in our closeness. When I'd woken up before dawn this morning, getting to work on time had been the only thing on my mind. Never once did I consider that I might wind up here, in a real-life Garden of Eden, wrapped in Owen's arms.

His fingers toyed with my braid while he talked. "Boot camp was at Fort Benning in Georgia. Then I shipped out straight to Iraq. First deployment was mostly in Baghdad. You probably heard about the Green Zone in the news, yeah?"

When I nodded, he continued. "I was there long after the US took command." He snorted. "Spent most of that time manning checkpoints."

"How many tours did you do overseas?"

"Nuh-uh." Owen's body swayed as he shook his head. "My turn. How long have you been an EMT?"

"Little over two years. Started training when I was seventeen so I could be certified and hired on the moment I turned eighteen. Took my first call a week after my eighteenth birthday. It was a car wreck. Drunk driver."

"Fatality?"

Technically it was my turn to ask a question, but I let it pass. "No, but the guy got a broken nose and double black eyes." I grunted. "His blood alcohol was almost triple the legal limit. He got off lucky."

Owen's fingers had reached the end of my braid, and he tugged the elastic tie until it slipped free. Combing his fingers through my hair, he loosened my curls until they sprang around my face and shoulders in a disarray of auburn, ginger, and strawberry-blond streaks. "God, your hair... you don't know how many times since I met you that I've dreamed of burying my hands in it. It's living fire when the sunlight hits it like this."

The burning coal returned to my throat and exploded into my cheeks. I swallowed, trying to put it out. "That—that's not a question."

He chuckled, and his laughter rumbled beneath my ear. I raised my head as he tugged me closer, until my face hovered over his. The sunlight did amazing things to his own hair, glinting in blue streaks. His eyes sparkled as if illuminated from within. "You also don't know how many times I've dreamed of kissing you." His stomach flexed hard beneath me as he closed the few inches between us. Before his lips met mine, he paused. "Unless you don't feel the same?"

I was feeling a million things, most all of which could be called desire or want or even need. I dropped my lips to his, answering his question.

His hand knotted in my hair at the nape of my neck while the other skimmed beneath my shirt and up my spine, burning against the bare skin there. I gasped, and he flicked his tongue over mine. Finding his shirt hem, I slid my fingers underneath, along his ribs, caressing skin as warm and smooth as I'd dreamed. He rolled, lowering me to the dock, taking his place on top of me. As he shoved a knee between my legs, I raked my nails up his back, grazing sleek muscles until he shuddered. He groaned and pulled away, his eyes half lidded.

Breathing hard, he stroked his knuckles from my temple to my jaw. "I know we said no expectations, Rikki, but I might go crazy from it... from wanting you."

He bent and kissed me again, his mouth urgent.

I was no delicate flower, but neither was I reckless, *or* desperate. If I didn't move, didn't do something to clip the wire on this ticking time bomb, I'd wind up naked beneath him, blissed out of my mind. And I'd wake up in the morning with one hell of a regret hangover. I'd never been good at separating my heart from the rest of my body, and in my relatively brief lifetime, I'd learned the people who held my heart were usually the same ones who broke it.

Unlike Mina's, mine didn't easily grow back.

I pulled back, shimmied away, and rolled to my knees. Owen turned over, tucked his hands behind his head, and gazed up at me, frowning, his brow furrowed. "Where are you going?"

Throwing caution out the window, I stood and hooked my thumb in my waistband. "I've got three months before I leave for Chapel Hill. It's not a long time, but there's no reason to rush either. I plan to make them the best three months of my life."

With a couple of swift tugs, I removed my shirt, shed my running shorts, and kicked them aside. Wearing only boy shorts and a sports bra, I skipped, hopped, and dove into the pond. When I popped to the surface, Owen was on his feet, staring at me with a look of half disbelief, half laughter. "Well, c'mon." I curled my index finger in a beckoning gesture. "What are you waiting for?"

I didn't have to ask him twice.

Owen licked his lips and, in a seamless maneuver, stripped off his shirt, revealing a stunning landscape of lean angles, flat planes, and deep valleys. Skin the color of a burnished penny hugged every well-defined bone and muscle. I sucked in a breath, and it hung in my throat.

My God, he was beautiful.

As if he could read my thoughts, Owen snagged his bottom lip between his teeth and held my gaze. He brushed a hand across the ridges of his abdomen before dropping his fingers to the fly of his jeans. With a twist and a tug, he released the button and zipper. His jeans slumped to the dock. How the water around me hadn't started boiling that very moment, I didn't know because my body had transformed into a living, breathing flame.

He leaned forward on his toes and arced into a graceful dive. He surfaced several feet away, sleek as a seal, his shoulders flexing as he swam closer.

"How come the water's so clear?" I asked, grasping for a neutral topic.

Stopping inches away, Owen reached and snagged my wrist. He tugged me closer, clamped onto my knee, and wrapped my leg loosely around his waist.

"How deep is it?" I asked. "You're touching the bottom, aren't you?"

His hands slid up my thighs to my hips, over my back, and stopped beneath my shoulder blades. I threaded my arms around his neck, and water like sun-warmed silk lapped our skin.

"The pond's clear because it's lined with white sand," he said. "At the deepest point, it's about seven or eight feet to the bottom."

"How tall are you?" I was trying my best to ignore his thumbs stroking circles on either side of my spine.

He smiled in a cagey way. "I'll tell you, but then you'll owe me three questions in return."

"Three? The questions about the pond shouldn't count."

"Oh, but they do. I'm six three. Now it's my turn. You've lived in Evansville your whole life?"

I huffed and rolled my eyes. I didn't hate Evansville, but it was so small, and it held so many painful memories of my dad. And of my mom, who was little more than a ghost herself, at least when it came to me. Owen was the first thing in years to make me not constantly yearn to leave, to experience the bigger world outside this small town. "My great-great-great-grandfather was a founding member. He was one of a group of Confederates who settled here after the Civil War."

"After you finish nursing school, will you come back home?"

"No, not if I can help it. One more question."

"No boyfriend?" He arched an eyebrow. "Really?"

I paused for a beat and snapped my eyes wide open. "I forgot all about him. He's going to be *so* pissed when he finds out about you."

Owen's laughter rang across the pond.

Throwing my arms out, I leaned back and floated, staring at the blue sky. "You're from New York?" I tilted my head so I could hear his reply.

He changed his grip, bringing his hands to my waist. His thumbs traced arcs over my ribs. "Rochester."

"Brothers and sisters?"

"One older brother, Rami."

"Are you going to live in that cabin?" I raised a dripping finger and pointed at the snug tin-roof structure squatting on the hill behind us.

"Figured I'd split my time between here and the distillery. Been staying there, mostly, while renovations are underway."

I raised my head and caught his eyes. "At the warehouse? Where do you sleep?"

"That's four questions in a row." His grip tightened on me. "This game has gotten out of control. You have no respect for the rules."

I laughed and flicked my fingers, dashing a gentle spray over him. He blinked at me as droplets trickled down his face. "You don't want to pick a fight, Albemarle." He bit his lip, clearly to keep back his grin. "I'm well trained in torture techniques."

"I thought you were a checkpoint guard."

"That was my first deployment." He waggled his dark eyebrows. "By the time I finished my last tour, I'd become an assassin, skilled in stealth and subterfuge. My hand-to-hand combat skills are wicked lethal."

I laughed. "I don't believe you." Unlocking my legs from his waist, I went under, kicked hard, and stroked, putting yards between us. Coming up for a breath, I prepared to heave a massive deluge in his direction, but he'd disappeared.

I kicked again, spinning around, searching for an indication of his position—bubbles, ripples, a shadow—but there was nothing.

Until a hand latched around my ankle and tugged.

I sucked in a breath before my head submerged. Arms like steel bands closed around me, crushing me against a hard chest. He pushed off from the bottom. We broke the surface, and he allowed me one breath before his lips were burning against mine, his tongue claiming me. "Tell me if this is too much. Tell me if I'm rushing you."

In reply, I twined my legs around him and circled my arms around his neck.

His mouth slipped to my jaw, my neck, his teeth nipping a path as he tasted and sampled sensitive spots, the hollow beneath the curve of my jaw, my collarbone.

Eager to touch him, I slid an arm free from his neck and pressed my fingers to his chest, dragging them lower, exploring each ridge of muscle.

His lips returned to my mouth. When his thumb swept over my breast, a moan escaped my throat in the shape of his name. "*Owen.*"

"Say it again," he purred.

"Say what?"

"My name."

Warm delight rolled up my spine. "Why?"

"Because I like the way it sounds when you're drunk from kissing me."

Heat flared from my core and bled into every extremity. I brushed my lips over his and complied with his request.

Owen's hand, the one that had claimed my breast, sank lower, wrapping around my thigh. His thumb stroked dangerously close to the point of no return. His hardness pressed against me, proving how ready he was to take things further, faster. *Too* fast. "God, Rikki." He gripped my hips and rubbed against me. "I want you so bad it hurts."

I tensed and broke our kiss.

His thumb froze. "Rikki?" he asked, his tone hesitant.

My heart, which had been thrumming with excitement, edged a step closer to panic. He'd asked if he was rushing me, and I'd wanted the answer to be no, but my sudden insecurity was saying something else. *Too fast,* whispered the little voice in my head. *Too out of control. He'll forget you once he gets what he wants. If you let him in, he'll break you for good.*

I unlaced myself from his body and submerged, swimming like a seal fleeing a shark. When I reached the dock, I gripped a board and hauled myself out. In time, perhaps, I would manage to silence that doubtful voice, but at that moment, the distrust, the fear, was utterly in charge.

"What's wrong?" Owen called behind me, still standing near the middle of the pond where I'd left him.

He was undoubtedly used to confident and self-assured women, and there I was, acting like a frightened little girl. Turning to face him, I threw back my shoulders and raised my chin. Tears of anger and frustration, mostly at myself, burned in my throat. "What the hell do you want with me?"

His brow furrowed. "What are you talking about?"

"I can't do flings." I snatched a towel and scrubbed it over my skin. "I can't do meaningless summer affairs that end when fall comes and I leave for school. I have to get out of Evansville. I *have* to. It might be easy for you to let me go in three months, but I don't work that way. I *can't* work that way."

"What? Why the hell would you think that?" Owen dashed a hand across the water, sending up a huge wave. "I'm lost here. Give me a clue."

"I'm not giving you a clue. I'm giving you an out." I grabbed my shirt, tugged on my running shorts, and hurried to the end of the dock, where I jammed my feet in my shoes and snatched my truck keys. "If you were smart, you would take it. You'd find someone who won't get hurt so easily, or... or someone who wouldn't leave in the first place."

I ran for my truck and threw myself behind the steering wheel. My hands shook as I shoved the key into the ignition. Dolly's engine roared to life. I wrenched the shifter into first gear and glanced out the window. Owen was already out of the water, striding toward me as I spun Dolly around and pointed her down the path leading to the road. *How could he have caught up to me so quickly? And why does it seem he walks in shadows when the rest of the clearing is burning bright with sunlight?*

I stomped the gas pedal and gripped the wheel like the reins of a bucking bronco, desperate to get away. Running was ridiculous and stupid, and Owen deserved the right to a calm conversation to explain himself, to sort things out, but my emotions were in command, and they overruled my common sense. Later, when the hormones and bad brain chemicals had worn off, I'd feel like the biggest fool on the planet, but for now, there was only instinct and reaction.

Dolly's old frame squeaked and groaned as we bumped over the rutted path. I beat my fist against the steering wheel. Tears burned in my eyes. "I'll never be able to face him again after this. Hell, he'll probably never want to *see* me again after this."

Reaching the main road, I checked for traffic and yanked on the wheel, turning toward Evansville and the security of home—never mind that home was the place I'd been so desperately trying to escape. Dolly's tires barked on the pavement when I stomped the gas. Her engine roared, protesting my demanding driving.

"Oh, shut up," I told her. "Just get me home. We girls have to stick together. Especially when one of us is being a humongous idiot."

Chapter Eleven
An Innocent Man

WHEN I'D LEFT OWEN, he was half naked, dripping wet, and alone. Although I expected he could've eventually caught up to me—if he hadn't already dismissed me as more trouble than I was worth—I didn't expect to find him in my rearview mirror minutes after I'd run from him like a doe escaping a hungry wolf.

He'd managed to put on his clothes, but his helmet was missing, and wind lashed at his dark hair. He whipped his bike to the left, gunned the engine, and roared past me, disappearing around the next curve in the road. *Where the hell is he going?*

I got my answer the moment I rounded the bend and found him several yards ahead, standing in the middle of the road, scowling, his arms folded over his chest, his feet planted shoulder-width apart. He'd parked his motorcycle perpendicular to the yellow lines, taking up both lanes so I couldn't easily drive around him, not without tumbling off the road's narrow shoulder and down the steep mountainside.

His statement was clear—he was ready to fight.

Slamming my brakes, I rolled as far off the road as I safely could. After shifting into neutral, I stomped Dolly's parking brake, threw open my door, and jumped to the pavement. "What's *wrong* with you?" I marched toward him, my hands fisted at my sides, my heart thrashing in my chest. "Every day EMTs like me scrape up the brains and guts of idiots like you who think they're immortal on a motorcycle."

A muscle throbbed in Owen's clenched jaw. He was breathing hard, like a bull preparing to charge. "What do you care? Running off like that without an explanation..."

I plowed to a stop several feet away but close enough to see darkness swirling in his eyes. "I might not have things figured out," I said, "but that doesn't mean I want to see you get hurt."

He rocked forward and bared his teeth. Like a wounded animal, everything about his posture indicated an urgent need to protect himself. He exuded the same bigger-than-life feeling I'd sensed when he'd saved me from falling in the warehouse. "If you don't want to see me get hurt, then why'd you leave me like that?"

"I thought you said you'd never chase me."

He gestured at the road farther ahead. "You're right, and there's a fine line between chasing and fighting for something you believe in. You're free to leave anytime, and I'll let you go, but I think I at least deserve a chance to defend myself." He edged a step closer. "I'm guessing you're just protecting yourself. No one can hurt you or lie to you if you don't give them the chance."

He was wrong. Life didn't wait for me to give it a chance to hurt me. It simply took whomever and whatever it wanted, and I'd been powerless to stop it. There was nothing wrong with wanting to keep myself from going through that again.

Open handed, his arms raised at his sides, he slipped closer. "You'd prefer to be alone because it's easier. Safer."

My throat swelled, and my eyes burned. I shook my head, refusing my tears, refusing his words.

"You'd keep pushing me away if I never called you out on it. Because it's hard to fight for something when you think you'll never win." He moved like a shadow, creeping toward me as though I were a frightened horse on the verge of spooking.

He'd come close enough to touch me, but he let his arms hang loose at his sides instead. *Look*, his posture said, *I'm not a threat.*

Don't be afraid of me. Unable to meet his eyes, I stared at the toes of his black boots. Scuffed and scratched, they looked like something he'd probably worn in the army.

"Believe it or not," he said, "I'm not a proud man. I've been broken before, so I know how it feels. If one of us has to bend to make this work, then I will. You set the pace. I'll follow."

My bottom lip trembled. I clamped it between my teeth. With gentle fingers, he cupped my chin and tipped my face up. "I won't expect or demand your trust—I'm not too proud to do whatever it takes to earn it."

"Why?" The word came out as an unsteady breath. "After today, I can't lie and say I'm okay and everything's going to be all right. I'm not going to be easy. Why am I even worth the effort to you?"

His eyes closed. He leaned in, pressing his forehead against mine. "Because maybe I'm as broken and difficult as you, and I recognize a kindred spirit when I see one."

"The blind leading the blind?" I chuckled, but it sounded more like a sad hiccup. "How could *that* go wrong?"

"You've been hurt. I can make a couple of guesses about who and how, but it's not really important right now. It's something we'll work out eventually. In the meantime, all I ask is that you don't put the blame on me." Pulling back, he offered me a sad smile. "I'm an innocent man." He winked. "Mostly."

With trembling hands, I wiped my eyes and stepped back. "I can't believe we haven't seen a car yet. Let's get off the road before someone gets hurt."

He squinted at me. "Only if you promise not to run again."

"I'm done running for a while, but what do we do now?"

"You choose."

"Lunch?" I suggested as I retreated to the shoulder beside Dolly. He backed toward his bike. "It's a little late for lunch."

"Early supper, then. I haven't eaten since breakfast, and I'm starving."

"Rose's?" he asked.

"No, let's go to my house. I'll call Luke and Mina—we'll cook out." Mina's presence would be a welcome distraction. She was often my shield whenever I felt vulnerable.

He gave me a surprised, wide-eyed smile. "You cook?"

"I think I can handle a few steaks on the grill."

Owen slung his leg over his bike, and the engine growled to life. He toed the clutch, teased the throttle, and rolled past me. Farther down the road, he turned around, but instead of zooming past me, he pulled to the narrow shoulder behind my truck.

"What are you doing?" I asked.

He gestured at the road, but the tone in his voice suggested his words had double meaning when he said, "Waiting for you to lead the way."

Chapter Twelve
Foggy Mountain Breakdown

PRESENTLY...

Rain was still falling when I reached Hickory Wood Cemetery, and I sat in my truck cab, listening to the comforting pitter-patter on my roof. The graveyard crouched atop a bald knob that offered extended views of the surrounding mist-frosted ridges. Heavy cloud cover smothered the sunlight, tinting the graveyard in gloomy shades of gray. Ghostly tendrils of fog skirted the old iron gate and danced like spirits between headstones.

Evansville's founding fathers had built the cemetery not long after they built the town. Over time, most of Evansville's citizens had established their final residence in Hickory Wood, making it a rather crowded place, but it also meant the town kept the grounds raked and trimmed. Floral arrangements in fall colors adorned most gravesites, suggesting the cemetery had received recent visitors.

Today, however, I had the dead all to myself.

I dug underneath my seat, found an old retractable umbrella, and pushed open Dolly's creaky door. Taking a moment to orient myself, I savored the cool, damp air smelling of decaying leaves, wet grass, and rusty wrought iron. I weaved around puddles and through the cemetery gates, maneuvering past rows of gray and white grave markers—some new and polished, some old, crumbling, and coated in moss.

My father's grave hunkered near the end of a row that, on a sunny day, would have been shaded by the eponymous hickories looming nearby. Someone had visited recently; the silk arrangement at the

112

foot of his headstone hadn't yet faded from sun exposure. Mom didn't like anyone knowing she sometimes snuck up here to cry. As the first female sheriff elected in Twain County, she thought she had something to prove, that showing emotion was revealing weakness. She could hide her grief from most people but not from me.

I crouched, set a bouquet of fresh yellow flowers at the base of his stone, and traced my fingers across his name, Eric James Albemarle.

"Hey, Dad." I swallowed the lump rising in my throat and blinked against the sting in my eyes. "Long time no see."

I pictured my dad arching an auburn eyebrow, crossing his arms over his chest, and giving me an expectant look—the same look he'd given me whenever I'd stayed out playing with my friends instead of coming home in time for dinner.

"I know it's been too long, but I don't have to tell you what's been going on. If you've been listening in on my prayers, you already know." My prayers were less formal petitions to God and more random mumblings of distress. Sometimes downright begging and pleading.

"Rose is pissed at me. She's not ready to hear *sorry* from me yet, and I don't blame her. I can't come to her empty-handed, and she wants more from me than a bunch of stupid flowers, but I can't give her what I don't have."

My knees complained about my prolonged crouch, so I grunted and stood up. The rain on my umbrella prattled in loud whispers, and the mists had thickened, blotting out all but a few dozen of the closest tombstones and monuments. Death had never frightened me, and although my surroundings were doing their best to create a horror-movie scenario, I remained undaunted.

"I'm too old to blame anyone for the mistakes I've made, including Mom, although she still has things to answer for. But you'd be proud of me. I'm here to do what I should have done three years ago.

I'm going to get the truth, and then I'm going to get on with living. I'm sorry it took me so long to figure it out."

Closing my eyes, I imagined him wrapping his arms around me for a big bear hug. I hadn't come here for absolution—not from him, anyway. There were others to whom I owed an apology but not my father. My devotion to him had never wavered. Guilt and blame never factored into our bond. I wished I could say the same about my relationships with the other residents of Evansville.

"I'd visit longer, but I've got a long to-do list today, and I'd better get on with it." I rubbed the arch of my dad's grave marker as if caressing his cheek. Instead of saying goodbye, I told him what we'd always said whenever we parted, "Miss you too much."

Without looking back, I worked my way deeper into the cemetery, down a steep hill to the rear corner where another hickory guarded a newer row of monuments. I'd never visited this section and wouldn't have known where to go if the florist hadn't kept immaculate records. He'd searched his old files and found the delivery forms for the wreaths and sprays that had been transported to Mina's gravesite on the day of her funeral.

Her parents had given her a black stone, simple, elegant, and a little edgy, like her. I propped a red rose bouquet at its base, took a step back, and wondered how to start. One more apology—how hard could it be? I was an expert in talking to ghosts and had spent most of my life inside my own head, conducting lengthy dialogues with both the dead and the living. But not with Mina.

I'd never had a sister—hadn't wanted one. Other people's relationships with their siblings had seemed like shoddy wannabe imitations of what I'd had with her. She'd deserved more than my empty, hollow words of grief and sorrow, but I'd stayed away because that was all I'd had to offer her. Until now. "Well, I'm finally here. I know, I know—too little, too late."

In my head, Mina scowled at me, folded her arms over her chest, and tapped her foot, which was sheathed in a black leather boot with a ridiculously high heel.

"So, you're going to puff at me like an angry dragon? Guess I can't blame you." I pointed at the roses. "Do those help? If not, I've got more." I removed a parcel from my coat pocket and set it beside the flowers. "It's Dove. 'Life's too short for Hershey's,' right? I would have brought Chunky Monkey, but that would've been sticky, and you'd look terrible covered in ants."

Mina rolled her eyes. She stopped tapping her toe and held out her palm, motioning for me to hand over the chocolate bar.

"I should have been there." I couldn't even face her headstone without looking away. "You know why I wasn't, though. You of all people understand best, but it's no excuse. I know that." My breath hitched, caught in my throat, and burned. "You were there when it counted, but I didn't return the favor."

Wiping my eyes, I chuckled sadly. "I bet you wish you'd never encouraged me to date Owen, don't you?" She glared at me, and I flinched. "Sorry. Low blow."

The Mina from my memories shrugged, peeled open her chocolate, and popped a piece between bright red lips painted with MAC's Rooby Woo. My appeals had done little to impress her, apparently. I was equally unimpressed with myself. Nothing new there.

"I know it was my fault, not protecting you when I should have." Pausing, I cleared my throat and waited for my chin to stop trembling. "There's no way to make up for what happened, not really, but I'm at least going to try, okay?" I closed my eyes, holding back tears. "I'm going to figure out what the hell happened, and when I do, I promise to come back and tell you. That'll be better than any lame apology, right?"

Mina's nostrils flared. She pursed her lips.

"Okay, okay." I flapped my hands at her. "You're right. You deserve the lame apology too. I suck, and I'm sorry... for everything."

I left Mina nibbling the last of the chocolate and returned to my truck, treading carefully through fog that had become more like stew than misty atmospheric backdrop. At least the rain had stopped. I folded up my umbrella and let the damp do its worst to the curls springing free from my braid.

I returned to Dolly and set the heat to full blast, shook off the umbrella, and stowed it. The fog swirled like a creature composed of secrets, reminding me again of my purpose and intent. I flipped on my headlights and rolled out of the parking lot.

Perhaps I was an idiot, coming back to Evansville like this, poking at sleeping monsters, intent on waking them up. Mina had died because we'd gotten involved in something we hadn't understood, and I didn't want to suffer the same fate. I left Hickory Wood hoping I wouldn't be adding my own grave marker to the cemetery's collection anytime soon.

Chapter Thirteen
Come a Little Closer

THREE YEARS BEFORE...

After stopping by the grocery store to pick up a few items for supper, I ushered Owen into my dark, quiet house. I asked him to wait in the kitchen while I ducked into the bathroom, combed out my damp hair, and exchanged my clammy T-shirt and shorts for a strappy green sundress that, according to Mina, set off my eyes.

"Where's your mom?" Owen asked when I returned to the kitchen, his heavy gaze following my every move.

"Work? The diner? Who knows?" I unloaded the grocery bags and set packages beside the sink.

He joined me at the counter, helping me unpack. "She leaves you on your own a lot?"

"We have our own lives."

"But has it always been like that?"

I opened an overhead cabinet and pointed at a casserole dish I couldn't reach. "Like what?"

"Were you two ever close?" Owen grabbed the dish and set it on the countertop beside me.

I cracked open a bottle of my favorite quick marinade and emptied it into the dish. "When I was young, Mom and I were inseparable. We rock climbed. We hiked. She taught me how to ride a bike and play volleyball."

Owen caught my hand and squeezed it. "What happened?"

Glancing away, I shrugged. "My dad died, and everything changed." Eager for a less troubling topic, I held up a Styrofoam

117

packet of rib eyes for his inspection. "How do you like yours cooked?"

He flashed a sharp smile full of teeth. "Rare."

I pointed toward the house's rear, in the general direction of the back porch. "You know how to start a grill?"

He arched a brow and pursed his lips. Clearly, my question had offended his manly sensibilities. "Propane?"

"Charcoal. There's a big blue box on the deck that has all the stuff you'll need in it."

While Owen worked his magic on the grill, I set the steaks in the pan to marinate and rifled through the refrigerator before digging out a head of lettuce, grape tomatoes, and cucumbers. The vegetables reminded me that Dad used to plant a garden every spring: squash, peppers, and heirloom tomatoes growing in a rainbow of colors. Sometimes he would fish the local streams and bring home stringers of trout. He'd dust off our ancient churn and make homemade ice cream. In winter, we'd hike into the national park and find our own Christmas trees, and he'd take me sledding when it snowed.

I'd had a lot of years to dwell on the nature of our relationship. There was the family Mom and I had been before Dad's death, and there was the one we were after. Once, we were like iron chains, but Dad's illness and death had been a constant barrage of air and salt water, and now she and I were mostly just rust.

Tires crunched on the gravel driveway, snapping me out of my thoughts. I peered through the front-door window and recognized Luke's old green Ford.

"Didn't think you could pass up a free steak dinner," I told him as he escorted Mina across my front yard. "But I wasn't sure if you got my message."

"Loud and clear." Charm and mischief twinkled in Luke's blue eyes. He'd recently shaved, and he looked less like a hardened war veteran and more like the charming boy I'd known before he'd joined the army. "I would have smelled your grill all the way from town and followed my nose out here if you hadn't invited me."

I hugged Mina, inhaling her jasmine and patchouli perfume. "Y'all are here just in time to help me make the salad."

Luke frowned. "I thought maybe I could light the grill or something."

"Already taken care of," Owen said, wiping his hands on a dish towel as he stepped onto the porch behind me. "Coals are lit."

Taking Mina's hand, I brushed past Luke and Owen. "You want to eat in this house, you've got to earn it. Luke, I know your mom used to make you work in the diner. I think you can handle shredding some lettuce."

"That was *supposed* to be a secret." He followed us into the kitchen. "I never wanted to be exploited for my culinary talents."

Pointing at the romaine hearts, I rolled my eyes. "Get to work, Iron Chef."

Like powerful medicine, their presence cured the discord in my soul. Their laughter and banter was a warm compress on my neck and shoulders, easing away the day's emotional and hormonal overdoses. Owen stepped away from his steaks and leaned close to me at the counter, where I was buttering a loaf of French bread. "You okay?"

I sniffed and dashed my hand across my watering eyes. "Great, actually."

"This was a good idea. I'm glad you thought of it."

Luke tossed aside his lettuce knife and bowed. "A more perfect bowl of chopped greenery, you'll never find. You're welcome." He caught Owen's eye and jerked his chin toward the kitchen doorway. "C'mon. Let's check on the coals before she finds something else for us to do."

Owen collected his dish of steaks, winked at me, and followed Luke outside. I didn't object because I'd been waiting for the moment when I could talk to Mina alone. "Girl, tell me everything," she said the instant they were out of earshot.

Quickly, I summarized the day's events, starting with Owen appearing at the EMS station and ending with our middle-of-the-road tête-à-tête. Mina bit her lip, obviously resisting the urge to butt in and ask questions, particularly about the events occurring in and around Owen's pond, which had made her eyes bulge and her mouth hang open like a broken latch.

When I'd finished rehashing everything, she gave me a hard look. "Your defense mechanisms can kick in pretty hard-core sometimes. You really like this guy, and it scares you."

I wiped off Mina's cucumber knife and worked on slicing a pile of grape tomatoes in half. "So? What's your point?"

"Why don't you just try trusting him?"

"You know what Ronald Reagan said when the Soviets promised to get rid of their nuclear arms in the eighties?" I only knew because it had been a question on my final American history exam, and I had studied like hell for it.

She rolled her eyes. "Oh my God, Rikki, you're such a nerd. That's ancient history, so of course I don't know what he said, but I'm sure you're going to tell me, anyway."

"He said, 'Trust, but verify.'"

"How're you going to do that?"

"Not sure, but until I figure it out, I'm not going to rush into anything."

"You've always been careful." She reached into an overhead cabinet for a stack of dinner plates. "Maybe too careful. If you live your life in fear, you'll miss all the fun. And since you like quotes so much, here's one from our philosophy class. 'That which does not kill us, makes us stronger.'" She set the plates on the counter with a clatter and cocked a crooked grin. "Who's the nerd now, bitch?"

BY THE END OF SUPPER, the sun had dipped below the tree line, and twilight tinted the sky in shades of violet and indigo. Buttery citronella candles flickered along the porch rails and in the center of the table, lending the night a sense of enchantment. The spectral colors and glimmering lights heightened Owen's allure, brought to life the flames in his eyes and the burnished glow in his bronze skin.

I could almost believe he was a magical creature from another realm, sent to tantalize me, tempt me, entice me into sharing a moment of pleasure that was, in reality, a curse. In the old stories, he'd turn out to be a goblin king who would lock me away in his underground lair. Or he'd be prisoner to his own curse, a slave to a fairy queen, doomed to serve her forever. Perhaps, if I grabbed hold of him tightly enough and refused to let go, he'd eventually turn into a hot coal, like Tam Lin. I could drop him in a well, turn him back into a man, and he'd be mine forever.

Mina had brought out the old portable radio I kept in my room and tuned in the local country station. A low, quiet voice crooned about convincing his lover to come a little closer. Following the singer's advice, Luke rose from his seat, pulled Mina from her chair, and tugged her into his arms. She giggled but didn't resist when he rocked her in time with the song's slow beat. He muttered something in her ear. She smiled, and her eyelids fluttered closed.

"I'm not a dancer," Owen said. "Hope you're not disappointed."

I shook my head. "If you haven't noticed, I'm not particularly graceful. Mom suggested ballet once when I was little. I asked for a bike instead."

As the darkness thickened, tiny spots of light flickered to life near the tree line's edge as if the stars had come down to dance with us. The Smokies were home to a rare species of fireflies that could synchronize their blinking, and the season's first arrivals were gracing my backyard with coordinated flickers of phosphorescent light. Twilight, gleaming candles, and fireflies—the innate magic of the mountains felt especially palpable.

I pointed at the flashing flecks of light. "When I was a kid, I pretended they were communicating in a magic language, and only those who were special enough to figure it out would learn some fantastic secret."

Owen scooted his chair closer. He took my hand, flipped it over, and brushed his thumb across the base of my palm. His lip twitched—not quite laughing at me. "Did you ever translate their message?"

Pointing at the tree line, I squinted into the gloom. "There's a deer path in the woods if you know where to find it. Follow it about two miles, and it leads to a clearing with a big crop of boulders in the middle. I found it when I was six—followed the fireflies there. Was hoping they were leading me to the entrance of Tir Na Nog, or Narnia, or Diagon Alley. I never found a magic door or portal, but it was a good place to hide when I needed to get away from my problems."

"If you'd found the entrance to that magic land, would you have run away?"

His touch tingled from my fingertips to my scalp. I closed my eyes. "Maybe for a little while. Not forever, though. There was a time, believe it or not, when I wasn't so anxious to leave home. I used to think this house and this backyard were the best places in the world."

"Growing up has a terrible way of ruining things, doesn't it?" He pressed a kiss to my palm.

My eyes popped open, and I caught him staring at me through dark lashes. He dropped my hand and yanked my chair, pulling it around until I faced him. In an impulsive display of affection, he scooped me up and dropped me into his lap. I crumpled against him, laughing. He brushed a cluster of curls off my cheek and tucked them behind my ear. "Just because I don't dance doesn't mean I want us to spend the whole night keeping our distance from each other."

"I was sitting right beside you."

He growled. "It wasn't close enough."

"I thought you said I was supposed to set the pace and you'd follow."

"You want to take it slow, and I'm okay with that, but don't tell me you don't like it when I touch you."

My heart tumbled an ungainly cartwheel in my chest. I pressed my lips together, remembering his kisses.

He laced his arms around my middle, and his thumb stroked my back along the top edge of my dress. "Nothing to say, hmm?"

"You said I didn't have to answer, but if I did, I had to tell the truth. I'm pleading the fifth."

Owen chuckled and nipped my jaw. He lowered his voice. "You look like a fantasy in that dress with your hair loose down your back." He ran his fingertips from my collarbone to my dress's thin strap and slipped it loose. He pressed his lips to my shoulder. "I'd say you've got skin like cream, but you have too many freckles." He kissed my neck. "Never knew I was a freckle guy, but I could spend hours kissing each of them, especially the ones no one else gets to see."

Involuntarily, my fingers clenched, knotting in his T-shirt's soft fabric. My breath was ragged. I'd been kissed before, but I'd never been seduced, not like this, and certainly not by someone who could undo me simply by whispering alluring things in my ear. I turned, bringing my mouth closer to his, but before we could connect, the radio traded its slow, romantic ballads for a rowdy party anthem about beer and tractors.

"Yee-haw!" Luke yelled.

I flinched.

Owen grunted.

Luke spun Mina in a fast twirl then bent and hauled her over his shoulder. Her surprised squeal dissolved into a fit of laughter, and Luke smacked her rear end. "I'd like to say we'd stay and help clean up, Rikki, but I got to get this little lady home. It's past her curfew."

"I don't have a curfew," Mina protested.

"Shh." Luke patted her butt again. "I'm trying to get us out of here before Rikki makes us wash the dishes."

Chuckling, I waved them off. "Y'all go on. I don't need help cleaning up. There's not that much, anyway."

"That's right." Luke nodded at Owen. "Now that you've made him into your love slave, *he* can wash the dishes."

Owen flashed his middle finger at Luke.

I unfolded myself from Owen's lap and stood. "Okay, now you're pushing it." I pointed at Mina, who was still doubled over his shoulder, her rear in the air. "You better go before I start stacking dirty dishes on Mina's butt."

Mina squealed again. "Run, Luke, run!"

Luke tromped down the porch steps. "Thanks for dinner, Rikki." He hurried through the yard, still carrying Mina. "We should do it again sometime."

Moments later, Luke's truck doors slammed shut, and an engine roared to life.

While I stacked plates and serving dishes, Owen collected silverware and empty beer bottles. He followed me into the kitchen, and we dumped our burdens in the sink. I leaned against the counter.

"When are you off work again?" Leaning close, he stroked a knuckle over my cheek. "This once-in-a-while thing isn't really working for me."

His words echoed my own feelings. "I'm on duty with the EMS through Wednesday morning, but I don't have to go back until Thursday evening."

His face fell. "So, the next time you're free is five days from now—that's almost a week."

"I'm sorry." I plucked the beer bottles from the sink and carried them to the recycle bin in the utility room. I raised my voice so he could hear me. "The shifts are all overnight ones—twelve hours each. I'm the low man on the totem pole, and I need a lot of hours, so I take what I can get."

He grunted and said nothing else. I searched his face for a sign of what he was thinking or feeling, but his expression was hard and unreadable. He cleared his throat, closed his eyes, and seemed to be collecting himself. "I guess I'm going to head out unless you need me to help with anything else."

I shook my head. "I'll just put everything in the dishwasher later. No big deal."

The silent space between us filled with unspoken wants and desires that felt like a burning fuse desperately seeking a keg of gunpowder. If I touched him, I knew we'd both explode, and I wasn't ready for that. Without a word, he grabbed his keys from the counter, but I didn't follow him outside. I suspected, like me, he wanted to go anywhere other than an empty house and an empty bed. But after the day's tumultuous events, I couldn't bring myself to ask him to stay or to let me stay with him. Not yet.

He said he would earn my trust.

I was going to let him try.

Chapter Fourteen
So Fresh, So Clean

I SLID BEHIND THE RIG'S steering wheel, buckled in, and ignored the exhaustion turning my muscles to sand and my bones to lead. Halfway through my fourth twelve-hour shift, I could feel each bump in the road, each sway and lurch our ambulance made as Toni and I raced into a remote holler at the county's northern edge.

Frequently, finding people in the Smokies was like putting together a jigsaw puzzle with missing pieces. Some mountain folk preferred living off the grid or, at least, on the grid's farthest possible corner. Our GPS often brought us close but not all the way. We used intuition and a good dose of luck to locate patients who would otherwise prefer avoiding the notice of outsiders.

Tonight was turning out to be a jigsaw-puzzle kind of night.

The address Dispatch provided led us to the entrance of a dark and overgrown gravel road, and the GPS announced we had reached our destination, although there was no sign of a house nearby. "Can we ask the caller for more info?" I asked. "Or do we just follow our noses?"

Toni relayed my request to the dispatcher, and we idled at the dirt road's entrance, waiting for a reply.

A hollow, crackling voice responded through Toni's radio. "You're looking for a white single-wide about a half mile down on the right. Caller said porch lights will be on. They'll flag you down in the driveway."

I eased off the brake, and the rig bumped along the rutted dirt road. Our headlights illuminated low-hanging branches. Choking brush entombed the pathway. Hairs rose along the back of my neck, responding to some instinctive menace, as if years of antagonism and hostility from the residents of this dark, narrow valley had created an imaginary force field discouraging intrusion from strangers.

As the dispatcher had said, a man stood at the end of his driveway, waving at us as though we were a 747 and his yard were a landing strip. I rolled to a stop in the drive and set the parking brake as Toni climbed down from her seat. "C'mon," said our contact, waving for us to follow. His salt-and-pepper beard hung to the middle of his chest, and an old International Tractor cap slumped low on his brow. "He's 'round back."

Toni and I collected our medical kits and hurried to catch up. Our host, who smelled like a beer keg gone sour, escorted us to the rear of a single-wide home set on a cinder block foundation. At the back of the house, we found a young man slumped on the steps of a weathered deck.

"What's his name?" Toni asked.

Our host scratched his belly. "Cricket."

"Full name?"

"Uh, Travis. Travis Wambach, but not even his momma calls him that."

An overwhelming and distinctly soapy odor flooded my senses as I popped on a pair of latex gloves and reached for Cricket's wrist. "What do you think?" I asked Toni as she wrapped a blood pressure cuff around our patient's bicep. "Original scent or Ocean Breeze?"

She snorted, ignoring my joke, and squeezed Cricket's shoulder. "Hey, man, my name's Toni. We're going to get you fixed up, okay?"

Cricket moaned and belched.

"What did you do?" I asked. "Drink some laundry detergent?" When Cricket only moaned again, I glanced at our host and raised an eyebrow. "Sorry, didn't catch your name."

He scratched his belly again. "I'm Dale." He pointed at my patient. "Cricket's my cousin."

"So, Dale, tell me exactly what happened." Cricket's pulse fluttered beneath my fingertips, regular but a little fast and light. I let go of his arm and dug into my kit for my otoscope and a tongue depressor.

"Well... we was, uh, sitting around on the back porch, after dinner, drinking some beers, shooting the shit like usual. Then my brother, Alan, he gets the bright idea to play truth or dare, like we was a bunch of teenagers or something."

Alcohol was involved. How unsurprising.

Dale shifted his weight, weaving from one foot to the other. "So we go a couple rounds, mostly harmless stuff, but then Alan dares Cricket to drink whatever's left in the bottle of his old lady's washing soap. I tried to stop him, but Cricket's real hardheaded, 'specially when he's been drinking."

I slid the tongue depressor into Cricket's mouth, peered down his throat with my otoscope, and wasn't surprised to see the tissue was highly inflamed. If he hadn't already suffered a few internal burns, he probably would before the night was over, especially when that soap started coming back up. "How much do you guess he drank?"

Toni removed a bag of IV fluid from her kit and unwound the tubing.

"It was about half empty," Dale said, "but it wasn't one of them big bottles." He raised his hands, forming a small boxy shape. "'Bout like that."

"So... maybe a quarter gallon or so?"

Dale shrugged. "Maybe."

Toni helped Cricket to his feet, and the two staggered down the steps and into the yard. Dale trailed behind us, wringing his hands.

"Don't know whether the doc will want to admit him for observation or not," I said, "but it'll be a while before they release him, anyway. You might as well get some sleep before you worry about coming to the hospital for him." *Sober up, too, while you're at it.*

Behind me, Toni had opened the ambulance's rear doors, but she paused as our patient fell into a coughing fit. Cricket hacked a raw sound deep in his throat, bent over, and groaned. Clenching an arm around his belly, he cursed, and his abdominal muscles contracted. With a horrible retching sound, the contents of his stomach splashed to the ground in a pool of thick, gooey blue.

When Mina's brother was little, I'd given him a battery-powered gun that churned out an endless stream of bubbles when he filled it with soap solution. Cricket looked as if he had ingested one of those bubble guns. He vomited again, and torrents of blue lather and gauzy bubbles gushed from his throat and foamed around his mouth, as though he were a rabid dog.

Toni propped Cricket against the side of our rig and bowed over, hands on her knees, gasping for breath. Laughter quaked in her broad shoulders, rocked her frame, and thundered from her chest. "Plop plop," she said between guffaws. "Fizz fizz."

I slumped against the ambulance beside Cricket, giving into the hilarity. "Oh..." I giggled. "What a relief it is."

I TUCKED THE AMBULANCE into its garage bay and handed the keys to Roberto, who had arrived to take over the next shift. Stumbling outside, I felt like a vampire shriveling beneath the pale dawn light. Although I lived miles away, I could hear my bed calling my name. My pillow was promising to make sweet, sweet love to me, and my toes tingled in anticipation. Or perhaps that was just numbness from over-exhaustion.

"You look like hell, Rikki," Roberto called as I shuffled to my truck. "Get some sleep."

"Thanks, Roberto. You really know how to charm a lady, don't you?"

"Why? You seen one around?"

I flipped my middle finger at him without looking back, but his laughter followed me to my truck. When I cranked her engine, Dolly grumbled as though I'd awakened her from a long nap. "Oh, don't complain. You've had plenty of beauty sleep. Now it's my turn."

But it was not to be.

After a drive that took less than half an hour but felt like three, I turned down my driveway and discovered my regular parking place had been taken by a sleek black car I couldn't have identified if not for the familiar blue-and-white logos adorning the trunk and tire rims. *Who the hell do I know who owns any kind of BMW, much less one that's been molded from hot, melted sex?*

Dolly's brakes squeaked as I parked beside the Bimmer. I cut her engine, and my ears hummed in the quiet while I studied the low-slung, curvaceous car painted in a glossy black that insinuated dark and naughty delights—as if it ate tight leather and stiletto heels for breakfast.

Curiosity temporarily diluted my exhaustion, and I searched the grounds for a clue about the car's owner. Never in my wildest dreams did I expect to find Owen, dressed in jeans and dark T-shirt, camouflaged in the shadows of my front porch.

He strolled to the porch's edge, where the early-morning sun painted him in pale-gold light, and he looked like something mystical and holy. A sly grin spread over his face. "Like it?"

I licked my lips and swallowed, stalling for a moment to gather my composure. "It's, uh... it's yours?"

He shrugged. "It's a long ride to Chapel Hill. I think you'd be more comfortable in a car, don't you?"

He might as well have spoken French, or Arabic, for all the sense his words were making. "What do you mean, 'Chapel Hill'?"

Owen crossed the yard and pulled me into his arms. Four days of working twelve-hour shifts, and sleeping poorly in between, had taken its toll, but his touch felt like a shot of B12 and caffeine, straight to my heart. "A buddy from my unit got out a year ahead of me, and he's been going to UNC on his G.I. Bill. I called and asked if he'd give us a tour—you know, from an insider's point of view."

I leaned back and blinked at him. This wasn't merely some last-minute surprise. He'd thought ahead and planned this outing purely for me. "A tour? Today?"

His brow crinkled with concern. "I know you're exhausted, but maybe you could nap on the way? I haven't seen you in days, and I really want to hang out with you. But if you're too tired, I can cancel. We can stay here, be couch potatoes, and binge on Netflix or something."

I shook my head, stunned. Overwhelmed. Amazed. A warm ray of sunshine curled around my heart and squeezed. "I don't know what to say."

"Say you're going to take a shower and get dressed." He frowned and wrinkled his nose. "I don't know why, but you smell like you've been swimming in laundry detergent."

I chuckled and tugged free from his arms. "I sort of have been."

He followed me across the front porch and into the kitchen, where my mom was pouring a cup of coffee. Her uniform shirt looked freshly pressed, her badge recently shined. Bacon, eggs, and hot grease perfumed the air. Mom sometimes cooked on weekends but rarely during the week. She had either grown a wild hair, or possibly, she was feeling sorry for me. She glanced at us, grunted, and took down two mugs from the cabinet. She nodded at Owen. "That one's been on the porch waiting for you since sunup."

He smiled sheepishly and twisted his ring around his finger. "Knew if you made it to bed, I'd probably never get you out again." He rolled a shoulder. "If it's selfish, I'm not sorry."

Owen refused when Mom offered him breakfast, so she dished a plate of bacon and eggs for me while I poured coffee. After handing Owen his cup, I slumped on a stool at the kitchen island and dug into my breakfast.

He leaned against the counter beside me, close enough for his arm to graze my shoulder. Even that small point of contact was enough to set my blood thrumming. I'd missed him more than I'd allowed myself to admit.

"So." Mom folded her arms over her chest and studied Owen with a hard eye. "Chapel Hill?"

"I thought we'd look around, get some lunch." Owen glanced at me. "Maybe it won't seem so far away once I've checked it out."

I wondered whether he was implying that we could make it work between us, even if we lived four hours apart. "I have a packet of brochures from some apartments around campus," I said. "Do you think we could check those out too?" I'd intended to spend the day catching up on sleep and laundry, but Owen's plans appealed to me more, though I wasn't sure I had the energy for trudging around campus all day in the summer heat.

He sipped his coffee and nodded. "Whatever you want, Rikki."

Mom cleared her throat and set her mug in the sink. "You kids have fun. Be careful on the road." Her eyes flicked toward the front of the house, and although she couldn't see it from where she stood, I suspected she was thinking about the fancy car sitting in our driveway. Like me, she was probably wondering where it had come from and how Owen afforded such things. I couldn't know for sure. Maybe he had family money, but the average soldier's pay couldn't possibly support a rich diet of Ducatis, BMWs, distilleries, and private mountain retreats. Between his desire for anonymity and his affinity for extravagant luxuries, Owen was turning into quite the enigma. "Don't do anything I wouldn't do."

I shoved a piece of bacon in my mouth and harrumphed. "That doesn't leave us many options."

"Exactly." Mom snagged her ball cap from the counter and slipped it on, covering her dark-brown hair. I should've offered to trim the long hairs on her neck, but I'd been too busy and distracted. We'd gotten good at neglecting each other, and the blame wasn't all hers.

On impulse, I stepped into her path and threw my arms around her. She paused as if surprised, but her hands slid across my back, and she drew me in for a tight hug. She'd always given the best hugs, and perhaps it was my fault that I hadn't indulged in them enough lately. "Be safe, and don't let any bad guys get away."

She rubbed her cheek against mine. "I'll try my best." Pausing, she sniffed. "Why do you smell like laundry detergent?"

"A game of truth or dare, half a bottle of Tide, and a couple of drunk hillbillies. You do the math."

She winced, shaking her head. "The stupidity in this county never ceases to amaze me." She was still chuckling as she let go of me and walked out the door.

Owen snorted as he refilled his coffee mug. "A Tide overdose? Is that the dumbest call you've ever been on?"

I gave him a wide-eyed look and shook my head. "Oh no. There have been much, much dumber ones."

"You'll have to tell me about them." He pointed at the kitchen doorway. "After you shower and get dressed." He set down his mug and took my empty breakfast plate to the sink. "Get moving, *ya albi*. We haven't got all day."

I paused in the kitchen doorway. "What does 'ya albi' mean?" It sounded like a play on my last name, but something in his tone, something tender, implied otherwise.

He waggled an eyebrow. "Maybe, if you're very sweet to me today, I'll tell you."

"Don't you know?" I winked. "I'm sweeter than a sugar boat on a syrup sea sailing around a planet made of cotton candy."

Chapter Fifteen
Carolina in My Mind

SOON AFTER WE HIT THE highway, the thrill of Owen's surprise wore off. His car—a BMW i8, I had learned—provided ridiculously plush seats, and while they weren't as seductive as the pillows and mattress on my bed, I had fallen under the spell of their buttery-soft leather. The monotonous hum of the road rumbling beneath the tires lulled me into a drowsy daze. Owen twined his fingers through mine and stroked his thumb over my wrist. The last thing I said before slipping into the abyss of sleep was, "I'll try not to drool on your seats."

He woke me three hours later as we exited the highway, following directions given by the polite Englishwoman whose voice was programmed into his navi system. I sat up, yawned, and rubbed my eyes. The sun had risen, and billowing clouds dotted the bright-blue sky. Outside the car's climate-controlled interior, the day was promising a super-strong dose of heat and humidity. North Carolina summers came in only two varieties, hot and sticky or *extra* hot and *absurdly* sticky.

"We there yet?" I asked.

"Almost. Thought you'd want to see the town as we drive through."

We left the four-lane highway crowded by big-box and chain stores, exiting onto a

smaller thoroughfare lined with quaint shops, cafés, and gourmet grocery stores. The road narrowed and wound up a steep tree-lined hill, carrying us past rows of grand old houses. Owen's car hugged the street's curves, and the engine purred like a panther stalking prey.

As we rolled past the university bookstores and shops lining Franklin Street, I watched our reflection in the store windows as if observing two strangers and tried to imagine the redheaded girl in the fancy car as someone more experienced and sophisticated than she felt. My stomach swirled, churned by excitement. "I can't believe I'll be going here," I said, slightly breathless. "It's like a dream." A dream I'd been harboring since I was old enough to say, "Go Heels!"

Owen clicked his tongue. "It's nothing like Evansville. That's for sure."

I studied him from the corner of my eye. "You don't like it?"

"I didn't say that."

"It's a long drive, though, isn't it?"

He patted his steering wheel. "Doesn't feel so long when you're driving something like this."

"I wouldn't know. It's always been just me and Dolly. We're an inseparable duo."

"If you want to drive on the way home, you can."

"Oh God, yes." I lowered my voice. "Just don't tell Dolly I cheated on her, okay?"

He laughed as the GPS announced our next turn. Tugging the wheel, he made a sharp left onto a narrow street running between a pub and an ice cream shop. "Beamon lives in an old house somewhere near here." His brow crinkled as he inspected the GPS screen. "Looks like we're close."

"Do you know what he's studying?"

He peered through the windshield, reading street signs. "I'm not sure... something to do with business, I think." He pointed at a little ramshackle house painted in faded maroon, squatting beneath a pair of fat pin oaks. The house sat on a small lot covered in dandelions, dirt patches, and dried leaves that gave the scene a sepia patina like an aged photograph. "That's it." His brows pinched together. "According to the GPS."

I studied the house as he pulled up next to the curb and parked behind a rusty blue Tacoma. My former excitement faded, apprehension taking its place. Here I was, a simple mountain girl, sure to look naïve next to a couple of worldly war veterans, one of whom was a student who'd already successfully survived a year of college.

As if he sensed my reluctance, Owen cupped my chin and locked his gaze on mine. "Hey, Beamon's a nice guy. It'll be cool. Trust me."

While most of me was excited about leaving home for the big city and busy campus, a small part of me believed I was crazy. That I would fail. That I should stay in Evansville, where things were safe, familiar, and easy. That I should stay with Owen.

Gathering my courage, I climbed out of the car. Owen met me on the sidewalk, took my hand, and led me to the house's front door. He knocked, and while we waited for someone to answer, he leaned close and brushed a kiss over my cheek. "Relax, ya albi. It'll be fun."

"Tell me what 'ya albi' means."

Grinning, he shook his head, refusing to say another word. The front door swung open, and a handsome young guy in a UNC ball cap, jeans, and a Braves jersey threw out his arms and tugged Owen into a backslapping bear hug. "Amir, long time no see."

They pounded each other's backs a few more times before pulling apart and turning their attention on me. I blushed and lowered my eyes, studying the tips of Beamon's fancy sneakers. "Beamon, this is Rikki Albemarle. Rikki, James Beamon."

Screwing up my courage, I met Beamon's sparkling brown eyes. His smile was warm and genuine.

"Good to meet you, Rikki."

"Nice to meet you too." I shook his hand and forced myself to relax. "Sorry if I'm a little nervous. Owen sprang this trip on me at the last minute. I'm still trying to wrap my head around it."

"Hey, it's cool. Come in. I'll grab you a Coke." He ushered us into his small, dark living room, furnished with secondhand couches, a plaid recliner, and an abundance of video game equipment. The room smelled of old beer, cheap cologne, and the distant ghost of marijuana smoke. Sitting almost hip-to-hip on the couch, a pair of college-age guys stared at the TV, both clutching game controllers like precious jewels.

"Amir, you know Latchford, right?" Beamon gestured at one of the young men whose head was shaved nearly bald. Tattoos twined around his forearm, and he wore a vivid red UFC T-shirt. "His unit was at Ayn al-Asad with ours for a couple of months, remember? He started classes here in the spring. Told him he could bunk here till he found his own place. Bastard still hasn't left."

Latchford cast a brief glance at Owen before turning back to the TV. An instant later, he paused and looked at Owen again, and his mouth fell open. He dropped his controller and stood. "Amir? *Owen Amir?*"

Owen narrowed his eyes, nearly scowling. He raised his chin. "You were Second Brigade, right?"

Latchford nodded, his mouth still agape. "I thought you were dead. Last I knew, they'd scraped you up from the roadside after an IED." He scratched his close-shaven head and squinted at Owen. "You were with the convoy that got attacked at—"

"No." Owen cut a glance at me before looking at Latchford again. An icy stillness filled him. His expression hardened, and his normally dusky complexion was pale. "I was in the back of that convoy." He shrugged. "We got a little shrapnel. That was it."

Latchford's face screwed into an expression of uncertainty. "I saw the medics bringing you in. That was a lot more than 'a little shrapnel.'" Scowling, he studied Owen a few more beats before he slumped onto the sofa and frowned at the TV. He glanced at Owen again and shrugged. "But whatever, man. I guess you got lucky."

Owen's nostrils flared. His lips thinned. "Lucky, yeah. I guess."

I studied Owen, analyzing his reaction. If I hadn't recently inspected his bare skin myself, I might have questioned his response. But he bore no traces of scarring or old wounds. His skin was fine, smooth, and perfect. Surely anyone who had suffered an IED attack and had consequently been "scraped up" from the roadside wouldn't have gotten away unscathed. Maybe his tension and rigid posture were an indication of his pain from remembering those who'd been wounded or killed in the attack—people he'd likely known and cared about.

A specter of grief settled on my shoulders, cold and heavy, but it didn't stop me from wondering. *What kinds of things happened to him overseas? What ghosts are haunting him? Do I even have the right to ask those questions when I'm still contemplating walking away at the end of summer?*

Beamon, who had disappeared into the kitchen during Owen and Latchford's conversation, reappeared, toting two cans of Coke. He passed the drinks to Owen and me, and we stood in awkward silence, waiting for someone to say something. I cracked the tab on my Coke, and the *snap-hiss* broke the tension.

Owen blinked, shook himself, and glanced at the red can in his hand as if he didn't know how it had gotten there. "You ready to go, man? You don't have to hang out long. Just show us the highlights."

Beamon glanced at me. "Nursing, right?"

I bobbed my head and sipped my Coke. Sharp, cold bubbles stung my throat, and my eyes watered.

"I dated a nursing student for a few months last semester." His smile widened. "I got to know my way around Carrington Hall. Why don't we start there?"

Chapter Sixteen
School Spirit

AFTER WE'D SPENT A few hours hiking around campus, my phone was loaded with photos of me grinning like a kid at Disney World, but instead of Cinderella's castle, I posed before slightly more austere landmarks, between the Old Well's pillars, at the base of Morehead-Patterson Bell Tower, on the front steps of the Greek revival temple housing Playmakers Theater.

Owen had trooped along dutifully. I'd watched him all day, gauging his reactions, but he'd said little and maintained an inscrutable expression. If it hadn't been his idea to come in the first place, I would have thought he didn't want to be there.

By midafternoon, my dogs were barking in pain. My hair tie strained to control my frizz-bucket braid. Sweat glued my tank top to my back, and my Chucks were melting to the sidewalk. Owen called for a time-out, and Beamon offered to take us to his favorite bar.

In Four Corners' blessedly cool interior, the gods of UNC basketball, Michael Jordan and Dean Smith, peered at us from a wall of autographed photos while the waitress took our orders. I thumbed through my phone, studying the pictures I'd taken throughout the day. At first glance, I noticed only myself and occasionally Owen, whom I'd had to beg, cajole, and threaten to get him to join me. But after looking through the photos for the umpteenth time, I noticed a reoccurring image.

A man in a black baseball cap appeared in several of my photos. He was never fully facing the camera, never standing close to me or our group, but I was certain it was the same guy each time. He wore a white polo shirt and khaki shorts—typical attire for a college student—but something about his posture was almost... *menacing.*

"You guys heading back to the mountains after this?" Beamon asked as our waitress set down a platter of gooey cheese fries. Until I cooled off, the thought of eating greasy bar food turned my stomach, but for politeness' sake, I scraped a few fries onto my plate. Owen's lip curled, suggesting he felt similarly.

"I kind of wanted to look at some apartments while I was here." I raked my fork through a grease puddle on my plate, marking patterns with the tines. "I already know what classes I'll be taking, but I have no idea where I'm going to live."

Beamon pressed his lips together and seemed to contemplate my situation. "I guess you don't want to live in the dorms?"

"Do most upperclassmen live in the dorms?"

He shook his head. "There's a ton of student housing, but it all depends on your budget."

"My budget's looking for something in the realm of dirt cheap."

"But safe." Owen studied me with yet another indecipherable look. "Somewhere with a low crime rate."

I pursed my lips and huffed. "Unfortunately, dirt cheap and low crime rates are harder to find than the lost ark."

Owen drained his water glass and stood as he tugged his wallet from his back pocket. He dug out a couple of bills and dropped them on the table. "It won't hurt you to look around, get an idea of what's available, but if you're tired, I understand. We can head home."

I raised a shoulder and dropped it. "Let's look around a bit more. If you don't mind."

"No, I don't mind." Owen flashed a quick smile, revealing a rare glimpse of his dimple. He was usually easy to smile and tease and flirt, but he'd been quiet and solemn most of the day. "You might as well take the chance while we're here."

Taking my hand, Owen pulled me up beside him and offered his friend an apologetic smile. "Sorry to run off on you, man."

Beamon pointed at the remaining pile of cheese fries. "I've got plenty to keep me busy. The Braves are on in a little while. I'll probably stay, watch the game, have a few more beers."

"Thanks, Beamon." I patted his shoulder. "I appreciate you taking the time to show me around."

"No big deal. Make sure you say hey if you see me on campus." He pointed at Owen. "And promise to be good to my man there, okay?"

Owen tugged me toward the exit and flicked a salute at his friend. "Don't start no trouble."

Beamon raised two fingers and touched them to his brow. "Won't *be* no trouble."

When we stepped into the heat outside, I sagged. "I've lived in this state my whole life, but I still melt every summer." We traipsed up the sidewalk, heading for Owen's car. I plucked at my tank top, ungluing it from my chest. "Sometimes all I want to do is lie at the bottom of a swimming pool and not come up for air until October."

Talking about weather was bland and safe. It was the appetizer to the meatier main course of topics weighing on my mind. We walked a block in silence before the question that had been teetering on my lips all day finally fell loose. "Why'd you bring me here?"

He flinched and blinked at me, his brows furrowing. My question had obviously caught him off guard. "What do you mean?"

Hunching my shoulders, I shoved my hands in my pockets and stared at my sneakers. "I know you're busy with the distillery, and your time is precious. But you took a day off and spent it letting me drag you all over a place you couldn't possibly give a damn about." I turned, facing him, and stopped in the middle of the sidewalk. "Why would you do that?"

He frowned. "Why would you think I wouldn't care about this place? It's important to you, isn't it?"

"Yes. But that doesn't answer my question."

"Maybe..." His stoic mask slipped, revealing a glimpse of uncharacteristic worry. His voice was low and strained. "I wanted to size up my competition. Maybe I wanted to see what I was going up against."

"Competition?" Despite the heat, shivers scattered across my arms. "What are you talking about?"

"If it were another man trying to steal your heart, I'd know what to do. I'd know how to fight. But you're in love with something a lot bigger and more powerful than me." He curled his fingers around my elbow and squeezed. There was no menace in his touch, only heartache. "Seeing you here today, I realize what this place means to you. I can't fight this. It's where you're supposed to be—what you're supposed to do. As much as I want to keep you in Evansville with me, I know I can't. I have to let you go, and it's *killing* me."

His words were a sucker punch to my solar plexus, emptying my lungs in an explosive burst. My mind spun in a whirlwind, disintegrating thought and feeling, tossing them together into a cloud of chaos and confusion. I gasped and stumbled back. "What? I can't..."

He caught me, cupping my chin. He dragged a thumb across my lower lip. "You accused me of wanting some casual summer fling. You're *so* wrong, Rikki."

"But we've barely had time—"

He kissed me, silencing my protest, and in that touch, I felt his want, his fear, his urgency. He could have been lying, could have been performing an Oscar-worthy act of deceit. *But for what purpose?* I had nothing to give him that was worth that much effort. Nothing except myself. His kiss tasted like truth, and I wanted to believe.

Pulling away, I locked onto his gaze and held it. He never flinched. Never looked away. He revealed himself, held himself open until I could no longer bear the rawness of his candor. Closing my eyes, I rested my forehead against his chest. "If you're thinking about trying to hang in for the long haul, I have to warn you that it's going to be hard," I said. "Inconvenient. Messy. I'm probably going to screw everything up."

"I don't need guarantees." He folded his arms around me and ran a finger down my spine. "Just say you're willing to give it a try."

"What about no expectations?"

"It was a naïve thing to say. I didn't expect to feel this strongly about you this soon."

That was it, the big question I'd been avoiding since Owen first strolled into Rose's Diner and asked me on a date. Did I want him? Did I want *us*? Doubts dripped through me like rain through a leaky roof. But a ray of sun shone behind the clouds. I wanted to embrace that warmth and light.

"I'm willing." Circling my arms around him, I held him tightly. "No guarantees, Owen, but I can agree to try."

Traffic whizzed by on the street. Pedestrians angled around us. The earth spun, oblivious to the two of us, but in the small realm of our embrace, my world was tilting on its axis. Everything was about to change, and I was terrified.

And I was thrilled.

Clearing my throat, I pulled away, ungluing myself from him. "God, I'm sticky. You're going to regret that hug."

He smiled, dimple at full power again, and my heart fluttered like a bird fluffing its feathers after the rain. He shook his head. "I've never regretted a moment with you."

Chapter Seventeen
Another One Bites the Dust

OWEN JACKED THE BMW'S air-conditioning to maximum power. I leaned in, holding my face close to the vent while he poked the control panel, bringing the navi system to life. "Where to next? You have some addresses for me?"

I stretched, reaching for the back seat, and snagged the folder of apartment brochures I'd printed off the internet. "I have these places organized into three categories: possible, unlikely, and you-must-be-dreaming."

He chuckled. "So where do you want to start."

"Where do you think?" I gave him a wide-eyed, ironic look.

"You-must-be-dreaming?"

I passed him a flyer advertising a newly renovated development with every amenity: pools, hot tubs, tanning beds, fitness room, and energy-efficient washers and dryers. "Unless you think it's a waste of time."

"Whatever the lady wants, the lady gets." Owen punched the address into the GPS. While the navigator calculated directions, I studied our surroundings, trying to lock the location of Beamon's house into my mental map. Knowing how to get in touch with an army guy in a hurry might come in handy in the fall, *if* I could remember how to find him.

As I turned to check the GPS's status, something glimmered in the corner of my vision. I flinched, and hairs rose along the back of my neck. I examined our surroundings, but nothing unusual stood out. Not until I glanced through the driver's-side window.

A solemn figure turned the corner, disappearing around the rear of the business across from us. In a court of law, I never would've placed my hand on the Bible and sworn to it, but I was almost certain the person I'd seen was wearing a black ball cap, white polo shirt, and khaki shorts—exactly like the guy in my pictures.

Owen tugged the steering wheel and swung into the street, as slick and quiet as a snake. I shook my head and rubbed my eyes, dismissing the sighting as nothing more than coincidence. Or my overactive imagination. I could probably have pointed out dozens of guys around town wearing an identical combination of clothes.

"What happened to the engine?" I glanced around, assuring myself we were accelerating. "It's so quiet."

He gestured at the dashboard. "It's in electric mode. This is a hybrid."

"It's a race car for the environmentally conscientious? How progressive of you."

After a short drive across campus, Owen turned in to the Academy Apartments parking lot and pulled into a spot marked for visitors. Regretting the need to return to the heat, I groaned and pushed open the car door.

From the outside, the complex was big and boxy, constructed entirely of brick, but each apartment offered a small balcony overlooking a grassy common area with an aquamarine swimming pool and landscaped with a colorful assortment of bushes and trees. "I can get a room here on my own, but the cost is steep." I wrinkled my nose and studied the fine print on my rental flyer. "Otherwise, I can apply for a multiple-bedroom unit, and they'll match me with roommates."

"Strangers?" Owen opened the door to the rental office, and a blast of cool air washed over us.

"I guess so."

"Coed?"

I shrugged. "I dunno."

He pressed his lips together, and thin lines formed at the sides of his mouth. "You'd be willing to live with some guy you didn't know?"

"No. That's why this place is on my 'you-must-be-dreaming' list. I'd want a single room, and the rates for that are ridiculous."

A cute young blond woman sitting behind a desk with a phone pressed to her ear looked up, appeared to notice Owen, and smiled. Pressing a hand over the phone's mouthpiece, she said, "I'll be with you in a sec." She jerked her chin toward a row of fat leather chairs lined against the wall. "Y'all take a seat, okay?"

After plunking into a plush armchair, I closed my eyes and let my head fall back. Exhaustion was creeping up like a sneaky nap ninja coming to sprinkle sleep dust over me. I had a feeling I'd go home the same way I'd come to Chapel Hill, asleep and oblivious.

"I know this isn't really any of my business," Owen said, "and you don't have to answer, but... do you have any scholarships?"

His question was similar to the ones I hadn't worked up the guts to ask him, but I'd just told him I was willing to try a long-term relationship. Maybe he'd earned the right to pry. "Yeah, a few academic based. A few need based. It's still going to be a stretch, but I can do it."

"I don't doubt that. I get the feeling once you put your mind to something, nothing can stop you."

"Hey, thanks for waiting," said a sweet Southern voice. I popped open one eye to find that the girl who'd been sitting behind the desk was now standing before us. She had focused solely on Owen, her gaze smoldering. "I'm Kelsey, and I'm guessing y'all want to look at an apartment because you certainly aren't one of our residents. I'd remember *you*."

He pointed at me. "You can show *her* an apartment. I'm just along for the ride."

Kelsey's glossy-pink lips quirked into a perky smile. "Bless your heart. Aren't you the sweetest thing?" She pivoted and click-clacked to her desk on towering heels.

Owen caught my glare and bit back a grin. *"Bless your heart,"* he whispered.

Kelsey bent, rifled through a desk drawer, and removed a ring of keys. "Follow me. I'll show y'all the model."

By the time the tour ended, the *click-clack* of Kelsey's high heels was ricocheting in my head like bullets, and her overly cheery demeanor had worn out my fraying nerves. Maybe the decision to stay and tour apartments had been a bad one, or maybe Kelsey was especially skilled at annoying me. I eyed her sleek pencil skirt and her flat-ironed ponytail and resisted the urge to stick out my tongue at her back. A small inner voice urged me not to judge too harshly. Maybe Kelsey was a future brain surgeon who worked in a soup kitchen on her days off. And I couldn't blame her for noticing a guy like Owen. A girl would have to be dead not to.

Back in the rental office, Kelsey passed me a form attached to a clipboard. "You said you weren't looking to move in right away, but if you'll fill out the preapproval application right now and put down a deposit, you'll be entered for a chance to live here rent free for a year." She eyed me again, arching a precisely plucked eyebrow. "Who couldn't use a free apartment for a year, right?"

My stomach sank as I glanced at the dollar signs on the application form. "I, um... I'm not sure I'm ready to hand over that much money yet. This is only the first place I've looked."

Her lips thinned. "The longer you wait, the less availability we'll have. This place fills up fast the closer we get to the start of the school year."

"Is the application online?" Owen asked. "If Rikki decides she wants to live here after all, can she apply on your website?"

She fluttered her lashes. "Of course she can."

"What about the contest? Does she still qualify for that if she applies online?"

"She sure does." Kelsey tilted her head, smiling at Owen as though he were her favorite flavor of ice cream. "As long as she pays the deposit before the end of the month."

"*She's* very grateful for your time." I returned the application to our cheery hostess. Plastering on my own big, toothy smile, I batted my lashes as I backed toward the exit. "But *she's* going to have to think about it before *she* makes her decision."

Kelsey dragged her gaze away from Owen. Her smile turned saccharine. "Of course. Call if you have more questions, and y'all have a nice day, all right?"

I leaned against the office door and stepped into the late-afternoon sunlight. The shadows had lengthened, drawing long lines across the walkways and common areas. Owen followed me outside, sliding a hand around my hip once he caught up to me.

I glanced at him, preparing to ask him what he thought about the place, but a man standing on the sidewalk near the edge of the driveway caught my eye. Black ball cap, white polo, khaki shorts.

I stiffened. A murmur of surprise slipped from my throat. "Oh."

Owen's grip on me tightened. "What is it?"

"That man standing near the street..." I whispered. "I know this sounds crazy, but I'm pretty sure he's been—"

"Following us all day?" Owen leaned in, touching his forehead to mine. From a distance, he might have appeared focused on me, but he'd trained his gaze on the stranger. "I've noticed him."

"Why didn't you say anything?"

"I didn't want to freak you out."

"Who is he? What does he want?"

"I don't know." Owen pulled away and set his hands on my shoulders. "I'm going to go find out. But please, Rikki, I need you to get in the car and lock the doors."

"What?" A cold shiver trickled down my spine. "No, let's just leave. Let's get in the car and go home."

He shook his head. A dark lock of hair fell over his eye, and he scraped it back. "Not until I know what he wants."

"Maybe he's just a creepy asshole. Why do you need to confront him?"

"Rikki, please, get in the car."

The cold fear warmed, veering toward anger. "Don't tell me what to do."

His grip on my shoulders hardened. "I don't want to fight you. And I sure as hell don't want to fight *him*. But I need to know who he is and what he wants with me without worrying about endangering you."

I gritted my teeth. "There's something you're not telling me. There has been from the start."

"Now's not the time. Please, I can't let anything happen to you."

My heartbeat pounded in my ears, but the desperation in Owen's eyes undid me. "Okay, but don't think you can hold out on me. You have to tell me what's going on."

He nodded. "I'll tell you what I can." I started to object, but he nudged me toward the car. "Go. I'll be back in a second."

A hot lump of panic surged into my throat. "Please be careful."

"Lock yourself in." He flexed his fist and glanced at his ring. "Stay there until I get back, no matter what."

As I edged toward the car, I kept Owen and our stalker in sight. He hadn't moved from the spot where he'd been standing when I first noticed him, and as Owen approached, he faced us as if welcoming the encounter. He smiled, and the coldness of it chilled me. Before Owen reached him, the stranger turned on his heel and strode away, not to escape but enticing Owen to follow, leading him somewhere less public, perhaps.

My pulse kicked into overdrive and pounded in my ears, drowning out traffic noise. My surroundings faded as my vision tunneled. Classic fight-or-flight response.

My hip bumped against the passenger door of Owen's car, and I glanced away long enough to reach for the handle with a shaking hand. When I looked up again, both men had disappeared. The towering apartment buildings around me obstructed a broader view of the street. I'd have to move closer to the sidewalk if I wanted to see where they'd gone. Owen's request that I stay put, stay safe, warred with my personal need to know why the stranger had followed us and why Owen felt compelled to confront him.

Reflexively, my muscles clenched. I gritted my teeth, waiting.

"Dammit," I rasped when the decision clicked in my head. I wasn't an EMT because I tended to avoid danger. Some people might've accused me of having a savior complex. Some people might've been right.

I sacrificed the extra minute it took to reach into the car, dig through my bag, and find my pepper spray. Mom had given me a can for my birthday every year since I'd turned sixteen, but until now, I'd never considered using it. *Thanks for looking out for me, Mom.*

Following the walkway from the apartment's rental office, I crept to the street and scanned my surroundings before turning in the direction I'd last seen Owen and our shadow. Except for a girl pedaling past on a bike, the shaded, tree-lined street was empty.

Cursing myself for waiting too long, I rushed to the end of the block, where the quiet drive spilled onto the bustling Franklin Street. Pedestrians strolled by, oblivious to my building panic. Revolving where I stood, I searched storefronts, landscaped green spaces, benches, and parked cars. My body had pumped so much adrenaline into my system, I could taste it. I swallowed, trying to ease the bitter, acrid flavor.

Unless I wanted to sprint around the surrounding blocks, searching every corner and crevice, I'd have to go back to the car and wait for Owen, but that idea soured my stomach. The stranger had waited for us to notice him before quietly luring Owen away. He'd avoided making direct contact or a noisy confrontation, which meant he hadn't wanted to draw attention. And while Owen hadn't tackled the stranger on the street in plain view, he also probably wouldn't have followed him far before losing his patience and forcing the man to talk.

So they'd most likely gone somewhere close by. Kicking into a run, I abandoned the sidewalk and followed the apartment's exterior walls, looping the property until I reached a rear corner. A thick copse of holly bushes, shrubs, and a tall fence concealed the complex's dumpsters and maintenance carts. Several oak trees clumped together, obscuring sunlight and darkening shadows. Hairs rose along my neck and arms, and chills slunk down my spine. *I have a bad feeling about this.*

Pausing, I closed my eyes, held my breath, and listened.

There.

A low murmur of voices drifted from behind the privacy fence. I crept closer, still holding my breath. The speakers, both distinctly male, argued in an unfamiliar, foreign language. While I didn't understand the words, I understood their urgency—and hostility.

A shout broke the tension.

Another shout replied, followed by a blast of heat and a blinding flash of light.

I shut my eyes against the glare, and fireworks exploded behind my eyelids. Someone coughed a short, harsh exclamation of pain, not quite a scream but close enough to jolt me into action. I dashed around the privacy fence and skidded down a short embankment that dropped into a paved area reserved for the apartment's dumpsters.

Alone on the ground lay Owen, curled into a ball, groaning in a broken, gruff voice. Beside him, a charred mark blackened the asphalt as if a scorching fire had struck and disappeared in an instant. Intense heat still radiated from the scarred pavement.

An avalanche of questions crashed through my head, demanding answers, but they'd have to wait until after I'd assessed Owen and taken him somewhere safe. One trick to staying sane as an EMT was learning to celebrate small victories. Another was to deal with one issue at a time, fix the problems I could and try to forget about the ones I couldn't.

I dropped to my knees and grabbed his shoulder. Blindly he lashed at me, clocking me in the jaw hard enough to make me see stars.

"*Ouch*, you jerk." I fell on my rear and heaved several deep breaths until the pain passed and the shooting stars faded.

"Oh, damn, Rikki. I'm sorry."

"I'm okay." Shaking off my daze, I rolled onto my knees and hovered over him, peering into his dark eyes.

He tried to smile, but his expression turned into a grimace. Gritting his teeth, he squeezed his eyes shut and clutched his ribs. Red oozed between his fingers, and my heart slammed into my throat. I tugged his fingers away and yanked up his shirttail, revealing a bleeding gash in his side. I hissed. "What did he do to you?"

"Stabbed me, I think."

Lacking a better solution, I whipped off my tank top, folded it into a compress, and pressed the fabric against his wound. A dry, broken whimper scraped from this throat, but he didn't resist. "It's not just a stab. The skin around it looks burned too. What the hell, Owen?"

"I don't know." He panted, gasping for breath. "It happened too fast."

"Where did he go?"

Owen glanced away and shook his head. "I don't *know*."

"We've got to stop this bleeding. I don't want to move you, but I don't want to risk that he'll come back and finish what he started. We've got to get out of here and get you fixed up."

"No hospitals."

I froze, my eyes narrowed, my jaw clenched. "If I weren't an EMT and a halfway-decent person, I'd leave you here and let you bleed until you gave me some answers."

Pain danced in his eyes. He grimaced but remained stubbornly silent.

I huffed. "Can you stand? I could try a fireman's carry, but you're almost twice as big as me, and I doubt you would like to have my shoulder jabbing into your stomach."

White lines formed at the corners of his mouth as he pressed his lips together. He nodded, sat up, and paused before swaying dizzily. When he recovered, he slung his arm around my neck, and together we stood. Another raw groan escaped his throat, but he was upright and still conscious.

Small victories, I reminded myself. *Celebrate them while you can.*

Chapter Eighteen
Bleeding Me

TOGETHER WE HOBBLED through the apartment complex, cutting across common areas and breezeways to reach the parking lot. We passed a pair of women lugging loaded laundry baskets and bottles of detergent. They gaped at us, their wide eyes shifting between Owen's bloody shirt and my utter lack of one. Gruesome red splotches had ruined my prettiest yoga bra, but at least I was halfway modest.

Without taking her eyes off Owen and me, one girl reached into her basket and fished out a bundle of wrinkled pink fabric. "Um... need a shirt?"

Still juggling Owen, I snatched the shirt from her and tugged it on, ignoring the cutesy cartoon on the front. I hoped Hello Kitty didn't mind blood. "Thanks."

"Hey, should we call an ambulance?" the other girl asked.

"Nope." I shook my head. "I *am* the ambulance. It looks worse than it is. I'm taking him to the hospital right now."

They stood in horrified silence, watching as we hurried to the car. I dumped Owen into the passenger seat, scurried around to the driver's side, and whipped us out of the parking lot.

"Where are we going?" Owen asked, still holding my folded tank top to his ribs. His complexion was pale, and even without checking his pulse, I could guess it was fast and weak.

"You need a hospital." I idled at the end of the drive, uncertain which way to go.

"You're as good as any ER doctor. You can fix this."

155

I balked. "You don't know that."

"I can't have the cops involved."

"You could tell the doctors it was an accident."

"Would they believe me?" He shook his head. "Would *you* believe me?"

"Not for a second." I scowled at him as he leaned against the door, his head slumped against the window. Throughout the day, despite the heat, he had maintained his crisp and impeccable good looks, but now sweat drenched his dark hair. His sweaty T-shirt clung to him. A gray pallor had stolen his golden glow. Pity, sudden and heartbreaking, overruled my irritation.

I took his free hand and squeezed his clammy fingers. "You're scaring the life out of me right now, Owen. If you die on my watch—"

"I'm not going to die, ya albi." His voice was hoarse, his eyes glassy. "Not if you take care of me."

After confirming my destination on the navi screen, I pulled onto the street. "Don't try to manipulate me."

He shifted and grimaced again. "What are you talking about?"

"Using my emotions to get me to do things I'm not comfortable doing." Hanging a left onto Franklin Street, I accelerated before shooting past slower-moving traffic. "In these kinds of situations, you'd do better appealing to my logic."

"I still don't understand."

"I mean that instead of telling me how great I am, just try telling me the truth."

After several blocks, I spotted a pharmacy, its familiar red sign glowing like a beacon of hope. I whipped into the parking lot and stopped the car in a spot near the front door. "Be back in a sec."

Owen slumped and nodded, closing his eyes.

In my head, I made a quick list of provisions. He needed stitches, but the average chain drugstore didn't sell sutures, so I raided the first aid shelves for alternatives and made a mad dash down the pain reliever aisle. After grabbing several bottles of purified water and Gatorade, I headed for the cash register.

The clerk rang up my purchases and handed me my receipt, eyeing me with a curious look. I beat a hasty retreat before he could ask any questions.

"Still alive?" I plopped into the driver's seat and tugged the door closed.

Owen's smoky scent was strong, concentrated, almost overwhelming. He peeled one eye open and peered at me. "Yes, but I'm starting to regret it."

"Drink this." I passed him a bottle of orange Gatorade. "Doctor's orders."

I tapped at the navi screen until it provided an address for our next destination. Following the map, I eased out of the parking lot and merged into traffic.

"What next?" he rasped.

"Finding us a room."

"Thanks for doing this."

"Don't thank me yet." I gunned the motor, and it responded with a disappointing electric wheeze. "This electric mode is BS. Dolly would eat your car for breakfast and poop out a tin can."

"Ow." Owen grimaced. "Stop making me laugh."

Switching lanes, I cut around a slow-moving car and accelerated. Several blocks later, I turned in to the parking lot of a humble motel and coasted to a stop. "I would have picked something fancier, but in those kinds of hotels, the rooms are all accessed from interior hallways. I think we both want to avoid being noticed, right?"

He nodded.

"Sorry if it offends your high-dollar tastes."

"Fortunately for me, practicality never goes out of style."

I rolled my eyes at him before ducking outside and dashing into the rental office. After reserving a spot on the ground floor, I drove around to our room and unloaded my patient. Owen groaned again as I helped him to his feet, and we weeble-wobbled to the door, but we didn't fall down. Another small victory.

Our room smelled musty, and the starched coverlet and bland art prints on the walls were dated, but at first glance, everything appeared clean and tidy. I eased Owen onto the bed and dumped my supplies beside him. After grabbing several wet washcloths and a bundle of towels from the bathroom, I settled on my knees beside Owen and tore open his blood-soaked shirt. The clinical part of my mind evaluated his wounds, but the shameless hussy inside me admired his body's fine build, the muscles, the ridges. *How does someone even get abs like that?*

"I've dreamed of having you in bed with me," Owen said, gripping my thigh. "But not quite like this."

If I hadn't been so worried about him, I might have blushed. Instead, I welcomed his flirting as proof he was still alive and aware of his surroundings. "I'm immune to your charming ways. You're not the first patient to flirt with me while bleeding to death, you know."

Although he kept his eyes closed as I cleaned his wound, he arched an eyebrow. "Oh? Guess I can't blame them."

With the old blood cleared away, Owen's injury looked less dire than before. A three- or four-inch laceration pierced his right side below his ribs. His bleeding had slowed considerably, suggesting his insides were in good shape and his assailant's weapon hadn't penetrated the abdominal wall. Yet another thing to celebrate.

I dabbed his skin with a dry towel and sprayed a disinfectant and numbing solution over the wound. Owen sucked a breath and clenched his jaw.

"That hurt?" I asked.

"No. Just cold."

"Grit your teeth. This next part is going to suck." I opened a package of superglue and a box of butterfly closures. "This needs real stitches. And you'll need antibiotics so you don't get an infection."

"I have a superb immune system. I've dealt with worse than this." When I pinched his wound closed, he flinched and grunted low in his throat. Superb immune system, maybe, but still a normal pain threshold. At least I could be reasonably sure he wasn't a cyborg.

"Worse? You mean, like an IED?"

He panted through his teeth while I closed his laceration and poured on a coating of wound-sealing powder. "What is that stuff?" he asked, ignoring my IED question.

Fine. If he didn't want to talk about it, I'd let it go. For now. "WoundSeal? You've never seen a field medic use this stuff? It's like a fake scab. People on blood thinners use it because they have a hard time forming clots naturally." After brushing off the loose grains, I pressed a gauze pad over the cut and adhered medical tape around the edges. "Now the best thing you can do is be still and try to get some rest."

I slipped off the bed and gathered scattered bits of paper and packaging. Owen grabbed my wrist. He peered up at me, his eyes still glassy, pupils enlarged. Mild shock, perhaps, but it was to be expected. "Yes, exactly like an IED."

I paused, surprised. "So, that guy... Latchford. He was telling the truth?"

Owen pressed his lips together and closed his eyes again. "Yes. But it's not like he said."

"Then how was it?"

"I survived. Do the details matter?"

I surveyed him, studying his smooth skin and sleek muscles again. He was perfect. Almost *too* perfect. I tugged free from his grip. "I'm going to get you a blanket and some more Gatorade. You need to stay warm and hydrated."

After trashing the packaging and bits of bandages, I balled up the bloody towels and rags, chucked them in the bathroom, and found a spare blanket in the closet. I tucked the blanket around him, handed him a bottle of Gatorade and a heavy dose of pain relievers, and went to work on his bootlaces. "I've seen a lot of your skin up close and personal, Owen. There's not a scar on you other than the one you got today."

He gulped the remainder of his drink and set the empty bottle on the nightstand. "It was bad but not as bad as Latchford thinks." He draped an arm over his eyes. "There was internal damage from the concussion of the blast, and it took a while to come back from that, but I guess, on the outside, I was lucky. I got to keep all my limbs. A lot of guys died that day. A lot went home missing parts and pieces."

I listened to his answer from behind an emotional wall, something I'd gotten good at building in the days when pain had driven my dad senseless. He'd begged and pleaded for me, for anyone, to make it stop. Even when he managed to sleep, he'd cried out, tossed and turned, gnashed his teeth. I'd improved those defense mechanisms in the back of a Twain County EMS ambulance. Those skills made it possible to listen to Owen's story without melting in a useless puddle of tears, although part of me would've welcomed the catharsis of it.

I removed his shoes and placed them on the floor by the bed. Returning to his side, I set my hands on my hips and studied his face. Greenish undertones tainted his skin, and purple bruises underscored his eyes. Only time and rest would improve his coloration. "You're okay with staying in your jeans, or do you want out of those too? I'm asking as a nurse, not a girlfriend, so keep the jokes to yourself."

A weak grin twitched on his lips. "Leave them on. I'll be fine."

Although his answers had moderately pacified me—he still had much more explaining to do—the immediate emergency had passed, and the weight of all the day's events, the fatigue, the fear, came crashing down. My knees wobbled, and I turned away before Owen saw tears in my eyes. I rarely cried when I was sad, but if something made me angry or drove me to the extremes of exhaustion, tears would pour like waterfalls.

"Rikki?" I could hear the concern in his voice.

Keeping my back to him, I waved him off. "I'm fine. I'm going to take a hot shower." Thinking of my lack of preparation, I swore. "Dammit."

"What?"

"I should have bought some shower stuff at the pharmacy." I kicked off my Chucks and tugged the elastic band from my braid. Bending over, I combed my fingers through my hair, shaking it loose. The simple tasks provided the distraction I needed to regain my composure. "My hair hates hotel shampoo."

"I could watch you do that every day and never get tired of it."

I turned and found Owen gazing at me through half-lidded eyes. "Do what?"

"Let your hair down. When your curls are all crazy and wild like that, I want to knot my fingers in them and kiss you until you moan my name the way I like."

Fire ignited in my cheeks, and I scurried for the bathroom. "You're loopy from blood loss. You should be quiet and go to sleep."

His laughter drifted under the door, but I drowned it out, turning the shower on full blast. While I waited for the water to warm, I peeled off my clothes and inspected the meager bar of motel soap and tiny bottle of two-in-one shampoo and conditioner. The stuff I used at home was specially formulated for curly hair and had industrial strength moisturizers. I wrinkled my nose and tapped the bottle. "Sorry, shampoo, but I don't think you're up to the task."

Frowning, I glanced at myself in the mirror, evaluating the damage. Dark, crusted blood coated most of my chest and stomach, but my hair had avoided the worst of the horror. Instead of risking the chance of making more frizz, I fastened my curls into a tight knot at the nape of my neck in hopes of keeping my hair mostly dry.

I scrubbed until the pink puddles at my feet ran clear. The soap smelled astringent and floral, nothing like the verbena blend I used at home, but at least I no longer reeked of sweat and dried blood. I washed every inch of my skin again for good measure. Who knew what pathogens and germs I'd picked up over the course of the day.

Spray pounded my neck and shoulders until the tension in my muscles receded. Closing my eyes, I reviewed the day's events and those that had occurred over the last weeks. Owen had just told me he had survived a close call with an IED attack, and now he was recuperating from what could have easily been a fatal wound. Was it a coincidence, or did he attract danger? And if so, was that a factor in my fascination with him?

I might have shied from risking my heart, but I'd never avoided danger and excitement. Not that I had a death wish, but I certainly had an aversion to wasting life, and over the past few weeks, I'd felt more alive than all my previous years combined. Metaphorically, I'd been living doped-up and numb, but the drugs had worn off and everything was coming at me sharp and bright, full of sound, color, and sensation.

Owen had brought my world to life. I didn't want to go back to the way things used to be—back to a life of ghosts and silence.

After rinsing off the last soap suds, I drew back the shower curtain, dried off, and tucked the one remaining towel around my chest. The short fabric barely covered my rear end, but I was too tired to care. Eyeing my bloody clothes, I huffed. "Yet another issue I should have thought of while I was in the drugstore."

Instead of putting my crusty clothes back on, I used what was left of the tiny soap bar to wash out my bra and underwear. Hello Kitty had avoided all but a few small stains, and my cutoff shorts had escaped the worst of the carnage. Knowing wet denim would likely still be damp in the morning, I skipped washing my shorts and hung the rest of my clothes on the towel rack to dry.

By the time I left the bathroom, the sun had set, casting the room in dim light. Owen was asleep, his dark hair a riot of messy locks across his forehead and pillow. My fingers itched with the urge to brush the hair from his brow, touch him, assure myself he was all right, but I didn't dare wake him. My stomach growled, and I considered ordering a pizza, but instead I shuffled to the window, drew the curtains snugly together, and slipped beneath the bedcovers.

I fell asleep before I had time to ponder the wisdom of being mostly naked in bed with an extremely wounded and yet somehow utterly enticing man.

Chapter Nineteen
Temptation

WHEN I OPENED MY EYES to total darkness, my groggy brain assumed morning was still a long way off. Owen shifted beside me, and I realized his body was pressed against mine and his heavy arm draped over my waist had awoken me. Sometime between falling asleep and finding him wrapped around me, I had lost my towel. *Figures.*

I wondered whether he was still sleeping. Maybe he hadn't noticed.

"I'd let someone stab me a hundred times if it meant I got to wake up like this afterward." His finger stroked my hip.

Nope, definitely not asleep. His rough and growly voice was hot enough to melt an ice cube in Antarctica. His scent enveloped me in a familiar smoky sweetness. Potential energy tingled beneath my skin, as if my body were an explosive device and Owen was the mercury switch that would set it off if I made the wrong move.

"How are you feeling?" I cleared my throat. "Hurting?"

"I woke up a while ago, took some pills, drank some more Gatorade. Got back in bed with you." He traced a fingertip along the rim of my ear and drew a line down my arm... shoulder... elbow... wrist. "I'd say I'm feeling pretty fantastic at the moment. How about you?"

Like my head might explode if I don't roll over and wrap my legs around you right this minute. "I'm, um—"

He pressed his lips to the back of my neck and stroked his knuckles across my ribs. I released a long, low breath.

He chuckled. "What were you saying?"

He knew the effect he was having on me, but I wouldn't give him the satisfaction of putting it into words. "You're a cocky bastard, aren't you?"

"In this situation? I think I'm behaving rather admirably."

"You're wounded."

He lowered his voice as his thumb brushed the underside of my breast. "Like I'd ever let that stop me."

"You might not, but I would." I swallowed, trying to relieve the dryness in my throat. "*Primum non nocere.*"

"What does that mean?"

"First, do no harm." Part of me wanted to kick our principles—his admirable behavior and my concern for his injuries—right out the door. A larger part of me wanted more answers first. "You said if I was sweet, you'd tell me what 'ya albi' meant."

"I did say that, didn't I?"

"I patched up your stab wound and probably saved your life. Does that count as being sweet?"

His body vibrated with silent laughter. "I guess it does."

"So... are you going to tell me?"

"It's Arabic, a term of endearment." He pressed his flat palm to my stomach and slid his hand up, stroking the length of my sternum, between my breasts, stopping to curl his fingers around my neck at the base of my jaw. He clutched me in a possessive embrace, and I couldn't work up the concern to object. "Ya albi. It means 'my heart.'"

My own heart thudded, swollen, aching.

It wasn't the only part of me that felt that way.

Throwing away caution, I rolled over to face him, pressing close, skin against skin. The pleasure of it briefly stole my ability to speak. I squeezed my eyes shut until the moment passed. "I told you not to manipulate my emotions. Just be honest. That's all I ask."

He ran his fingertips down my arm again, tracing bones until he found my fingers and brought my hand to his chest. Leaning back, he pressed my palm over his heart. "I *am* being honest, Rikki. I'm going out of my mind over you."

"We're not really in the right situation for clear thinking."

He growled. "That's not what I'm talking about. I won't deny that having you here like this, soft and warm and bare skinned against me, is something I've wanted since the moment you threatened to punch me in Rose's Diner. But I also want you here..." He tapped my hand where it lay over his heart. "And here." He tapped his temple. "I'm not lying."

"But you keep things from me."

He lifted my hand and kissed my palm. "I've never lied to you, though. I'll admit to keeping some things concealed, but we've known each other how long? A few weeks? I might already adore you, but I'm not a forthcoming person by nature. I'm earning your trust and learning to give you mine in return."

"Everyone's entitled to their secrets. I'm not asking you to bare your soul. But what happened earlier..." I licked my lips. I wanted to look into his eyes, but the darkness obscured him. Ambient light leaking in from around the curtain edges outlined him, but shadows hid his face. "If what happened today is the sort of thing you're hiding from, I don't blame you. But if it affects me, I think I have a right to know what's going on."

Owen groaned and plopped onto his back. He grunted a half-hearted sound of pain. "You're completely right."

"So, who was the guy that attacked you?"

"I don't know who he was, personally. He works for someone, an... *organization* I encountered while I was in Iraq. I got messed up in some bad trouble while I was over there. I'm still trying to figure out how to get out of it."

His words chilled me, but they vaguely explained how he might have come into his money. He spoke some Arabic, maybe more than I realized, and he had Palestinian ties through his family. Maybe he had worked for Middle Eastern warlords, anti-Israel rebels, or crooked politicians. Maybe he'd sold state secrets and betrayed his country. *No. I don't believe that.* Those were stereotypes I refused to buy into.

"How the hell did he find you in Chapel Hill of all places?" I asked. "It was kind of a random trip. How would anyone know you'd be there?"

"There are... *forces*, powerful circles of influence that operate in the shadows. They have their fingers on the pulse of the world. The question isn't how they found me but how I've managed to escape them this long."

"Are you bullshitting me?" Although he couldn't see it, I gaped at him.

"Scout's honor." His dark figure made a vague, inscrutable gesture.

I pulled my covers up, rolled onto my back, and let my head fall against the pillow. "You've got to know how irrational that sounds."

"And yet, you saw the proof, didn't you?"

Replaying the events in my mind, I searched for some clue or hint of betrayal in Owen's words, but I could find nothing to discredit him. *For now.* More things had happened during his encounter with the stranger than he'd confessed, such as the bizarre burst of heat and flash of light. Some kind of weapon, perhaps? If I pressed him on those details, though, I suspected he'd shut down again.

Start with the simpler explanations and work your way up.

"If you're telling me the truth," I said, "then are you safe going back to Evansville? How do you know they won't follow you there?"

"I've gone to great lengths to hide myself. The distillery's not in my name, and neither is any of my property. Everything's owned by shell companies with offshore banking accounts."

"How did you figure out how to do all that stuff?"

"My brother."

"Rami, right?"

Owen's shadow bobbed its head. "He's a lawyer—the big-money, New York City power-broker kind. So far his arrangements seem to be working."

"For now." I heaved a breath and turned onto my side, facing him. "But that doesn't explain how they found you in Chapel Hill."

"I can't explain that either. Bad luck? Coincidence? Maybe Beamon mentioned my name to the wrong person. Maybe I wasn't careful enough when I bought the BMW and my name raised a flag in the system."

Maybe there was more to it than he wanted to admit too. "Was that man trying to kill you?"

"I don't know. He made a lot of threats. Mostly, I think he wanted to scare me."

"Why?"

"Because they want me to come back and finish what I started."

"What exactly did you do?"

"Some things I'd rather not talk about right now."

The urge to compel him to answer pressed against my sternum, struggling to get out, but now was not the time or place for a demanding inquisition—the medical professional in me insisted I leave him alone and let him rest. "So, you don't want to finish whatever it was?"

He shifted closer. His breath warmed my cheek as he brushed his knuckles along my jaw and captured my chin. He leaned in and kissed me once, hard. "No, ya albi. I don't want to go back. I want to stay here. I want to open my distillery, fix up my cabin, and try my damnedest to make things work with you."

I pulled away. "It's all a little too fantastic to believe, you know."

"I know." He latched onto my shoulders and pulled me close again. "But time will tell, so please, just give us some time."

I wrapped an arm around his ribs, high above his wound, and pressed my ear to his chest, listening to the steady thump of his heart while he combed his fingers through my hair as if I were his exotic pet. He had asked for time, and I wanted to promise I'd give it to him, but the words wouldn't come.

Is it possible to fall in love with someone who keeps parts of himself hidden?

Is it possible to trust a man who holds so many secrets?

WHEN I WOKE AGAIN, pale sunlight glowed around the curtain edges. For a moment, I reveled in the pleasure of waking up in bed next to the sexiest man in the world, but when my brain snapped on, memories swept in like a tidal wave. I sat up jack-in-the-box fast. "Oh no."

Owen jerked awake beside me and grimaced, clamping a hand to his ribs. "Ow, ow, ow."

I fumbled for the blanket and wrapped it around me as I slid from the bed.

"Where are you going?" he asked.

"We have to go. I'll be late for work."

He groaned and slowly, carefully sat up. His dark hair stuck up around his head, and I paused long enough to dole out another serving of pain pills and smooth his ruffled locks. He leaned against me, pressing his cheek against my hip as I dragged my nails over his scalp. "Forget work," he said. "Come back to bed with me."

"As tempting as that sounds, I'd be a lot more interested if, um, a vigorous round of physical activity wasn't likely to reopen your wound."

He snorted. "Why do you have to be so reasonable?"

"You told me yesterday that practicality never goes out of style."

"It doesn't when you're talking about walking shoes, overcoats, and sneaking bleeding men into motel rooms. When it comes to sex, practicality should jump out the window."

I pinched his shoulder. "Go take a shower and try to keep your wound dry. I want to clean it and put on a new bandage before we leave."

He glanced up at me, giving me a playful grin. The green cast had faded from his skin, and his eyes were bright and shiny rather than glassy and dull. "You could give me a sponge bath. You know, to be extra careful."

I pulled away from his roaming hands and headed for the bathroom to grab my clothes. "Nice try, hot stuff. Quit procrastinating, and let's get moving."

Owen gritted his teeth, stood, and saluted me. "The army nurses have got nothing on you, Rikki."

I paused in the doorway and cocked an eyebrow at him. "Be nice, and I'll stop and buy you breakfast."

"Coffee?"

I nodded.

He grinned. "It's a deal."

Chapter Twenty
Love Is a Battlefield

THE RIDE HOME STARTED with a visit to a discount store, where I grabbed us both clean T-shirts. Next came a stop at Dunkin' Donuts that left us high on sugar and caffeine. But as the miles rolled by, my buzz wore off and dread crept in. After the previous day's turmoil, I'd avoided confrontation. I hadn't pressed Owen as hard as I might have under favorable conditions. The urgency of his injuries and my sympathy for him had discouraged hostility.

Simply put, I'd been too tired and too psyched out to pick a fight, and I was too worried about him to cause him further pain.

But now I was rested, and Owen was no longer in danger of bleeding to death. When I'd changed his bandage, the wound looked days old rather than hours old, and it showed no signs of infection. I was stunned, and the miraculous rate of his healing had me scrambling to come up with logical explanations. But I couldn't find any.

The uncertainties I'd been harboring about Owen resurfaced and strengthened as if they'd been festering in my subconscious. The angry mob shouting questions at me after Owen's attack had returned in force, and they refused to go away until I'd appeased them with answers.

I'd held my tongue as long as possible. Starting a fight—and I assumed a fight was the inevitable conclusion, considering his reluctance to explain himself—was a bad idea while cooped up in a car neither of us could easily escape.

By the time Owen and I pulled into my driveway, I was bursting with the need to know, to demand answers, to hold him accountable for all the strange and inexplicable things that had happened.

"You were quiet the whole way home." Owen parked next to Dolly and cut the engine. "Something's still bothering you."

I huffed. "You could say that."

"What is it?"

"Either I'm going crazy..."

"Or?"

"Or there's more to your story than you're telling me." I raised a hand, stopping his obvious objection. "When I caught up to you after you and that guy disappeared, I only heard the tail end of the fight, but something happened. Something more than a simple brawl between two business rivals."

The muscle under his eye twitched, and color rose in his cheeks. "What do you think you saw?"

"I don't *think*. I know. There was something like an explosion—a burst of light and heat. When I found you, there was a huge char mark on the pavement. The asphalt was pitted, maybe even melted. The edges of your stab wound showed signs of a burn too." I turned in my seat, facing him fully. "What the hell happened? How did you heal so fast?"

Owen's brow puckered. Deep lines scored his face around his mouth and nose. The muscle in his jaw tensed. "I—" He squeezed his eyes together and shook his head. His throat worked. He tugged on his ring. "I can't."

His shoulders slumped. When he opened his eyes, despair shown in their dark depths. "I can't tell you."

My anger simmered like bubbling lava. I needed to get out of the car before I erupted. "You mean you won't."

He shook his head, and his hair fell into his eyes again. He swiped it back and leaned forward, his voice low, earnest, almost desperate. "It's not that simple."

I threw open my door, scooted out, and set a foot on the ground while keeping my gaze pinned on him. "You keep secrets that get you bloody and almost dead, and I'm supposed to patch them up with no explanation. That might work if you were a random patient in the back of my ambulance, but if that's all you are, then you might as well go home and never speak to me again. I don't fall for patients."

"What's that supposed to mean?"

I rolled out and stood. Owen cursed, grunted, and climbed out too. We stared at each other over the roof of his low-slung car. Strong emotions burned in his eyes—regret, maybe. Fear, perhaps.

"It means I need to decide if I can keep doing this... whatever it is... with you. Is it possible to trust you and let you keep your secrets at the same time? As long as impossible stuff keeps happening around you, and you keep refusing to explain it..."

Stepping back, I shook my head as though I could shake off my doubts. I stubbed my toe against the gravel, a better alternative to kicking his high-dollar car. "Maybe there are people in the world who can take the crumbs you're willing to offer and be satisfied. I don't know if I'm one of them." If I walked away from Owen, I'd have to know exactly why. And if I stayed with him, I'd also have to know why. "That's what I've got to figure out."

His face fell. His obvious hurt and dejection struck me like a physical blow. The urge to apologize, to take back everything, burned on my tongue. Instead, I dashed into my house and slammed my front door behind me. In my pocket, my phone buzzed like a hive of angry bees. Mina had texted, asking if I was home yet. I texted back, telling her to grab some Chunky Monkey and meet me at the EMS station, stat.

Peering out the window, I checked to see if Owen had taken my hint. Other than my rusty old Chevy, the driveway was empty. *Well, that wasn't nearly as much of a fight as I thought it would be.*

MINA AND I SAT HIP-to-hip on Dolly's tailgate, our legs dangling. The sun beat down, but a cool mountain breeze kept me from melting into a puddle of ginger curls and soupy ice cream. I longed for the air-conditioning inside, but the EMS station parking lot was the only place private enough to talk without my nosy coworkers overhearing us.

"So you just walked off and left him?" Mina asked.

I scrubbed my eyes as if I could remove the vision of Owen's crestfallen face. "I told him I needed to think about some things."

She slid her sunglasses down her nose and peered over their rims. "Girl, did you really just tell a man who is that fine and that into you that you need to 'think about some things'?"

"Did you not just hear what I told you? Are you saying all the secrets and weird stuff don't matter?"

Mina sighed and scooped up another spoonful of ice cream. "I'm saying my brain is melting from information overload, and I'm not sure what to tell you. You have every right to be freaking out." She dropped her ice cream spoon into the carton and gave me a long, contemplative look. "If what you saw was real..."

"Yeah, I know."

"There's got to be an explanation."

"That's what I thought, but if so, then why won't Owen tell me?"

"Maybe he's a top secret superagent." She gasped. "Or a spy with double-oh-seven gadgets!"

I smacked her arm. "Be realistic."

"The question isn't whether you can accept that he has secrets. It's whether you can trust him in spite of them. Either way, I'd hate to be in your shoes right now."

I had no reply for her because it was the same question I'd been asking myself on repeat for the last twenty-four hours. So much uncertainty and doubt were banging around inside my head that my brain felt swollen and bruised. Desperate for a break from my problems, I changed the subject. "Tell me about you and Luke."

Since Owen had walked into my life, I'd been living inside my head, self-absorbed and mostly oblivious. But not so oblivious that I hadn't noticed changes in my best friend.

"There's really not much to say." Mina flapped her hand at me dismissively and scooped another bite of our melting ice cream.

"I don't believe that. I saw the two of you together the other night. There was something going on there."

She paused as if considering how much to tell me. "Luke and I are... talking."

"You're doing more than *talking*, I bet."

She huffed, jabbing her spoon at me. "In the past, I put my relationships in neat little boxes tied up with neat little bows. Whatever it is between Luke and me, it doesn't fit in a box, and I don't want to screw it up by trying to put some label on it." She grinned sheepishly. "But yeah, there's more than just talking." Peering at her sticky fingers, she frowned. "I promise to tell you more when there's more to say, though. You know I don't keep things from you."

A shrill alarm blasted through the EMS station, making both of us flinch.

"Dammit." I jumped down from the tailgate and shoved the remains of our afternoon ice-cream binge into Mina's grocery bag. Dolly would not appreciate me leaving Chunky Monkey melting all over her truck bed. "This day's going to suck. I can already tell."

"When do you get off?" Mina palmed her Mustang keys and backed toward her shiny red convertible.

"A couple hours after dawn."

Her lips thinned in obvious distaste. "That's cruel and unusual punishment. How can you stand to work like that?"

"I love my job." I shrugged. "It doesn't bother me that much."

"Come crash at my place when your shift is over." Mina slid into her sleek car, and I tried not to envy her easy grace and effortless style. "When you wake up, we'll hang out and talk. No interruptions, I promise."

Chapter Twenty-One
Basket Case

"Contrary to popular belief, I'm actually *not* crazy." My boots thudded on the hay-strewn floor as I paced back and forth, my loose curls bobbing like flags on a breezy day. My breath puffed in white clouds as I jabbed a finger at myself. "I like to think of myself more as an old doll that's started coming apart at the seams, you know? Stuffing hanging out, loose strings, maybe an eye that's dangling by a thread"—my arms flailed as if I were conducting an invisible orchestra—"but I still have enough wits to know Owen is stone-cold evil, no matter what anyone else says."

A derisive snort made me flinch and turn on my heel.

"What?" I threw my hands out at my sides. "You disagree?" I narrowed my eyes. "Has he gotten to you too? Been winning you over to the dark side by bribing you with carrots?" I stroked the velvety gray nose of the horse poking his head over his stall door. Named for the color of his coat, Foggy blinked at me with big, mournful eyes. "You think I'm nuts, too, don't you?"

I'd come to Jack Huddle's stable not only to satisfy my sense of nostalgia but also because I needed to sort through my thoughts, and his horses had always been good listeners. I could confide in them without worrying they'd go gossiping around town, unlike most of the two-legged citizens of Evansville. Also, grooming horses had always been one of my favorite ways to de-stress. I'd found a curry brush and mane comb hanging in Mr. Huddle's tack room, and after letting myself into Foggy's stall, I stroked the brush over his shoul-

177

ders and flank. He expelled a sputtering breath that sounded like a sigh of pleasure.

"I'm like the girl in *Stranger Things*. Owen is the big bad evil, and even though no one believes me, I've got to do whatever it takes to save this town from itself." I only wished I had made this determination sooner. The guilt of having abandoned Evansville for three years haunted me almost as much as the memory of Mina's death.

I closed my eyes and let myself drop through the black hole in my mind, returning to that horrifying night. Reliving that terror *hurt*. It *burned*. Each time I remembered, my soul shredded into finer tatters and scraps. Soon only a few gossamer threads would remain, and then I'd be as much of a ghost as the specters roaming in Hickory Wood Cemetery, except I wouldn't be a mere figment of imagination.

"Then they really will have to call for the men in white coats to take me up and lock me away."

The only thing I knew to do was to confront Owen and try to stop him from hurting anyone else, but the thought of facing my best friend's killer made my knees turn to water and my stomach churn like the ocean in a hurricane. I dropped my forehead to Foggy's shoulder and smothered my watering eyes against his warm flesh. "From the beginning, something told me not to trust him. Not to let him get close. But my stupid heart was louder than my common sense." I hiccuped. "I *loved* him. And he killed her. She was my best friend, and he destroyed her."

Picking up on my distress, the horse whickered and stomped a hind hoof. Fearful of having my foot crushed, I backed away, wiped my eyes, and ran my brush over Foggy's back until he calmed. His eyelids fluttered, and he snorted in a drowsy way. If only finding peace were as easy as letting someone brush my hair. Life would be so much easier if I were a horse.

"How about you and I trade places, Foggy?" I exchanged the curry brush for a comb and concentrated on working the knots out of his mane. "You be human for a while, and I'll stay here eating oats and going for long walks in the mountains."

"Rikki Albemarle, are you in here?" Jack Huddle's call roused me from my morose woolgathering. "Saw that old Apache parked outside. Don't know anybody else who drives a truck like that, so I figured it had to be you."

I plastered a smile on my face, leaned over the stall door, and waved at the silver-haired man striding down the aisle between the horse stalls, carrying a pail and a pitchfork. He wore an old canvas work coat and faded jeans that hugged his long legs. Jack Huddle had always reminded me of Sam Elliot without the mustache. "Hey, Mr. Huddle. Sorry for the intrusion."

He stopped outside Foggy's stall and leaned against the doorpost. "You're always welcome here. No need to apologize. I had no idea you were in town."

I rolled my eyes. "Then you're the only one."

"Evansville gossip spreads faster than warm butter on hot toast, don't it?" He winked. "But it takes a little longer for news to travel all the way out here. Don't get into town much, not unless I need supplies."

"Thought I was overdue for a visit." I waved at Foggy. "I've seen most of the townsfolk. Thought it'd be rude if I didn't say hello to you and the horses too."

"You aren't in any big hurry to leave, are you?"

"I'm cooking dinner for the sheriff tonight, but other than that, I'm free."

Mr. Huddle pushed his pail into my arms and smiled. "You feed the horses." He raised his pitchfork. "I'll shovel the manure."

"That sounds like a fair deal." I returned his smile, grateful that he seemed to understand my need to hide from Evansville a little longer and have something to occupy my time while I was at it. "I won't even charge you for my time."

Chapter Twenty-Two
Can't Fight This Feeling

THREE YEARS BEFORE...

Late in the afternoon, I shuffled into Mina's small apartment kitchen, wearing a borrowed pair of cutoff shorts and the jade-colored tank top she'd picked out for me. She frequently tried to dress me in green, and I wondered if somewhere in the back of her mind, she suspected my red hair and freckles meant I was part leprechaun and I should do more to dress the part. She didn't need me to lead her to a pot of gold, though. Her parents kept her flush in cash when her part-time pharmacy job wasn't enough to pay the bills.

Desperate for a hit of caffeine, I filled a mug with old, cold coffee and shoved it in the microwave. Mina must have heard me puttering around. She turned off her living room TV and joined me in the kitchen. Her sleek black hair fell in a glossy sheet down her back, and her white linen sundress made the gold tones in her skin glow. Next to her, I felt frowzy and disheveled, like a rag doll trying to hang out with Barbie.

Leaning a hip against her counter, she folded her arms over her chest and gave me a scrutinizing look. "How'd you sleep?"

"Not well." In truth, I'd suffered hot and explicit dreams about Owen that left me aching, unsatisfied, and even more confused. "I think you keep rocks under your mattress."

Shaking her head, she grabbed a jug of milk from the refrigerator as the microwave dinged. "You want cereal?" She passed me my steaming coffee. "Or I could make you a peanut butter sandwich."

181

"Cereal's fine." Warily, I climbed onto a stool at her counter and sipped my nuked coffee while I watched her open cabinets and drawers. She'd never been much of a cook, and her mostly bare kitchen was proof, but that didn't stop her from trying to be a good hostess.

She set an empty bowl and a box of Cap'n Crunch in front of me. "Bon appétit."

I'd barely started eating when a knock at Mina's front door disrupted our quiet breakfast. She glanced at me, her brow furrowed. "I wasn't expecting anyone. Were you?"

When I shook my head, she rose from her seat and disappeared down the hallway. A cold sweat rose on my neck and the backs of my knees. An excited voice whispered in my head, suggesting that perhaps it was Owen showing up to surprise me. *And if so, how do I feel about that?*

But it wasn't Owen who followed Mina into the kitchen. It was Luke, and he smiled smugly as if he knew what I'd been thinking. "Hey, Rikki," he said. "Funny running into you here."

"Why don't I think your being here is just a coincidence?" I dropped my spoon into my cereal bowl and glared at Mina. "You said we were going to hang out, just you and me."

"I had no idea he was coming over." She placed a hand over her heart. "Swear to God."

I glanced at Luke and scowled. His lips thinned as he nodded toward the living room. "Let's sit and talk."

"Be nice to her." Mina shook her finger at him.

He held his hands out at his sides. "Why wouldn't I be?"

"I know you're devoted to your boy, and dudes stick up for each other, even when they don't deserve it. You don't have to criticize Owen, but just make sure you didn't come over here to make Rikki feel guilty either. She told me what happened, and I think she had a right to freak out. I would have done the same in her situation."

Abandoning my cereal, I followed Luke out of the kitchen, and we claimed seats on opposite ends of Mina's sofa, like rivals taking opposite sides of a boxing ring. My resentment at his presence stemmed not so much from fearing what he might say but rather from feeling conspired against.

"First," Luke said, "I should tell you Owen hasn't said a word to me. When you've been through the hell the two of us have survived, neither of us has to talk for one of us to know the other's seriously messed up about something. And seeing as how everything is going fine with the distillery, that means it's either his family life or his personal life that's bothering him."

Luke swiped his honey-brown hair off his brow. A muscle flexed in his square jaw. "I've seen him with women before, Rikki. I'm not calling him a saint. In our career, love-'em-and-leave-'em was pretty much the only option, and neither of us lost much sleep over that. But now we're out, and he's putting down roots, which is good for him. We could both use some stability in our lives."

Suspecting I knew what he was going to say next, I stood and rounded the sofa's corner, moving to the open area in front of the empty fireplace. I was better at processing things—feelings, emotions, problems—on the move. "And I'm giving him the opposite of that. I know. I told him when we were in Chapel Hill that I was willing to try something long-term with him, but then he was attacked, and a lot of things happened he won't explain."

"I know there're things about Owen that don't always make sense." Luke stood, as if remaining seated in my presence put him at a disadvantage. He smoothed the wrinkles from his T-shirt. Something clattered in the kitchen as Mina pretended to be occupied rather than eavesdropping. "It's been like that since his last tour in Iraq, ever since he was…" He cut his eyes to me, obviously wondering how much he should say on that subject.

"Ever since the IED?" I asked. "He mentioned it."

Luke's hands fisted at his sides. His shoulders stiffened. "He saved my life that day. Did he mention that? Put himself between me and that explosion, made himself a human shield. Bastard was lucky he didn't die. He *should've* died, but he's got angels on his shoulders.

"He's not going to chase you—he respects your need for space too much. So, you've got to be the one to go to him."

A stew of anger and longing simmered in my veins. Making the wrong step with Owen could ruin all the plans I'd so carefully laid. It would shatter all the walls I'd so expertly built. I wanted him, but he could break me. "It's not that easy."

"Do you care for him or not?"

"Of *course* I do." I gritted my teeth. "I want Owen more than anything I've ever wanted before, but how the hell do I trust him?"

"Sometimes you have to take a leap of faith. Stop playing it so damned safe all the time, and just jump." He crossed the space between us and took my hands, forcing me to stop pacing. His eyes were shards of sapphire ice, pinning me in place. "I'd trust Owen with my life. He's the closest thing I've ever had to a brother, so believe me when I say you can believe in him."

Luke's words had sliced me, and my heart was bleeding for Owen. So much for the toughness of scar tissue. But Owen had repeatedly proven to be my weakness, my kryptonite, my Achilles' heel. I'd made lists in my head, pros and cons, reasons for and against, but quantifying my attraction to Owen was like trying to quantify all the light in the universe—it was impossible.

"It's not just Owen," Mina said behind me. "You have to trust yourself too." She crossed the room and yanked me into a fierce hug. Her familiar perfume was a tendril of comfort, and I melted in her arms. "You are one of the bravest people I've ever known. You've never let fear stop you from doing the things you've wanted before. Don't let it stop you now."

I trusted Mina.

I trusted Luke.

Perhaps it was time to trust Owen.

INSTEAD OF HEADING straight to Moon Runners or El Jannah, I drove to the other end of town and stopped at the local bakery to grab a box of chocolate chip cookies—a peace offering and a reminder of our first date.

After the bakery, I raced up the steep hill heading to Hickory Wood Cemetery. I parked in the gravel lot, my hands shaking as I tugged the keys from the ignition. Ever since leaving my house, I'd fought the urge to turn around and run far away from the truth I needed to face—I was falling for Owen. I needed to get on with my life, stop sheltering my heart. Time to put on my superhero cape and face some fears. Take some risks. Live my life. I had a lot of flaws, but until Owen came into my life, I hadn't realized self-doubt was such a big one.

I followed the gravel path through the cemetery gates. Even in the dark, or completely blind, I could have found my way. My father's grave pulled me like a magnet. I crouched, bracing a hand on the curve of his stone for balance, and pictured my dad the way I preferred to remember him, not skin and bones in a medical bed—with tubes plugged into each of his nooks and crannies—but strong and vibrant. He'd often kept his red hair, so much like mine, clipped short to discourage his curls. He'd loved wearing rock-concert T-shirts and ragged jeans full of rips and tears. Colorful streaks and smudges from his latest painting covered him like tattoos.

"Hey, Dad." I plucked a few strangling weeds from the base of his stone and imagined him smiling at me. "I bet you'll never guess why I'm here."

Over the years, his grave had become my confessional. He could've listed at least a dozen existential crises that had brought me here in the past: questioning my college path, my career goals, my decision to move away from home, my disagreements with Mina, the coldness between me and Mom. But never had I talked to him about love, not this kind, anyway.

I closed my eyes and told him everything that had happened since the day Owen showed up at Rose's Diner and asked me out. "He's a good man. He's been patient, understanding, and honest—when he's willing to open up and talk, which isn't very often."

I pictured Dad pursing his lips with a look that said, *So what's the problem?*

I told him about my doubts, Owen's secrets, and the things about him I didn't understand.

Dad rolled his hand, gesturing for me to continue.

"And somehow, I don't care. I mean, I *do* care but not enough to walk away. Every time I think about walking away from him, it hurts. Like... if I leave him, my heart might claw through my chest and run back to him regardless of what the rest of my body is doing. Remember when you told me sometimes the wrong boy is the one who knows how to say all the right things?" Owen kept a lot of things to himself, but his actions had spoken clearly. He'd listened to me, hadn't tried to stand in my way, manipulate me, or tell me what to do. He'd supported my goals, respected my wishes, and given me space. "So, maybe you'd agree that the right boy is the one who doesn't say much at all."

Silence, I could respect, but lies were poison, and as far as I knew, Owen had never told me anything other than the truth.

"And in case you were wondering, I'm not here to ask your advice, Dad. I've already made up my mind." I stood, brushed my hands against the seat of my shorts, and stepped back from his monument. "I just thought you'd like to know."

Chapter Twenty-Three
Hardly Wait

BY THE TIME I LEFT the cemetery, twilight had arrived, and deep shadows gathered beneath awnings, haunting the spaces between buildings on Main Street as I rumbled through Evansville's sleepy downtown. Luke hadn't been certain whether I'd find Owen at the distillery or at his isolated little cabin. Because the drive to Moon Runners would take half the time of driving out to Owen's cottage in the hills, I decided to start my search at the distillery.

On my way, I passed Rose's Diner. Flower baskets dripping pink geraniums and sweet potato vines hung on either side of the doorway. Her neon Open sign glowed brightly in the window. Hers was one of the few businesses that remained open in the evenings, serving a hungry dinner crowd.

Other than the diner, downtown Evansville was as quiet as an empty library. Few people would have witnessed me turning onto the side street leading to Moon Runners. Dolly bumped over the rutted entrance, and I wheeled into an almost-vacant parking lot. I pulled into a spot next to an unfamiliar black Tacoma and killed the engine. I wondered if Owen had added another vehicle to his collection or if it belonged to a subcontractor working late.

My nerves were firing, crackling like exposed wires. I was anxious, eager to see Owen, and worried he wouldn't feel the same about me. Standing straight, my shoulders back, I brushed lint from my shirt and scanned the distillery's brick exterior. Owen had removed the warehouse's old signage, but he'd hung up nothing in its place to indicate the new business coming to life inside. Through the window in the warehouse's side door, a single bright light burned. A shadow crossed in front of it.

My breath caught.

I grabbed my cookie container and inched forward, avoiding parking lot potholes, and stared through the window, hoping to catch a glimpse of whoever was inside. Once I reached the door, I raised my chin and took a deep breath. *Here goes nothing.*

The night Owen had brought me to the warehouse for a sneak peek, darkness had concealed many interior details, so I couldn't compare before and after. I suspected the space had been dank, musty, and dirty, but he'd put a lot of effort into cleaning up and clearing out. The concrete floors looked freshly scrubbed. Rustic barnwood had been installed over the bare brick walls in strategic spots, adding accents of warmth and texture. I rounded the corner of a huge wooden frame—like a giant bookcase—and stopped.

There stood Owen, both hands braced on either side of a set of blueprints spread atop a vast raw-wood structure that would probably become the bar. His T-shirt clung to him, outlining firm muscles flexed in his back. Sawdust speckled his coffee-dark hair.

My earlier reluctance and uncertainty receded.

This was where I was supposed to be.

I only hoped he agreed.

"It looks amazing," I said. "I can only imagine how beautiful it'll be when you're done."

On the bar's plain tabletop, his hand fisted briefly before his shoulders relaxed. He stood straight, turned around, and faced me. His eyes flickered over me, taking in details. A guilty smile crossed his lips, and a subtle blush colored his cheeks.

"Hope you don't mind me showing myself in." Although my insides were twisting and turning, I smiled. "I would have knocked, but I was afraid you'd tell me to leave." I presented my cookie container. "I brought a peace offering, if that helps."

His eyes dropped to my feet and scraped up the length of me, like a tiger eyeing his prey.

I stalked closer, feigning confidence while ignoring my racing heart. I gestured at the cookies. "I was hoping to win myself a reprieve."

A slight grin slipped across his lips. "Then your plan worked."

I stopped inches before him, close enough to smell his smoky scent, to feel his warmth. His eyes were as dark and brown as the rich chocolate Mina preferred. Long, sooty lashes framed his gaze. His heartbeat fluttered in his neck, fast and vital. I wanted to kiss that pulse point, taste his skin. "All the way here, I debated what to say to you. I thought I might apologize, but that wouldn't be right—not completely. I'm sorry for the way I left things, but I'm not sorry for taking a step back."

He said nothing, merely flicked an eyebrow.

"From the moment you walked into my life, everything's been a blur. I'm either working or squeezing in time to be with you when I'm not working. There hasn't been time to stop and let it all sink in. It's been the world's craziest roller coaster. I just wanted to get off and let my head stop spinning long enough to figure out what I wanted to do next."

His scrutiny was sharp. I felt like an ant under a magnifying glass, pinned by a beam of sunlight.

"And have you figured it out?" he asked.

"I know what I want. Question is whether it's too late for me to get it."

He frowned. "What do you mean?"

"I want your kindness and generosity and patience. I want your charm and laughter." I brushed a thumb across his stubbled jaw. "I want your secrets too."

His eyes blazed. "You're sure?"

"As sure as a tightrope walker stepping out on a very thin rope on a windy day." I smiled. "If you're the man I think you are, and that everyone insists you are, then I should be able to rely on the fact you'll have my best interests at heart, no matter what else is going on in your life."

"Everyone? Who's everyone?"

"Well, mostly just Luke and Mina."

His lip twitched, revealing a hesitant grin.

"Is it too little, too late? Do I still have a chance?"

"Unlimited chances, Rikki." Owen gestured to his ribs, to the place he'd been wounded. "I owe you my life, and you owe me nothing in return. Especially not apologies."

I pointed at his abdomen. "I'm not sure that counted as a mortal wound."

"Thanks to you, I never had to find out." He leaned in, resting his forehead against mine. I can give you time to process things, if that's what you need. What I *can't* give you is a promise that things will always make sense or that I'll always be easy to be with. I get how challenging it is to be with someone who has secrets. But I swear on my life I'll protect you and never do anything to hurt you."

Relief flooded me as though I'd been suffocating and he'd given me air. "That's what I'm counting on."

He took my cookies and set them down. He cupped my jaw, tilting my head back. I gripped his shoulders, trying to keep my balance as my world slanted. His lips brushed mine as he spoke. "Stay with me tonight?"

Because staying with him was the very reason I'd come back, and because I couldn't have formed the words to deny him, not if my life depended on it, I kissed him—burning fuse to powder keg. He exploded, taking me with him.

His hands fisted in my hair. I dug my nails into his shoulders.

There were smoke and flames, and maybe it was all in my head, but I was burning, turning to ash in his hands.

He broke away, his chest heaving, and dragged his wrist across his mouth. When he looked at me, his eyes burned, full of blue flames and amber sparks. Thick, impenetrable shadows swirled around him before dissipating in a breeze of cool air that smelled of sawdust and varnish. Excitement surged through me, bright and sharp like the touch of a live wire.

"Not here. Not here, where everything's hard and cold and too open to interruption." He closed his eyes and raked his hands through his hair. His voice was rough, his breath labored. "When I make you cry my name, I want to be the only one who hears it."

A wave of arousal rolled through me, but I let it drift away. Stepping back, breaking all physical contact, I smoothed my hair with trembling hands and brushed wrinkles from my shirt. My head cleared, and my bones settled in place, my body reforming around them. The burning hadn't been real, but no other words described the sensation, the utter loss of myself in Owen's touch. I had to put some distance between us before his heat and my hunger overcame my self-restraint.

I stuffed my shaking hands in my pockets and cleared my throat. "You're still letting me set the pace, right?" I wasn't trying to tease him, but if things moved too quickly, I might panic again. I did stupid things when I panicked.

Slitting his eyes, he gave me a wary look. "Of course."

"Is there any reason you can't take a minute to give me a tour?" I waved, gesturing around the room. "If this place is half as important to you as UNC is to me, then I want to see it." A tour would also give me the chance to calm my racing heart and gather my composure. "Introduce me to my competition."

Letting out a long breath, he offered me his hand. I took it. Heat radiated from him, and I might have been projecting, but I felt his desire like warmth from a campfire banked for the night—still there but low and smoldering. "There's not much to see yet, but I'll show you what I've done so far." He pointed at the massive wooden unit behind us. "This'll be the back of the bar, shelves and cabinets for storing bottles and glassware." He patted the heavy wooden base he'd been leaning on. "This is the bar. I'm having the top made from a single oak slab. It's a custom piece, and I'll put it in last so it won't get damaged."

He ushered me to the front of the warehouse, stopping at the tall roll-up doors. "The seating area will go here. I'm looking at table-and-chair combos, but I haven't found anything I like yet. Thinking about getting something custom for those too." He nodded toward the garage doors. "I'm building a deck out there for outside seating. There'll be an area for live music."

Tugging my arm, he guided me across the room to the rear, where walls and floors were still bare. "Copper distilling tanks go here. They're coming in on a truck tomorrow." He faced me, grinning, enthusiasm lighting his eyes. "Wait until you see it after they're installed. They'll change the whole look of this place."

Slowly, I spun, taking in the full scope of the warehouse. "It's going to be amazing. It's already come so far." Owen's pride was evident in the way he held himself, chin raised, shoulders back, eyes shining, thousand-watt smile blazing. "I couldn't dream of starting with an abandoned old warehouse and turning it into something like this. Your ingenuity is incredible."

His gaze dropped, and he rubbed the back of his neck. "It's not like I'm saving people's lives, though."

I bumped my shoulder against him. "Don't make me a saint. I've been doing everything I can to abandon Evansville. This town has been good to me, but all I've thought about for the last five years is getting away. Since I've met you, it's starting to feel like I might be betraying this place a little. This old town needs new blood if it's going to survive. What you're doing is important."

Taking his hand, I led him to the exit. "Is there anything else to see?"

His brow wrinkled, and he shook his head.

"Take me to dinner?" I hadn't gotten to finish my bowl of cereal that morning before Luke interrupted, and my stomach was growling. "I'm starving, and Rose always makes lasagna on Wednesdays."

He grinned, tugged his keys from his pocket, and opened the door. Gesturing to the parking lot, he bent in a brief bow. "Right this way."

"Is the truck yours?" I followed him across the parking lot as he headed for the black Tacoma. "Another for your growing collection?"

"Borrowed it from a friend." He guided me to the passenger side and opened the door. "Needed to haul some stuff."

I climbed in, but he caught my hand as I reached for the seat belt. "You came back to me, ya albi." His face was serene, his gaze bottomless. "I wasn't sure you would."

A short trip through downtown brought us to a parking spot in front of Rose's Diner. Owen held his hand out for me after I climbed from the truck, and we strolled inside together. The clink of cutlery and glassware accented the busy dinner crowd's low, rumbling conversation.

"Well, don't you two go together like peas and carrots?" Rose hurried out from behind the counter and escorted us to the only empty booth in a dining room that smelled of coffee and hot grease. "Wednesday night lasagna, right, honey?"

I nodded.

She glanced at Owen and arched an eyebrow. "You gonna order something different?"

"Wouldn't dare."

"Good answer," Rose said, backing away from our table, already on her way to the kitchen. One of her waitresses deposited water glasses on our table before rushing to greet a new group of customers stepping through the door. Another waitress flew by, pausing only long enough to drop a basket of bread and butter on our table.

Even though my own drumbeat had recently changed rhythm, the pulse of Evansville remained steady and regular, marching at the same small-town pace it had always kept. The diner buzzed around us at a blinding pace, but Owen and I were caught in a bubble where time flowed according to our own private momentum.

He tilted his head, and the muscles around his eyes tightened. "You've got a funny smile on your face. What are you thinking about?"

"Just wishing I could make time stop." I grazed a finger over his knuckles and traced the insignia on his ring—like a Star of David inside a circle. "A month ago, I would have told you this summer couldn't be over soon enough, but now I think it's going to go by way too—"

A blast of sirens and a blur of blue and red lights blew past the diner's front windows. I counted two, three, four sheriff's cars racing by—almost half of Twain County's fleet. My heart thundered into my throat. I rocketed to my feet, sprinted across the dining room, and hit the front door as Rose caught up to me. We stumbled onto the sidewalk together.

While most deputies had long ago switched over to newer, flashier Dodge Chargers, my mother had preferred to keep her comfortable old Crown Victoria. Her car hadn't been in the pack, but still my heart hammered, and a sick sensation simmered in my stomach. I wondered what kind of call had required the immediate attention of most of the county's on-duty officers. The possibilities made me shiver.

Rose grabbed my arm and clutched the base of her throat with her other hand. Streetlights cast stark shadows on her face, emphasizing the lines of worry around her mouth and eyes. "Mike's on duty tonight. I'm sure one of those cars was his."

I stared down Main Street as if the reason for their emergency might make itself known. But the deputies had no jurisdiction inside Evansville's limits, so they were most likely headed out of town, somewhere I couldn't follow on foot. "Where are they going in such a rush?"

A warm presence appeared beside me. Owen slid his arm around my shoulders and tugged me close. His eyes were closed, his brow furrowed. He raised his chin and pressed his lips into a hard line. His pose was pensive, contemplative, as if he was thinking hard about something.

Rose tugged her cell phone from her pocket. "I'll call Darla and find out."

Darla was one of Rose's best friends and, coincidentally, a dispatcher for the county's emergency services. As she waited for the call to go through, I glanced around and noticed most of the diner's patrons had joined us on the sidewalk. Those who hadn't made it past the traffic jam in the doorway pressed against the windows, their attention focused on Rose and me.

"Hey, it's Rose." She caught my gaze and held it as she listened to the response on the other end of the line. "Yeah, I saw them drive by. What's going on?"

Her brow crinkled. Her mouth popped into an O. She looked at me, and her eyes widened, filling with fear. My already unsettled stomach turned over again.

"Thanks, Darla." Her voice wobbled. "Keep me updated if you can, okay?"

"What is it?" I clutched her hand.

She looked away, purposely avoiding my eyes—a sure sign of bad news. "Hostage situation out on Old Mill Road. Your mom..." She closed her eyes, her throat working as she swallowed. "Sh-she was serving a restraining order and divorce papers on a guy who pulled a gun on her. He's got your mom at gunpoint, and he's refusing to let her go."

Chapter Twenty-Four
Kryptonite

PULLING FREE FROM OWEN'S embrace, I shifted into first-responder mode, shutting down emotions as adrenaline flooded my veins. *Deal with one issue at a time. Fix the problems you can, and try to forget about the ones you can't.* "Can you make this truck fly, Superman?"

"I can try."

As we raced through town, a dark thought struck me. "You're taking a risk, you know."

He scoffed. "I'm a pretty great driver, even on mountain roads. Trust me. I'll get us there in one piece."

"I'm not talking about your driving. I'm talking about this hostage situation. Not just the literal danger of a potential shooter but, you know, the attention that's going to attract. Going there is a risk to your anonymity." My panic bubbled over and sent pulses of fear stabbing through me. "You're sure you want to expose yourself?"

"Rikki, it's your mom. What else were we supposed to do? You think I don't know how precious she is to you and how afraid you must be right now? You honestly think I would leave you to find her on your own?"

I shook my head and rubbed my watering eyes. I'd said I trusted him, but some small doubt must have lingered inside me, or else I wouldn't have been so amazed by his gallantry. "Do you even know where Old Mill Road is?" I knew the road, but Darla hadn't given Rose a specific address. I expected we'd have no trouble finding a collection of deputies' cars once we reached the general location, though.

He flashed his phone's screen at me, revealing a GPS map. "Nope, but I think I'm on the right path."

Darkness blurred past our windows as Owen flew over the blacktop. His headlights bounced off trees as he whipped around curves. I gripped my door handle until my knuckles strained against my skin. I gritted my teeth as he cut corners and caught air at the crest of one steep hill. "Can't help my mom if you kill us before we get there," I muttered through clenched teeth.

"Trust me, Rikki. I can handle it."

"You got an Earnhardt in your family tree?"

He snorted. "Does it *look* like I'm driving in circles?"

The chatter kept me distracted, held my fear at bay. In the back of my mind, I was screaming, but I had long since learned to ignore the voice of panic. "What does a Yankee know about NASCAR, anyway?"

"I know it got its start in moonshiners outrunning the law on back mountain roads like these." The Tacoma's tires squealed as he rocketed through the turn onto Old Mill Road. "Besides, haven't you ever heard of Watkins Glen?"

I forced a tense smile. "So you're getting some practice, just in case you decide to make a career change?"

We crested a short rise, and a parade of red and blue lights lined the roadway, their spotlights burning bright, illuminating the scene like a Hollywood movie premier. Four Twain County patrol cars sprawled along the shoulder in front of a white fence. Behind that fence stretched a dried lawn filled with rusting mechanical fragments—car parts, truck frames, an old lawn mower body. In the doorway of a crumbling white clapboard stood my mother. Behind her stood another man, one arm cinched around my mom's neck as he pressed a pistol barrel against her head.

My heart spasmed. *Please, no. I can't lose her too.*

Owen rolled past the deputies' cars before tugging the wheel, bringing us to a stop on the shoulder several yards beyond the last vehicle in the procession. I yanked my door handle, but Owen grabbed my arm, pulling me back before I could haul myself out. "Wait, Rikki."

I bared my teeth at him like a wild animal caught in a trap. "Let me go."

"Don't rush in there and spook him. That guy's already on edge. He doesn't need much of an excuse to pull the trigger."

"I *know*. I've handled people in desperate situations before. I'm not going to confront him. I just want to get close enough to see what's happening."

He held my gaze, and worry showed in the lines around his mouth and eyes. "I'm coming with you."

"Fine." I eased open my door, slid to the ground, and met Owen behind his truck, my heart thumping in my ears. Together, we crept toward the closest patrol car and hunkered low before peeking around the trunk. I recognized the three deputies staggered along the peeling white fence at the edge of the yard: Tanner Nobles, Mike Heinlein, and Unberto Gallardo, the rookie.

Owen grabbed my shoulder, leaned close, and whispered, "I could help your mom if you'll let me."

I tore my attention away from my mother's pale face and met his earnest eyes. "How?"

"Do you trust me?"

"You know I do, or you wouldn't be here."

"Then you trust me to help her?" He pointed at my mom.

I nodded.

"Then please, no matter what, stay here and don't move."

I furrowed my brow. "What are you—"

Owen kissed me, hard and quick, before he peeled away and trotted to the Tacoma. I watched him until he crept around the bumper and the darkness swallowed him. The temptation to follow him, to demand answers and offer my help, pulsed through me until my muscles quivered with the urge to move, but my curiosity paled in comparison to my fear for my mother. He was a soldier, someone specifically trained to deal with hostile situations like this, and he had a knack for accomplishing the uncanny. Whatever he was up to, I would trust him, and I wouldn't abandon my mom.

"Mr. Greer," Mike said, his attention again on the perpetrator. "I can guarantee that if you let the sheriff walk away unharmed, we will all get in our cars and roll out of here. We'll leave you in peace. No one has to get hurt today."

"Y'all are liars," Greer said. "If I let her go, y'all will shoot me down. I seen it too many times on TV."

From the corner of my eye, I caught a flash of movement. At the yard's edge, where the patrol cars' lights didn't quite reach, a dark, nebulous figure drifted toward Greer's house. Presumably, it was Owen, creeping closer to Greer and my mother, but he was dim, camouflaged among the shadows.

He'd been wearing a bright white T-shirt when I'd last seen him. Unless he kept a change of clothes in the truck, I didn't understand how he could hide himself so well, even in the darkness. His shirt should have reflected the ambient light. Maybe it wasn't Owen at all. Maybe it was a trick of the wind and moonlight. But I knew better. It was simply another example of his inexplicable nature.

"This isn't television, Mr. Greer." Mike raised his hands, fingers splayed, palms out. "There isn't a movie director calling the shots here. Nobody's writing a script to make things more interesting. You're the one in charge, and you can decide how this ends."

"I'll tell you how it *don't* end," Greer shouted. "It *don't* end with me going to jail."

"You're saying you don't want to go to jail. I'm telling you we can make that happen. The sheriff was serving court papers on you—that's all. You weren't being charged with a crime."

Greer paused. His wiry eyebrows furrowed as he contemplated Mike's statement. "The only one committing a crime is my wife. Leaving me and trying to take my kids too. I'll let you have the sheriff back if you tell me where I can find Donna and my kids."

"No one wants to let your wife take your kids away. But you've got to let Sheriff Albemarle go. Think of how this will look when you go to court."

Greer jerked his chin and bared his yellow teeth. He was gaunt, and sores marked his cheeks and forehead. I had a feeling he'd had a long-term relationship with drugs—meth most likely. If he was currently high, which seemed plausible, there would be no reasoning with him. "I want full custody, and I want that woman in jail for kidnapping!"

My mom stood stiffly in the doorway, her face stark white in the spotlights, her expression grim. Her mouth was set in a firm line. Her chest worked like bellows. Greer was a little man who'd extended himself to keep his forearm hooked around my mom's neck. If not for the gun, my mom would have long ago disabled her assailant. If not for the gun, Greer probably wouldn't have tried holding her hostage in the first place.

Truthfully, I hadn't expected to rescue my mom. I'd only come in case the worst happened. I'd fight to keep her alive, no matter what, but a gunshot to the head was something even God would have trouble fixing. I wasn't even a full-fledged paramedic, much less a god. I was a relatively inexperienced EMT with a lot still left to learn. The only thing I could do for my mom was be there.

I squeezed my eyes shut and muttered a silent prayer, begging Greer to listen to reason, put down his gun, and surrender. But a reasonable man would've avoided this situation from the outset. *If I can't have reason,* I prayed, *I'll take a miracle instead.*

"Y'all think I'm stupid?" Greer's voice was high-pitched and anxious. He pressed the gun against my mom's temple hard enough to make her grimace. "Y'all think I don't know you're just trying to fool me? If I let the sheriff go, that'll be the last anyone sees of me. I've gone to jail before. I *ain't* going back."

Mike shifted a step closer, his hands still up in a passive position, showing he was nowhere close to reaching for his gun. "Mr. Greer, I—"

A sudden flash of blinding light burst from the house's doorway and windows.

I squeezed my eyes shut, stumbled, and fell to a knee. Someone cried out. I'd seen light like that when Owen and the stranger fought in Chapel Hill. That a similar phenomenon had happened here, in Owen's proximity, was certainly no coincidence.

How the hell does he do these things?

When my vision cleared, Greer lay facedown in the front yard, and my mom was gone.

I jumped to my feet and staggered forward. Mike's reflexes had kicked in, and he lunged, throwing himself on top of my mom's assailant. Unberto and Tanner surrounded them, ordering Greer not to move. Mike jerked Greer's arms and hooked cuffs around his wrists. The little man muttered nonsensically and offered no resistance, his body flopping like a rag doll. Mike yanked Greer to his feet and shoved him toward Unberto before turning and searching behind him, presumably looking for my mom. I'd already cleared the fence and reached Mike's side when my mother stumbled around the corner of the house.

"Mom!" Relief surged through me, as cool and refreshing as a mountain spring. Tears of relief prickled in my eyes. I ran to her side and threw my arms around her. "Are you okay? Are you hurt?"

"Rikki?" She stiffened. "What the hell are you doing here?"

"I came to make sure you were okay."

"How did you know—"

"Josie, what happened?" Mike grabbed my mom's shoulder. "There was some kind of light... an explosion?"

"I don't know any more than you." Blinking, my mom shook her head and pulled away from me. I almost yanked her back. "One minute I was standing there with a gun barrel pressed to my head and a crazy man's arm around my throat. Next minute, I was standing at the backdoor steps. I don't think there was an explosion, but... there was a kind of a hot smell, like ozone."

"Maybe he had a flashbang or something?" Mike glanced at the empty doorway at the front of the house, as though he expected an explanation to reveal itself.

Internally, I rolled my eyes and huffed. Flashbang, indeed. I searched our surroundings for a glimpse of my mother's mysterious savior, but Owen apparently preferred to avoid recognition. "Mom." I took her hands in mine and gave her my best I'm-a-medical-authority-you-better-listen-to-me glare. "I think you should go to the hospital and get checked out."

Unintimidated and unimpressed, she patted my head and gave me a patronizing grin. "I feel fine, Rikki. Much better than I did two minutes ago, that's for sure."

I stabbed my finger against her shoulder. "You don't know what that light blast was about. You could have internal injuries or... or..."

She smirked. "Or what?"

"Or radiation poisoning." Tossing my hands up, I made an exasperated sound. "I don't know, but I don't think you should shrug it off."

"I promise I'll go if I start feeling poorly. Right now, I have a job to finish." She grimaced as an ambulance siren and more flashing lights approached. She arched an eyebrow at me. "Friends of yours?"

"At least let them give you a quick exam." I gestured at the rig pulling up on the scene. "It'll give me peace of mind."

She gave me an inscrutable look. Her shoulders slumped. "Fine. I'll do it for you. But tell her to make it quick." Her gaze shifted to the local news van rolling up behind the ambulance. "I have a feeling it's going to be a long night."

After handing my mom off to Toni, I sneaked away, avoiding the deputies and their unanswerable questions. If they hadn't noticed Owen's presence before, there was no reason to risk alerting them now. If we were lucky, he'd get away without his name appearing in any police or news reports.

I circled to the Tacoma's driver's side and opened the door. Owen sat behind the wheel as if he'd always been there. As if he hadn't somehow done the things I knew he'd done but that I still didn't understand.

"News vans are here," I said. "Might be a good idea if you keep a low profile and let me drive."

Grimacing, he nodded and scooted over. I climbed behind the wheel and started the engine as he slumped low in his seat. Instead of turning around and driving past multiple witnesses, I followed Old Mill Road away from the excitement. Taking that route meant taking a longer path back to town—going around my ass to get to my elbow, as my mom would say—but I figured neither of us was in a rush to get anywhere other than far away from Greer's house.

Once the last patrol car had disappeared from my rearview, I released a long, trembling breath and pulled onto the shoulder. The emotional wall inside me quaked—a crack crawled through the mortar. "That was..." I pressed my heels to my eyes and waited for the shaking to stop. My mom was the only real family I had left. I'd been taking her for granted, and I could've lost her.

Owen dragged me into his lap and stroked my back.

"He could have killed her," I rasped, my throat swollen with unshed tears. "He could've put a bullet through my mom's head and killed her."

Owen pressed his forehead against my temple. "That wasn't going to happen."

Although he didn't say it, I knew he meant he wouldn't have *let* it happen. Somehow, in his inexplicable, mysterious way, he would've saved my mom's life.

He *had* saved my mom's life.

I didn't know how, and he'd likely refuse to tell me, but I would let Owen have a thousand secrets if it meant that, in return, I got to have him at my side, keeping me safe, protecting my family, saving the day. I wouldn't let curiosity overrule my appreciation for the miracle he'd given me. I owed him that much, at least.

"What are you thinking?" Owen asked.

"I'm thinking about not looking a gift horse in the mouth."

He leaned back and cocked an eyebrow. "Am I the horse in this analogy?"

"No. You're the hero." I cupped his jaw and pressed my lips to his cheek. "Thank you."

He said nothing, neither accepting nor denying my gratitude. He merely tightened his arms around me and held me as though I was something to be treasured.

"I'm also thinking I never got my lasagna." Lack of food and an overabundance of adrenaline and fear had left me feeling sick and shaky. I gave him a serious look so he'd understand the importance of my next statement. "I might drop dead on my feet if I don't get something to eat."

Owen chuckled and glanced out the window, staring at the dark night surrounding us. "How about I cook dinner for you at my place?"

"Your place, Moon Runners? Or your place, El Jannah?"

"My place where I live, where I keep my things, where I have a stove to cook on and a bed to sleep in."

An image of him sleeping, hair tousled, at the motel in Chapel Hill flashed in my mind, and I blushed, remembering that night's barely restrained intimacy. "What are you cooking?"

He glanced at me from the corner of his eye. "It's a surprise."

"I don't know..."

"Say you'll come home with me? Eat supper with me and stay the night, okay?"

My blush expanded, its warmth spreading into my fingers and toes, tingling down my spine. I had no excuses left to offer—no misconceptions or fears left to cling to. Here Owen was, laying himself open for me to accept or deny. My choice was as easy as breathing air.

I squeezed his hand and peered into his dark eyes. "Okay."

Chapter Twenty-Five
Unsteady

A HIGH-VOLTAGE POWER line hums a deep vibrating tone that sinks into your teeth and burrows into your bones. That same sensation filled the truck's interior as we left behind Greer's house and Evansville, taking the winding, back-mountain road to El Jannah. Heavy cloud cover hid the moon. Darkness, as thick as crude oil, oozed over mountaintops and flooded valleys, obscuring and concealing until all that remained of the world were a few square feet illuminated in the Tacoma's headlights. Owen and I might as well have been the only two people left in the universe.

As soon as we'd left the roadside beyond Greer's house, Owen had laced his fingers between mine and hadn't let go.

A thousand thoughts and questions crossed my mind, but I didn't know what I could say. The moment was too surreal, almost transcendental—like a dream, one I didn't want to wake up from. Words were too ordinary and could only ruin the moment, so I kept them to myself. Owen stayed silent, too, though probably not for the same reasons. He glanced at me and squeezed my fingers.

I wanted to ask what he was thinking, what he was expecting, but more than once, he'd said he preferred to show rather than tell, and tonight was likely no exception. Anticipation coursed through me like an amphetamine, spiking my heart rate, shortening my breath.

Once we reached El Jannah's winding pathway, I drove past the clearing at the pond and climbed the hill leading to Owen's cabin. The Tacoma's headlights illuminated the cottage's deep front porch and peaked tin roof and made the surrounding pines into pale, spectral giants. When I turned off the engine, an orchestra of crickets, tree frogs, and cicadas played a staccato symphony.

Without a word, we exited the truck and crossed the gravel drive. At the top of the porch steps, I caught his hand and tugged hard enough to make him stumble against me. I kissed him, searing and hot. He was all hardness and strength, long angles and flat planes. A piercing shot of desire pulsed through me, like touching an exposed wire. After pushing him against a porch post, I straddled his leg and nipped the sensitive spot beneath his ear, and he groaned.

"When you walk through that door, ya albi, I'm yours. Understand?" He rubbed against me like a cat, a big, hungry mountain lion. His voice was a low, rough purr in my ear. "Once you choose to walk in, there's no backing out, no leaving without doing real damage. I can't let you in if there's any possibility you'll have regrets."

Unsteady and shaken, my heart pounding in my chest, I wrenched myself away, crossed the porch, opened his screen door, and rattled the front door's knob. "You'll have to unlock it if you want me to go in."

He stood where I'd left him, and despite the darkness obscuring him, he radiated intensity and urgency. "You're sure?"

"At some point, you'll have to stop asking me that."

He crossed the porch and slid a key into the door lock. "I'll stop asking once I'm deep inside you."

Stunned by his bold response, I gaped at him as he pushed open the door and stepped inside. He reached for the light switch, and several lamps blinked on, throwing low, warm light around a cozy, open floor plan connecting living room and kitchen in one sweeping space. Still a bit shaken, I wandered in behind him, treading over a braided entryway rug. A larger version of the same rug filled a living room outfitted in overstuffed furniture—a sofa and two big club chairs squatting around a rustic pine coffee table. Bookshelves, crammed with paperbacks and knickknacks, lined the walls. His home was comfortable and masculine, and it smelled like him—hot oil and incense, sandalwood and cedar.

Owen wandered into his kitchen, opened a cabinet, and took down a pair of glass tumblers. "Whenever I visited my dad's parents as a kid, my grandmother would make *musakhan*. It was my favorite." He opened his freezer door and scooped ice into glasses before filling them with water from a pitcher in the refrigerator. "I hope you're hungry."

He set a full tumbler on the counter next to me, turned back to the refrigerator, and retrieved a packet of raw chicken. From a small closet pantry, he selected an onion, a bottle of olive oil, several spice containers, and a bag of round flatbreads. He piled his items on the counter and pulled out a pan from a cabinet beside the stove.

"Can I do anything to help?" I asked.

"Nope." He pointed at a stool at his kitchen island, and I sat, watching him move around with ease and familiarity. "It won't take long. I've got it under control."

"He cooks, he builds cabinets, he rescues the sheriff from desperate criminals. Is there anything Owen Amir *can't* do?"

He paused, his dimple flashing. "I'm sure, if you try hard enough, you'll think of something."

He lit one burner on his stovetop, and a ring of flame flared to life. After setting his pan in place, he drizzled in a generous portion of olive oil. While it warmed, he chopped the onion.

"Did your grandmother teach you to cook?" I asked.

"Yes." He added the onion to his pan, sending up a plume of steam and an enticing sizzle. "She did, and so did my dad. He loves cooking."

"You don't talk about your family much."

"I guess it's because I haven't been home much over the last few years." He slit open a pair of chicken breasts, rubbed salt and pepper over them, and let them sit while he stirred the onions. "But I call them whenever I can. My *sitto* loves emailing me. She's obsessed with funny cat videos." He snorted. "She doesn't even *like* cats."

"Your sitto?" I'd heard him use the word before.

"My grandmother."

"Are you fluent in Arabic?"

He nodded. "My father insisted Rami and I know it well enough to talk to our overseas family. I spent a lot of summers with my grandparents, and my grandmother has never had a very good grasp of English."

"Is your ring a family heirloom, by chance?" I pointed at the signet ring he always wore on his left middle finger. I'd wondered about its significance from the first day I'd met him but had never found an appropriate time to bring it up. Its age and tarnish suggested he wore it more out of sentimentality than fashion. "I never see you without it." I raised his hand, studying his ring.

"It's been in my family for generations. It's kind of superstitious, but everyone believes it's a lucky charm. My uncle wore it when he went to Iraq. Then he gave it to me when I went on my first deployment."

"Tell me about the etching on it. It looks like a Star of David, but you're not Jewish."

He glanced at the ring again and nodded. "It's actually called the Seal of Solomon, but since Solomon was David's son, I'm sure the similarity isn't a coincidence."

"Maybe it isn't superstition. You seem to have had some good fortune in your life."

"Yes," he said, suddenly serious. "You're the proof."

As the evening progressed, our conversation flowed like a slow and easy river. Owen plated his concoction of spiced onions, flatbread, chicken, and sliced almonds and sat down beside me before passing me a knife and fork.

I cut into the chicken, forked up a bite-sized piece, and sniffed. "Tell me what I'm smelling. What are the red flakes?"

"Sumac. It gives it a kind of tart flavor, like lemon. There's also cardamom and saffron."

"Cardamom. I was wondering why it smelled a little like Christmas cookies." The herbs blended into a complex, savory flavor that was foreign yet familiar. It wasn't macaroni and cheese or mashed potatoes and gravy, but I got the same comforting sensation from eating it. "Unbelievable," I said around a mouthful.

"You like it?" He held his fork poised over his plate, his gaze intent. My opinion seemed to matter a great deal to him.

"I think it might be my new favorite thing." I frowned. "The onions aren't the best for my breath, though."

He stole a quick kiss. "Hmm. You taste sweet to me."

Resisting the urge to lick my plate, I scraped up the last bite and savored it as Owen collected dirty dishes and arranged them in the dishwasher. Although he had refused to let me help with the cleanup, he didn't resist when I offered to make coffee.

I poured him a cup but clicked my tongue.

"What?" he asked, accepting his mug.

"I forgot the cookies."

He wrapped a hand around my hip and leaned close. "You're still hungry?"

A brazen impulse surged through me. I met his gaze and lowered my voice. "Yes. But not for food."

His breath caught. Interest sparked in his eyes. "You started a fire when you showed up at my warehouse, telling me you wanted me and asking for second chances. Now you're throwing more fuel on it? You like to live dangerously, Erika Albemarle."

"No." I set down my coffee mug and wandered into the living room, studying my surroundings again. Rough-sawn lumber paneled the walls. Plain calico curtains framed a pair of windows, one facing the porch, the other looking out over the hillside and, presumably, the pond below. A memory of our previous swim flashed through my mind, and the heat simmering in my stomach rose into my cheeks. "I'm just tired of being afraid."

Soundlessly, Owen stepped behind me. "You're not the only one, ya albi." His hands, hot through my shirt's thin cotton, slid around my waist. He pressed a flat palm to my stomach and stroked me from navel to collarbone, pulling me against him. "You're afraid of staying. I'm afraid of leaving. I'm afraid of the things I can't control, and you're afraid of heartbreak." Combing my hair aside, he bent and pressed his lips to my neck. My eyes slipped closed. "When I'm with you, I forget all of that. I'd consume you completely if I could. But remember..." he said, almost a whisper. "*You* get to set the pace."

As if Owen had pulled the trigger on a starter's pistol, I turned in his arms and rocked up on my tiptoes, bringing my mouth to his. Uttering a groan, he wrapped himself around me. He opened to me, and my tongue flicked against his, teasing, tasting. Honey sweetness, red pepper heat, fire, and smoke blended into a flavor that was exclusively his.

My previous inspection of his house had revealed two doorways leading from the main room. Presumably, one went to his bedroom. I tugged free from his grip, grabbed his hand, and pulled him behind me. A bold move, perhaps, but I'd made up my mind, and I was committed to finishing what I'd started when I'd walked through his front door. Chuckling, he scooped me up and toed open the door. He carried me into a dark room, and I yelped when he tossed me, but I landed in a mound of softness—linens and pillows and a downy mattress.

A lamp flickered on beside me, filling the space with soft yellow light. Out of respect for his clean bed linens, I sat up and tugged off my Chucks. Barefooted, I folded my legs beneath me and examined his room with quiet awe, as though it were a sacred place. Maybe it was—I planned to worship him thoroughly before the night was over.

His quarters were sparse, a few dark pieces of furniture and a bed big enough to hold a large family, mounded with pillows and an indigo quilt embroidered in gold and silver threads. His scent was intense here. I closed my eyes, breathing him in like an addict inhaling her favorite drug.

"Rikki, look at me."

My eyes popped open and locked onto his dark, smoldering gaze that left me feeling, again, as if we were the only two people in the world. Brilliant blue sparks flickered, and more things shown in his eyes than simple desire, but I wouldn't ask him to name his emotions. *Let him show me, not tell me.*

His smoky scent intensified, and his shadow seemed larger than it should've been. In the past, those shadows had disturbed me, but now I accepted his mysteries without doubt—they were simply another element that made him unique and extraordinary. He kicked off his boots and hooked a finger in his shirt hem. I rocketed up on my knees. "Wait."

He froze, his head tilted in an inquisitive pose.

With a trembling hand, I beckoned him closer. He complied, cracking a wry grin. I reached for him, pushing his hand away from his shirt hem. "Let me." My voice wavered, but his smile widened, turning him into an alluring imp—a satyr anticipating his Bacchanalian rites.

"Eager thing," he rasped, nipping my ear.

I smoothed my hands beneath his shirt, over the ridges of his stomach, along the sleek planes of his chest, his skin like golden charmeuse warmed in the sun. When I reached his shoulders, he raised his arms, and I tugged his shirt over his head, ruffling his hair in the process. A pale-pink line underscored his ribs, the only remaining evidence of the wound he'd suffered. It had healed too fast, too clean, but I wasn't in the mood to question it.

He held himself still as I inspected his skin. "What are you thinking?" he asked.

"I don't understand everything about you, Owen, but until you prove me wrong, I think the universe may be giving me a chance to have someone in my life who's a little less... *fragile*."

I bent and kissed his scar. In the past, he had spoken boldly, voicing the intimate things he wanted to do to me. While I had found the courage to touch him like this, I didn't have the nerve to confess how much I wanted him, how badly I needed to feel his hands, his mouth, his body.

Maybe he'd read my wishes in my eyes because he tugged the elastic tie from my hair and combed his fingers through my braid until my curls sprang free. He paused to kiss me before pulling my shirt over my head. With a snap, he flicked the clasp on my bra and slipped it off, leaving us skin to skin, my paleness pressed against his bronze heat. The contrast was breathtaking. *He* was breathtaking, like some powerful being barely hanging onto his control—a bull pawing at the ground, a cobra coiling to strike.

Something wild lived in him, waiting for the opportunity to break loose.

Owen bit his lip, and his eyes darkened as his gaze slipped over me. I was exposed and vulnerable, but... I wasn't afraid. There was no room for it—I was too filled with want and need to be frightened. I pressed a hand to his chest over his heart, and its rhythm matched my own racing pulse.

Cupping my breast, he drew a thumb over its swell, and I wondered if I would blister from his hot touch. "I've tried a thousand times, trying to picture this moment, but my imagination is pathetic, apparently. Nothing I imagined compares to this." His thumb curved over my breast again. "I didn't know skin could be so soft."

I curled my arms around his neck and leaned into his hard chest, which was corded with muscle. "You're no choir boy. I'm not the first woman you've ever touched."

His dimple appeared when he smiled. "Maybe not, but you're certainly the finest, finer than I deserve. But I'm selfish. I don't think I could ever willingly walk away from you."

He knotted his fingers into the curls hanging down my back. "God knows no one else has had hair like yours. With your skin, it's like opals and garnets. You'd be almost too perfect to touch if it weren't for the freckles..." He kissed my shoulder. "Here." Cupping my chin, he brushed his lips over the bridge of my nose. "And here." His hands slid to my knees, and he yanked, tugging my legs around his waist. "Bet I'll find more if I look in the right places."

He shifted, setting his knee on the edge of the bed, and leaned until gravity took over and pulled us down. He held himself over me, studying, touching, dragging fingers from my collarbone over my breast, down my ribs, stopping at the top of my shorts. He followed the same path again but with his lips. Anticipation throbbed through me, painful in its intensity. Blood roared in my ears.

His touch would be the only relief for my aching, but I refused to rush him.

"Probably no freckles down there," I rasped as his finger traced under my waistband. "Doesn't get much sunlight."

He chuckled. "No nude beaches in your past?"

"I'm not quite that daring, sorry."

"I don't believe you. I'll have to see for myself." He pulled at my cutoffs, slipping the button and zipper loose. I raised my hips, and in a couple of swift tugs, he had rendered me bare beneath him. He shook his head as he studied me, his fingers tracing my hipbones. "Guess you were right, not a single freckle."

I fingered the waistband of his jeans. "I'm ahead of you, now. Time to catch up, don't you think?"

"You're sure?"

I couldn't blame him for asking again after all the times I'd run away when things got tense. But not this time. "Never been surer."

He grinned and rolled aside, leaving me long enough to strip off what remained of his own clothes. The foil wrapper of his condom packet glinted in the light. He returned and slipped between my legs. Reverently, he bowed his head and brushed his knuckles over my cheekbone. "*El kamar helou wa inta ahhla.*"

I searched his face for a clue, but his expression was inscrutable. "I hope you said something nice."

"I said you're beautiful."

My heart surged into my throat. *No going back now. No more running. The only way from here is forward.*

Owen shifted, pressed himself against me, hard and hot, and I welcomed him in. Lingering touches and slow kisses took the place of talking as, together, we made the first tentative moves, establishing a rhythm, progressing in a steady ascent toward a high-rising peak. As the summit neared, I gave in to frenzy, like embers swirling inside a blistering firestorm.

He'd said when I walked through his door that he would belong to me, but now I belonged to him too.

He'd wanted to consume me. I realized I wanted to be consumed.

I'd set the pace and gotten lost in him and didn't care if I found my way back out. I was with him, he was with me, and we were both exactly where we were supposed to be.

I UNDERSTOOD OWEN'S fascination with hearing his name cried out in an ecstatic moan. By the end of the night, my name had become his canticle, his holy chant. Maybe I wasn't a goddess, but hearing him supplicate to me had certainly made me feel powerful, as though something more than blood coursed through my veins.

He lay beneath me, panting, his eyes still glazed. Anatomy had been one of my favorite subjects in school, and I enjoyed applying what I knew to his body. I dragged the tips of my nails up from his elegantly formed umbilicus, over finely wrought obliques, serratus anterior, and the chiseled plains of his pectoralis major.

When my fingers reached the divot between his collarbones, the fossa jugularis, he snatched my wrist. He rolled over and pinned me down. From the moment he'd brought me into his room, blue and gold sparks had filled his eyes. Those lights hadn't dimmed throughout our time together, and I met his electrifying gaze, boldly and unafraid. Otherworldly or not, he was beautiful, and somehow, he was mine.

"I wasn't expecting this when I moved here—finding someone like you," he said. "I wasn't supposed to find someone who makes me feel the things you make me feel. It wasn't part of the plan."

"I tried to give you an out, Owen." My lids fluttered closed when his lips touched my cheek. "More than once. Yet here you are."

His teeth tugged my earlobe. "And here *you* are, despite all your efforts to resist."

"I had made up my mind a long time ago to not let anyone get to me the way you have. You weren't part of my plan either. But I guess plans change."

He eased onto his side, snugged me against him, and pulled the covers over us. He turned out his bedside lamp, and darkness settled like a thick blanket. "Change isn't necessarily an ending." He nuzzled my neck. "You'll still leave for school at the end of summer the way you thought you would. But now you'll come home on the weekends more than you might have before. Now you'll make sure your apartment comes with a bed big enough for two."

With my ear pressed to his chest, I listened to his heartbeat. "You'll be busy getting the distillery going."

"You'll be busy taking classes and studying. Working, too, if I know you."

"How's this going to work?" I tightened my arms around his ribs. "How will we find time?"

"Time is subjective, really. It's all a matter of how you perceive it. If you think we don't have enough, we never will."

"You have *so* many facets." I smothered a snicker against his chest. "Distiller, carpenter, mechanic, soldier. Who knew you were a philosopher too?"

He tugged one of my curls but said nothing.

I shifted, stretching up to kiss him. "This is still only the beginning. I'll give you time, and someday you'll tell me your secrets."

Maybe in the morning light, under the glare of sunlight, my convictions would fade, my doubts would return, but as I fell asleep, listening to Owen's steady breathing, I believed every one of my words.

Chapter Twenty-Six
White Lightning

"WAKE UP, YA ALBI." Owen stood in the doorway, freshly showered, judging by his slick hair. Barefoot in jeans and T-shirt, he padded to the bed, bringing me a cup of coffee so hot that steam curled from its surface. I sat up, drawing the covers around me, and cleared the remnants of sleep from my eyes.

Taking the coffee from him, I inhaled its blessed aroma. "I didn't hear you get up."

"Do you always sleep like the dead?"

"No." I sipped, careful not to burn my tongue. "Almost never."

"I wouldn't have woken you up so early, but I've got to get back to the warehouse today. They're delivering the distilling tanks, and I need to be there." He gave me a mournful smile. "And you go back to work today, too, right?"

Peering into my coffee cup, I nodded. "I've got to swing by Mr. Huddle's stables and help him unload a hay delivery. Then I've got to head to the station. I'm scheduled for the next three days. Twelve-hour shifts."

He tucked a finger under my chin and raised my face, urging me to look at him. "When you get home, pack enough things so you can come back and stay here awhile, okay?"

Smiling, I blinked at him. "You're sure?"

"Didn't I prove how sure I was last night?" He pointed at a doorway in the corner of his room. "There's stuff in that bathroom if you want a shower before I take you home." His gaze shifted to the pile of clothes crumpled on the floor by his bed. He grinned and scratched the back of his neck. "I could give you a T-shirt and a pair of my gym shorts to wear until you get something from your house, I guess."

I had planned for a lot of possibilities last night but not for what I would do the morning after. Besides, no one would want to take a shower and then put on dirty clothes from the day before if they were presented with a better option. "Um, yes, please."

After he left me to finish my coffee and clean up, I slid out of the bed and tiptoed into a tidy, compact bathroom tiled in calming beiges and creams. A stack of white towels waited on a rack attached to the wall, much like a hotel bathroom. I found soaps in his walk-in shower and lathered up under a warm spray. The lather smelled masculine—cedar and sandalwood—but nothing about it explained his typical smoky aroma. Although I didn't understand it, and it made me uneasy when I thought about it too much, the smoke seemed to be a part of him as much as his sweat and blood. After drying off, I returned to his room and found he had left me a plain white T-shirt and a pair of gym shorts.

I padded barefoot into the kitchen and found him drinking coffee and studying his laptop. He glanced at me and chuckled. "You look like the Incredible Shrinking Woman in those."

I plucked at the T-shirt, which fit me like a dress. "But I guess it's better than nothing."

"Oh, I don't know about that. You look pretty fantastic in nothing." He closed the cover on his laptop and drained the last of his coffee. After rinsing his cup in the sink, he pulled something from his pocket and held out his hand. A silver locket the size of a nickel hung on a slim chain dangling from his knuckles. "Before we go, I want to give you something."

He let the chain slip from his fingers to pool in my palm. The silver was warm from his touch, and the patina on the necklace suggested it was old. "What is it?"

Owen plucked the necklace from my hand and pushed my hair off my neck. "It's a *ta'wiz*. A charm. I want you to promise to always wear it, okay?"

When he finished fastening the chain around my neck, I fingered the locket. "What's inside it?"

"A paper inscribed with a prayer from the Qur'an for warding off evil."

"Are you sure it's okay if I wear it? I don't want to do anything disrespectful."

"Just be careful with it. It's older than it looks." He shrugged. "I know it sounds superstitious, but my sitto sent it to me when I told her about you."

My eyebrows arched high. "You told your grandmother about me?"

Nodding, he bit his lip and avoided my eyes. "She wanted you to have it."

"Okay." I couldn't quite decide how I felt about him discussing me with his family, but the warm flutter in my chest suggested I liked the idea. "I'll wear it."

He met my gaze, his expression hardening. "Promise me."

His sudden seriousness was uncharacteristic and a little troubling, but I nodded and stroked the charm again. "I promise."

Grabbing his keys from the counter, he jerked his chin toward the kitchen door, and I followed him to the truck. Dust kicked up behind us as we rolled away from his cabin. It was a warm, balmy morning, so Owen rolled down the windows. I closed my eyes, turned up the radio, humming along with George Jones, and drank up the sunshine. A few moments from my life were sealed into my memory like tattoos, impermeable, forever a part of me. I had a feeling the previous night would become one of those forever memories. Riding in the truck with Owen, with wind that smelled of green growing things and sun bathing us in golden warmth, might become another.

With little traffic to interfere or slow us down, we made a quick trip across the county from his house to mine. In my driveway, Dolly sat alone—my mom's car was gone. I wondered what she'd thought about the events from the day before. When I'd left her in Toni's hands at Greer's house, she hadn't seemed aware that Owen had played a role in her rescue, and I'd try to make sure she remained blissfully ignorant.

Owen parked the Tacoma and followed me inside. In my house's small foyer, he wrapped his arms around me and held me close. "I'm not ready to let you go yet. Last night wasn't enough." He kissed the pulse in my neck. "Not even close."

Although I should have been bankrupt after the energy I'd exerted the night before, need and desire buzzed in me as though my bones were electrical wires. My heart beat a rapid, stuttering rhythm against my ribs. "I've still got an hour before I have to be at the station, and my mom's at work," I said.

Owen groaned, slanted his mouth over mine, and walked me backward until I came up hard against the wall behind me. Without a word, he slid down my shorts. I kicked them aside and tugged his jeans around his hips.

His breath was hot in my ear. "I didn't bring anything—"

"I've been on birth control since I was sixteen. It's okay."

His fingers gripped me, lifting me, wrapping my legs around him as he rocked into me. I threw back my head and exhaled a breathy scream.

"I like that song," he growled in my ear. "Sing it again."

Another deep stroke and I crooned a long, sad note—a mournful cry, grieving the fact that all too soon, our time together would end.

Forget responsibilities and pragmatism. Who needs the real world, anyway?

Our coupling was quick and fierce and over almost as soon as it had begun, but I had a feeling this would be the memory I'd play on repeat most often throughout the long day before me.

"*Ana bahebak*, Rikki," Owen said, panting against my neck, still holding me against the wall.

I stroked his back, waiting for the stars to fade from my eyes. "What does that mean?"

"Ask me tonight. If you really want to know, ask me later tonight, and I'll tell you."

WHEN I PULLED INTO the EMS station's parking lot, an older Ford Crown Victoria adorned with the Twain County Sheriff's logo sat in a spot near the entrance. I parked Dolly beside the patrol car, turned off my engine, and sat for a few moments, gathering my composure. There was no mistaking which member of the sheriff's department had decided to pay me a visit.

I couldn't remember the last time, if ever, my mother had been to the EMS station, and her unexpected appearance stirred cold currents of worry in my stomach. I had a feeling she hadn't stopped by for a mother-daughter chat. Gritting my teeth, I strode through the station's front door with my head held high and my defenses raised.

I found my mom sitting in an old recliner in the employee lounge, holding her hat in her lap, keeping company with Roberto and Bonnie Jo Stuckey, their eyes all glued to *The Price Is Right* on the big-screen TV. I frowned at her as I folded my arms across my chest. "To what do I owe the honor, Sheriff?"

She flinched, apparently so engrossed in the Plinko game she hadn't noticed my entrance. Wearing a dour expression, she rose from her seat and held her hat over her chest as if preparing to make a vow. "Rikki. I need to talk to you."

"I figured out that much on my own."

She glanced at Roberto and Bonnie Jo, who were both urging the Plinko chip to bounce closer to the big-dollar prize. "Is there somewhere more private?"

"In the office. Follow me."

Mom closed the office door while I took a seat at the desk. She plopped into a visitor's chair, smoothed down her uniform shirt, and set her hat in her lap. "I'll get straight to the point. After all the hubbub yesterday—oh, your paramedic gave me a clean bill of health by the way." She gave me an annoyed grimace, apparently irritated that I'd subjected her to unnecessary medical poking and prodding. "I went back to my office to write my report, and while I was reviewing the details, I realized I'd watched you drive off in a black Toyota Tacoma." She sniffed. "Last I recalled, neither of us owned a truck like that, nor do any of your friends. Who does it belong to?"

I cursed a string of foul language in my head. "Whose do you think it was?"

"Hmm," she grunted, narrowing her eyes. "Don't play coy with me. I'm not here as your mother. I'm here as the sheriff, and this is part of my official investigation into yesterday's events."

"What investigation?" I fisted my fingers together on the desktop and leaned on my elbows. "Greer held you hostage. Some freak event happened, and you lucked out and got away."

"Freak of nature, indeed." She scowled and scratched her jaw. "That truck belongs to your boyfriend, doesn't it?"

"Boyfriend?" I arched an eyebrow. "You mean, Owen?"

She waggled her fingers at me and grumped. "That young man who's been sniffing around your heels. Owen Amir. He's opening the distillery in the old furniture warehouse."

"If you already know who he is, then you already know if he owns a black Toyota Tacoma or not."

Leaning forward in her seat, she gave me her best bad-cop glower. "The DMV records don't reflect him owning such a truck, but Rose Heinlein says she saw the two of you together yesterday evening and that you left the diner in a black pickup after she told you what the dispatcher said."

"So, you already know the answer to your question." Her inquiry had wound me tightly, as if I were a spring and needed to release some tension. I stood, pushed back my chair, and paced the room. "Why are you bugging me about it?"

"Why are you protecting him?" Mom stood, set her hat on the desk, and folded her arms over her chest, watching me walk circles like a caged tiger. "What's he hiding?"

"He had nothing to do with what happened yesterday. He doesn't need to be in your report."

"I'll be the one who decides that, Rikki."

"He was inside the truck the whole time."

"Are you sure about that?"

I froze midstride and met her icy stare. "Why wouldn't I be?"

"Because." My mom looked away and hunched her shoulders. She lowered her voice. "I could swear I saw him inside that house."

My insides turned to ice. No. Mom couldn't know that for sure. And she sure as hell couldn't put Owen in her report and endanger his anonymity. "That's ridiculous."

Her jaw clenched, her nostrils flaring. "The explosion—or whatever it was—nearly knocked me out. My ears were ringing, and my head was spinning, but someone helped me get outside. At the time, I was too dazed and disoriented to realize it, but the more I think about it, the more I keep seeing a flash of memory. There was a tall, dark figure leading me out."

"You think it was Owen?" I harrumphed and shoved my hand on my hip. "Maybe you just want to think it was him. Maybe your imagination is making things up to make sense out of something that was just a fluke. A lucky break. A miracle."

Mom's gaze swung back to me. Her eyes were pleading, her mouth a thin, grim slash surrounded by lines of strain and distress. Obviously, she was desperate to make sense of the impossible. I almost felt bad enough to confess what I knew. Almost. "He's the only one unaccounted for," she said.

I shook my head and leaned against the cinder-block wall beside me. "Owen was *in* the truck, Mom. That's all I can tell you." I scrubbed my hands over my face. "I don't know what you think you saw—shock can do crazy things to a person. But whatever happened in that house... Owen had nothing to do with it."

She huffed, reached for her hat, and tugged it on. "I'm on my way over to his place now—the distillery. I wonder if his story will match yours."

I crossed the room and opened the door, a not-so-subtle hint that I was more than ready for her to go. I planned to text Owen and warn him about the coming inquisition as soon as she left the station. If the two of us stuck to our story, surely my mother would have to relent. "Mom, you made it out safe and alive. Isn't that all that matters?"

Her hazel gaze locked on mine as she stopped in the office doorway. "Maybe it is. Maybe it isn't. I won't know until all my questions are answered, though."

My concern for maintaining Owen's anonymity had made me react harshly to my mom's interrogation, but I could have lost her if things had gone badly at Greer's house. Realizing that, I regretted being so cold. "I'm glad you're okay, Mom."

She cuffed me under my chin as she squeezed by me. "I can take a lickin' and keep on tickin.'"

"Don't be too hard on Owen. I like him. Try not to scare him off, okay?"

She sauntered down the hallway toward the exit but flicked a smile over her shoulder. "What kind of mom would I be if I didn't give my daughter's boyfriend a hard time?"

"Just promise to keep your gun in your holster at least." I paused in the hallway, watching her leave. The sunlight streaming through the exit door outlined her, drawing her in a dark silhouette, turning her into a mythological hero, some Athena-like warrior goddess. But I knew what lay beneath her hard jaw and stubborn exterior, and it wasn't all grit and steel.

I wasn't the only one in our house who still carried scars.

Chapter Twenty-Seven
Monster

AFTER A COUPLE OF HOURS of cleaning Jack Huddle's stables then working a twelve-hour shift for the EMS, I was exhausted, and my brain felt like a fuzzy ball of cotton. I should have been going home and getting in bed, but as the saying went, I could rest when I was dead. If I had to choose between sleep and Owen, my choice was easy. I pulled into Moon Runner's lot and parked next to Owen's Ducati. Luke's green Ford occupied a parking place on the other side. Mina had called everyone and asked us to meet at Moon Runners for dinner. I hoped she was thinking of takeout because I was too tired to go anywhere else.

Construction lights lit the warehouse's interior and reflected on newly installed copper distilling tanks hunkering in the rear of the warehouse. They glowed warmly, throwing off a pinkish-gold gleam. When Owen had described them before, I'd failed to appreciate how lovely they could be. I'd imagined industrial pipes and sterile barrels with nozzles and gauges, but these tanks were works of art—sculptures worthy of a gallery. "They're beautiful," I said as Owen joined me. "Who knew?"

"*I* knew," he said, buffing his knuckles on his shirt. "I've had a vision for this place from the start. There's more to me than good looks and hot sex, you know."

I snorted. He ignored my mockery and tugged my elbow, drawing me away from the tanks, maneuvering me toward the bar, where Luke and Mina hovered over a menu from the Panda Garden.

"Nice of you to show up." Luke shot me a wry grin. "We're starving."

"You didn't have to wait," I said. "You could have ordered for me. I'll eat anything."

"Don't let him fool you," Mina said. "We only got here, like, two minutes before you did."

Luke gritted his teeth, making a pained expression. "Two minutes of nearly starving to death."

Owen opened a cooler sitting at the foot of the bar and popped the lids on two bottles of beer for Luke and Mina. "How about you, Rikki?"

"Water, if you have it."

He grabbed two bottles, handing one to me.

After calling in our order, Mina caught my eye and gave a pointed look to Owen, who was distracted, looking at pictures of something on Luke's phone. She waggled her eyebrows. I understood what she was asking with her dramatic expressions. I nodded toward the rear of the warehouse, where the bathrooms were located.

Grinning, Mina followed me. After closing the bathroom door behind us, she grabbed my shoulder and squeezed. "Tell me everything."

"I won't tell you *everything*," I said. "Some details are just between Owen and me."

She tugged my hands between hers and held them to her chest. "So, you're saying there *are* details. Hot, naked details?"

Nodding, I grinned. "Lots of details."

She bounced on her toes. "You're happy?"

"I am. More than I thought I could be."

"Do you love him?"

I looked away as a blush scalded my cheeks. "I don't know. Maybe?"

She furrowed her brows. "Maybe?"

"Yes?" I covered my eyes as if I could hide from the truth. It was an ingrained response, avoiding my emotions, especially the strong ones. I'd come a long way in the last few weeks, but admitting my feelings still required a concerted effort. But I'd known the night before, when I'd been lost among the stars in his eyes. "Yes. I do."

"Does he know?" She tugged my hands away from my face.

"Not in so many words. But we're getting there. I'm staying with him again tonight. If the time is right, I'll tell him."

"Again?" She grinned. "Staying with him is going to be a regular habit?"

"Maybe." I returned her smile. "Probably."

Mina's phone buzzed. She pulled it from her pocket and glanced at the screen. "Delivery guy says he's here, but he's not sure he's in the right place." She looked up at me and snickered. "He's freaked about making a delivery to an old warehouse in the middle of the night."

Following her out of the bathroom, I leaned close and whispered. "How about you and Luke? Any hot, naked details of your own?"

She flicked a single eyebrow. "Maybe a few."

Mina skipped across the warehouse and hurried into the parking lot, where she consoled the delivery boy and assured him he was in the right place and that no one was playing a prank on him.

Owen leaned against the bar and crooked his finger at me. Smiling, I snuggled up close to him as he wrapped his arms around me.

"How was work?" he asked.

"Uneventful, which is mostly a good thing, except it can make for a long day. But at least it means nobody died."

He nuzzled my ear and sniffed. "You smell like disinfectant."

"We cleaned the rig. It picks up all sorts of nasty bugs on the job. Don't want to pass them on to the patients."

He squeezed me tighter. "You call me Superman, but you're the real superhero around here."

His compliment warmed me from the tips of my toes to the roots of my hair. "Not even close. I still have a lot to learn. But maybe you and I can form our own local Justice League." I smoothed a loose lock of dark hair from his brow and marveled at having the privilege to touch him like this. Touching him as much as I wanted. I wondered whether that was something I'd ever get used to. "We're like Batman and Robin. The people of Evansville are lucky to have us."

He tilted my chin up and pressed a gentle to kiss my lips. "I think..." He lowered his voice. "I think we're lucky to have each other."

Something about his tone and tenderness triggered a memory from earlier in the day. "You said something to me this morning in Arabic. Ana... something."

He paused and seemed to tense. "*Ana bahebak.*"

"That was it. You said if I wanted to know what it meant, that I should ask you tonight."

"Are you saying you want to know?"

I met Owen's dark stare, which seemed to reveal the depths of his heart, and I nodded. "I want to know."

"Once it's said, there's no unspeaking it. No taking it back."

My heart throbbed, swollen and heavy, sending warmth out with each pulse. Of all the things I'd done so far, of all the crazy impossibilities that had happened since his arrival, nothing scared me more than this moment. And yet I wanted it more than anything. Swallowing, I nodded again. "Tell me."

Owen cupped my face and stroked a thumb over my cheek. Blue sparks flared in his eyes. "*Ana bahebak*, Rikki. It means 'I love you.'"

Light and warmth surged through my veins as if the sun had risen inside me and starlight blazed in each nerve ending. But before I could form a response, before I could tell Owen I felt the same way, the warehouse's main entrance flew open, the door hitting the wall with a bang.

I jumped at the sound and inhaled a quick gasp. Owen jerked away and spun around, shoving me behind him. I peered around his shoulder and watched Mina step through the doorway. Her hands were empty, no Chinese takeout bags, and she stared ahead, blank eyed, as she entered the room.

"Mina?" Luke asked, stepping toward her.

Her head jerked around, and she threw up a hand. As if she'd slapped him, Luke flew back, crashing against the bar. Dazed, he slumped to the floor.

"Luke!" I rushed to his side and checked for a pulse. His heartbeat fluttered faintly, and his breath was shallow, but he was alive. Keeping my attention half on him and half on the impossible scene unfolding before me, I checked him for injuries.

Mina turned her gaze on Owen and gave him the same empty stare. There was no light in her eyes. *No soul.*

My insides turned to ice.

Run, said a scared little voice in my head. *Run, run, as fast as you can.*

"Mina, what are you doing?" I asked.

"Son of Suleiman." Her voice was dull and flat. Her blank eyes were focused on Owen as if the rest of us didn't exist. "I've been looking for you for a long time."

Lights flickered, and the shadows around Owen thickened. His smoky scent bloomed strong and hot. "Mina, what's going on?"

She chuckled coldly. "I've had many names, but I don't think Mina suits me." She stalked closer and stopped several feet away, crossing her arms over her narrow chest. She had always been slight and fine boned, but now her presence seemed as substantial and ancient as the surrounding mountains. "For the time being, why don't you call me Al-Mudhib?"

Owen tensed, his hands fisting at his sides. He glanced at me, and blue sparks were raining like a comet storm in his eyes. "It's not Mina."

"What do you mean, 'not Mina'?" I gaped at him. I waved my hand at her as if to say, *Look, clearly, it's Mina.* "Are you *crazy*?"

Beside me, Luke moaned and shifted. I stroked his hair from his brow and held him close, searching my mind for something I could do to help him.

"How did you find me, Al-Mudhib?" Owen's attention shifted back to Mina. Despite accepting that Owen had revealed some uncanny things to me in the past, my mind struggled to believe what my eyes were showing me. There stood my best friend, but... *not.* Reality was splintering like a pane of glass in a hailstorm.

Mina cracked a wry smile that made me feel only coldness and trepidation. "You've done a good job keeping the shadows wrapped around you—until yesterday. We have eyes everywhere. When you do things to draw attention to yourself, the humans aren't the only ones who notice."

Humans? Yesterday? Is she talking about Owen saving my mom? We had been so careful. But not careful enough, apparently. In Chapel Hill, Owen had told me there were powerful forces, circles of influence operating in the shadows, who kept their fingers on the pulse of the world. When he'd said it, I'd underestimated the meaning of his words.

But how does Mina know about any of that? What's happening to her? This is insane. She and I were just in the bathroom, giggling about sex and love.

"What do you want?" Owen asked. "Why are you here?"

Luke grunted. He was awake but remained slumped on the floor next to me. He'd pinned his eyes on Mina and stared at her as though the devil himself had walked into the room. Perhaps he had. "Mina?" he croaked. "Baby? What's happened to you?"

She ignored him and raised a finger, pointing at Owen. "I want the ring, of course. Give it to me, and I'll leave peacefully. Everyone walks away unharmed. This is my promise to you."

What ring? Owen's lucky charm? He'd said it was a family heirloom, but evidently, it was more than that. Mina had called Owen "Son of Suleiman," and the emblem on his ring was called the Seal of Solomon, but I didn't know what any of it meant. Or how the hell she had known about it. My head spun with confusion until I was dizzy and lightheaded.

Although he was already tense, Owen held himself even tighter, like a snake coiling for a strike. "You know I can't do that."

"Then the blame for whatever happens next is solely yours." Mina shifted, dropping her arms, spreading her feet. Like air pressure falling before the start of a storm, the atmosphere in the room forecast an inevitable fight.

"Mina... Owen... *please,*" I said. "Both of you, stop it. You're scaring me." Nothing made sense, and fear burned like acid in every nerve ending, but it would be a cold day on the face of the sun before I'd leave my friends. Blame my big, stupid ego.

"This is between you and me, Al-Mudhib," Owen said. "Let the others leave."

"Surrender the ring," Mina said, "and be spared. I won't offer mercy a third time."

Starting low and dim, a fire, like a snake, slithered around the baseboards and crawled up the walls. The flames reflected in Mina's eyes, glowing, pulsing. Heat bloomed through the open space, sudden and scalding, reminding me of the attack in Chapel Hill that had left melted pavement and burn marks on Owen's skin. Where had this fire come from? Were these Owen's strange abilities at play?

Owen's voice was an almost animalistic growl when he replied. "If I take this ring off, we're *all* dead. You'll never let us out of here alive." He looked at me once, and his face was a mask of torment.

"I'm sorry, Rikki. I'm so, *so* sorry." The words were an apology, but they sounded more like a eulogy. Like death, grief, and goodbyes.

Stalking toward Mina, he gritted his teeth, and a bloom of black plumes burst from his skin, engulfing him completely. Hopelessly, I reached for him, clawing the thin air as though I could catch one of his shadows and draw him back. "Owen, no. Whatever you're doing... *don't*."

His darkness expanded, billowing like smoke, forming the shape of a massive beast, a demon so huge and opaque he devoured the light—a monster made of cold rage and black holes.

Teeth, fangs, horns, and claws all as dark as the pits of hell.

He roared, and the walls shook. The windows rattled.

Mina gasped, and fire erupted around her so bright and blinding I couldn't look at her.

Only the day before, Owen had risked himself to save my mother, so I couldn't understand why he wasn't playing the hero now. I glanced overhead at the sprinklers, but they remained rusted and disappointingly dry. The beast's black shadows twined with the flames, and they danced an infernal waltz. "Owen," I pleaded at him. "*Please.*"

Please what? Please save us? Please stop scaring me and help Mina? Please wake me up from this horrible dream and tell me none of it's real?

Struggling to his knees, Luke knelt beside me. "Go, Rikki. You've got to get out of here."

"Like hell. I'm not leaving Mina."

Flames exploded outward, circling the room, racing to block all escapes. Powerful and searing, the blaze guzzled air and moisture like a thirsty beast. Luke and I leaned into each other, supporting each other. Sweat dripped into my eyes as I threw my arm up to protect my face from the heat. The scent of burning hair filled my nose. *The fire's too big. Too wild. We'll never make it out. None of us are going to walk away.*

In the shadow beast's eyes, fury burned like Saint Elmo's electric-blue fire. I'd seen hints of that creature inside Owen before, but never like this, wild and unfettered. Ferocious, angry, and terrifying.

Fear, icy and cold, clamped frigid teeth around my heart and sank its fangs in deep.

"Owen!" I yelled again, but the beast's roar drowned out my voice. Despite my terror, despite the flames and the heat, I let go of Luke and crawled toward the demon, forcing myself to approach his ever-expanding darkness. If Owen were somewhere in those shadows, I had to reach him, had to beg him to stop this, save us, whatever it took. *"Owen."*

My fingers brushed his darkness, and it was like touching the heart of a glacier—a cold so brutal and devastating I lost myself in it.

Like a tornado, blackness churned through my vision, relieved only by icy, sapphire stars—no warmth, no compassion, no mercy in those cold pinpoints of light. Whatever humanity Owen had possessed was gone, and whatever remnants of reality I'd been clinging to shattered into dust and blew away.

"Stay away from me," Mina shrieked at the dark beast that had been Owen. "Stop!"

"Owen, *please*," I begged. "It's Mina." *It is, isn't it? Isn't that my best friend, pleading for her life?* "Please don't hurt her."

The blue stars around me exploded, bright as a nuclear bomb. I squeezed my eyes shut and buried my face in my hands, but still my eyes burned. Luke threw his arms around me and held me while the darkness tore at us and howled in our ears.

Mina screamed as though she were being eaten alive.

Crushing blackness, like a tidal wave, crashed down and rose around me like a flood.

I sank, falling into the eternal depths, until my breath faded, and I drowned.

Chapter Twenty-Eight
Silent All These Years

PRESENTLY...

I set my grocery bags on the kitchen counter and unpacked everything: cube steaks, flour, Crisco, eggs, milk, potatoes. All the ingredients required to make a batch of mashed potatoes and chicken-fried steak, my mom's favorite. By the time my mom sauntered into the kitchen, I was dropping battered steaks in a pan of hot oil.

Her boots scuffled over the worn linoleum, her nostrils flaring as she scented the air. "You weren't kidding, were you?" she asked.

"'Bout what?" I lined a plate with paper towels for draining the steaks after they'd finished frying.

She set her hat on the counter and shrugged off her uniform coat. "About making dinner." She shuffled into the hallway and hung her hat and jacket on the rack by the front door.

When my water bubbled, I raked in a pile of peeled and chopped potatoes. In another pot on the back of the stove, field peas simmered in a ham hock broth. I'd ask my heart and arteries for forgiveness later, but for tonight, we would feast.

"I heard you made the rounds through town today." She took down two glasses from a cabinet and filled them with ice.

I huffed. "This town gossips too much."

She opened the fridge and reached for the tea pitcher. "And you're surprised?"

"No." I checked the underside of my steaks and decided they needed to cook another minute before flipping. "Maybe I hoped they'd make an exception for me this one time."

"Are you kidding?" She filled the glasses, set them on the kitchen island, and returned the pitcher to the fridge. "You showing up back here is the most exciting thing to happen since, well..."

I waited to see if she'd finish her sentence, but she didn't. I studied her from the corner of my eye and interpreted the meaning behind her puckered brow and downturned lips. "Since the fire at Moon Runners?"

As if my words were a magic spell, a chill flooded the room. Mom's shoulders tensed. Her gaze flicked up to me, questioning. Never once over the past three years had I mentioned that night. Not since I woke up in a hospital bed to find my mom sitting beside me, her head hanging heavy in her hands, her clothes rumpled, the wrinkles on her face deeper and starker, as if she'd aged ten years in a matter of hours.

"Why do you think I'm back here, Mom?"

"Hmm. Had my suspicions but didn't want to push. Was afraid you'd run away again."

"I want to make amends for running out without an explanation, but you have to admit, you haven't been the easiest to approach."

She slumped on a stool at the kitchen island, her shoulders bowing in. "Easier to run from your feelings than face them, I guess. I didn't set the best example for you."

The steaks sizzled and popped when I turned them over. A tinge of black pepper and garlic flavored the air. "But now you suddenly want to talk?" I tried to keep my voice free from irony. "What's changed?"

"You coming back to town, I guess. It was a surprise, you showing up on the doorstep the way you did. It brought up a whole bunch of feelings I wasn't prepared to deal with. But I've thought about it all day and realized I'm the mother in this relationship. Maybe this is my chance to act like one for once."

A wave of guilt lapped against my heart, eliciting my sympathy. "I'm sorry for showing up unannounced. I guess that wasn't fair of me."

Mom sipped her iced tea. "Maybe not, but I haven't been totally fair to you over the years either. If I'd done better, maybe you wouldn't have felt the need to leave without a warning or to stay away for three years."

"You know where Chapel Hill is. It's not like you couldn't visit me."

"You didn't need me." Her gaze dropped to the countertop, and she peered into her tea glass. "And I guess I was afraid I was one of the problems you were running from."

I crossed the kitchen and leaned on the island, facing her. This was all going a bit easier than I'd anticipated, but time had a way of wearing away sharp edges. Maybe my mom and I weren't iron chains anymore, but perhaps we could be something else. Something more flexible. "I panicked," I said. "Fight or flight. I chose flight. I was always planning to leave Evansville but not like I did. Not in the middle of the night without saying goodbye. Not without ever coming back to visit or picking up the phone just to chat. I abandoned you and Rose and Luke, and y'all have every right to feel hurt and betrayed."

"I know a lot about survivor's guilt and PTSD, Rikki. More than you think. This line of work hasn't always been easy, and I've seen things that have made me want to run too. You don't have to explain it to me. I wanted to leave after your dad died. I guess a part of me *did* go away. I wasn't exactly here for you, uh, emotionally speaking."

I bit back a smile. "Someone been watching *Dr. Phil* lately?"

She blushed and ducked her head. "I almost lost you in that fire. Instead of Mina, it could have been you. I couldn't have survived it. Losing you would have killed me too."

A drop of condensation rolled down my tea glass. I caught it on my thumb and rubbed it between my fingers, considering my mother's grief. She wouldn't want me to make a fuss or offer consolation. She'd never needed coddling from me. "So, what do we do now?"

She looked up and pointed at the frying steaks. "Now we eat dinner. We go slow and appreciate being together."

I rounded the island and threw my arms around her. She wrapped me up in her embrace, and I inhaled her scent, baby powder and Ivory soap. We'd never said these things to each other before, not during the past three years and certainly not in the years after Dad's death.

"In the hospital, I was too overwhelmed, too shocked to talk. By the time I'd gathered my wits, the doctors were releasing me, and all I could think to do was grab my things and run to Chapel Hill as fast as I could. I didn't understand what had happened, and I couldn't deal with it, not with losing Mina..." And accepting that Owen was to blame.

To the rest of the world, the fire marshal, and the federal agents assisting with the investigation, the fire had looked like an accident, something about the gas lines being disturbed when the boilers for the distilling tanks were installed and the sprinklers not being up to code.

I knew better.

I knew the truth, or as much of the truth as anyone would probably ever know.

But no one would have believed me if I'd talked of a man turning into a demon made of shadows and darkness. In the years since leaving Evansville, I'd explored the details I'd gleaned from my last moments with Mina and Owen. With an almost obsessive devotion, I'd researched King Solomon, Suleiman in the Islamic tradition, his ring with its star-shaped seal, and Al-Mudhib, the name Mina had given the night she died.

The results led me to a vast and arcane collection of resources, all focused on mystical, demonic creatures from Islamic lore. In the US, we tended to call creatures like Al-Mudhib genies. Elsewhere they were known as jinn and their various alternate identities: wraithlike ghouls, rebellious marid, and powerful, fiery ifrits. I wasn't yet sure which of these beings Owen was, but I intended to find out.

The acrid scent of scorching flour drifted over us. Mom released me from her embrace, and I scurried to rescue our steaks from the grease before they burned.

"How long are you staying in town?" she asked.

I shrugged and reached for the colander in the overhead cabinet. "I don't know." And I didn't know what I was supposed to say. Last time I'd tried to explain what happened, I narrowly escaped a psych consult. How could I predict what would happen next or whether I would survive it? "I've taken a bit of a sabbatical so I can deal with some things."

"You stay as long as you need. There's always room here for you. It's nice to live with a living, breathing person instead of ghosts."

I chuckled as I set the colander in the sink and searched for a pot holder. As I strained the potatoes, sticky warm steam enveloped my face, and the potatoes' earthy scent perfumed the air. "I know what you mean. I've been living with ghosts for a long time too."

PATTING HER FULL BELLY, Mom urged me to leave the dirty dishes to her. "It's the least I can do." She paused, covering her mouth as she burped. "Especially if it means I can get you to cook like that again."

"My repertoire isn't very big." I stepped into the hallway, grabbed my peacoat from the rack, and shrugged it on. "And I tend to eat a lot less grease than you."

Her brow furrowed as she rolled up her uniform's sleeves. "Where are you going?" She glanced out the window over the sink, most likely taking note of the murky darkness outside. The rain had let up, but thick clouds concealed the moon. It was a demon's kind of night.

Unconsciously, my fingers rose to stroke the ta'wiz charm beneath my shirt collar. As promised, I'd never taken it off—not as a favor but as a reminder of the horrible things that had occurred and what could happen if I let my guard down. "To see one of those ghosts we were talking about."

Her brow twitched. "There was a ghost in Greer's house that night he held me hostage. Is that the one you're planning to visit?"

"Possibly." I grabbed my keys and purse from where I'd tossed them on the counter when I'd first walked in.

She turned on the hot water and squirted dish soap into the sink. "That boy saved my life, Rikki. I couldn't prove it, and I couldn't put it in my report, but we both know it's true."

"'Et tu, Brute?'"

"What's that supposed to mean?" She folded her arms over her chest and jutted a hip.

"Everyone acts like Owen's the Saint of Evansville." Exasperated, I tossed my hands in the air. "It's his fault Mina died. Why am I the only one who sees that?"

"I'm not the only one he's helped. In the past three years, there've been more than a few times when something tragic could've happened, but by some miracle, everything turned out all right."

I scowled. "It was coincidence."

"You're not listening." She shook her finger at me. "Evansville has its very own superhero. You know that old single-lane bridge that crosses the Nantahala out on 74? Couple months after you left town, there was a bad accident. Two cars collided late at night—one of the drivers was drunk. The other car was a family—they crashed through the barricade and fell in the river. Should have drowned, but by the time emergency response got there, they were standing on the side of the road, dripping wet. Scraped up and bruised but alive. Their car was mangled. The doors wouldn't open. When we asked them how they managed to get out, they couldn't explain it. Just said that one minute they were in the river, certain they were going to drown, and the next minute, they were free. It's exactly like the night Greer took me hostage. And that's only one example. I can give you a half dozen more."

I bit my lip, refusing to say anything. Refusing to give Owen credit, despite the voice in my head insisting it was true. *What happened to Owen being so concerned about being discovered by his enemies, anyway?* It was almost as if he was daring them to come find him. "So, he wanted to ease his guilty conscience." I shrugged. "He's still a monster."

"If you're so afraid of him, why are you so intent on going to see him?"

"Because he has to answer for what he did."

She tossed out her hands. "What exactly did he do?"

Oh no, I wasn't falling for that trap again. One close brush with the hospital's psyche ward was enough for me to keep my mouth shut. Even if Mom was convinced Owen was a comic book hero, she'd never go all in when it came to believing the truth. Unable to come up with a satisfactory response, I jingled my keys at her. "Don't wait up."

"If you need backup, give me a call."

I smiled and tossed her a wave, but the gesture was more light-hearted than I felt. Dread as thick as tar slogged through my veins. Still I plodded forward, determined and stalwart.

Once upon a time, Owen had loved me. If any of those feelings remained, he'd let me talk to him, and he'd give me the answers I

needed to fill in the missing pieces of an incomplete picture. Whatever happened after that was up to fate.

Or to the god who'd created him. This nightmare.

This jinni.

ALTHOUGH THE RAIN HAD stopped, moisture hung in the
air in a watery mist that beaded on Dolly's windshield. Her headlights burned through murky fog clinging to the blacktop and roadside, swathing everything in cold, damp gloom. As it had earlier in
the day, the weather matched my temperament, and I took it as a
strange sort of encouragement. If the night had been bright and
warm, I might have turned around and gone home. A woman didn't
face her demons on clear, moonlit nights. There was too much romance and hope in those sorts of things, and I was in the mood for
neither.

Perhaps my reluctance made the trip seem longer than usual, not
that El Jannah had ever been a quick drive from my house. I nearly missed the turn for Owen's driveway. I slammed the brakes, and
Dolly skidded past the graveled entrance. After reversing, I backed
up several yards, shifted into first, and pulled off the road, angling my
truck so her headlights burned down the pathway, illuminating overgrown greenery encroaching on the drive.

No wonder I'd nearly missed it—brambles and vines camouflaged the path. As I trundled over the rutted road, branches and bri-
ars scraped the sides of my truck. *Does Owen really still live here, or
has he abandoned El Jannah and moved some place neither Luke nor
Rose has wanted to tell me about?* Their loyalty to him should have
heartened me, perhaps, but a ball of ice had formed in my stomach
the moment I left my mom's house. Not even Rose's and Luke's favor
for Owen could thaw it.

My doubts about his presence faded when I rounded the curve leading to the pond. Here, the overgrowth thinned, and the lawn around the hot spring had been weeded and trimmed. Memories flared, and my heart surged as I remembered happier times. I chased that joy away with an image of a dark, angry beast and the echoes of Mina's screams.

I wondered why he hadn't moved after the fire. That event had certainly drawn a lot of attention. Instead, he'd rebuilt and opened Moon Runners as he'd always intended. Luke had said Owen wanted to put down roots, and maybe that meant he didn't easily dig them back up. His stubborn streak ran deeper than I'd known—maybe even as deep as my own.

The gravel path wound around the backside of the hill on which Owen's cabin perched. I followed it until it dead-ended in the empty parking area at his front porch. The glow of his porch light lit his Ducati sitting by itself at the side of his yard. I turned off my head-lights and sat, listening to Dolly's engine tick as it cooled.

My truck had never been quiet, not like some modern electric hybrid. Her growling motor and her tires crunching over gravel should have announced my arrival if Owen were nearby to hear it. I wondered whether he was somewhere else, driving another vehicle, maybe his BMW, if he hadn't already replaced it. With the power of a jinni at his personal disposal, he could have anything he wanted.

Anything but me.

I'd sat for so long in silence that I'd almost talked myself into leaving when a light flicked on inside the cabin. My heart stuttered to a halt. I froze, my muscles clenched, like a doe who knew a wolf had spotted her.

A shadow shifted at the window in the front door—someone peering out. Without realizing it, my hand drifted to the key still sitting in Dolly's ignition switch, but I caught myself and fisted my hands in my lap. If Owen came out of the house as a raging, roaring beast of darkness with blue flames in his eyes, maybe then I'd run. Would he take that approach after everything we'd once meant to each other? I wanted to say no, but part of me wasn't so sure.

Slowly, almost hesitantly, the cabin's front door swung open, followed by the screen door. A tall, lean shadow stepped through the doorway. *Nope, definitely not a demon.* Porch light caught the gleam of his dark hair and revealed a glimpse of skin. Although an unfamiliar beard and stark shadows concealed the details of his face, he was unmistakable as he leaned against one of the posts supporting the porch's roof. Our three years apart suddenly felt like three seconds. Equal parts of longing and trepidation, like fire and ice, warred inside me.

Swallowing, I screwed up my courage and threw open Dolly's squeaky door. Pebbles crunched beneath my boots as I stalked forward on wobbly legs, rounding the corner of Dolly's bumper. Fragrant with pine and cedar, the air was damp and frigid against my cheeks. My breath puffed in anxious, smoky swirls. I fingered my necklace again.

Stopping halfway between my truck and the steps leading up to the cabin's front porch, I shoved my shaking hands on my hips, striving not to hunch my shoulders, trying not to give away my fear. "We need to talk."

He made me wait several anxious heartbeats before answering, and his voice was deeper and rougher than I remembered. "Aren't you afraid I might eat you?"

I studied him, his worn red flannel and blue jeans, his broad shoulders and long legs. He looked warm, unthreatening, and approachable. So did black bears, from a certain perspective, before you got close enough to see their teeth and claws. "Yes, actually, I am."

He stood straighter and folded his arms over his chest. "Then why are you here?"

"You know why."

"Death wish?"

Is he joking? Really? "I want to know what happened."

"You know what happened." He scrubbed his hands over his face. "You were there."

"I was..." I shook my head. "And I wasn't. At the end, there was only cold and darkness and Mina screaming. None of it made any sense. At the end, I woke up in the hospital with third-degree burns on my arms, and Mina was dead."

"So you ran. No surprise."

"Isn't that what you're supposed to do when you're a regular, mundane person? You don't fight the monsters, you run from them. That's how you survive."

"If that's true, then why did you come back?" He flashed his teeth, not quite a smile. It was too menacing for that. "Have you decided to fight the monsters, after all?"

Shaking my head, I stepped closer, ignoring my flight instincts. "No, I can't fight them, but it turns out I can't run from them either." I tapped my temple and moved forward another step. "Once they get inside you, there's no getting away. They follow you everywhere you go. They hide in the dark places in your house, in the shadows at the hospital where you work. They infest your dreams and refuse to let you sleep." My voice quavered, threatening to break. "They don't gobble you up in one big bite. They devour you slowly, bit by bit, atom by atom, until you're nothing but a shadow, the absence of light and all the things you once were."

Raising his hands, he stepped back. "So I'll ask you one more time. Why are you here?"

"Because I want my life back. I want *Mina* back."

On reaching his door, he pushed it open and turned his back to me. Pausing, he glanced at me over his shoulder. "I can't help you, Rikki. I can't give you what you want, and I don't know why I ever thought I could. Go home and forget you ever knew me."

I scrambled forward several steps then caught myself and stopped. *What am I going to do? Chase him?* "Don't you think I've already tried that? They don't make a pill strong enough to make me forget. I know because I've tried them all."

He shook his head and stepped through his doorway.

"What about your magic?" I yelled before he let the door shut. He froze, his figure a dark shadow standing at the cabin's threshold. "What can the jinn do? They can take life, but can they give it? Can they erase memories? Can they go back in time and stop a nightmare from happening in the first place?" And that was the heart of it. I hadn't come to Evansville merely because I wanted to hold him accountable and make him confess. Knowing the minutiae of what had happened that night wouldn't bring Mina back or rid me of my suffering, but perhaps a jinni's magic could. I had come because I wanted him to fix me, heal me, whatever it took. "Can you make my pain go away?"

He had once told me that time was relative, and at that moment, nothing was truer. A thousand years passed in each of the seconds I waited for his response. He said nothing, though. Instead, he stepped deeper into his house, pushed his door closed behind him, and turned out his lights.

My fear drained away like air from a punctured tire, and I sagged on my feet, dejected and frustrated. "I hope you don't think that's how this ends." I marched to his front porch and banged on his front door. "You owe me an explanation."

I banged again. "*Owen.*"

After I'd knocked and called for him several more times and he still refused to answer, I admitted defeat. I slumped back to Dolly and climbed behind the wheel. Her engine came to life with a stuttering cough. "This was just one battle." The words were directed at Owen, even though I knew he couldn't hear me. "It takes more than that to win a war."

That night, after driving home, climbing into bed, and falling asleep, I didn't dream of monsters.

As far as I could tell, I slept like the dead and dreamed of nothing at all.

Chapter Twenty-Nine
Holding Back the Years

ROSE SET AN EGG-WHITE-and-spinach omelet on the tabletop before me and refilled my coffee. "Anything else?"

I shook my head. "Thanks. This looks great."

"Looks like rabbit food." Her nose wrinkled.

"Rabbits don't eat eggs, last time I checked."

Her lip twitched, but she had enough customer service ingrained in her to keep from revealing her dismay at my choice of breakfast. She raised her eyes and glanced around the bustling dining room. "Things will slow down before long. If you're still here, maybe I'll take a break. We can sit and talk if you'd like."

I nodded and smiled. "I'd like that very much."

She winked and scurried off, hurrying to refill empty coffee cups and deliver stacks of pancakes. Rose treated me like family, which meant that if she didn't forgive me immediately, she was at least willing to give me a second chance.

I slid my plate closer and sliced my fork through my omelet. Intent on devouring my breakfast, I didn't notice the din around me going quiet. Not until Owen slid into the seat across from me did I realize everyone had stopped talking, and all eyes had turned on us. Startled, I swallowed wrong, and a lump of egg lodged in my throat. My eyes watered. Owen slid my mug closer as I pounded my chest and coughed.

He leaned in. "I won't say I wasn't trying to surprise you, but I didn't mean for it to go quite like that."

As if sensing my distress, Rose swung by the table and refilled my mug. She brought a cup for Owen, too, then disappeared again without saying a word. I guzzled coffee until my throat cleared, and I heaved a breath. "You get a ten for effectiveness," I croaked, "but a five on execution."

He poured sugar into his coffee and stirred. "I'll try to do better next time."

Next time? Despite the trite banter, nothing about Owen's presence was as blithe as his demeanor suggested.

Three years was a long time by some standards but not so much by others. If I'd expected to find him greatly changed, I would have been disappointed. He'd grown out his beard, and perhaps his eyes seemed a little deeper set and the hollows in his cheeks more noticeable, but he still smelled of hot oil and incense smoke. He was still beautiful enough to steal my breath—until I remembered the creature lurking underneath that enticing exterior.

When I'd envisioned confronting him, I'd anticipated feeling nothing for him except fear. What a naïve lie I'd told myself, but if I'd thought seeing him again would remind me of past feelings and stir up old longings, I never would've come back. *A girl doesn't fall in love with the devil and come away unscarred, but she also doesn't have to make the same mistake twice.*

"You want something to eat?" I raised a hand, trying to get Rose's attention.

Owen shook his head. "I'm not hungry."

"That's usually why people come to diners, though."

"I came to find you. I want you to come back to El Jannah with me."

"I went to El Jannah last night. You weren't particularly hospitable, if you'll recall."

"I never expected to see you there. I was stunned, and after you left, I had to convince myself you hadn't been a hallucination. It took me a while to process, I guess. I didn't sleep much."

Guess Luke didn't tell him I was in town after all. I cut up the rest of my omelet but didn't eat it. The shock of Owen's presence had robbed me of my appetite. "Welcome to my world." I paused. "Actually, I slept fine last night. First time in years."

He shifted, his gaze darting away.

I froze. "Wait. Don't tell me you had something to do with that."

"I can't take your pain away, Rikki, not like you want. But I could do that one small thing for you, at least."

"Why would you?"

He shook his head. "Please. Come back to El Jannah, and we'll talk."

"Don't say you'd rather show me instead of tell me. If I'm going to El Jannah with you, I want to know exactly why."

"How about if I said we could go swimming?" He arched an eyebrow, his dimple flashed, and for a second, I almost thought he was serious.

"Been there, done that."

Rolling his eyes, he huffed. "I want to talk to you. That's all. But not where we'll be overheard."

I pushed my plate aside, wrapped my hands around my mug, and studied him. He wore more flannel today, blue with a pale-green check. He'd kept his hair the same, sides trimmed close but long enough on top to fall in his eyes—although it was a bit shaggier than before. On the whole, *he* was a bit shaggier than before, as if he couldn't quite bring himself to care about the details of his appearance. Before I could answer him, my phone rang. Joseph Khan's face appeared on the caller ID.

Owen's gaze flickered to my phone. "Who is that?"

"Nobody." I swiped the reject icon.

"Boyfriend?"

"You don't have the right to ask me that."

His smile dropped. "You're right. I'm sorry."

My phone buzzed again.

"You better take that," he said. "Seems important."

I rolled my eyes but scooted out of the booth and gathered my phone, swiping the accept button as I strode out into a cool fall morning. "Hello, Joseph."

"Good morning," he said, his voice irritatingly chipper. "I see you survived the storm."

"What?" I strolled to Dolly and leaned against her front bumper.

"The storm that came through when we talked yesterday. You said you'd call back, but you didn't."

I glanced at the sky and noted the utter absence of clouds, a stark contrast to the day before. The air was crisp and dry. The winds were still, no whipping festival banners or swaying trees. "I've been busy."

"Are you busy now?"

I glanced through the diner window. Owen had removed his wallet from his pocket and was tossing bills on the table. He leaned over and unhooked my purse from the back of my chair. "I was eating breakfast." *But not anymore, apparently.*

"I won't keep you, then. I thought I'd tell you I'm coming to Evansville to see you."

My stomach dropped like a broken elevator. "What? Why?"

"I thought if I visited, saw you in your home environment, I'd get to know that part of you better."

"I don't think that's a good idea." Owen ambled to the sidewalk, stopped in front of me, and handed me my bag. "I'm a little preoccupied."

"I get that. I won't stay long. You know I don't get much time off. I'll be there tomorrow before lunchtime. I saw online that there's a festival this weekend. You can give me the grand tour."

"Joseph—"

In the background, a voice over the intercom called for Dr. Khan. He must have been at the hospital. "They're looking for me. Gotta go. I'll see you tomorrow, Erika." The line went dead.

I stared at my phone, baffled. "Talk about getting steamrolled."

"What's the matter?"

Shaking my head, I stuffed my phone in my bag. "Unexpected complication."

"It's not a good sign of long-term potential when you're calling your boyfriend an unexpected complication."

"He's *not* my boyfriend." I folded my arms over my chest. "Not that it's any of your business."

His only response was to flick an eyebrow.

"You know what?" I shifted my weight and set my hands on my hips. "I *will* go to El Jannah with you." I waved off his surprise. "But you have to do one thing for me first."

His posture turned wary. His shoulders tensed. "What?"

"Take me to Moon Runners. I want to see it."

His brows arched high, and he blinked, obviously surprised. "You think that's a good idea?"

"My mind has turned it into some kind of house of horrors, but that's ridiculous, right?" Owen couldn't be that much of a monster, or the town would have run him off with pitchforks and torches by now. Luke and Rose vouched for him. Even my mom seemed to be on his side. So what was I missing? "I think if I saw it again, maybe it would help."

"You want to walk?" He tilted his head, gesturing down the sidewalk. "It's nice out."

I glanced at the cerulean sky. No clouds had popped up since I'd checked a minute ago, so I shrugged. "Lead the way."

Our footsteps filled the silence during our walk through town. So many times, I'd imagined what I would say to him if I ever saw him again, but all those words now seemed insufficient and feeble. And if I couldn't say the important things, I wouldn't need to bother making chitchat.

When we turned the corner onto the street leading to Moon Runners, my gaze fell on a familiar yet utterly strange sight. It was the same old warehouse, but not. The signage that had been missing before now announced the distillery's name in a large, bright font. He'd built the outside seating area and platform for live music the way he'd planned. Strings of lights hung over the deck, and pots of mums bloomed in big planters positioned around the building and resurfaced parking lot.

It was his dream, and he'd made it come true to the last detail. Vivid and alive, Moon Runners was nothing like the fiery inferno from my nightmares. Owen walked several more paces before apparently realizing I'd stopped. He turned back, caught sight of the surprise on my face, and smiled sadly. "Nice, right? Luke's been sprucing up the place, getting it ready for the festival tomorrow."

Stupid, ridiculous, involuntary tears rose in my eyes. I blinked and scrubbed them away. I clamped my lips shut and marched forward, intent. *Mina died here. Don't forget that.*

When we reached the front door, Owen removed keys from his pocket and unlocked it. His lip twitched. "You're sure?"

My thoughts went straight to the last time he'd asked me that question, right before we'd spent the night together. I narrowed my eyes at him. "Don't ask me that ever again."

Nodding, he pushed open the door and held it for me. The warehouse's old rolling garage doors had been replaced with huge windows that let in enough light to illuminate the room. Glasses and bottles glinted on the shelves behind the large wooden bar. Soft golden light gleamed on glossy tabletops. Banners advertising the Fall Leaf Festival hung from the rafters. I closed my eyes and inhaled, but it had been three years, and nothing from the night remained.

Instead of smoke and burning hair, the bar smelled of alcohol and something sour and astringent. My throat burned, but I wasn't sure alcohol fumes were to blame.

"Rikki?" The concern in Owen's voice was thick.

I waved him off and strode farther into the room. Weaving a path through the tables and chairs, I trailed my fingers over their polished surfaces. Stopping before the big glass windows, I closed my eyes again and listened. No roar of fire or angry beasts answered, only the steady beat of my heart.

Yet out of nowhere, my tears resurfaced, falling of their own free will. So much for my emotional barricades. The last few years had been a constant barrage of artillery, and the defenses I had worked so hard to build in the time since my dad's death had suffered—big chunks had broken loose. There were holes now, and more pain got through than before.

Had I been hoping to find Mina's ghost here? Was I relieved I didn't? The tears fell faster, thicker, hotter. I dropped into a crouch and hugged my knees, burying my face against my legs. Owen shuffled closer but had the sense not to touch me. "I should have saved her," I said, my words muffled against the fabric of my jeans. "The things that happened to me were my own fault. I knew there was a risk that came with deciding to be with someone who kept secrets, but Mina was innocent. She didn't know. She didn't have the chance to walk away, and she was the one who died. It should have been me."

The leather of his boots creaked as he shifted to kneel beside me. "Don't tell me you spent the last three years blaming yourself." His voice was low and hoarse. "It wasn't your fault."

I glanced up through blurry eyes. "I could have walked away from you, but instead I stayed and dragged her into your orbit. It was my fault, and it was your fault too. Of course it was your fault. *You're* the monster, Owen. *You're* the beast in my nightmares."

He jerked as if I'd slapped him. He didn't defend himself, though. He stood and backed away. His eyes were hollow black wells, empty and bottomless. "Why do you think I left you alone all these years, Rikki? From the beginning, running away was the smartest thing you ever did, and I told you I wouldn't chase you. Maybe you shouldn't have come back."

"But did you really leave me alone? Did you *really* stop chasing me?"

He paused, his brow furrowing.

"When I ran to Chapel Hill, I thought I was going to burn through all my savings, but after a week of living in a motel with no idea how I was going to find a place I could afford, I got a call from that apartment complex we visited. The girl, Kelsey, the one who gave us that tour... she told me I'd won their contest—the free apartment for a year. But I'd never filled out an application or put down a deposit, so how did I win? Was that you?"

His jaw flexed as he clamped his lips tight. Looking away, he shoved his hands in his pockets and backed farther away from me.

I stood, my fists clenched at my side. "Both years, I got scholarships I didn't apply for. By the time I graduated, I had almost no loans left to pay. Was *that* you?"

He stiffened more. He turned his back and strode to the door.

I hurried after him. "I didn't *ask* you for that. I didn't want your help. I tried to forget you, but there was always something that kept bringing me back."

He picked up his pace and rushed into the parking lot. *Now who's running away?*

I followed him outside. "Tell me what happened, Owen. After everything went dark, tell me you didn't kill her."

In the middle of the parking lot, he froze and dropped his head. I stepped around and faced him, waiting for him to look up at me. An eternity passed in the seconds it took for him to collect himself.

When he did look up, the expression on his face was devastation. "I broke my promise to you, and it killed her. In my dreams, it isn't Mina, though. It's you. Every time in my nightmares, the one who dies is *you.*"

With that, he disappeared like a soap bubble bursting—instant and with no evidence that he'd ever been there. Maybe I should have been more awestruck, but after the things I'd seen, a disappearing act was too lame to register. At that same moment, a shiny Ford truck wheeled into the parking lot. As it lurched to a stop beside me, the driver's tinted window slid down, and Luke gave me a hard look. "Was that Owen you were talking to?"

I nodded. "Does he do that often? Out here in the open for anyone to see?"

"He doesn't get out much. Or at all, actually. Guy's been a freaking hermit."

Maybe that explained the town's reaction to his appearance in the diner. Or maybe it was the paparazzi appeal of seeing two cast members from the biggest tragedy in Evansville's recent history. We were local legends—the ones who got away.

"But you two are still close?" I asked.

"We went through some horrible things overseas, and surviving them together only made our brotherhood stronger. This time was no different."

I silently digested his answer as I fiddled with a loose string on the hem of my shirt, uncertain of what to say next.

"So... what brings you here?" Luke tilted his head toward the bar.

"It's happy hour somewhere, right?"

He blinked at me, obviously uncertain about whether I was joking. When I said nothing more, he huffed. "Come on, then. Let me pour you a drink."

Because I had nothing better to do, and because the thought of getting numb for a while appealed, I waited for him to park his truck and lead me into the distillery.

He motioned to the stools at the bar. "Take a seat."

I perched on a stool, leaned my elbows on the solid slab of oak serving as the countertop, and watched him shuffle around with the confidence and ease of someone who had spent a lot of time there. Several dozen boxes with Moon Runners' logo on them were stacked on the floor at the end of the bar. I pointed at them. "Extra stock for the festival?"

Luke nodded. "Those are going out to our booth at Wallers Park, where they're having the concerts. The mayor suggested it, and Owen thought it would be good for us to have a presence closer to the heart of the action."

"You'll be there?"

"Nope." He shook his head. "I'm glued to this place. Owen will man the booth."

"You said Owen was a hermit."

"He is. That's another reason I insisted on staying here tomorrow. He needs to get out and remember what it's like to be human."

That seems unlikely. "Your mom told me you run this place now."

Luke set four shot glasses in a line on the bar before me. "She's right. I do."

"I didn't know you were planning to work for Owen."

He set two mason jars filled with clear liquor onto the counter. "You never asked."

"Was that always the plan when you came back to Evansville with him?"

He poured two shots from one jar then poured two shots from a second. "No. I was drifting around for a while, especially after the..."

"Fire?"

Without meeting my eyes, he nodded. "Owen offered me a chance to manage the place, and I took it." He slid one shot glass to me and kept the other for himself. "I was barely treading water. If he hadn't offered me this job, I think I would have drowned. There are more than a few folks in this town who now have good jobs, thanks to him."

I abstained from making a judgment about Owen's supposed generosity and pointed at my shot glass. "So, this is moonshine?"

Luke raised his shot. Glancing pointedly at my glass, he waited for me to pick up my drink. When I did, he touched his glass to mine. "Cheers."

I drank, and fire lit a trail down my throat. My eyes watered. I pounded my chest, coughing. Luke, however, had swallowed his like water. "That's our original blend," he said. "Straight corn liquor. You know the difference between moonshine and whisky?"

Still coughing, I shook my head.

"Whisky is aged." He slid the second shot to me. "Moonshine isn't. Simple."

"What's this one?" I pointed at the next drink.

"Neutral grain blend. Supposed to be mostly flavorless. Good for mixing drinks. Smooth for a shot."

"Don't you have anything more...?" I let my gaze wander to the collection of bottles on the shelves behind him, reading labels, considering flavor options.

"What?" He quirked an eyebrow.

"Sweet."

He grinned and reached for another bottle full of yellowish liquor. "Lemon drop. That's next. Finish this one first." He tapped the bar next to my glass. "Drink up."

My second shot went down smoother than the first. I pushed my empty glass across the bar. "Okay, bartender, fill 'er up."

I was on my fourth shot—something that'd had peaches brining in it—when Luke's charming façade slipped. "You blame Owen for Mina, don't you?"

I looked up quickly, and it took a moment for my vision to catch up. The moonshine was fraying my senses, turning everything soft and fuzzy. "'Course I do."

"Do you blame *me*?" He pointed at himself.

Frowning, I tentatively sipped my drink. "Why would I?"

"Mina was my girlfriend. I loved her. Every day I ask myself if I could have done something to save her. Every day I remind myself she was gone long before anyone could have helped her. When Mina walked into the parking lot that night, she never came back. That thing, that *monster*, took her and used her, made her his puppet."

Without pausing long enough to question the wisdom of drinking so much in such a short time on a mostly empty stomach, I tossed back my fourth shot. *Wisdom be damned. Bring on the numbness.* I gulped my drink, and the world spun around me. "Owen should have cut her strings. Turned her back into a real girl like the Blue Fairy did for Pinocchio. What's the point of all that strength, all that magic, if he can't do anything useful with it?"

Luke shook his head, and suddenly, he had two of them. I swayed on my seat and blinked. "Every move he made was to save us," he said. "That darkness—that was him fighting back. If we hadn't been inside that darkness with him, Al-Mudhib would have killed us or let the fire finish us off."

"Did Owen not have enough strength to save Mina too?" I shoved my glass toward Luke and gestured for a refill. Screw numbness. I wanted oblivion—it was the only release from the guilt and anger. He poured more peach 'shine, and I gulped it like a thirsty woman in the desert. "Was there not enough room in Owen's darkness for all of us?"

He frowned at my empty shot glass. "Maybe you should take a break, Rikki. Last I recall, you aren't much of a drinker."

"Screw your recall." I ignored the slur in my words. "A lot has changed in three years."

"And now you're a lousy drunk?"

"Now I'm a whatever-it-takes, don't really care." Stars sparkled in the periphery of my vision. I closed my eyes, but that only amplified my dizziness. Folding my arms on the bar, I put my head down, hoping it would help. "Okay... maybe that last one was a bad idea."

"When was the last time you ate?"

I shrugged. "Owen dis... distracted me from my omelet."

"What?"

I waved him off. Talking required too much effort.

Luke was quiet for a moment, but then he was at my side, gripping my shoulders. He helped me to my feet, but when I stumbled and sagged, he cursed and shoved his shoulder under my armpit. He hefted my dead weight into his arms. The last thing I heard him say before the world became a gray, soupy swirl was "Owen *did* pull Mina into his darkness, but it was too late. That fire jinni had already taken her, *killed* her. Owen was the only reason there was something left of her for her parents to bury. He's the only reason either of us survived."

Chapter Thirty
What Good Can Drinkin' Do?

I WOKE WITH A START, as if someone had crashed a pair of cymbals over my head. Shooting up straight, I caught my head in my hands before it rolled off my shoulders. At some point while I was out, a hot, blazing ember had replaced my brain. "Oh, dear God," I muttered, peeling one eye open.

Dark and hazy, the room around me slowly sharpened into focus. Although I hadn't seen it in three years, I recognized my surroundings—Owen's cabin. And I was on his big, overstuffed sofa, tangled in a soft chenille throw. *How'd I get here?*

Someone cleared his throat. I jerked my head in his direction but whimpered when my head exploded. "Your moonshine is rotten."

"I can't speak from experience," Owen said, "but my understanding is you aren't supposed to drink that much that fast."

I opened my eyes again and found him crouched before me, offering a tall tumbler of iced water. I took it and pressed the frosty glass to my fevered cheek. Behind him, a window revealed the sun had nearly set. Deep shadows crept through the room, relieved only by a pale light shining over the kitchen stove. I sipped my water, and the coolness eased my dry, sour throat. "What am I doing here?"

"Luke brought you." Owen rose and pointed at an empty spot on the sofa beside me. "Mind if I sit?"

I shrugged. "It's your house."

A muscle under his eye twitched, but he took a seat, keeping a wary distance between us. "Luke had to get back to work—he's still got a lot to do to get ready for the festival, and it's not like he could let you sleep it off at the bar. He didn't think he should take you home and leave you by yourself... or for your mom to find."

"So he brought me here?" I gulped the rest of my water and set the glass on his coffee table.

"I promised him I wouldn't eat you." His nose wrinkled. "You smell like sour pickle, anyway."

I scowled at him. "How long have I been out?"

"Most of the day."

"I've been sleeping on your sofa the whole time?"

"Snoring on my sofa, yeah."

I flashed him a hard look and caught him grinning, dimple and all. It sent my heart thrumming, like someone strumming a guitar, playing a beloved old song. He quickly replaced his smile with an unreadable expression, and we sat in silence for several heartbeats before I groaned, slumping against the back of the sofa. "Well, I'm here now. So, what did you want to tell me?"

"It can wait." He leaned closer, peering into my eyes. "How are you feeling?"

"Like a garbage truck ran over me."

He raised a hand to my face but paused. "Can I?"

I studied his gaze, searching for a sign of his intent, but the only thing in his eyes was the usual amber specks on a field of dark brown—no sign of blue flames. I nodded. He touched his fingertips to my temple. A wisp of his smoky scent wafted over me, but cool relief filled my head. My headache faded away. "Thought you said you couldn't ease my pain."

"A headache is nothing. The only cure for heartbreak is time, I'm afraid."

"It's been three years, and it's only gotten worse."

He looked away. "I believe that."

Folding my fingers together in my lap, I studied my knuckles. Owen picked at a loose thread on his shirt cuff. If he'd owned a grandfather clock, it would have ticked loudly, counting the seconds, but instead there was only silence, awkward and thick. He inhaled and glanced at me. Then he stood and crossed the room. "If you're feeling up to it, let's walk. It's a nice evening. Dry. Not too cold yet."

I rose, eager for the distraction and fresh air. Following him through the front door, I stepped into a brisk fall evening. A thick tree canopy concealed the sky, and fading sunlight cast everything in gloom. Owen's boots crunched over the gravel in his drive as I marched behind him, focusing on the sweet air and the relief of no longer feeling nauseated and achy.

Instead of taking the driveway, he followed a small path descending the steep hillside to the pond. Several yards down, the trees thinned and the sky peeked out, revealing a stunning field of deep indigo. Stars sparkled, bold and flamboyant. "Luke told me his side of the story," I said. "He blames himself for Mina as much as I do."

"Neither of you should be blaming yourselves." Owen studied the path instead of looking at me, but I understood why. Our history was a difficult thing to face.

In that moment, he wasn't a monster but a regular man who had made some terrible mistakes. If I believed Luke, and if I believed the urgings of my own heart, Owen hadn't killed Mina. He might have failed her, but he didn't kill her. My anger softened.

"It was my fault," he said.

"Oh, I still blame you, don't worry about that. Helps me deal with my own guilt, I guess."

"I'll take all the guilt you'll give me, Rikki, if it eases your burden."

"Tell me." Our footsteps set a rhythm for our conversation, like a metronome on a piano—*crunch, crunch, crunch.* "From your point of view, I want to know what happened that night. That's why you wanted me to come back here, wasn't it? To tell your side of the story?"

"I actually wanted to go further back than that night and tell you the things I should have told you after that day in Chapel Hill. It didn't take much to scare you away, and I knew the truth would do that. I wanted to keep you, so I told you nothing, and that was selfish."

Our steep descent eased as we neared the flat yard circling the pond. The skies reflected on its surface, turning the waters dark and inky. The water's damp mineral scent beckoned me closer.

Owen cleared his throat. "Growing up, I'd heard my family talk about King Suleiman, or Solomon as you know him, and how we were supposedly his descendants, but it was always told like a bedtime story. Not something real but a fable about a king who could control the jinn with a special ring Allah had given him. I knew about jinn, but they were just boogey men. I believed in them as much as you probably believed in demons."

When I was younger, our family had attended the local Pentecostal church. The pastor and Sunday school teachers spoke of angels and demons, but like Owen, I'd equated their existence with that of Santa Claus and the Tooth Fairy. When Dad died, Mom and I stopped going to church, and I lost my belief in a lot of things. "So, when did you know jinn were real?"

We reached the dock, and I paused at the edge, watching him stroll to the end, moving with long-legged grace. An old fire flickered to life in my stomach, but I stomped it out. My body recalled his touch, but my heart still remembered my fear.

He crouched, chucking a pebble into the pond, and the moon's reflection rippled. "I knew when I almost died in Iraq."

"The bomb?" Quietly, I stepped up behind him. "The IED?"

He stared into the water and nodded. "It was a lot worse than I'd let you believe. It gutted me, Rikki. Literally. I should have died, but my last thought before I blacked out was a prayer. A wish, I guess."

"So, jinn really do grant wishes?" I squatted beside him and watched the stars flicker on the pond's glassy face. His story sounded too fantastical, too unbelievable, but I'd seen enough to know he was telling the truth.

He snorted. "No, not like Aladdin. But with the ring, I guess it amplified my will. I made a subconscious, desperate plea, and the jinn answered—one in particular. He calls himself Shadhan."

"Oh yeah? And he waved his magic genie wand and saved you?"

He shook his head. "It's more complicated than that."

"It has something to do with the shadows and darkness and the blue flames in your eyes. It's whatever came out of you the night of the fire."

"Yes." He nodded. "Shadhan offered to keep me alive, and in exchange, I had to allow him to take possession of me. The jinn like making deals. It makes their magic stronger."

"Why would he make a deal like that? Why would he want to possess you?" Owen had avoided and evaded in the past, but he'd never lied to me. His answers also meshed with my research and filled in missing pieces of a puzzle that had frustrated me far too long. I believed his story, and realizing that was like untying the knot that had been wrapped around my heart for the last three years.

He sat down and folded his arms around his knees. Moonlight glinted in silver streaks on his dark hair. He looked supernatural, as if his jinni was sitting close to the surface, ready to make an appearance. "They have a hierarchy—the minor jinn and the seven kings who rule them. Al-Mudhib, the jinni who came to Moon Runners that night, is one of those seven kings." He held out his hand, waggling his ring finger. "Shadhan, the jinni who possesses me, wanted to break away from the kings' rule. He thought if I brought him with me back to the States, he might have a chance at freedom."

"And...?" I asked.

"It's not as easy as either of us thought it would be. The kings aren't happy about losing a member of their fold, and they don't like that, with the ring, I can keep them from easily getting what they want."

An unexpected shot of coldness pierced my heart. "What happens if they succeed in taking your ring?"

"I won't be able to control them anymore. They'll take Shadhan back."

My blood chilled, turning to frozen sludge. "What does that mean for you?"

He shrugged, and although darkness concealed his face, blue flames bloomed in his eyes. "Without the jinni's magic sustaining me, I'm pretty sure I would die."

Chapter Thirty-One
The First Cut Is the Deepest

OWEN'S REVELATION HURT more than I wanted to admit. I'd wanted to hate him, blame him, *rage* at him, but the thought of losing him opened a cold and yawning hole inside me where frigid winds howled. During the three years I'd been away, I'd lived in haunted fear. Yet a small part of me had clung to the comfort of knowing he was still out there somewhere. The part of me that had loved him hadn't died the night of Mina's death, but it had buried itself so deep down I'd convinced myself it never existed in the first place. A flicker of those old feelings bubbled to the surface, and hot tears rose in my eyes.

He'd always been sitting on the edge of death, and I'd never known.

Scrubbing my eyes, I stumbled to my feet.

"Rikki?" Owen jumped up and reached for me but stopped short and balled his fingers into a fist that he shoved in his pocket. "You okay?"

I backed away. "I-I'm fine."

"Could have fooled me."

"I'm as fine as someone can be when she's lost her father and best friend and then finds out she might lose you too." The words slipped out, and I snatched for them as if I could grab them from the air, shove them back in my mouth, and swallow them before he could hear, but I wasn't the one who had the magic to make desperate wishes come true.

"What?" Owen's shadowed figure froze. His tone was quiet but confused.

Shaking my head, I stumbled farther back. Faster than either of us could react, my heel slipped over the edge of the dock, my weight shifted, and my arms flailed.

I fell, plunging beneath the pond's dark surface.

Before the full realization of what had happened sank in, I was in Owen's arms, and we were standing on the dock, both of us sodden. I scraped wet hair from my eyes and scowled, panting from excitement and panic. "Magic... couldn't catch me... *before* I fell in?"

"It happened too fast."

I plucked my sweater away from my chest. "Likely story."

"C'mon." He chuckled. "Let's get to the house and dry off. The pond might be warm, but cold air and wet clothes are a bad combination."

"You don't have to tell me. *I'm* the medical professional here." He chuckled again, and when he grabbed my hand and tugged me forward, I didn't pull away or tell him to let go. "Couldn't you dry us off with magic?"

"I could." He frowned. "But every time I use Shadhan's powers that way, he gains more control over me. I don't like using his magic any more than necessary."

"Then why use your magic to get us out of the pond?"

"Gut reaction, I guess. Just acted without thinking."

Together we scrambled up the hill to Owen's cabin, and he led me inside. Standing on the braided rug at his front door, we kicked off our boots and wet socks. Owen unbuttoned his flannel, and despite telling myself not to, I watched his muscles flex beneath his damp white T-shirt. And when he stripped that off, too, my mouth went as dry as if I'd been sucking on hot desert sand. I hadn't forgotten how beautiful he was. I'd just convinced myself I no longer cared. *What a lie.* He was dusky skinned and lovely as ever, although he seemed a little leaner, gaunter, as if he hadn't been eating enough.

He studied my sodden sweater, frowning. His eyes flashed, and he reached for my throat. When I flinched, he stopped and pointed. "You're still wearing the ta'wiz?"

I tugged the chain free and let the locket dangle from my fingers. "I've been too afraid to take it off. I don't know if it really works or if I've just been lucky, but I don't want to find out the hard way."

He reached again. "May I?"

I nodded, and he clasped the locket between thumb and forefinger. He closed his eyes, and a few moments passed before he said, "It definitely works, and the more you believe in it, the stronger its magic."

"What does it do, exactly?"

"I told you when I gave it to you." His dark eyes opened, and he held my gaze until a warm sensation fluttered in my chest. "It protects you against evil. More specifically, it'll keep you from being possessed, and no jinn can use harmful magic against you."

"Too bad Mina didn't have one too."

Owen tensed, released the charm, and stepped back. "Let me get you some dry clothes." Barefoot, he padded across the room and disappeared through his bedroom doorway. Minutes later, he returned wearing dry jeans and an Appalachian State Mountaineers T-shirt.

"This okay?" He held out a bundle of clothes.

I took them, nodding. "Mind if I use your bathroom?"

"You don't have to ask, Rikki. Make yourself at home."

I shuffled into his bedroom, purposely ignoring his massive bed and the concentrated scent of him that suffused my every breath. Memories of what had happened in that room the last time I'd been there shoved against my barricades, chipping at the already crumbling mortar. I'd never been good at resisting Owen's magnetism, and staying there much longer was probably a bad idea.

After I'd changed, I joined Owen in the kitchen, and he poured a cup of coffee. He raised a questioning eyebrow and held out a mug. Nodding, I took the coffee and settled on a stool at his kitchen island.

"I already put sugar and milk in it," he said. "I hope that was okay."

"It's perfect, actually."

He turned his back and poured another cup. "Are we going to talk about it?"

"Talk about what?"

"What happened at the pond."

"I lost my footing and fell in." Shrug. "What more is there to say?"

"You were upset when I told you what would happen if I lost the ring. Why were you worried that the monster might die? Isn't that what you want?"

I stared into my coffee, refusing to look up. "I don't want you to die, Owen. Not even close. But I'm not sure I've figured out how to stop being afraid of you."

He slid onto the stool beside me, and his body heat warmed my clammy skin. "You have every right to be scared. That was a terrible night, and you couldn't have expected things to happen the way they did."

"Luke said you tried to save her, but the jinni had already killed her."

Owen's head drooped. He clutched his coffee mug tightly. "No one is possessed by a jinn king without being damaged by it. Even if it had been a lesser jinni that took her, Mina wouldn't have come away unscathed. Al-Mudhib was one of the seven most powerful of all the jinn. He probably killed her the instant he took her, and if not, she wouldn't have survived long without him."

"But you killed Al-Mudhib"—I pointed at Owen's finger—"with the ring?"

He rolled a shoulder dismissively, as if killing a powerful magical being were no big deal.

"And that's why they want it back, right? They're afraid of your power."

"Suleiman used the ring to enslave the jinn to his will. They'd do anything to keep a human from wielding power against them again." His lips thinned, and his gaze darkened. "Including hurting those closest to me."

I touched his shoulder. "You saved me and Luke."

"I should've shielded you both the moment Al-Mudhib walked through the door." He squeezed his eyes shut and gritted his teeth. "I should have never let any of you get close to me in the first place, but I was too... *selfish*. Too human at heart." He touched his chest. "I wanted you too badly."

My heart thudded a slow, shuddering beat. "Did you know that would happen? That he would have fire like that?"

Owen's head drooped, and a dark swath of hair fell over his eye. "The Qur'an says angels are made from light, men from clay, and jinn from fire. Shadhan warned me Al-Mudhib was a powerful being, an ifrit, but I underestimated him. I was overly confident in my abilities, and Mina suffered the consequences."

"Why did you stay?" I started to reach for his hand but stopped and drew back. "After the fire, why did you stay in Evansville? Surely more of the jinn, the other kings, know where to find you."

"This is my home. They won't make me leave it. If they had come, I would have fought them."

"But no one else has come? Not in three years?"

"No." He drained the last of his coffee and stood. "I killed Al-Mudhib, and I'm guessing it's made the other kings wary. I don't expect them to stay away forever, but they won't come without a plan, and I doubt any of them will come alone."

He collected his keys from the counter. "C'mon. I'll take you home."

"What about my truck? It's still at the diner."

"Don't worry." He folded his arms and bobbed his head, presumably in imitation of Jeannie in *I Dream of Jeannie*. "It's been taken care of."

I was in no mood to laugh. "What will you do if they come? The other kings?"

"I'll fight if I can. They'll kill me if I can't. But whatever the outcome, I'll only risk myself. I've told you everything because I owed it to you, and you deserved the truth. You deserved better than what I gave you." His voice turned sharp. "As long as the kings want this ring, it's not safe for anyone to be close to me. You've got your answers. Now it's best if you walk away for good this time."

The vehemence of his words surprised me, and I had no immediate response or comeback. Instead, I silently followed him to his motorcycle, and when he handed me a helmet, I slipped it on, fastening the strap without his help. He threw his long leg over the saddle and drew the bike up straight. I hadn't ridden behind him since the night we'd shared a picnic dinner in the hayloft above Jack Huddle's stables. My heart quavered, remembering the rush and thrill of it.

Owen apparently noticed my hesitation and arched an eyebrow at me. "Problem?"

I swallowed, but it did nothing to relieve the ache in my throat. Shaking my head, I climbed behind him and situated my weight. He pulled his helmet on, flipped up the face shield, and raised his voice over the Ducati's roar. "You remember how to do this?"

Leaning forward, I wrapped my arms around him and squeezed my eyes shut. His warmth bled into me. Taut muscles moved beneath his skin as he maneuvered the bike. My blood sizzled traitorously, remembering his body. Remembering how much I'd loved him. It had been brief but so, so real.

"Ready?" he asked.

I nodded, and my arms acted of their own volition, sliding tighter around his ribs. I vowed not to savor this, swore not to enjoy it. The ride was simply necessity—transportation and nothing more. *Who the hell are you trying to convince?*

He lowered his face shield, shifted into gear, and revved the throttle. The motorcycle growled. He released the clutch, and gravel crunched under the bike's tires as we rolled forward. Although he'd taken his time reaching the road, once we hit the blacktop, he abandoned caution and worked the bike through its gears until the world screamed past us in a blur of shadows and moonlight. Blood roared in my ears. My heart rammed against my sternum, demanding more, farther, faster.

Too soon, though, he turned onto my driveway and slowed. The magical spell of El Jannah faded, and the real world crept in. I loosened my grip, and when he stopped his bike at the end of the driveway, I climbed off and removed my helmet. "You weren't wrong when you said it was dangerous to be around you. I don't have a problem with you making that statement." If he'd been the inconsiderate and careless type, I never would have fallen for him in the first place. But there was a difference between being careful and being overbearing, and it seemed he needed a reminder of what I was willing to tolerate. "What I have a problem with is you making pronouncements on my behalf."

Owen raised his face shield and scowled. "What are you talking about?"

"One of the reasons I fell in love with you is that you wanted to protect me, but you never tried to control me. You asked me to trust you and let you handle the danger. You could have locked me up, tied me up, kidnapped me, or done a million other things to get your way, but you simply asked me to trust you."

He ducked his head. His throat worked. "You—you never told me you loved me."

"I never had the chance. Al-Mudhib took more than my best friend from me that night." I handed my helmet to him and backed toward my house. More tears burned in my throat, but I swallowed them. I'd had enough crying for one day. "What's the point of fighting to keep your home if you have to live in it by yourself? What's the point of staying alive if you're damned to spend the rest of your life alone?"

I turned on my heel and marched away but not before I heard Owen's answer.

"Because, Rikki, I don't know how to give up."

I PROBABLY SHOULD HAVE taken a hot shower and gone straight to bed, but my blood was still humming, and my thoughts were a whirl. Instead of burrowing under the bed covers, I changed into a clean pair of leggings, a long sweater, and dry socks. I found a pair of rain boots under my bed and grabbed one of my dad's old wool coats from the hallway closet. After finding a working flashlight in the utility room, I tiptoed outside and climbed into Dolly.

Once I reached Hickory Wood Cemetery, I made my way through the maze of headstones. The flashlight beam, which had burned brightly in the gloom of my utility room, dimmed in the cemetery's oppressive darkness. The air had cooled since my walk with Owen at El Jannah, and my breath puffed in foggy clouds. Undaunted, I pressed on, following the path I'd walked so often in my younger years I could've done it blindfolded.

The sharp, astringent odor of cedar and pine infused the air, ridding my senses of Owen's scent. Wary of roots, rocks, and ruts, I picked my way deeper into the graveyard until I reached a sleek black tombstone. There, I turned off my flashlight, crouched, and brushed my fingertips over the stone's engraved surface.

Despite trying to clear my head of Owen, the night sky reminded me of his dark eyes and their flecks that glittered like stars, sometimes gold, sometimes blue. I had come back to Evansville believing he was a monster who'd killed my best friend, but out in the clear night air, I reevaluated those beliefs, analyzing them like microbes under a microscope.

"I don't have any chocolate," I said, "but I've brought you something better, I hope."

In my mind, Mina wore black leather leggings and suede knee boots. I pictured her pursing her bright-red lips at me as if she doubted there was any better gift than chocolate.

"I told you I'd bring you the truth, and the truth is that Owen isn't the monster I thought he was. Maybe he's partially responsible for what happened. I mean, it was his fault for bringing us into his world without telling us everything first, but I believe he never meant to endanger us. Would you ever be able to forgive him, Mina? Would *you* give him another chance?"

Mina's haughty expression softened. Her stiff posture relaxed.

"You've always given people the benefit of the doubt, haven't you? You gave Luke a second chance after that horrible prom night." Laughter lit up her face.

"I know what Owen did doesn't compare to that, but you've always seen the good in people. I think he's suffered for what happened. He paid a penance, but has it been enough?"

The Mina in my mind bent, crouching beside me, and peered into my face, her eyes serious and dark.

"You said I shouldn't live my life in fear, that I have to trust myself."

She folded her hands together over her heart and nodded.

"I think you *would* forgive him, Mina. I think you'd say love is worth the risk."

I ached with the urge to hug her, but she wasn't real, wasn't even a ghost, only an avatar my brain invented for imaginary conversations. Still, imagination was better than nothing, and I chitchatted with Mina's memory until I lost track of time and my chattering teeth startled me back to reality. The cold night air had drawn away my warmth, draining me like a battery, and I shivered. The longer I crouched, the more my muscles protested. My rigid joints popped and creaked as I stood and gave Mina's headstone a farewell caress.

My flashlight beam flickered across the cemetery, scanning for the path leading back to the parking lot. I stomped my feet until warmth bled into my tingling toes. Dried hickory leaves crackled under my boots as I hiked out, and an owl's eerie hoot echoed through the trees, raising goose bumps down my arms.

Despite my efforts to remain detached and calculating about Owen, my memories insisted on evoking his beauty—his lush kisses and warm touches, the pleasure of his body on mine. He was gorgeous, and for three years I had sought any remedy to make me forget, to stop the constant wanting. Even now, at the thought of him, my lips tingled, my fingertips burned, my breath turned sharp and short. I'd tried everything, nearly ruining my life in the process, but if a cure existed for being addicted to Owen, I'd never found it.

As I drove home, I surrendered, allowing the one indulgence I'd been denying myself the past three years. Wrapping the past around me like a warm blanket, I enveloped myself in memories of Owen. By the time I'd returned to the house, I was drunk on him, my desire intense and undiluted. A hot shower took the edge off, and when I crawled into bed, I fell asleep without fearing my dreams.

For the first time in a long time, I welcomed them.

Chapter Thirty-Two
Uninvited

DESPITE IT BEING NEARLY lunchtime, I sat at the kitchen counter in my pajamas, sipping coffee and reading headlines on my laptop. Late-morning sunlight shone through the kitchen window, casting the room in a warm yellow glow. I hadn't slept that late or that well without the help of a prescription since... I couldn't remember when. For the first time in years, I felt relaxed and rested—at least until a knock at the front door shook me out of my rare moment of peace.

My thoughts went first to Owen, and only Mina could have made me admit out loud that a part of me was hoping he might show up—that when he'd dropped me off last night, he'd regretted driving away. Maybe I wasn't ready to pick up where we'd left off, but like him, I wasn't quite sure how to give up.

Instead of Owen, I found Dr. Joseph Khan standing on my front porch. My stomach turned cold and sank to my feet. Unease stirred through me like some creature slithering beneath a puddle's dark surface, and I fingered the ta'wiz around my neck. Between getting piss drunk, finding out about Owen's life-and-death jinn conundrum, and going on a midnight visit to the cemetery, I'd forgotten about Joseph's impending visit. Now he was here, and I dreaded his presence.

"Erika." His smile was wide and toothy. *Like a hungry hyena.* Clean-shaven and meticulously groomed, he wore his dark hair clipped close, discouraging the mild waves that appeared when it grew out. He wore khakis, hiking boots, and a fleece pullover, likely

all designer brands. He inspected me, taking in my bedraggled pajamas and frizzy hair. Ever so slightly, his cheery façade slipped. "Did I
wake you?" He checked his gold watch. "It's almost noon. I told you
I was coming before noon."

"And I told you not to come at all."

His face fell, and a flash of hurt shimmered in his eyes. "I just
thought you were playing hard to get. Did I misinterpret?"

"Joseph, I—"

He squeezed my shoulder, and his gaze softened, going big and
round—total puppy-dog-in-the-pound effect. "I can see I was
wrong, Erika, but now that I'm here, can't we make the most of it?"

I could've kicked him out, cold and final, but his visit provided
a long overdue opportunity for a rational, adult conversation about
the state of our relationship and his lack of respect for my bound-
aries. Rolling my eyes, I motioned for him to follow me into the
kitchen and pointed at one of the stools at the island counter. "Wait
there, and I'll get dressed."

When he sat, I hurried to my room, cursing under my breath.
Joseph had never once thought to let me set the pace. Months before,
I had desperately wished for even the smallest spark to ignite between us, but my wishes weren't magic, and Joseph would not...
could not... *ever* replace Owen.

I slipped into jeans and a long-sleeved, skinny T-shirt and laced
up my boots. Quickly, I weaved my hair into a braid and tied it off.
Foregoing makeup, I stopped by the hallway closet and found an old
crocheted scarf to go with my dad's wool coat.

In the kitchen, I grabbed my bag. "Ready?"

Joseph stood and glanced at my attire. Arching a single eyebrow,
he nodded and gestured at the front door. "Lead the way."

In the driveway, Joseph's silver Lexus SUV gleamed in the sunlight. I frowned and caught myself wrinkling my nose. Blanking my

face, I held out my hand and waggled my fingers. "Give me your keys. I know my way around here better than you do."

He glanced at me from the corner of his eye, nostrils flared, posture haughty. "I have GPS, Erika. How do you think I got here?"

"If you want me to go with you, then you'll let me drive."

Shaking his head, he passed me the keys, and we climbed into the SUV's buttery-leather interior. Bland instrumental music streamed through the Lexus's expensive speakers. I bit my tongue, refraining from making snarky comments—my cynicism would only make things tenser and wouldn't help us get to town faster.

"So, tell me what you've been up to," he said, turning down his stereo. My ears rejoiced.

"Visiting with friends mostly. I went to my father's grave." *I got trashed on moonshine and found out my old boyfriend is possessed by a jinni.* "I cooked supper for my mom, and we talked."

"And?" He glanced at me.

"And it was fine. It was all fine. A lot of it was personal. I don't want to talk about it." *Not with you, especially.*

"Erika." His tone was full of exasperation. "I'm sorry if you think I'm prying—"

"I *do* think you're prying." I cut him a sharp look from the corner of my eye. "I came up here to take a break and get away. If I recall, you agreed it was a good idea, but I've been here less than three days before you show up with barely any notice. You've been good to me, Joseph, but my personal relationships aren't something I'm willing to share with you."

We'd met the first day of work, when I'd accepted a full-time position at UNC Hospital's oncology ward. Joseph had sought me out and asked me to lunch along with a group of other doctors and nurses, making it seem like a professional courtesy. As the weeks passed, he'd stopped inviting the others, and our professional relationship had evolved into friendship but nothing more. We were nei-

ther physically nor emotionally intimate, despite his urgings otherwise. I'd simply needed a friend, and he'd made himself available.
"Plus, I'm not naturally the open and sharing type. You know that."

"You're right." He gripped his door handle tighter, and the
leather creaked. "I know I can be aggressive sometimes, but I've always gone after the things I want. Some women like that in a man."

"I'm not *some* women. Haven't you figured that out by now?"

He offered no response, and we rode the rest of the way into
Evansville listening to the torturous drone of his elevator music.

A few miles from the center of downtown, parked vehicles lined
the highway on both sides. The farther we drove into town, the more
the traffic—both car and pedestrian—increased. Banners, balloons,
and inflatable dancing creatures advertised food, games, and concerts. As we passed Wallers Park, music from the main stage blasted
loud enough to drown out the insipid melody on the Lexus's stereo.

"Where are we going to park?" Joseph asked.

I pointed at the intersection ahead of us. "We'll go to the sheriff's
station. I'm sure my mom won't mind if we take a visitor spot."

After we'd secured his SUV in the sheriff's lot, we joined the
crowds milling through downtown. Music drifted on the breeze
along with the scent of roasting corn, grilled meat, and deep-fried
junk food. Scanning the parking lots and open areas around us, I
spotted a food truck parked near the entrance to Wallers Park. "How
about kebabs?"

He nodded and gestured for me to take the lead. We wove
through throngs of people sampling candied apples, churros, and
cotton candy. Some toted purchases from the craft booths. We
passed a young father carting a huge stuffed bear on his shoulders
while his wife pushed their toddler in a stroller. Joseph and I took
turns ordering lunch. After he insisted on paying and I relented,
mainly because I was too exasperated to argue any more, we nibbled

kebabs as we drifted farther into Wallers Park, drawn by the lively strum of guitars and banjos.

On stage, a bluegrass band was jamming to "Orange Blossom Special." The fiddle player sawed his bow across the strings, mimicking a train's sad whistle. Some in the audience clogged, and others stomped their feet and clapped. Joseph and I stood on the edge, watching and listening. He leaned close, raising his voice. "I'm trying to imagine what it's like around here when there's no festival."

"Much quieter and a lot less crowded." I licked my fingers clean and balled up my paper plate and tinfoil. "Come on. I'll introduce you to some folks."

We picked a path between lawn chairs and blankets until we reached Moon Runners' booth at the edge of the grassy lawn. While we waited in line, I studied the menu board, scanning the fall-themed drinks Luke had chosen for the festival: a caramel apple mule, a pumpkin-spiced hot toddy, and a ginger-pear cocktail that might have appealed if I hadn't overindulged the day before.

"Moonshine?" Joseph pursed his lips and checked his watch. "I'm not sure I'm ready for liquor this early in the afternoon."

"I know the owner, and he's supposed to be here today. I thought we'd say hello."

The couple in front of us collected their cocktails and stepped away, leaving room for us to scoot in. A brown-haired girl I didn't recognize smiled at us as she shoved a stack of dollar bills into her apron. "What can I get you?"

I shook my head. "We're not here for drinks. I was hoping to talk to Owen."

"Oh no, I'm sorry." Her smile fell. "He had to go back to the distillery to get more supplies. Said he'd be back in a half hour or so." She cocked her head and gave me a quizzical look. As she took in my red curls and freckles, her eyes went big and round. "Hey, aren't you Sheriff Albemarle's daughter? You were there at the distillery when—"

Stepping back, I waved her off. "We'll see if we can catch Owen later, okay?"

"Oh, okay." She blinked, and her smile returned. "You want me to tell him you were here?"

"No. I'm sure we'll find him around somewhere."

With Joseph silent and looming behind me, I weaved through the crowd and joined shoppers perusing arts and crafts booths that lined the sidewalks around the park's perimeter. "She was talking about the fire, wasn't she?" Joseph asked. "Has that happened a lot since you've been back? People recognizing you and bringing up bad memories?"

At a booth selling handmade silver jewelry, I inspected an elaborate silver wire ring studded with turquoise. "Ever since I was a kid, I've been recognized for one reason or another. At first, I was the girl whose father died. Then I was the sheriff's daughter. Now I'm the woman who survived the town's most recent tragedy." I set down the ring and leaned in close to study a pair of hoop earrings. "I'm used to people whispering about me whenever I walk by."

"I guess I can see why you were so anxious to get away." He slid his hand over my shoulder and squeezed. I resisted the urge to jerk away. "And not so willing to come back."

He thought he understood me, but he was wrong. Eager to change the subject, I pointed at a pottery display several tents over. "I know the artist in that booth. She and I went to high school together. I'm going to say hello."

By late afternoon, we'd seen all the sights and visited all the booths. The sunlight had softened to pale gold, hinting at the approaching sunset. Evansville's maintenance crews had strung lights around the park and along the sidewalks on Main Street, and the bulbs flickered to life above us.

The day was getting late, Joseph would have to drive home soon, and we still needed to have a serious talk before he left. "Come on." I tugged his elbow. "Let's get a coffee and sit for a while. My feet are tired."

I led him on a shortcut through the rear of the park, cutting behind the music stage and the row of food and drink booths beside it. We'd almost reached the sidewalk across from Rose's Diner when someone shouted my name. "Rikki!"

Like a magnet, Owen drew my gaze. He stood beneath the boughs of a massive ginkgo tree, and its golden leaves littered the ground. For a moment, those vivid bits of debris resembled flames, and it was as if a ring of fire had engulfed him.

Stepping forward, I gasped, but Joseph caught my shoulder and yanked me back. I stumbled against him. "What are you doing? Let me go." I tugged, but his grip tightened.

His expression had gone dark, his jaw rigid, brow furrowed. Flames burned in the depths of his dark eyes the same way they had once burned in Mina's. My knees turned to water, and a scream built in my chest.

"Rikki." Owen raced toward me, his hand outstretched, reaching. "Get away from him! He's not—"

In a blink, the world whipped away. Owen, the park, and the rest of Evansville disappeared. In another blink, I was standing among a crop of tombstones. Light, like a campfire, rippled across their surfaces in the fading evening light. *Hickory Wood? What the hell are we doing here?*

Behind me, an intense heat warmed my neck and shoulders. I refused to turn and look, fearing what I knew I would see—a being of fire. A jinni. He roared, and the air shook with his fury. "What infernal magic is this?" asked a voice that sounded like Joseph but older, deeper, angrier. "Where are we?"

Afraid to look, terrified of what I would see, I glanced at him from the corner of my eye. He still resembled the man I knew, mostly, although his skin glowed as though he'd swallowed fire, and it was burning through him, layer by layer. He grasped my arm, and his touch blazed as hot as a branding iron, yet I didn't burn. "What spells are you working, Erika? What magic has that wretched man given you?"

Magic? My mind blanked, but then Joseph hissed something unintelligible in my ear, and a ring of heat encircled my neck, pulsing against my chest. I clutched my throat, and my fingers brushed the thin silver chain I'd worn since the day Owen gave it to me. *The ta'wiz.* It felt alive beneath my touch, as if Joseph's words had awakened it. Perhaps it had intervened, bringing me here, to a place I'd always felt safe and where there was less chance of innocent bystanders being harmed. And if so, I wondered where Joseph thought we would wind up when he'd snatched me from Waller's Park.

I jerked my arm free. "Something wrong, *Joseph?*"

"It's no matter," he spat. "He'll come for you, and that's the important thing. I wasn't sure until I saw him myself, but the look on his face when he saw me was pure terror—not for me or for himself but for *you*. You still belong to him, Erika, and he *will* come for you."

"And then what?" I balled my fists at my sides. I'd be damned if I'd give in to my fear the way I had the night Mina died. I'd be damned if Joseph—or whoever he was—used me as Owen bait. *But what can someone like me do against a being like Joseph?*

"Then we take the seal and kill the Son of Suleiman."

My throat went as dry as dust. *We?*

Swallowing, I worked up my nerve and turned all the way around.

Behind Joseph stood two brilliant pillars of fire—ifrits, according to Owen and my previous research—holding themselves together in the vague shapes of men.

Just as Owen had predicted, a jinni king had come for him, and he hadn't come on his own.

Chapter Thirty-Three
I Won't Back Down

"I'M GUESSING YOUR NAME'S not really Joseph, and those"—I pointed a shaky finger at the fiery beings flanking the one who'd pretended to be my friend—"aren't some tourists you picked up in town." Although the words sounded light, my voice quaked, and my heart hammered against my ribs. The revelation of Joseph's true nature explained much about his intense interest in me. It also explained my aversion to him. My subconscious had been warning me about monsters all along, but I'd been too focused on the wrong one.

"I am Malik Al-Abyad." The being I'd formerly known as Joseph gestured to himself. "My companions are Abu Ya'qub and Al-'Ad-ja'yb."

"And you're three of the six remaining jinn kings." I backed away a step, angling for the cemetery's exit. "Your introductions are very polite for three creatures who'll most likely kill me once you're done using me to bait Owen, but I don't care about your real identities. I have a feeling that by the day's end, I'll never think of you again."

Joseph's fire flared brighter and hotter. "And why do you say that?"

"Because Owen will destroy you all as he did the other king who challenged him." Maybe that was a bold statement for an ill-fated woman who'd found herself standing in a graveyard and surrounded by three malicious jinn, but I was a fervent believer in the philosophy of fake-it-till-you-make-it.

Fighting an ifrit—much less three—was beyond me. In all my research, I'd never discovered a definitive way to defeat them. Part of me wanted to crawl into one of the cemetery's old mausoleums and never come out again, but a larger part of me—the part with the superhero complex—refused to run away and hide. I'd never get out of this situation without Owen's help, but maybe I could buy us some time. The ta'wiz was no weapon, but I could do a lot with a good shield against a being who'd underestimated my potential.

Not stopping to think, not giving Joseph a chance to read my decision in my eyes, I leapt—not for the exit, as he might have expected, but straight for him. Surprised, he was slow to react. I rammed into him, and we toppled, Joseph taking the brunt of the fall.

Before he could recover, I was on my feet, running, ducking into the deep shadows between the old monuments and gravestones. I sprinted, squinting into the fading light, searching for the path leading out of the cemetery. Trusting that a being made of fire and magic could easily navigate the darkness, I wasted no time looking back or worrying if Joseph and the others were on my heels.

I won't be that girl in the horror movies, falling and tripping. The monster might catch me, but I'm going to make him work for—

"Oof!" I plowed into a warm, firm body, smashing my nose against a sternum as hard as rock.

Before I could scream, a pair of arms latched around me. The scent of hot oil and incense flooded my nose. "Rikki, shhh, it's me."

"Owen." Digging my fingers into his biceps, I clung to him. In the darkness, he was a shadow—huge and impenetrable. Blue stars burned in his eyes, and my heart shuddered, but I ignored the frantic screams in my head. "How did you find me?"

"The ta'wiz. It's like a homing beacon."

"They're right behind me."

"Then we'd better get out of here." He folded himself around me, and his jaw brushed against my temple. His breath warmed my cheek. "Trust me, okay? And don't let go."

Nodding against his chest, I held fast to him. "I do. And I won't."

As I had with Joseph moments before, Owen and I moved imperceptibly through space and time, disappearing from the forest in one breath and appearing on his front porch in the next.

"Won't they follow us here?" I asked, stepping back after he released me.

"Eventually, yes, but thanks to your ta'wiz, they can't follow your trail like I could. This is naturally the next place they'll come looking for us, though. Not that it'll be easy for them to find."

He opened the front door and turned on the lights. I followed him inside, my heart still fluttering high in my throat. "So why doesn't the ta'wiz seem to work on you the way it works on them?"

He tugged me farther into the house. "It's like a security system only my family and I know how to disarm."

After pulling out a stool at his counter, he motioned for me to sit. Too nervous to be still, I shook my head and paced instead. Floorboards creaked beneath my feet, echoing the anxious voices in my head. "And how come they'll have trouble finding El Jannah?"

He pointed at my necklace. "The prayers on that necklace act like a spell, blocking harmful magic, right? I've spent the last three years surrounding El Jannah with more of those spells, setting up magical barricades to keep the jinn from easily finding or spotting this place. If I did things right, it should weaken their power too."

I crossed the length of his living room, turned on my heel, and marched in the opposite direction. "You have the ring, and they fear it because Solomon used it to enslave them. Can't you just do that now?"

Owen leaned against a counter and folded his arms over his chest. He wore a long-sleeved Moon Runners T-shirt. His dark hair hung in his eyes, and his beard was shaggy. Gone was the well-groomed soldier I'd known years before. In his place stood something a little less tame, as though the human disguise had thinned, revealing more of the beast inside.

Is the jinni taking over, or has something else worn him down? I knew how it felt to stand inside a storm of grief and have the grit of sadness scour away my humanity.

"Solomon was gifted the ring directly from Allah himself," he said. "Thousands of years have passed since then. The magic has dimmed, and my family's bloodlines have been diluted. We're an echo of what Solomon was."

"Can someone who isn't a descendent of Solomon use the ring?"

"I'm not sure what would happen. Maybe nothing." He raised a shoulder and dropped it. "Or maybe its power would be too much for anyone else to bear."

"So why would the kings care about the ring?"

He let loose a cold grin. His eyes blazed amber and blue, a blend of man and monster. "Because even an echo of Solomon's power is still something worth fearing."

"So, what now? Do we stand here and wait for them?"

His expression hardened. "I never wanted to involve you in this, but I don't know how else to protect you. I thought pushing you away would keep you safe, but I'm not sure that's right, anymore."

I stopped pacing, shoved my hands into my pockets, and inspected the toes of my boots. "I could have walked away in Chapel Hill. Maybe I *should* have. But I didn't, so now I'm involved, and I'll see tonight through to the end, because otherwise, I'll be looking over my shoulder for the rest of my life. I did that for three years already, and things haven't gone so well."

"And if we do manage to end this, and we both survive, then what?"

Looking up, I locked onto his eyes. My fingers itched to brush the hair off his brow, smooth his beard, stroke away the dark circles under his eyes. Three years ago, I wouldn't have hesitated, but he wasn't the same Owen anymore, and I wasn't the same Rikki. "I don't know... I really don't know."

WE KEPT VIGIL LATE into the night. Owen brewed coffee, and I accepted a mug mostly to keep my hands occupied. El Jannah was quiet. Peaceful almost. It felt like a lie. We sat on the couch, letting the silence pile up like rocks on a cairn, until Owen cleared his throat. "So you never suspected your, uh, *friend* was an incognito jinni king?"

I shook my head and stared at the ripples my breath stirred on the surface of my coffee. "I thought *you* were the monster I was hiding from. I never thought to look at the one standing right beside me."

"Do you still think I'm a monster?"

Carefully, I considered my words. "My mom thinks you're a superhero."

"You don't agree with her?" He winked.

"Weren't you afraid of attracting the jinn kings' attention with your heroics?"

"Maybe I got tired of hiding. Maybe I was ready for them to come so we could put an end to it all... one way or another."

His words were so hopeless. My heart wrenched for him, for what he must have suffered and how alone he must have felt—even with Luke at his back. "Did you really do all those things? Have you really been saving people?"

Glancing away, he studied the floor and shrugged one shoulder.

He was happy to let me call him a monster, but when I accused him of being a hero, he was shy and reluctant. His humility could have been an act, but I was tired of doubting him.

"I think Owen Amir is a man with flaws like everyone else, but he's also loyal, brave, and driven." My smile fell. "But it's the thing inside you I'm not so sure about." Perhaps the jinni had saved Owen's life in Iraq and had helped protect us from Al-Mudhib's attack in the warehouse years before, but my instincts contradicted the wisdom of trusting the jinn. From what I'd learned in my studies, they were tricksters by nature, self-serving and capricious.

Instead of offering assurances about his jinni's trustworthiness, Owen continued his original line of questioning. "I would think your jinn radar would be sensitive after everything you've been through. You really didn't suspect his true nature?"

"Don't think I haven't been beating myself up for it. Joseph was persistent but careful. Looking back on it now, I think he knew his pursuit made me uncomfortable, and he used that to keep me from looking too closely at him."

Owen leaned forward, resting his forearms on his knees, and twirled his ring around his knuckle. "How long did you know him?"

"About five months. I met him when I started nursing full-time at the hospital after graduation." Giving in to my jitters, I stood and went to the kitchen to pour out my coffee. Caffeine was the wrong choice when I was already jumpy and on edge. "He was pretty new too. Had just started a few months before me. I thought he was looking for a friend."

Owen arched an eyebrow. "*Just* a friend?"

"He made plenty of implications otherwise, but I never..." I waved my hand, implying he could figure out on his own what I'd never done. "Maybe my jinn radar was working after all. I always felt there was something not quite right between us. It's why I never took the next step."

"Was he the only one?" Owen stood. "I'm asking from a purely analytical standpoint, of course. Just wondered if there were any other potential threats we should be aware of."

Is he actually jealous, even after all these years? I gave him a smug smile. "Well, for the sake of analysis, the answer is no." I huffed. "The last three years have been lonelier than I'd like to admit."

He set his mug on the coffee table and prowled toward me, his face hard to read. "It shouldn't be that way for you, Rikki. You deserve happiness and love."

A pang of regret cut through me. "I think fate tends to disagree."

"You might have had them if I hadn't gotten in your way."

"I *did* have those things, once upon a time... with you." Perhaps the jinn kings would come, and we'd die fighting them. I had nothing to lose by speaking plainly, openly.

He froze, mere inches away, his eyes sparkling. "And look what happened."

"You know what Mina said the night of the cookout, when you grilled steaks on my deck and the fireflies came out?"

"What?"

"She quoted Nietzsche to me, of all things. 'That which does not kill us—'"

"'Makes us stronger.' Everyone knows it. It's cliché."

"But it's true to some extent. Ever since the night Mina died, I felt like I was coming apart, piece by piece, but since I've been back here, since I've faced you and found the truth, I..."

The muscle in his jaw flexed. "You what?"

"I feel stronger than I have in a long time. I'm ready to face these bastards. I'm ready to take my life back."

Owen flinched, his head jerking up like a dog hearing a curious noise. "It's good you say that."

Icy dread filled my stomach. "Why?"

"Because I think they're here." Narrowing his eyes, he pointed at his bedroom. "I've secured that room most of all. You'll be safest in there." He strode to the front door and yanked it open, but he didn't cross the threshold. I wondered if he had put spells around his house, too, like a fortified zone to retreat to if the front line of defense fell apart.

"And do what?" I frowned at him. "Leave you to fight on your own? We did this before, in Chapel Hill, remember? Maybe I can't fight, but I can't sit by and do nothing either."

He paused, his throat working as he seemed to consider my words. Finally, he nodded, having apparently come to a decision. "In Chapel Hill you came for me but not before you hesitated. That hesitation saved your life. Trust me when I ask you to hesitate again." He crossed the room and pulled me into his arms, his hands rough on my shoulders. I felt like a brittle leaf blowing about in the wind, but his dark look pinned me down. "I know you don't like to be the damsel, and there may come a time before this ends when I'm going to need your help, but stay here and be my secret weapon. Stay safe long enough to be there when I need you."

I held his gaze, wondering if he could see everything I was feeling but couldn't say, not just my fear but my hopes too. Maybe there could be something for us on the other side of this if we hung on long enough to reach it.

For another beat, he held me, our focus locked on each other. I would have given my right eye to know what was going on in his head, but other than his obvious dread, he was unreadable. He cupped my chin, his fingers hard but not cruel. "Promise me, Rikki. Say the words."

I cleared my throat. "I promise."

His shoulders relaxed, and he brushed his knuckles over my cheek. "I'll be okay. And if I'm not, you'll be there to patch me up, right?"

"I thought that's what your jinni was for. Now that I know the truth, you don't have to hide him."

"I told you I don't like using his magic any more than necessary. One of these days, there won't be anything of me left. It'll be Shadhan in my body, controlling the ring." He grimaced. "That's likely been his plan all along, and maybe he thought I wouldn't suspect his motives. I might be slow, but I'm not stupid."

"I can't bring people back from the verge of death like a jinni can. If you want to stay alive, you'll have to try to keep all your parts and pieces intact."

"I'll do my best." He flashed a grin, revealing a glimpse of his dimple. Then he disappeared, leaving me standing in the doorway of his bedroom alone.

Chapter Thirty-Four
Battle Cry

I LISTENED TO MY PULSE thump in my ears and tried to ignore the urging of my heart insisting I wasn't the type to sit by, waiting to be needed. This was no car wreck, though. No heart attack, acute appendicitis, or code blue emergency I could rush into with a crash cart and resuscitation team. So far, my encounters with the ifrits had only proven how ill-equipped I was to intervene in Owen's unfamiliar world.

Despite the intense itch driving me to get involved, I slumped on the edge of Owen's bed, popping my knuckles, gritting my teeth, tapping my feet. But when the silence continued after five... ten... *fifteen* minutes, my patience cracked. Surely more than enough time had passed for Owen to fight and win, or lose, this battle.

From his bedroom window, I peered outside, but the limited view provided only a small glimpse of his driveway and the trees beyond it. His bathroom window revealed even less—more forest and a stretch of star-studded sky. I tiptoed out of his bedroom, silently padding to the living room window.

From there, I spotted the first glimmer of the jinn.

Three fiery beings blazed in the flat yard beside the pond. Their light, like three dancing bonfires, wove in and out between a billowing black plume.

From this distance, the fight was difficult to follow, and Owen's ghostly shade blended into the darkness. Only the occasional flicker of blue flames and play of shadows across the ifrits' bright fire revealed his presence. Quietly, I eased open the front door and listened to the cacophony of battle. Grunts and shrieks filled the air, accompanied by a never-ending roar—not an animal cry but the raging of an angry forest fire.

From the front porch, I watched four monsters attack each other, fall back, reposition, and attack again. Against three opponents, Owen's dark jinni was a whirling dervish, a tornado of shadows spinning, twisting to face one opponent then the other. Sometimes the four figures moved like strobe lights, flashing faster than my eye could follow—here, there, visible, invisible.

Owen's shadowy beast bared his teeth. Moonlight gleamed, sparking off the tips of his horns in explosions of cobalt light. Like a bull, he bellowed and lowered his head, charging for one fiery opponent. The ifrit's flames billowed, but he held his ground, and when the two beings collided, the night tore apart in shrieks like rending metal. Shadows swirled with brilliant yellow flames, forming a cyclone of churning darkness and light. Another bellow resounded. The fire and shadow tempest blew apart, flames flying like shards of glass, sparking hundreds of tiny fires across Owen's lawn. Then the ifrit's remains flickered feebly before dying out, one by one.

A blue spark danced across the yard, a single firefly blinking high above the ground, then a dozen sparks, a hundred, a thousand. They spun, swirling together. Like a constellation, they formed the familiar outline of Owen's shadowy demon—horns, claws, fangs. My lizard brain squealed, urging me to retreat and hide. Instead, I gritted my teeth and squeezed my eyes shut until the panicked voices in my head subsided.

I realized I'd been holding my breath when I inhaled reflexively, sucking in an anxious gasp. I also realized I'd decided to leave the cabin only when my steps crunched in Owen's driveway. My promise to stay inside, stay safe, flashed through my mind, but another earth-shattering roar rent the quiet, tearing apart the night. I was sprinting down the hillside path before my thoughts could catch up and try to stop me.

One of the two remaining ifrits lunged for Owen's shadow monster while the other attacked from his rear. His dark, cloudy figure bloomed bigger, thicker. Sapphire flames blazed in his eyes as he gnashed his sharp teeth and howled. He was the beast of my nightmares, the being who'd terrorized my dreams for three years, the demon I'd blamed for Mina's death. My legs turned to water, and I stumbled to a stop as alternating waves of hot and cold panic smashed into me.

My heart beat an erratic, frantic tempo. I braced my hands on my knees and held my place, fighting to restore my calm and control, urging my terror to recede. I watched Owen's shadow monster shake off one ifrit like a grizzly shaking off an overzealous opossum. While he was distracted, the other ifrit punched through his chest, a laser beam ripping through smoke, and the dark beast bellowed.

He stumbled back, sinking to his knees. Slow to regain his footing, he moved as though his shadows had turned to sludge.

Fear for myself fled, replaced by dread for Owen. If the ifrits defeated his shadow monster, what did that mean for Owen?

You know exactly what it means, said a cold, emotionless voice in the back of my head. *Owen won't survive without his jinni.*

The scents of ozone, smoke, burnt grass, and hot metal—like an overheated iron skillet— tainted the air. The ifrits' heat reached for me, tendrils of a monstrous vine drawing me closer. I had barely reached the bottom of the hill when Owen's beast let loose another roar that shook the surrounding trees. The two remaining ifrits wailed like train wheels screeching against iron rails, their voices combining into a hellish orchestration of rage and hate.

A flash of white light and a burst of intense heat erupted from Owen's jinni, slicing through the darkness like a whip, turning the night into brilliant, blinding daylight for a heartbeat before fading to black.

When my vision recovered, I saw the ifrits' flames guttering, losing substance, flickering like a paper match on the verge of going out.

Whatever had happened to generate that energy burst, it had obviously exhausted the ifrits' power and essence—depleting their light and heat, draining their presence until they resembled a distant desert mirage. But that blast of power must have come at a great cost to Owen's jinni too. His monstrous demon of shadow and storm clouds contracted. He howled as his towering mass swirled like water circling a drain, spiraling to a single point—the Big Bang in reverse. His expansive darkness sucked inward to a pinprick of blue starlight that blinked once and disappeared.

All that remained was Owen, lying prone and still in the short grass at the edge of the dock.

He didn't get up. Didn't move.

A hot bolt of electric terror tore through me. Adrenaline flooded my bloodstream, and my legs pumped as I sprinted the remaining distance, reaching Owen's side as one ifrit rallied, gathering strength to raise up, his fiery fist clenched to deliver a potentially brutal blow. I screamed at him, and my shrill cries were no match for his terrible howls, but I distracted the ifrit long enough to draw his attention away from Owen.

The ta'wiz had shielded me against Joseph before.

I hoped it would protect me again.

Lowering my shoulder, I dropped my head and plowed into the fiery demon.

Chapter Thirty-Five
Don't Surrender

DESPITE APPEARING TO be made of diaphanous flames and unsubstantial particles of light, the fire jinni felt as solid as a full-grown man. He went down as hard as one too. Like Jack and Jill, we tumbled, rolling down the pond's bank. Gaining momentum, we toppled over the edge and splashed into the shallows.

Beneath the pond's dark surface, I clung to the writhing, howling, burning ifrit, holding on until my arm muscles screamed.

Until my skin blistered despite the Ta'wiz's protection.

Until black spots poked holes around the edges of my vision and my lungs shrieked for air.

Until, finally, the monster's fire was extinguished. Fading into steam and mist, the jinni evaporated from my grasp. In the thigh-deep water, gasping and gulping for breath, I sprang to my feet, searching for my opponent. Instead of flames, a thick fog dispersed across the pond and drifted away like a ghost—a jinni's ghost, perhaps. *Let's hope that's what it is, anyway.*

A warm surge of triumph welled up in me, but I shoved it down. *It's too soon to celebrate. The fight's not over yet.* One jinni king remained, hovering in the yard near the dock. Glimmering dimly, the ifrit was less of a fiery monster and more like heat shimmering off the blacktop in summer, his light thin and watery. Maybe the ifrit was nearly defeated by Owen's final attack, or maybe it was biding its time, gathering its strength. I wasn't dumb enough to assume it wasn't a threat, but Owen was my more immediate concern.

Scalded, drenched, and dripping, I raked my hair back and climbed out of the pond. I scrambled across the dark lawn and crouched at Owen's side, lowering my ear to his mouth. His breathing was shallow, tremulous, and wet. In the hospital, we sometimes called that kind of breathing the *death rattle*. His skin was cool and clammy. I pressed my fingers against the inside of his wrist, but his pulse was so faint, I couldn't be sure I was feeling anything other than my own blood throbbing in my fingertips.

My throat tightened as if an invisible hand were choking me. "Owen?" I croaked, shaking his shoulder. "Wake up."

When he didn't respond, didn't move, didn't gasp for a breath, time ground to a halt. The world froze, and everything inside me went still and silent. With clinical, robotic detachment, I slipped into emergency responder mode—raising his chin, tilting his head back, pinching his nose. I pressed my lips over his, and rather than honey or red pepper, he tasted like cold ashes and extinguished fires.

"Hear me, woman, and stop what you're doing."

A disembodied voice, a whisper, skittered over me like cold wind, raising hairs on my neck and arms. I froze, my hands braced on Owen's chest, and listened.

"The one you're fighting to save is still alive but only just so."

The only thing in the yard besides Owen and me was the flickering remnants of the last ifrit, who seemed to have recovered some of his substance. Occasional tongues of yellow-and-gold flame flickered along his edges. *Is that who's talking to me?*

As if reading my thoughts, the voice answered, "Malik Al-Abyad, the White King, will be upon you soon. Wait any longer, and he'll be too strong for you to defeat. Now's the time to strike him down."

Still straddling Owen's hips, I sat back, unwinding my rigid posture. I searched my memory for a name to match the voice. *What did Owen call his jinni?* "Shadhan?"

"Indeed." A translucent nebula of pale-blue stars blinked to life, floating several feet above Owen's head. I wondered if that was all that remained of Owen's roaring, monstrous beast. If so, then Owen's chances of survival seemed even more uncertain. More desperate.

"You're still here?"

"Scarcely, but yes."

"Owen's alive?"

"I've already answered this. Waste no more time asking useless questions."

My fists clenched, but I didn't think I could choke a nearly invisible jinni. "So, answer this one instead. How do I save him?"

"There's nothing you can do, woman. Save your fears for Malik Al-Abyad. If you don't defeat him, none of us will survive this night."

I eased off Owen and stood on trembling knees, facing the tremulous cloud of blue stars.

"What the hell can I do against him? I'm just a regular person."

"The ring..." Shadhan's voice was fading, and so was his light.

Fear clamped down on me with jagged sharp claws, and my breath shuddered. I knew about intubation and defibrillation. Epinephrine and naloxone. Chest compressions and Heimlich maneuvers. I knew nothing about magic, though, and the thought of using that ring scared me more than if he'd asked me to crack open Owen's chest and perform open heart surgery. "But Owen said if he ever took it off, he'd die."

"I can sustain him... but not for long."

Panic seized me, heart sprinting, blood baking, air thinning. I couldn't catch a breath. "But... he wasn't sure anyone else besides a descendent of Solomon could wield the ring. He said it might be too much for me to bear."

I waited for Shadhan's quiet, wispy voice, but when the essence of blue stars faded away without a reply, my mouth went dry. My knees turned to quicksand, and I dropped into a crouch beside Owen,

stroking his arm with trembling fingers, tracing the long sinews leading to his wrist. Following the veins branching the back of his hand
like a map, I reached the ancient ring. The coldness of it burned,
and I recoiled. Letting out a scream of frustration, venting my fears,
I grabbed the ring again and tugged. His hand flinched, and he uttered a feeble groan. I waited a hopeful moment, praying for a miracle, but he remained unconscious.

Desperate, I grabbed the ring, wrenching it over his knuckle.

Darkness concealed the ring's details, but it felt significant, as
though it weighed more than it should have for its size, as though
it had captured and held thousands of years of history in its core.
Maybe nothing would happen. Maybe too *much* would happen, and
wielding the ring would mean we all died, but I *had* to try. Giving up
was no option, and letting Owen die was even less of one.

Despite their crumbling mortar and missing stones, my emotional barriers went up, and I locked my fear and panic behind them.
Later, I might have a chance to deal with my feelings—*if* I survived.
For now, there was only time for action and doing whatever it took
to save us both.

Rising, I stood and spread my feet. I faced the being I'd once
known as friend and colleague. He'd managed to regenerate enough
flame to form a thin, wavering outline of a man—nothing like the
raging inferno he'd been before. If I'd stood before a jinni king fully
in control of his powers, I would've fought him because it wasn't my
nature to surrender, but I wouldn't have dared to hope for success.
This thing before me, though, was reduced and weakened.

I slipped the ring on my finger.

Maybe I *could* beat him.

Maybe.

Thrusting my shoulders back, I raised my chin. "You wouldn't
consider calling a truce, would you?"

The ifrit's flames pulsed, but he offered no response.

"I take that as a no."

Other than begging for mercy, which I didn't think he was receptive to, I didn't know what else I could say. Joseph had been a lie, a straw man, and I was a pawn on his chessboard. The only way to show him he was wrong was to beat him with my actions, not my words. *Show, don't tell, right?*

I stilled my breathing and reached for a calmness inside myself I wasn't sure existed. *What am I supposed to do now?*

Owen had said that after his IED attack, the ring responded to his unconscious desire to survive, so I focused my thoughts on my most burning wish—defeat Joseph, save Owen. The calm I had been searching for slipped over me like a cool spring shower, and my mind cleared. I stepped forward, pinning my gaze on the ifrit's countenance where his eyes might have been if he'd had any.

"Malik Al-Abyad." I had known him as Dr. Joseph Khan, but using a fake name seemed like a bad way to start when it came to commanding a jinni. I clenched my fist, raising the ring toward him, with visions of the *Green Lantern* dancing in my head. Hal Jordan's alien ring had worked by making the things in his imagination manifest as reality, but I doubted the Seal of Solomon worked that way.

A quiet hum filled my veins. My nerve endings tingled. Perhaps it was wishful thinking, but I felt something happening. "I command you to kneel."

Start small. If I could make the ifrit do that much, I'd move on to greater demands.

He didn't kneel, though.

Instead, the quiet titter of funeral chimes rippled from him. He raced forward, propelling himself on who knew what. Magic and myth? Anger and hate? I retreated several steps, refusing to give him my back. If I let him out of my sight, let him have any advantage, the fight would end before it began.

Reaching the edge of the pond, I had run out of room to retreat. I braced myself and squeezed the ta'wiz charm at my throat, asking for protection from anyone, any*thing*, who could hear me. Like a linebacker, the ifrit tackled me, and the back of my skull bounced against the hard ground. Darkness spun across my eyes. I bit my tongue, and blood filled my mouth, bitter with adrenaline and cortisol—the human body's favorite fighting drugs.

When my vision cleared, I could see the stars shining through the ifrit's nebulous form, yet his strength was substantial, overpowering. He pinned me to the ground, a cockroach beneath his boot heel.

He chuckled again.

"You think this is funny?" I spat a wad of bloody phlegm at him, hardened my resolve, and wrapped my will like a fist around my next command. "If it's funny, then laugh some more, Al-Abyad. I *order* you to laugh."

Unfazed, he gathered me in his arms and yanked me to my feet. Wrapping one clawed hand around my neck, he squeezed. Desperate and losing air fast, I struggled to break free and regretted not asking my mom for tae kwon do lessons instead of another summer of volleyball camp. I stroked my thumb over Owen's ring and wheezed the command again, choking on my own words. "*Laugh... you bastard.*"

A shiver, prickly and sharp like sandburs and thorns, undulated through me. *More magic from the ring?* The sensation was unpleasant but bearable, and if it didn't get worse, I'd be able to handle it. *But when have I ever been that lucky?*

The ifrit's grip eased, and I stumbled away. His flames wavered, rolling like ocean waves in a storm. Was he struggling? Trying to resist my order? Perhaps so, because he went still, and laughter trickled from him, light and tinkling like a mountain stream—not the laugh of a monster but of someone carefree and full of joy. It reminded me of the way Mina had laughed.

I'm sorry for not protecting you or saving you, Mina. Sorry for the pain and grief and anger. But tonight, I make things right.

Holding Mina's memory close, I drew strength from our friendship and fed it into my next command. "Now, Al-Abyad," I rasped. "Let's try this again. I want you to—"

Moving too fast to perceive, the ifrit backhanded me, whipping my head around, cracking my neck with the force of his blow. My teeth clashed together. White spots bloomed in my vision, and I fell, landing hard on my tailbone. It snapped, and I shrieked.

"Do you wish to surrender yet?" The ifrit loomed over me, and for an instant, Joseph's familiar face appeared among the flames.

"As if..." Panting, I scrambled back a foot or two. "As if you'd let me just walk away."

"Not walk away, no, but I can offer you a painless death."

Instead of debating his offer, I fisted my ring hand again and finished the command he'd prevented me from completing before. "I don't want to surrender. I want you to kneel, Abyad. I want you to get on your knees and *kneel.*"

My last word ended in an excruciating scream through my clenched teeth, but Al-Abyad complied, his snarl of protest matching my bellow of pain. Slowly, an inch at a time, trembling with the effort to resist, he dropped to his fiery knees, submitting to my will. Agony tore through me as though someone had threaded barbed wire through my body and ripped it back out. Wheezing, I curled into myself and thought of my father, who'd borne the torture of his dying body for months, simply so he could have one more minute, one more hour, one more day with me and my mom.

I vowed to also endure—for him, for Mom, for Mina, *and* for Owen.

Gritting my teeth against whatever agony was coming next, I flung my hand out, pointing at Owen, who still hadn't moved, hadn't drawn a breath or uttered a sound. "Heal him, Al-Abyad. Whatever it takes. Even if it requires sacrificing all your power and magic to do it, make Owen whole again."

A horrible bellow, like a million missiles hurtling toward the earth, shattered the air. I bellowed as well and lost my grip on the world as my bones turned to hot, molten lead and my blood boiled. An eddy of blackness churned around the edge of my awareness—not Shadhan or Owen but a demon of oblivion, coming to devour my consciousness. My body was likely going into shock, but I pushed on, determined to see this battle of wills to the end. *Who's a pawn on the chessboard now, you asshole?*

Al-Abyad must have felt something similar to my pain because he twisted and churned, struggling against my command, but he was losing. Inch by inch, he stumbled closer to Owen.

"Heal him," I said again, my voice a hoarse croak. "Whatever it takes."

"Whatever it takes?" asked the ifrit, his words a raw whisper. Both of us were suffering, but who would break first? "What it takes is a sacrifice. An agreement. A contract."

Owen had said something similar, that deals made the jinn's magic stronger, but making such a deal required trust. "Jinn are tricksters. I can't believe anything you say."

"Then the Son of Suleiman dies." Abyad pointed at Owen, and he opened his eyes and made a horrible choking sound. Owen writhed as if fighting for a breath he couldn't catch.

"*Heal* him," I begged, and my skin felt as though it was tearing from my muscles. My body squirmed, a primal effort to escape the pain, but there was no getting away from the ring's torture.

"To save the one you love, you must give up something you love in return."

"What do you want?" Tears of desperation spilled down my cheeks. "Tell me, and you can have it."

The ifrit said nothing, and his silence was more than the passing of a thousand years. It was more than I could bear.

"Will it... will it cancel his contract with Shadhan?" Anguish raged and screamed, shattering my control. My body was tearing in two. *Do something, fast. You're not going to hold out much longer.* I dragged in a breath that felt like fire in my lungs. "If I make a deal, will Owen be completely free?"

"Yes."

Owen groaned and raised a hand toward me, his chest heaving as he continued to struggle. "No, Rikki. Don't."

"How can I trust you?" I asked the ifrit.

"How can you afford not to?"

Whimpering, grinding my teeth, thrashing on the ground, I offered the first thing that came to mind. "Let him live," I moaned as the pain sank deeper, setting like a hook in the base of my spine, "and you can have Dolly."

The ifrit laughed. "Nice try but not even close."

With only the briefest hesitation, I submitted my next offer, the sacrifice I was certain Abyad was truly after. "My life, then. Take my life for his."

"You haven't loved your own life in years. Your offer is still not good enough."

What did he want? My mind spun to come up with something that could satisfy him. "I'll give you—"

"I want every *tendresse* you shared with him—every feeling of fondness or love. Every touch. Every caress. Every whispered declaration. I shall save his life, and in return, you will have no memory of loving him. No one else will remember you were ever together, and it shall be as though your love never existed. Only the Son of Suleiman will retain the memories of your devotion, and he alone shall suffer the loss of your love—a wound even greater than death."

"No." His eyes filled with pain, Owen pleaded with me. "It's not worth it. Please, Rikki, don't. "

"To save your life? I'd give him anything." I'd lost enough people already. There was no way I'd let him die too.

"Including *us*?"

"If you die, there will be no 'us,' anyway." As long as he remembered, he could remind me. He'd made me fall for him once. I had to believe he could do it again. I had no other option to save him. I clasped the ta'wiz between my fingers, hoping its magic might still shield me somehow, and before I could change my mind, I said the words Abyad had been waiting for. "I accept the deal."

Owen bayed like a wounded animal while the ifrit cackled, his satisfaction evident in his horrible joy.

In the last seconds before my body gave out, I saw Abyad, like a shimmering ghost, lean over Owen, extend one fiery tendril, and touch it to Owen's forehead.

What happened after that, I didn't know, because the demon of oblivion claimed me and dragged me away to his lair of unconsciousness.

Chapter Thirty-Six
Just Like Starting Over

LIKE DOLLY'S ENGINE trying to start on a cold winter morning, awareness returned in fits and starts. Periods of light followed fragments of blackness. Flashes of sounds—screams and howls mixed with the clatter of someone opening kitchen cabinets and moving things around in the refrigerator. Flickers of color and smells—hot metal, burning grass, coffee, and fabric softener.

When my mental engine finally caught and thrummed to life, I blinked until my surroundings came into focus. Pale morning light streamed in through a nearby window, illuminating the Princess Leia poster hanging on the wall next to me. *Home sweet home.*

As I sat up and stretched, a streak of pain lanced from my hips up the length of my spine. Swallowing a yelp, I rolled onto my side and pressed tentative fingers to my tailbone. A breathy wheeze burst from my throat, and stars swam across my vision. *Broken tailbone? How the hell did that happen?*

Deciding that standing was preferable to sitting—or curling up into the fetal position—I crawled out of bed. My hair was loose, a natural disaster of frizzy red curls, like knotted piles of debris after a hurricane. I raked the ruddy avalanche out of my eyes and hobbled into the kitchen, where the scent of coffee plowed into me like a bulldozer.

Mom stood at the counter, sipping coffee and staring out the kitchen window. She flicked a glance over her shoulder then immediately looked back. Her gaze scraped over me, from hurricane hair to rumpled pajamas and back up again. "Rough night?"

I honestly couldn't remember. The last thing I recalled was going to the diner with Joseph after the festival and insisting he had to go home. *But what happened after that? Did I pass out? And if so, how did I wake up in my bed with injuries? Would Joseph really have abandoned me like this?*

This wasn't the first time I'd blacked out and lost memories, usually after a night of too much drinking or too many pills. I'd hoped coming back home and making peace with Mina's death, my survivor's guilt, and my remorse for basically deserting my mom and Rose would've been my first step toward recovery, but maybe I was expecting too much too soon.

Her brow creased. "Are you all right?"

"I've given myself a thorough medical evaluation, and I passed."

Grimacing as if she didn't quite believe me, she filled a mug with coffee and set it on the counter in front of me before taking my hand and giving it a squeeze. Her forehead puckered, and the lines around her mouth stood out, deep and harsh. "Heard you had a friend with you at the festival. He didn't try anything funny, did he? Didn't get out of hand or anything?"

"Nothing like that, I swear. Just a party that got a little crazy." *That must have been what happened, right?*

"Hmm." Mom's eyes flicked to the front door. "You didn't drive home, did you?"

"Nope. I hitched a ride." Or so I hoped. *Maybe Joseph drove me home before he left.*

"Don't take this the wrong way"—she sniffed, her nostrils flaring, her lips tightening into a pucker—"but you smell rank." She reached for a bottle of generic naproxen on the counter, shook out several blue pills, and passed them to me. "Go hit the shower."

Nodding, I backed away from the counter and swallowed my pain pills with a sip of coffee. "I think I'll clean up and head to the diner for breakfast." From there, I hoped I could sort out my memories from the night before. If not, then maybe I could eat enough greasy food to make me not care so much.

"I've got to head to work. You going to be around for dinner?"

I searched my mental calendar but could think of no reason to refuse. "Yeah, I should be. I could cook again."

Mom set her coffee cup in the sink. "Sounds good. Let's make it a date."

She started past me but paused and pulled me into a hug. "I'm glad you're home. I hope you can stick around for a while."

"I'm glad to be home too. I missed you, Mom."

She pulled away, swiped at her eyes, and hurried out the door. Maybe she was crying, but she wasn't one to show softness if she could help it.

After a long, hot shower, I coiled my hair back in a twist and dug a clean pair of jeans and a cable-knit sweater from my luggage. I knotted my Doc Marten laces extra tight and shrugged on my trusty peacoat. Then Dolly and I took a ride into town, following familiar old roads I could've navigated in my sleep. I wondered whether that was what I had done last night. *God, I hope not.*

I reached Rose's Diner at peak breakfast rush and had to drive two blocks past her restaurant before a vacant parking place appeared. But an empty barstool waited for me at the counter, almost as though Rose was expecting me. Careful of my bruised rear end, I eased into the seat as she hurried out of the kitchen, carrying a plate laden with eggs, tomatoes, biscuits, and a thick hunk of cheddar cheese. She set the plate down in front of the man sitting beside me. I glanced at him, and the hairs on the back of my neck stood up.

I swallowed thickly. "Hello, Owen."

He gave me a strangely intense look, his eyes searching mine. "Rikki."

"Long time no see." Not since the night of the fire at his distillery. Not since Mina's death. We'd been a group of young, carefree, innocent friends hanging out, ordering Chinese takeout, talking about our futures. We couldn't have known that a faulty gas line would ruin everything in a blink.

The knot in his throat bobbed. "Heard you were in town."

"Sorry I haven't said hello sooner." I searched his face, taking in the angles and planes, the knife-straight nose, the gold flecks in his eyes, the lovely bronze shade of his skin. We'd hung out some in the past because he was best friends with Luke, and Luke and Mina had started dating, which meant we'd often founds ourselves in a group together. *So how have I never noticed how good-looking he is?*

Before I realized what I was doing, I'd leaned a fraction closer to him and inhaled. He smelled like shower soap—sandalwood and a hint of cardamom. It was pleasant but not what I was expecting. *What* was *I expecting?*

"I don't blame you," he said. "It's not like we share a happy history. I'm not sure what you remember when you look at me, but I thought it was best to leave you alone if that made things easier for you."

I waved his comment away as Rose appeared with a mug full of coffee and set it before me. He was right that I still got shaky every time I thought about that night, but I didn't want to make him feel any guiltier than he probably already did. It hadn't been his fault, anyway. A subcontractor had installed those gas lines, and he'd paid a heavy penalty for his mistakes, according to the news reports.

"I actually went by Moon Runners day before yesterday." My head throbbed at the memory. "Luke was there. He gave me a few samples." A few too many. I'd woken up at home, groggy and headachy. After popping a couple of pain pills and going back to bed, I'd slept through the next morning. I had a history of losing chunks of time, and I was tired of it. Something had to give, and I hoped coming back home really was the first step toward recovery.

"That must have been hard for you, going back there. I admire your bravery."

I shrugged. If you could call getting blackout drunk being brave, then I was on my way to becoming the next great American hero. "They say the best way to defeat your demons is to face them."

He barked a sharp laugh. It sounded a little bitter and cold. "You don't know just how right you are."

"You've faced some demons, too, have you?"

"You could definitely say that."

Even after he'd cleaned his plate and Rose had taken away his dishes, Owen lingered, drinking more coffee as I finished up my breakfast. I got the feeling he was working up the nerve to ask me something. A few times, he'd glanced at me and inhaled. But then he let the breath out and looked away. He toyed with an old brass ring on his finger as if he were anxious.

Rose brought us our bills. She glanced at Owen, looked at me, and quirked her eyebrow. "This might sound random and totally out of the blue, but... y'all look pretty good together—as a couple, I mean. Owen, you ever thought about asking Rikki out on a date?"

Heat rushed into my cheeks and blazed in a furious blush. "Way to put someone on the spot."

"Actually, um..." He rubbed the back of his neck and gave me a slightly apologetic wince. "I was trying to think of a way to bring it up."

I furrowed my brow at him. "Bring what up?"

"How do you feel about taking a motorcycle ride on a pretty fall day?"

I glanced out the diner's big plate glass windows. A bright sun blazed in the sky. A gentle breeze ruffled the leaves of the ornamental trees planted along the sidewalk in front of the restaurant. It *was* a pretty fall day. "Are you asking me out?"

Owen's hesitant smile brightened. He looked at me through his thick black lashes, and my heart did a little flip-flop. *Really... how have I not noticed him sooner?* "You ever ridden on a motorcycle?"

"No. Never."

He stood and tilted his head toward the door. "Come on. It's an experience you really don't want to miss."

Hesitating, I looked into his eyes, wondering whether I should trust him. Something inside me, something instinctual, insisted I could. Still, I wavered. Motorcycles were dangerous and deadly—a type of risk I usually avoided. Also, there was my sore tailbone to consider.

Rose rolled her eyes and grunted a sound of exasperation. "You only live once, Rikki. Might as well have fun with it. I'll vouch for Owen. He's good people."

Sorting through my memories, I searched for anything that might support Rose's claims and remembered the Raven's Knob fire. Owen had been there that night, working tirelessly among the smoke and flames to save a local family. It also seemed he'd tried to save us the night of Mina's death, and though my memories remained trapped in a haze of trauma, I suspected he'd played a larger role than I'd known in keeping me safe. Nothing else explained how Luke and I had been found in the Moon Runners parking lot, burnt, smoky, and unconscious but alive. He'd saved us the same way he'd saved the Buckleys.

When I'd come to town, I'd been looking for breakfast, not a love connection, but Rose's determination was compelling, and Owen's charm was inexplicably magnetic. I couldn't be as certain as Rose that he was "good people," but the only way to know for sure was to find out for myself.

Owen arched his eyebrow and grinned, revealing a single dimple that melted my already wavering resistance. "I should warn you..." I smiled sheepishly. "I, um, might have a broken tailbone."

He flinched, and his expression darkened. "Oh God, I should have known." Brow puckered, concern brimming in his eyes, he reached for me but stopped short. "We don't have to—"

"I'm not an invalid." His concern was sweet if not a little intense for someone who barely knew me. And I wondered what he meant by saying that he should have known about my tailbone. "I'm just telling you to take it easy on me."

Nodding, his expression still intense and full of worry, he said, "If you're sure."

Rising from my seat, I took his hand in an effort to reassure him. "I am, but you'll have to tell me what to do."

"There's really only one main rule." He led us toward the door. "Hold on tight, and never let go."

With my heart in my throat and my arms bound tightly around his ribs, we whipped down Main Street and raced to the outskirts of town, following Highway 74 as it wound beside the Nantahala River. The white water rafting companies had packed up and left for the season, and the river was quiet and empty.

Owen eased off the throttle. He leaned, and the bike coasted around the corner of the next turn, rolling onto a narrow road that crossed a bridge suspended over the water. He stopped the bike parallel to the road beside a barrier and dropped the kickstand. When the motorcycle settled, he flicked the ignition switch, and I tugged off my helmet and handed it to him. He slid off his seat, and I followed as he strode toward the bridge. The river tumbled over rocks, forming eddies and white-capped waves. Sunlight sparkled, dancing and jumping in the currents.

He stopped midway across the bridge and leaned against the railing, peering at the clear waters.

"You brought us here to show me the bridge?" I asked.

He shook his head but didn't look my way. "I brought you here to tell you a ghost story."

I shivered, overwhelmed by a distinct and powerful sense of déjà vu. "If it's the one about the Nantahala Lovers, I already know it."

He flashed me a brief, sad smile. "My story *is* about two lovers, and it's tragic, too, but mine has a happier ending."

I arched an eyebrow and leaned against the railing beside him. "Oh? I thought ghost stories don't have happy endings."

He chuckled. "I guess you're right. I guess mine is more like... a legend. The legend of the Soldier and the Three Jinn Kings."

"Sounds like something from *A Thousand and One Nights*." I poked his shoulder playfully. "Are you my own personal Scheherazade?"

His smiled sweetly at me. "Will you let me tell it to you?"

His earnestness warmed me. I wanted to hear his story. In fact, I *needed* to hear it, but I couldn't explain the source of that intense urge. "Yes. Please do."

He took my hand, folding it between both of his. A simple touch, yet it was comforting and familiar. "Once upon a time, there was a young man who was a soldier. He went to war in the deserts of Iraq because his king had commanded it of him. While he was there, he was mortally wounded when the enemy staged a surprise attack. In desperation, he made a deal with a jinni to save his life. Do you know what jinn are?"

"Like genies, right?" I had leaned close, his story drawing me in like a net. I hung on every word as though he was revealing the secrets of the universe rather than entertaining me with a simple story.

Owen nodded. "But not like the ones in the movies. The jinn are beings made of smokeless fire. They can take on different shapes, and they can possess a man. The jinni in this story promised to save the soldier's life, but doing so would require the jinni to take permanent possession of him. Having no other option, the soldier agreed."

Owen went on to explain how the soldier later discovered the jinni had used him to escape the tyranny of seven powerful jinn kings who ruled over all of jinn kind. But of course those jinn kings hated that one of their subjects had attempted to escape.

Owen tucked my hand into the bend of his elbow. We strolled along the bridge, back to the road, and took a pathway leading down to the river's edge. The county had installed a paved sidewalk for tourists to enjoy along the banks, but we had the river to ourselves as far as I could see.

"The soldier went home and left the army and tried to start a normal life. He met a girl, the bravest, most clever and beautiful woman he'd ever known. He fell in love with her the first time he saw her. She, however, took a little time to come around to him. She'd lost people she loved before, and she was afraid to risk her heart again. But he won her over, their love burning bright and hot."

"That doesn't sound like the kind of relationship that has long-term potential." I crouched, picked up a loose rock beside the sidewalk, and hurled it into the river. It crashed into the water with a satisfying *spelunk*. "The hot ones burn out fast."

"You'd think that, yes, but you'd be wrong." He glanced at me, his eyes searching, intent, piercing—as though he could see deep inside of me. "Theirs was a love to last throughout the ages."

Still holding my attention, he continued his story, telling of the troubles the lovers had faced and overcome together. How the soldier's beloved lost her best friend to a jinn king's wrath. How his beloved's grief ravaged her and turned her into a hollow wraith for years. But in time, they found their way back to each other, the ember of their love reigniting until three jinn kings returned for a final reckoning.

"The soldier and his lover fought fiercely. They destroyed two jinn kings and weakened the third. But the battle took a turn, and the soldier was mortally wounded before the third jinni king was destroyed. Desperate, the soldier's beloved begged the jinni king to heal her lover and save his life." Owen's gaze locked onto mine, and perhaps I was imagining it, but a universe of emotion—pain, sorrow, and regret—seemed to swirl in his dark eyes. *What hurts has he suffered? Is he a survivor like me—one who's a little scarred and jaded but still harbors a seed of hope for finding happiness someday?*

"The jinni king agreed, but for a price. The jinn always require a bargain in exchange for their help. The jinn king told her, 'To save the one you love, you must give up something you love in return.'"

The sense of déjà vu retuned again, stronger than before—powerful enough to make me dizzy. I closed my eyes and swayed on my feet. Owen clutched me closer, steadying me. "She did it, didn't she?" I asked, breathless. "She gave up something precious and saved the soldier's life."

He nodded, gently resting his forehead against mine. His warm breath mingled with my own. "The jinni king asked her to give up her memories of her love for her soldier. A sacrifice so absolute it would erase their love from the collective memory of the universe, from anyone who'd ever known them. Meanwhile, the soldier would be cursed with the memory of their love while knowing she had forgotten it. He begged her not to do it, but she'd lost too many loved ones already—she couldn't stand to watch him die too. The choice to save his life was easy for her."

I huffed. "I doubt if it was *easy*. If it had been easy, then their love wasn't real. Are you saying it wasn't real?"

"I'm saying that she loved him so much she was willing to give her own life for him. She loved him so much she didn't have to stop and think about it."

"And is that how the story ends? She agrees to the price, and the jinni takes her memories, and they both live but not so happily ever after?" I pulled away and narrowed my eyes at him. "This story *sucks*."

He threw back his head and laughed. It vibrated through his chest. "No, that's not how it ends. Or that's how the jinni king thought it ended, but he was wrong."

"What happened to that third king after he granted her request?"

Owen shrugged. "He disappeared. Perhaps the strength required to heal the soldier finished the king off. Perhaps he went back home to lick his wounds and recover. That's not the important part."

"What's the important part?"

He released me from his embrace and took my hand, and we walked farther down the bank toward a small, empty park. "The important part is what the soldier decided to do next." He stopped abruptly and faced me again. "He vowed to return to the desert and find the other jinn kings. Perhaps they were angry with him, or perhaps they were afraid of him after he'd killed so many of their kind. Either way, he promised to find those kings who remained and command them to return his beloved's memories."

"Did he do it? And did it work?"

Owen cocked his head and gave me a curious look. "What do you think?"

"It had to work. All love stories have to get their happily-ever-afters in the end."

He nodded. "The legend isn't clear, but I believe he'd keep his promise."

I was beset with an inexplicable need to take ownership of the story and ensure it got the ending it deserved, as though I had something personally invested in it. Rationally, it was a ridiculous compulsion, but Owen seemed pleased by my enthusiasm. When he smiled the way he was smiling at that moment, I would've done anything to keep him happy, and no, it didn't make sense, but I didn't care. "And even if he hadn't found the jinn kings, he would have courted her again, right? He would have stayed with her and been gentle and patient and kind until she fell in love with him again. Even if she had no memories of the past, they could form new ones together, right? They could still have a second chance."

Owen brought my hand to his lips and pressed a kiss to my knuckles. His touch burned, and I wanted more of it, of him. "Yes." His voice was raspy. Broken. Heavy with emotion. He was obviously feeling it too—whatever this was between us. "They would have their second chance, no matter what."

The atmosphere thickened, filling with unspoken sentiment. Owen's words had mesmerized me. I was in his thrall, and as he led me to his motorcycle, a panicky feeling crawled up my throat. He would drive me to town, and we'd part ways. How long would it be before I saw him again? Whatever the answer, it wouldn't be soon enough.

"Rikki, I know you barely know me." He handed me a helmet. "And I don't want to rush things and risk scaring you away, but I'm really hoping you'll let me see you again."

I let out a shaky breath. "I was afraid you'd take me back to Rose's and never ask."

His smile gutted me. "You mean it?"

"I'm not good at dating... or relationships. I can't promise you anything or that I won't make a mess of it."

"Then we take it slow. You set the pace. I'll follow." His fingers skimmed my jaw as he adjusted my helmet straps. "I want to earn your trust. I'll do whatever it takes."

My heart warmed, glowing like an ember. *How does he know all the right things to say?* "You hardly know me. Maybe you'll find out I'm not worth the trouble."

"You're definitely worth it, and someday, if you're very sweet to me, I'll tell you how I know."

"Then I should warn you that I'm sweeter than a sugar boat on a syrup sea sailing around a—"

"Planet made of cotton candy?"

I gaped at him. "How did you know I was going to say that?"

"Maybe I remember you better than you think." He winked, threw his leg over his bike, and patted the seat behind him. Still babying my tailbone, I eased behind him and balanced on my perch as he thumbed the starter and gunned the throttle, making his engine snarl.

I latched my arms around him, eager to keep him close. Who knew where we'd end up going, but I was determined to stick around long enough to find out. Burning golds and fiery reds from the surrounding trees blazed by. Bright leaves swirled around us as we blew through piles that had gathered on the road. I closed my eyes and drew in a deep breath that smelled of damp forests and fresh water.

For the first time in years, Evansville felt like home.

Mina had given me hell for my affinity for remembering quotes, but I couldn't help it. My mind was like a crow, hoarding shiny bits of information that attracted my attention. I'd always remembered from my American Lit class in college that Thomas Wolfe had gotten the title of his famous book from a writer named Ella Winter, who had once told him, "Don't you know you can't go home again?"

She was wrong, it turned out. You *could* go home again.

All you needed was a little grace and a strong belief in second chances.

Acknowledgements

MANY THANKS GO TO THE crew at Red Adept Publishing, especially Lynn McNamee for giving me my first chance years ago and for continuing to be a publisher of outstanding integrity, for welcoming my family into yours, and for all the awesome Oculus Rift games. Thanks to Sara N. Gardiner for her spot-on editing and for helping me bring a better balance to Rikki's and Owen's relationship. Thanks to Angela Webster McRae for putting on the polish, but also for being a friend and one of the nicest people I know.

Much gratitude goes to my writer cohorts who provided invaluable feedback in the early stages, especially Erica Lucke Dean who held my hand word-by-word, chapter-by chapter, draft-after-draft. And to Mary Fan, whose notes and suggestions made the characters and their world much richer and truer. Also to Nicole Platania, a brilliant and tireless youth librarian, for reading early drafts and for championing local writers in general.

Thanks to Glendon Haddix at Streetlight Graphics for the gorgeous cover, and to Jessica Anderegg for helping facilitate its design.

All my heart goes to my family for their continued love, patience, and support. I couldn't do it without you, and without you, I wouldn't want to.

Don't miss out!

Visit the website below and you can sign up to receive emails whenever Karissa Laurel publishes a new book. There's no charge and no obligation.

https://books2read.com/r/B-A-NETB-JTEX

BOOKS 2 READ

Connecting independent readers to independent writers.

Did you love *Touch of Smoke*? Then you should read *My Soul Immortal* by Jen Printy!

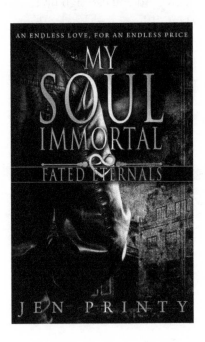

An endless love, for an endless price.

Jack's immortality is exposed when he prevents a liquor store heist, forcing him to flee to protect his secret—a secret not even he understands. But when he meets Leah Winters—a mirror image of his decades-lost love, Lydia—his very soul is laid bare. He begins to question his sanity. Is she real, and if so, what does that mean for Jack and his secret?

Jack's not the only mystery man in town. A stranger named Artagan hints at knowledge Jack is desperate to possess. But can he trust Artagan, or does the dark newcomer harbor deadly secrets of his own?

As Jack's bond with Leah grows, so does the danger to her life. Jack must discover just how much he is willing to risk in order to save the woman he already lost once.

Also by Karissa Laurel

The Norse Chronicles
Touch of Smoke

Watch for more at www.karissalaurel.com.

About the Author

Karissa Laurel always dabbled in writing, but she also wanted to be a chef when she grew up. So she did. After years of working nights, weekends, and holidays, she burnt out and said, "Now what do I do?" She tried a bunch of other things, the most steady of those being a paralegal for state government, but nothing makes her as happy as writing. She has published several short stories and reads "slush" for a couple of short-story markets.

Karissa lives in North Carolina with her kid, her husband, the occasional in-law, and a very hairy husky. She loves to read and has a sweet tooth for speculative fiction. Sometimes her husband convinces her to put down the books and take the motorcycles out for a spin. When it snows, you'll find her on the slopes.

Karissa also paints and draws and harbors a grand delusion that she might finish a graphic novel someday.

Read more at www.karissalaurel.com.

About the Publisher

Dear Reader,

We hope you enjoyed this book. Please consider leaving a review on your favorite book site.

Visit https://RedAdeptPublishing.com to see our entire catalogue.

Don't forget to subscribe to our monthly newsletter to be notified of future releases and special sales.